iCon

WILDMAN 101

CONSTANTINE O'DONNELL

ISBN: 978-1-63950-202-8 (sc)
ISBN: 978-1-63950-203-5 (e)

This publication contains the opinions and ideas of its author. It is intended to provide helpful and informative material on the subjects addressed in the publication. The author and publisher specifically disclaim all responsibility for any liability, loss, or risk, personal or otherwise, which is incurred as a consequence, directly or indirectly, of the use and application of any of the contents of this book.

Writers Apex

Gateway Towards Success

8063 MADISON AVE #1252
Indianapolis, IN 46227
+13176596889
www.writersapex.com

iCon

by Constantine O'Donnell

Writers Apex

Book review by Kat Kennedy

*"This introduction is about my last 18 years
of strife since I was labeled Bipolar."*

In his book, the author relates episodes in his life that led to his diagnosis of bipolar disorder. It offers candid details of his many stays in mental asylums and his years working on ships and yachts, which allowed him to travel the world. His is a tale of alcohol and drug abuse which eventually led to his abhorring the use of both. Of his first time being admitted to the St. Pats mental asylum, he states, "While drunk in 2003, I pretended to have Bipolar to get off with breaking a window in a 5-Star hotel in Dublin's city center." Thus began the author's eighteen years of voluntary and involuntary admissions into asylums. O'Donnell openly tells the story of his life and his fight in order to prove that he isn't mentally ill.

This autobiographical work is a fascinating look into the mind of the author. Parts of the book are disturbing in their honesty concerning his time in mental asylums and struggles with drugs and alcohol. According to O'Donnell, aliens are communicating with him and have relayed the message that mental illness doesn't exist. He takes a firm stand against the use of psychotropic drugs as he believes they and alcohol have been the source of his problems in life. In this engaging treatise, the author states, "This book is going to explode on to the world at large and I am about to tell you to throw away your psychotropic medication." He asserts, "The alien race are going to help me. There will be no more illness on planet earth." The book contains explicit descriptions of sexual encounters, making it more appropriate for adults. This one will likely stay with readers long after they have finished reading.

CONTENTS

AN INTRODUCTION TO MY NEMESES

This book was written to get everyone off my case. You know who you are! My name is Juan, and I'm from Shrove, Ireland. What you are about to read is the story of my life. I have been watched by aliens since I was born. They were surveilling my father and my mother's family for generations before I was even born. The O'Donnell's in Shrove and the McLaughlin's in the Waterside, Derry are the smartest clans of people in the world. The crusade I went on was always going to happen. I got addicted to drink and drugs but got clean. I have a real penchant for women but that'll always be the same!!

O'Donnell Motto: Under this sign, you shall conquer.

"The O'Donnells are one of the most eminent families whose forefather was Niall of the Nine Hostages. Tirconnell, meaning "Connell's territory" (now Donegal), was their base, and from Domhnaill (world mighty), they took their name. Their Chieftains were inaugurated on the Rock of Doon near Letterkenny.

Theirs is a history of the battle. They built strongholds around Donegal and defended themselves first from their neighbours, the O'Neills, and then, in a losing battle, from the Tudors.

As a youth, the O'Donnells heir, the great Red Hugh, was abducted and imprisoned in Dublin castle. His escape through the snow-covered Wicklow Mountains is one of the great sagas. He was the leader in the Triumphant battle of the Yellow Ford but died in Spain following the exodus after Kinsale.

The O'Donnell's established an Austrian line with a Major General Henry Count O'Donnell. Count Joseph, his son, was finance minister following Napoleon's depredations. Another O'Donnell account was aide-de camp to the Emperor Franz Josef. Their kinsman reached the highest rank in Spain – Prime Minister in 1858.

Many O'Donnell's have been illustrious churchmen, including the "Apostle of Newfoundland" and Cardinal Peter O'Donnell in Ireland. Their present chieftain is a Franciscan missionary whose heir will come from the duke of Tetuan's family in Spain."

"And I am Don Juan O'Donnell, an adventurous man who got caught up in the mental health system and cannot fucking get out of it!!! This book is going to explode on to the world at large and I am about to tell you to throw away your psychotropic medication. They pile the weight on you which makes you feel depressed! They ruin your personality. Big pharma is poisoning you. I am going to close them DOWN!!!!! The Alien race are going to help me. There will be no more mental illness on planet earth. Mental illness does not exist!!!"

This introduction is mainly about my last 20 years of strife since I was labelled Bipolar. The latest diagnosis of persecutory delusions from paranoid schizophrenia from Doctor Noir is part of an I.R.A gaslighting conspiracy against me. They all want to be mentally ill. I think it's the rep of being intelligent you get from it. I never had the Jesus condition, I thought I was God. Jesus was the biggest con-man the world has ever seen. I do not believe in God. God is an invention. Jesus and I have a lot in common, we both have our doubters, we both fell in love with hookers, we talk in fables, we care for the sick and also fought a government. I never walked on water but if pushed I could swim through land! They tried to crucify me for fighting them but I came back from the dead and ascended to the throne! I am like Moses and his 10 commandments. The aliens are helping me write this book.

I do not agree with a lot of human laws and the aliens are honing my instincts for a worldwide take over.

At present I am being gaslighted by the I.R.A all over the world. They are ridiculing and poking fun at me with information they are getting on me from every source they have. Well it's about to stop Mr. Ira cos every little cunt snitch and tout is going to turn on you. The I.R.A are jealous I'm writing this book about myself. It shows their level of consciousness.

Gaslighting is a form of emotional abuse. It's the act of manipulating a person by forcing them to question their thoughts, memories, and the events occurring around them. These people are pushing me to question my own sanity (which I bloody well don't!). These fucking dickheads say things to me and then deny saying anything when I question them. It's a fucking nightmare. They are probably taking bets on when I commit suicide. It ain't going to work mi compadres. I know it is their underworld operation doing it. The derogatory things they say are so private to my life that it bloody shocks me how they know. If I complain to anyone, I look schizophrenic because the wank stains deny saying it. It's exactly what they are after. I was told to wear a camera by a Dublin crim called Wolf Tone in Letterkenny mental asylum. He was the one who told me the whole of the I.R.A(Irish Republican Army) and Sinn Fein were responsible for the gaslighting. This book has annoyed them so much. I heard one idiot of a taxi driver shout out in the street outside my house in Rathmullan "who does he think he is calling himself an iCon?" It shows their level of intelligence. Wolf Tone said "record what's going on around you and catch them in the act". I can't afford the camera at the minute but I definitely will wear one when I can. Fuck it but I don't know what else to do but write about it. The gardai don't believe me. They asked me was I taking my medication? They looked like they were going to keep me in Letterkenny Garda station when I went in to report it! I reckon by their reaction they were in on it.

The Gardai called me the ghost of na h-eire in court in 2018 trying to scare the shit out of me. It was a nickname. Someone roared it in the court room door "Ghost of na h-eire, get out!!!" I was up for a drunk and disorderly. Another one of their scams to annoy the hell out of me.

There was only a couple of us in the court room. I don't know where the nickname came from?! Possibly Sint Maarten? My nickname in Sint Maarten was Guinness. The gaslighters have been caught by other members of the public saying random things to me in public. Listen out for these plebes and put two and two together. My photo must have done the rounds around Ireland and beyond. They recognize me instantly. It's great craic. I know they are jealous as fuck. I heard the fuckers boast to one another of what they said to me. It's like a badge of honour giving me shit. They all feel superior doing it. SO many Chief's and no Indians. One female patient said in Letterkenny mental on this admission (05/10/21) "I don't like the Real IRA – too many bosses!" "I'm letting Juan in on it" she said. She was about 15 feet from me in the open-air smoking area, talking to another female patient in the underground way they speak. Loud enough for you to hear it. Then she went into the nurses and screamed at them "I'VE HAD ENOUGH OF THE REAL IRA! THE WHOLE LOT OF THEM COMING DOWN ON ONE MAN -JUAN!!! IT'S NOT FAIR!!!" I could see them through the windows to the corridor. And nurse Mr. Saint C said "If you roar that again, we'll ECT (Electroconvulsive-therapy) you!!!" And he meant it! I could see the evil cunts eyes. They were plain as day as I sat in the smoking area. It was all the outward confirmation I needed. I already knew it was them. But Mr. Pandy, my roommate and I.R.A C/O (commanding officer) of Bloody Sunday said when I said "Tiocaidh ar la!" to him for a bit of mild amusement, "they're crumbling too!" The whole thing has come to a halt because of them bullying me. That will learn them LOL. They are vile creatures the lot of them. They said they will thwart this book using all the English and Irish people. I'd love to see them try. There is so little going on in their miserable little fucking lives. I can see the pleasure in their ego driven eyes every time they give me abuse. JEALOUS LITTLE CUNTS LOL. "Juan's got friends in the RYA!" is one I got today (02/10/21) in the asylum from one of the I.R.A nurses (they're all IN said nurse Mr. little T). She was slagging me off about my Superyachting background. "Oh, la la!" was the one I got when I walked into the pubs in Letterkenny. I heard the gaslighter's say things like "I said this to him…." And have a little laugh amongst the other deviant assholes.

It's their claim to fame in their little itty-bitty lives. Whoo hoo! High five! It's the same abuse as I get in the mental asylum from the nurses and doctors. They started giving me abuse when they were told to, for whatever reason that could be. They are all getting away with bullying me. They enjoy every little power trip they get. They love to get one over on a famous guy. I'm not blowing my own trumpet but I have a lot of fame around Letterkenny and beyond. The cunts are squeezing my emotions with all their worth, inside and outside the mental asylum. It's a real-life conspiracy but now it's out in the open for one and all to hear.

The gaslighting was at a high in Letterkenny in 2020. A lot of people in Letterkenny have ties with the mental asylum. I have ruffled a lot of feathers with my conspiracy talk amongst the nurse sympathizers and fucking layabouts. The layabouts carry stories back to the mental asylum and paint me in a bad light.

My current Doctor, Doctor Noir, is one of those deviants. He throws out mental illnesses to everyone that comes in the asylum doors. Nobody ever gets a clean bill of health from him. I plan to be the first. I was warned about Doctor Noir for years by other patients that he just threw out diagnosis's Willy Nilly. Doctor Noir blackmailed me into taking what's known as a depot injection. I said I would take the tablet form but he said "no. You have to take the depot." I was sure that's illegal, I've heard since it's not. I was angry and he laughed at my anger. This was the year 2020 after I got thrown out of Ariadne's hostel for fighting as you will read. I did not want that poisonous depot medication in my body. Doctor Noir was enjoying the little power rush. The depot is medication in a vile injected in to the muscle. A Doctor and a nurse said when they were administering it to my ass, "rape?" laughing to each other. I looked around and they were looking at the scar I have from an ingrown hair removal operation on the crack of my ass. They were patronizing me and treating me like a nobody. They do not know my mission. I am going to end mental illness forever.

End Bipolar, it's only emotions. Bipolar is a series of ups and downs in mood. Fucking bullshit personified. The higher your intelligence, the larger the range of emotions. And as for schizophrenic, it is the spirit world talking to the living. It does come from alcohol abuse, drug abuse and dysfunctional parenting. Children should have a good up-bringing. They should not be subjected to below par parenting. The diagnosis of schizophrenia is a fucking bullshit diagnosis. It was given to me when I complained about getting abuse on the street in Letter-FUCKING-kenny.

The depot injection is the biggest scam going. The injection costs the health system 1800 euro each patients injection each time!!! The doctors are getting everybody on them. They are even bullying the dysfunctional young to take them as mandatory, telling them they have no choice. They tell them they will section them if they refuse. I would say a few of those dysfunctional kids will come forward after reading this book. They should not be on those injections. The injections are poison.

The doctors and nurses are in cahoots to get everybody on them. The health system is being drained. The system is kaput. The nurses love the injection because they do not have to remind patients to take their medication when they leave the asylum. It lightens the work load of the nurses. No more dispensing tablets. They do not care about the patients involved. The fucking injection leaves you unable to ejaculate. What a nightmare?! So long to a good sex life! I told my younger brother this and he just went "SO?!!" I thought fuck sake! He could not give a rat's ass about my human rights.

The mental asylums worldwide need a protest to get off all medication. I told Doctor Noir I didn't want the medication. I was experimenting with him. I wanted to see how he would try and manipulate me in to taking it. That was when he threatened me about not getting out of there. They have lots of ways of coercing you. They are a law onto themselves. That is about to change!!!

I took the medication anyway, just to get out of there. And after a couple of days, I got some leave to go into town. I got back from the town after some hours out and upon my return, I was summoned to the interview room by Doctor Noir. He told me when I went in that he had had reports from my excursion down town that I was snapping at people for no reason. It really fucking annoyed me. I only snapped back at the one person who gaslighted me. I remember the fucking evil little smile on the prick that I snapped at. I knew immediately when Doctor Noir challenged me on it why the gaslighting prick smiled. He was going to report me to the asylum. I have fame in the underworld. Everybody in Letterkenny seems to be criminal. I said to Doctor Noir "how did you hear?" He said laughing "we have eyes everywhere!" Great for paranoia! I thought. The whole fucking drill of gaslighting is to lock me up and throw away the key. The public involved are trying to get me committed forever. INSANE!!! How fucking cruel are these people? Doctor Noir also threatened me with Dundrum, an asylum for the criminally insane, when he heard about my fight in the hostel a couple of days before my admission. It was old news by that stage!

A guy staying in the hostel was gaslighting me and I put him in his place. I wanted the town to know I meant fucking business. I kicked him down 3 flights of stairs. It worked for a little while.

Doctor Noir tied my hands, the ignorant cunt. The gaslighting was also impressive in a corner shop near the Aura in Letterkenny in 2019. I was in getting some beer when a delivery guy, a complete nobody, said "you're out. High five". He was so condescending! Fucking jumped up cunt, as all of them are. Never been anywhere. I'd a fair idea he was on about the I.R.A. I ignored it taken aback, it was so unexpected. I should have just said "Never been in!!!"

Letterkenny is a buttfuck of a place to live. It gets lots of tourists because of my O'Donnell ancestors. The Letterkenny people do not deserve this. The Letterkenny be grudgers, of whom there are a lot of (talking from experience!!!), who aren't of O'Donnell descent have put downs they like to say to demoralize any O'Donnell's who have a confident air about them. They say things like "another O'Donnell who wants to rule the world!" or if you say something that sounds to them like you're blowing your own trumpet, the little inferior cunts, they say "ah…he's an O'Donnell!". I only lived there for a short while but I'd say the jealous belittling shit the mongrel cunts who aren't of true royal blood of the O'Donnell clan say has been going on for centuries. Another one the "five eighths" as they call themselves, as in, they say "I'm one of the five eighths" in other words "on the Dole". They also use "he's an heir!" In other words, you come from money or you have had money handed to you. WE IN A NORMAL SOCIETY LETTERKENNY "5/8 SCUMBAGS" CALL IT A GOOD UP-BRINGING! They are the most ignorant, incestuous people I have ever encountered. Maybe they will stop gaslighting me if challenged by you! There are O'Donnell supporters there too and I salute you but a few good people among all them bad ones makes it hard to combat. The bad ones will lose however because an O'Donnell is about to rule the world again!!! The general feeling if you are an outsider is one of complete discomfort. The Letterkenny mafia are so insular. The majority of them do not even have fucking passports. They are from generations of social welfare payments. They have no hopes or dreams and shit upon anyone who does. That includes their own people. I feel sorry for people growing up Letter-FUCKING-kenny. I have had the pleasure of having sex with a few nice women from there. I know they are not all bad. They cum like THUNDER.

Sinn Fein/IRA are trying to kill me and sell the rights of this book to Hollywood. They already did this with an old manuscript of iCon that I released to my friends about 10 years ago. I was at an all-time low emotionally because I could not get the money together to publish it. They fucking thieved it. And had it made in to the stupid cunt of a movie called Iron fists. I watched it and I was so pissed off. It does NOT show how feeble minded the powers that be are. A Sinn Fein party member told me they did it. I wondered what sort of response they were hoping for? I was fucking livid. I never made a penny! They probably made a Billion. It was a T.V series spin off as well. They made fucking tons of money!!!

I made jokes about someone stealing it after I released it but I never thought it would happen. They can fucking burn in hell. Top to bottom. They are the worst kind of people you could rely on.

On top of this, another reason I had the scummy political party people on my case was because I was accused in the wrong of hitting an ex-girlfriend called Fanjita in the face with the back of my hand in 2010. I didn't do it! She lied. She told me she lied about 3 months after she accused me. Her brother Leeroy told me not to write anything about her. He's a useless gobshite. And a fucking thief. He should be run out of Moville forever!!! He threatened me because he knew I was writing this book. Boohoo! Leeroy this is going down. Leeroy, what a hillbilly name?!! It, is all coming out in the open. No fucking way am I taking it lying down!!! Fuck you and fuck whoever has a problem with me. Fanjita always gets leniency because the whole surrounding area of Inishowen has been told they had a hard up-bringing. It is all a load of Alcoholic anonymous bullshit. Their parents were not that bad to them. They might have been alcoholics but they looked after the kids well. The AA spread that their parents were not fit to look after them. Fanjita had loads of good memories. The family may play the goodie two shoes but they are an illiterate delinquent bunch.

Poor Fanjita! Always playing the victim. AA was her go to for sympathy. Her parents showed her the way! Their Father, Lambo (Larry Lamb and Rambo!), used to tell the cops on everybody in the town, he probably still does. My heart was broke trying to control Fanjita's loose lips and vicious tongue. She had a problem with everybody in town. Loose lips, sink ships!!! I tried to get her to save her tongue for my cock. I should have given her a cunt punt and got fucking rid of her before any problems arose. I knew she was bad. AA was not enough. She told the lie that I hit her throughout Inishowen. She used her hillbilly family in Redcastle and her mongrel family in Glengad to spread the lie. Her family in Moville done the same. She went in to the local supermarket where I am going to sell this book in Moville and told the owner that I hit her. She was doing it to bring me to my knees. Well it did not work you twisted little cunt!!!

I am about to create a catharsis of epic proportions to cleanse her soul and clear a dead man's name. Fanjita told everyone that she was raped. I know for a fact that she lied about it. She more or less admitted it to me. The story of her rape was so much bullshit. It was another ploy to get sympathy. That lady has lived off rumours her whole life. It seems to be the way in Moville among the dole dwelling people. The story of me hitting her grew legs over the years until I heard back in 2017 after I returned from being out of the loop in Moville town, that I'd beat the shit out of her. It was a total lie and an exaggeration of the lie she originally told. People love fucking rumours. Fanjita was loving the rumour. The rumour did not stop when she told me the truth and I told people that she admitted lying to me the few months after the accusation. Her father Lambo made fucking sure the lies were believed. It didn't matter what I said, they are a big group of paedophiles that live in that housing estate, OGV. I think Lambo is a paedophile himself. He uses their tears as lubrication.

I was in Letterkenny general in 2019 when Scissorhands, Fanjitas older sister, threatened me in front of my mother in the waiting area. Scissorhands thought I was on my own. She does not know my mother who was sitting beside me. It was pretty funny. She was caught red handed. I know she would have lied if I had of reported it to the law but I am leaving that for another time

My mother was desperately trying to get me on medication again. A different nightmare that ended short and sweet when I convinced the admissions Doctor that all I needed was somewhere to live. My mother had to fucking help me instead of dumping me on the mental health services again! All I needed was family support! Scissorhands said to me "I'm going to destroy you!" She was sitting opposite me. My mother asked me what was wrong with her? I said they're all mental, referring to her family. She was with her father, mother and her younger brother boneboy. He's another useless tool. Scissorhands flipped when I said this and walked off. Boneboy said apologetically "no trouble!" I said "whatever!" Hosanna in a Hiace! They are tinkers.

Fanjita told me the minute they turn 18 years old, their Father, Lambo, takes them to the Dole office to sign on. Way to parent them Lambo. You should be taking them to college. Lambo's no fool himself, he works as a plumber in Moville in secret and he is on the Dole too. He has pictures on his phone to prove it. I often thought to myself when I was at sea why do seagulls have wings? My mate Farren said it's to beat the tinkers to the tip! My god the Bumbleweeds, as I call Fanjita's family, must have beaten the seagulls and rummaged long and hard to furnish that house of theirs. Fanjita's mother and father are ex-drunkards like I said. They are Born again Christians. BUT so much for God in their life! They are Satan incarnate.

I do not believe in any religion anyway because the aliens have told me it doesn't exist. God is make believe. It was made up by the well to do to keep the fucking savages in order. And grown adults should not believe in fucking stupid fantasy tales about water into wine, parting of the seas or the ridiculous ark story.

People in the sky dictating? Unfortunately for you humans who are terrible, there are. We will exterminate your father, your mother and all your kids.

When people die, they move into the spirit world. All deaths on earth in the future will be accidental. There will be no murders. Murdering another human being will carry a death sentence. Grief should be dealt with in minutes and got over really efficiently. There should be no more burials. Everybody should be cremated and have their ashes spread somewhere memorable. It is much more sodding humane. It is fucking savagery at the minute. All the disease that can come from dead bodies seeping into the earth, then animals feeding on it.

We are Aliens. We are now talking through Juan. All earthlings talk to their dead and they should really let them exist outside their realm for eternity. As aliens, we plan to help you humans to a better existence.

Back to me, Juan...I am learning every day from my alien mates. They speak to me every second of the day. It's a running commentary in my head. So much fun to listen to. Far better than listening to the dead. San Pedro, the cactus narcotic, opened up my cerebral channels in 2006, enabling me to speak with the dead. It was torturous. The aliens have hampered the dead talking to me. Only the good dead get through to me now. I find it all very comforting. I work and I live in harmony with the aliens. I have a wonderful relationship with them. They have been watching me since birth. They knew I would go on a crusade to rid the world of mental health illnesses. It is one of the best crusades ever to have taken place on earth, hands down. FYI I Juan am a genius. The aliens have told me so. FYI this book is going to sell more copies than the bible! LOL. This book contains a fraction of the women

I have had sex with. I hope it's not too over the top for you. In bed I am subliminal. Women fucking love having sex with me!!!

A limerick from Donegal. It is from my poetry book Anonymous in the town that talks. Find the book on Amazon.

14/08/04

Animal

In bed, I'm described as an animal,
Cos my intuition is almost subliminal,
And as I give her what she wants,
we have a jolly old jaunt,
and she gasps for air like a mammal.

This book is a ride and a half! Roll your own?! I don't think so. There's a big wide world out there and I've licked more than half the pussies on it, on my travels. The Born-again Christian entire support group in Moville town area and Inishowen spread the rumours of the wife beating for years. They were trying to destroy my reputation. It bloody worked. It took me nearly a decade to get over the wrongful accusation. It was slander. I tried to get Fanjita done for it, but the solicitor told me to wise up! Oh my God! Nobody believed me! I want justice from them and the Gardai Siochana. The guards knew she lied. They told me so. I could have her and her father put in jail for mental trauma of slander to me in years to come. I'm letting them sweat!!! I want a letter of apology from Fanjita to the Derry Journal. It has to say, "I lied and I'm sorry...." and explain the story of how she lied. She told me that she said to everybody that I flipped and hit her when she taunted me about being Bipolar. She laughed, recounting the lie. She knew the world would fucking believe her.

Her sister Scissorhands and I had running battles in Letterkenny mental asylum. She wanted a fling in the asylum with me even though she was angry with me. It shows how fucking twisted they are! She wanted to suck my cock. She told me so. She said her family would disown her. I don't think she cared. She used to flirt like crazy when I was with Fanjita. I wouldn't fucking touch her with a barge pole. She is a fucking skank of EPIC proportions. She played games with everybody in the asylum and eventually got barred for abusing me.

I call her Scissorhands because she is a suicide brunette – dyed by her own hand. She cut her own throat with a pair of scissors for Jesus sake!!! What a nutjob?! Safety scissors for her from now on…. The rumours of wife-beating nearly bloody ruined me over the years, and their Father Lambo nearly got me locked up for it in 2010 when Fanjita accused me of it. When Fanjita lied in her statement to the Gardai, old Lambo got a barring order against me from her house and his. They are both in the same housing estate. A garda told me that her statement was so disjointed they knew she was lying. It didn't make a difference. The rumour was spread, and she took me to court. I told my mum she would drop it on the courthouse steps. I was right. She held me back from working back on the yachts in the South of France for six bastarding months because of the court case. They all say "Ah! Poor Bumbleweeds, they had a hard up-bringing". It is the biggest let off they have going. They are fucking criminals and that is the end of it.

Fanjita then, like I predicted dropped the charge before we went in to court. I knew the game. I'd overheard her and her auntie who is dead from over dosing on medication, talking admiringly about some skank that had done it in Buncrana. Lying fucking bitches. I believe the IRA underworld took Fanjita and her father's side. After all they were in the underworld. They turned everyone in the underworld against me in every town in Ireland.

All of her family have an inferiority complex. I did my homework on it. It is probably the reason why they tried to destroy me. They are poisonous wretches, all of them. There are hundreds of Bumbleweeds. All over the United States and Australia. Leeroy, her pimp, and her brother's a waste of space. He is allergic to work. He has never worked a day in his life. He is on the dole and deals drugs, and that is it.

I honestly believe that all drugs should be legal but he is a lazy cunt. The IRA underworld has been beating down on me for years for this and other capers of mine too. They love to brow beat a hero. It makes them feel in charge. I think her father Lambo knew she was lying about the incident. I know her brother leprechaun leper knew. He told me as much. He is a drug dealer too. Old Fanjitas pillow talk consisted of her years of sexual abuse. It turned her on. She told me she wanked her uncle off in a car one night outside the local hotel in Moville when she was 9. She told her parents about it BUT they were TOO drunk to give a fuck about her. They thought she was lying. I could see her eyes light up, recounting the tale. She was fucking wet telling it. We fucked like devils after she told me. We always had great sex after her stories of abuse.

She told me about the rape. She said the guy was really into her for a long time. It happened at a nightclub when she was 17. She said, like the depraved cunt that she is, that she wanted me to re-enact it. I thought this girl is fucking mental. I'd heard of women like this. I thought it might be fun but I feared she would shout rape again! We never did it. Thanks be to Jesus! I think what happened with Ol' rapey when she was raped in the forest was over-enthusiasm on his part. I read between the lines in her story. She told me he bit her on the cheek when he was riding her but judging by the violent sex, she wanted with me, I'm not surprised. He probably just got over-excited. She wanted, in her own words, the adrenaline pumping during sex. She used to shout in my ear and grab me by the ass, digging her nails in, pulling me in deeper and deeper when we were fucking screaming "FUCK ME!" "FUCK ME!" "NO FEAR!" The sex was AWESOME but I hated every minute of it if the truth be told. She was a little scum bag. I'd no other circle to live in. Mine was poisoned with the Bipolar rumour and the Bumbleweeds and the OGV scum lived outside of society. She used to make me lick her fanjita every damn night. It was fucking boring. She loved to orgasm. Who doesn't I suppose? But what got me through it, was the thought that it was training for every woman I'd ever have after her. I knew I wasn't going to stay with her.

I got a Colombian hooker off in Sint Maarten in the Caribbean, in 2012 licking her pussy. She had stacked orgasms. She was lifting off the bed as she came. I had to put my hand on her belly to hold her down so I could keep licking her as she was about to cum but she pulled my head up towards her to kiss her and put my cock in her pussy as quick as she could then she fucking exploded in moans of pleasure. She was glowing after it. It was all thanks to the nights fondling Fanjitas lady parts with my tongue.

The sex with Fanjita kept me with her for a whole two years, but it wasn't worth the headache of dealing with her alcoholic drug taking crap. She said to get Ol' rapey done for rape, that she punched herself in the mouth and said he done it. She had a cut on her lip when she talked to the gardai. It was the clincher to get him arrested. She was so proud of herself. She is a psychopath. My auntie Aine feared she would stab me in my sleep. I told my Aunt not to worry. I wouldn't be with her long. Fanjita told Scissorhands after the so-called rape happened what 'Ol rapey had done and Scissorhands didn't believe her. I don't either. Either does Stev-o, a good OGV man. There are a few of them.

On the night I was supposed to have hit her, we were drunk in her house, and she got violent. I was sitting in a chair in her sitting room of her little council house in the suburbs of Moville. She was ranting and raving about why I didn't get jealous in the pub in Greencastle when she was flirting with a Russian fisherman. He never took her on and I ignored her when she was doing it. It pissed her off completely. I took the piss out of it and said "why would it bother me? Sure, we're broken up!". We'd broken it off at this stage. We'd gone on the piss again trying to make amends after getting our dole money as we did every fucking time, we got it. It was such a Loserville lifestyle. One they still live. When we got back to her house, she picked an argument.

She didn't get the reaction she wanted, so she jumped on top of me and started punching me on the top of my head. I grabbed her tiny little wrists in my two hands, she's 5 foot nothing – a spinner and put on her back on the kitchen floor. Her eyes looked afraid, but she got turned on in an instant. She said, "what are you going to do to me? Rape me?" I pulled her back up to her feet and said, "what's going on in that twisted fucking head of yours?" I let her go, and she socked me right in the eyeball with a jab. She then stood back grinning with her fists up, admiring her handy work. That tiny fist fitted right in my eye socket. I roared at her, "THAT'S FUCKING IT! ENOUGH!" She ran at me for another go. I sidestepped her, and she slipped on the beer on the lino floor. She ran head first into the clothes horse falling, flat on her face. SLAP! I broke my balls laughing. She was in her socks. She was a bit dyslexic. At night she used to cook my sock. OMG! Did she get up in a temper? Full of alcohol and venom. She stamped her right foot and said, "RIGHT! THAT'S IT!!" And stormed out the front door. Somewhere between her house and her parent's house where she stormed off to, further down the estate, she got a bust bottom lip. The same as the rape scenario. She'd fucking done it again. She'd punched herself in the mouth again. Lambo went on the full assault and got his barring orders and began ruining my reputation. He's been doing it for years. Lucky I'm thick-skinned and didn't top myself as well. Then she would've been two for two. When 'Ol rapey was in prison after she got him arrested for the rape, she got her entire family behind her to support her. Bunch of fucking losers. She protested outside the jail 'Ol rapey was in and caused him to commit suicide. She was SO delighted with herself when she told me.

In another cathartic outpouring, she also told me she shagged her brother Leprechaun leper, or Lepy as I call him, when she was 14 years old. He lost his virginity to her. Fucking hell!! It was just after their parents got back together after a few year's separation. I think all her brothers were having sex with her. They are thieves, drug takers and drug dealers. It wouldn't surprise me. The drugs they sell are complete dung as well! The Cocaine they get from Dublin, smuggled up in Bears car, is only 5% Cocaine. They sell it for 100 euros a gram. The main ingredient is the gum numbing agent for babies' gums. What a waste of fucking dosh. The weed they sell is poisoned with fibre-glass. The main dealers spray the plants, when they are growing them, with the glass so it makes it heavier. They do this so they don't have to put as much weed in that little 50-euro baggy you buy!! You can get emphysema from smoking it. The fibre glass sticks to your lungs permanently. You can tell the glass on it by the sparkle off the leaves. It is common all over Donegal. The foreign cunts are poisoning everyone! They put diesel in the hash as well to swell it so it becomes heavier as well. Nice people eh?! Think of all that poison you're taking in! And the ecstasy tablets the Bumbleweeds have been putting out there are so fucking bad, you have to take four or five of them just to get the MDMA buzz out of them (So fucking dangerous!!! They can kill you with one tab. Evil little Moville cunts. The ecstasy tablets come from Derry! Bottoms up you drunken Derry scumbags. No more poisoning Moville!!) The heroin they have been trying to bring in ever since I stopped them in 2010 is nothing but dirty, contaminated morphine. Who the hell wants to put that filthy, diseased, scumbag drug into your veins? There is no prestige in it at all. It is vile.

Here is a little poem I wrote about the Bumbleweed's. They are scum.

The dreams that drug dealers have

When I was young and had no sense,
My so-called Spartans were sitting on the fence,
They thought I'd lead them to the vineyards of France,
They'd sell below par drugs,
And off they'd prance,
Well, they were wrong,
From me they got the gong,
And now they'll live without their freedom,
In a maximum-security prison with a throng!

07/10/21

That poem was inspired by my poem Ni neart go cur le cheile and the Bumbleweeds. Leeroy told me their dreams. LOL fucking numpty dickheads. They don't even have passports!!! LOL. Everybody said they were the Spartans after reading my poem about the Spartans. I did not mean everyone. That's why only a few were chosen.

Her other brother, Lepy's twin brother, Jesus Christy, they call him, is a long-time drug dealer. He is the ring leader. Fanjita told me Jesus Christy gives money to their parents that he earns from selling drugs to Moville kids. The other siblings do the same with their drug money. It's a real family fucking business. Their dysfunctional parents know exactly where the money is coming from! It bumps up their dole money. It should NOT be allowed. The Gardai Siochana in Moville know the Bumbleweeds are the drug dealers of the town. Fanjita thinks her father and brothers are untouchable. She told me so. It goes back to them giving the Gardai information on other crims in the town. Fanjita has lots of dirty little secrets. She should have thought about who she was accusing in the wrong of hitting her – poets are the most feared men in history for a reason!

The Bumbleweeds are a real close nit family. Incest is rife with them. Roll your own is their motto! Fun for all the family is their credo! Lambo was trying to bring me down because he never amounted to anything in his life himself apart from being a piss head soldier that got groomed (what's that mean Fanjita? Fucked up the anus?!!) when he was drunk on a night out with the army, according to Fanjita. He woke up in the bed naked with another man and a sore arse. He had a serious upsetting case of ring sting for days afterwards!! She was really cleaning out her closet with me. She had nothing intelligible to talk about apart from her fucked up father and mother and weird bloody siblings.

She didn't drink when I met her, but she started one Christmas. I did coax her to drink a little, but she went full steam ahead. I thought at the beginning, how bad can she be? I soon found out!

During the first few weeks of hard-drinking and heartfelt out-pouring (she yapped without drink too!), I thought to myself, I would get to the bottom of her problems and be left with a good wife. I was so wrong. She turned nasty on me numerous times. She called the fucking guards all the time. I forgave her for her past but couldn't get by the assault charge she brought against me. It took a decade to get over the feeling of injustice. They framed me!!!

She was enjoying every minute of my framing, the sadistic, twisted little cunt. I was told by a nosey neighbor of theirs not so long ago that Old Lambo lies about the assault, and when he is telling it, he gives me nowhere to go with it. He was getting the story out. Lambo said if I, Juan, didn't remember it, then I must have had an alcoholic blackout. It was a catch 22 he was creating. The nosy neighbour said I must have had a blackout. I was exasperated trying to convince the nosey neighbor that I did not do it and that I remembered everything about the night it was supposed to have happened. The nosey neighbor wouldn't budge on it. I imagined half the town of Moville would be the same, that was my feeling at the time. She was going around telling everybody. Most of them thought she deserved it. Some were praising me; others were giving me shit. It was fucking pointless trying to get the truth out. I hope this sets the record straight. Lambo, her mother and her siblings were spreading shite about me for years. It is a full-scale assault on me, Scissorhands is perpetuating it and I want it to end. 14 years later and they're still fucking barking about it. They have nothing going on in their so-called lives. Lambo wanted to break my stare. I started dropping my eyes in the street when I met one of their neighbors. They were always trying to stare me down. Fucking imbeciles. It then became a habit. He was trying to make sure my life was over. He's a bully.

When I finally got rid of Fanjita, it was a terrible thing that happened. Finishing with her was nearly impossible. I'd moved out of her little council house and got a flat in town but she broke her own barring order to visit me. I'm sure a judge would not look kindly on that. She used to turn up on my door step when the relationship was over, dressed in her most provocative clothes. I'd give in to her saucy moves and let her in. She would suck my cock for nothing. She told me she used to charge! She told me years before that she had prostituted herself as well. It was in another outpouring of her dirty little slut of a mind. She said she enjoyed it. She said an Indian guy from Moville gave her 50 euros to sleep with her. I thought you dirty skank. I was kind of supportive to her because it was a catharsis so I told her I thought of hooking for women as well for a bit of craic. I'd been with a lot of woman, and I did not see the problem. I think it should be legal.

She arrived on my doorstep one morning drunk around the same time, looking to come in. I told her no but she begged to get in. I let her in and she said she was going to Dublin to meet a guy she had met on line. She was trying to make me jealous. I told her to leave. She said she was going down there to fuck him. I told her I didn't care and started pushing her out the door. She shouted no! Then with a psychotic laugh she bent over in front of me and pulled her leggings and knickers down. She put her hands flat on the floor with her ass in the air, just like the hookers do it and said "Fuck me before I go!" I had no condom but thought fuck it. She's on the coil. She had such a sordid history. I couldn't help but fuck her like a wild thing!!! I dropped my trousers and rode the ass off her!!! I thought to myself as I was doing it "Enjoy my spunk Dublin jackeen!!!". I kicked her out straight after I had cum. I'm sure he was a top-notch Gentleman!!! LOL.

She was trying her best to get back together with me. She came down all the bloody time. There was no conversation so I was pretty content with just emptying my bag into her and kicking her out the door again. I never thought about contraceptive. She'd been on the coil contraceptive. It was about a month into it, when she fell fucking pregnant. She told me she'd had the coil removed. The nasty fucking bitch.

The day she told me, she called me to an alleyway. I thought it was a bit strange but I figured the shadows are where her people feel the most at home. It was mid-afternoon in downtown Moville. I walked from my flat to meet her. She was strangely excited. She said I have something to tell you. "I'm pregnant!" she said. "It's 70% yours, 30% someone else." I said, "where do you get those percentages?" Jesus Christ! What a fucking craic addict!!! She told me she had slept with someone else from Shrove on the same night as me, the night she thought it happened. A couple of days later, she was in my apartment. She pulled out a measly gram of off the rock cocaine and was all excited. I asked her where she got it. She told me a friend of hers sold it to her. She'd spent half her dole money on it. She more than likely spent the other half on cigarettes. She did that every fucking week. She was such a stupid cunt. She was taking her tablets for pregnancy at the same time as the Cocaine and alcohol. I thought, what a fucking lunatic? I told her I didn't want any. I said it was a waste of time, and money. She said she didn't give a flying fuck. I asked her what about the baby? She said "Ah, it'll be okay". I thought what a tit of a woman.

I'd given the relationship a chance because the baby could have been mine, but it was too much for me to get my head around. On top of another man, she was killing that baby with drugs and drink. It was fucking awful to watch!!

I phoned my father a few days later for some advice, and he said without hesitation, "get rid!" It was all the advice I needed. She was destroying my very core.

Around this time, Jamima, whom you'll meet later, gave me 500 euros back that she owed me from the three grand I lent her in 2006 to get her life back in London. It was a nice little return but it was all I ever got back from her. She conned me out of three thousand euros. These two women have been a very destructive influence in my life.

Jamima convinced me to put in the foreword of my first ever poetry book that I was Bipolar because it would be good for sales. I didn't want to do it. I said it goes against the very thing I am fighting! She said she didn't believe me that I wasn't. It hurt like fuck. Putting in the book I was Bipolar went against every fibre of my being, but I wanted inside her knickers! I don't know what was going on in my mind at that time. She ain't nothing special. Fuck it, I thought, I'll do what she is saying. When I did it, it caused a major shitstorm for me. I had to then tell everyone individually I wasn't Bipolar after the book came out. It was torture. I had to tell them how them how the Bipolar diagnosis came about in the Dublin mental asylum. Now I'm writing this book to tell you the truth. It is such a relief. Telling the story over and over again wore my brain down and burnt me out. I became a recluse after publishing my first book because of the fucking Bipolar slant in the foreword. I was living in my parent's old house with the curtains closed and no bloody contact with anybody. I started drinking again as well. That was 2007. I'd been off alcohol for a year. You can read all about those days later.

Fanjita came down again and I told her to leave my flat and never darken my door again. My dad said, "why didn't she do that to the other guy?" He thought she was playing on my good nature. She eventually miscarried. I'm not surprised and I was very relieved. She is unfit to be a mother. She was really cruel to the son she has, a tiler, when I was with her. She said "you can beat him if you want". He was only 8 years old! She was not even able to look after him. He grew up with her parents. She was too busy drinking and doing drugs. He is a drug dealer now as well. When he was 9, he fondled another kid's penis in school. Fanjita didn't know how to handle the situation. I just thought he's taking after his mother!!! Lol.

When Fanjita was playing her games with her scumbag fuckbuddy's, Leeroy would scam them for enough money to buy a few beers. Fanjita would suck their balls out through the end of their knob and her brother Leeroy would hang out with them. He would be supping on his cheap lager when Fanjita and her boudoir buddy were fucking in the bedroom. I think he got off on it. It happened when I was going out with her. She wanted a hall pass, and I reluctantly gave it to her. I don't think I had much choice in the matter. It fucking ate my insides out. It hurt my pride. She was a little fucking slut. I'd been warned how bad she was by Stev-o, the O'Gara Villas(OGV) good guy, but I didn't believe him.

Lambo was probably also annoyed with me because his wife, who cheated on him when they were split up, with his best friend, the coalman, was always flirting with me when I was in their house. Lambo knew the Coalman had been at her because her pussy was all slack. She is mutton dressed as lamb! What were you ever thinking, Lambo?! 9 fucking kids with her. 1 of them is the Coalman's (another of Fanjita's little outpouring's). Jesus!

Fanjitas mother, Talula, is a fat hillbilly that dabbled in psychoanalysis. I heard in Letterkenny mental asylum from one of her classmates that she cheated on Lambo again when she was in college for it. She has her work cut out analyzing a family like that! Talula used her psychoanalysis for evil and tried to destroy me. She wouldn't even shake hands properly with me when I tried to make amends. She manipulated the truth and believed her lying bitch of a daughter. Talula is a hussy and an evil bastard. Fanjita doesn't lick it off the grass.

Another of my ex's, Riverdance, a psychiatric nurse joined teams with Scissorhands to take me down in Letterkenny in 2018. I call her Riverdance because she loved anal sex, and when the shit flew out of her, I put on my tap dancing shoes, came in her ass, and did a jig on the shit!! I think she felt freedom having a crap and getting fucked up the arse at the same time. She shit all over my lap one time and totally unperturbed said when I'd finished "I think you need a shower". I felt like Michael Shatley. She looked a bit ashamed but I said nothing. I thought it was funny and I didn't want to put her off the idea of ass-fucking. Her ass was so bleeding tight. It was the tightest little hole you could imagine! It was disgusting and erotic, and I guess I took one for every patient in the audience!

She was a horny 40-year-old spinster, I'd never had one before. She has three kids, and her little 6-year-old daughter Angel is a little nymph. She copies her mother's flirtations. One morning Angel came into our room and jumped into bed beside us. Riverdance was between Angel and I. Angel was hugging and kissing Riverdance then she reached out between her mother's legs with her bare foot and touched my bare leg. She was testing boundaries. Her mother said so. I don't think she wanted to leave me out.

Another morning she came in, and Riverdance and I were spooning, I was fucking her from behind, under the covers. Angel surprised us. I didn't withdraw. She got in beside her mother, and when Riverdance was talking to her, I pushed my cock up, deep inside mum. I did it for a joke. I imagined her eyes lighting up and Angel wondering what was up. I was about to pull out when Riverdance subtly reached back under the covers and grabbed my ass with her hand, and pulled me in again. It was funny and erotic. I had so many mixed emotions. It was very naughty. She told Angel to leave and we carried on fucking!

She was a psychiatric nurse with a little twist in that fucking brain of hers. The sex started with her about two weeks after I moved in. We'd been flirting over and back. Then one afternoon I got angry at her mother for hinting that I do more work in the garden. I was doing it for free and she annoyed me by insinuating I wasn't doing enough. I phoned Riverdance at work and told her what happened and that I was moving out. She calmed me down and told me don't be doing that, she said she'd have a word with her mother. She came back that evening and came down to my room. She stood with her back against the open door of the room and was a little bit flirty. I was sitting on the bed. She asked was everything alright now? I said it was grand. I asked her what she's been at all day? She said with a saucy smile on her face "fantasizing about you!" I took my chance and walked over and kissed her full on the lips. Then I sat back down on the bed again. I was getting her wet. She smiled and said "I should not be doing this…" Then she walked over to where I was sitting and standing between my legs, pushed me back on the bed. She lay on top of me, kissing me on the mouth. Before she had time to think, I rolled her on to her back and pulled her trousers and knickers down. She looked a bit shell shocked. Like she didn't know what was happening. I pulled my bottoms down. I was rock hard. It was all very steamy. I was about to enter her pussy when she said what about a condom?! I didn't have one and I definitely didn't want to stop. So, I said "you told me you were on the coil" She said she was but what about diseases? I said "well I'm clean! What about you?!" She said she was, so, I jumped on her. We fucked ferociously. She was clawing at my back and moaning really loudly. That was the beginning of a very, very erotic couple of months.

Things were going really well until one day she gaslighted me. We'd just had sex and she was standing with her back to me, putting on her trousers when she said "You're in jail, and I'm here with you!" I asked her immediately what she meant but she turned around and said with an evil smile, "I didn't say anything!" I thought, not another fucking gaslighter! Then she tried her NLP on me. BUT she had already told me she had done an NLP (Neuro linguistic programming) course as part of her recent up-grade for her psychiatric nursing SO I was aware of it. I knew already what it was. She was SO fucking obvious. She was trying to manipulate me into being mentally ill. Rot in Hell bitch!

What she said about being in jail with her, really tweaked my morbid curiosity. It made me think about what she got up to in Dundrum, the hospital in Dublin for the criminally insane, where she'd worked for 15 years as a nurse. I wondered if she fucked any of the patients? She seemed like that kind of woman. I asked her later did she ever fuck any? She denied it but she was laughing. I wasn't sure if she was telling the truth or not. She said the staff fucked each other though. She said all the staff were riding one another, married men and all.

I challenged her again, later on that evening when we were both relaxing in the sitting room about the jail comment. I was hoping she would admit it. She said she didn't know what I was on about. It really fucking pissed me off. It was bad enough getting it in the street but now the woman I was sleeping with too. She was blatantly gaslighting me. I think she thought no one would ever hear about it.

How wrong was she? A Billion are going to hear about it, Riverdance, you soul destroying slut of a human being. I'm so glad you are disbarred.

Riverdance was struck off and no longer allowed to practice as a psychiatric nurse for having a fling with me. It is a little justice for me for all the games she played and it makes me laugh a little too.

That first bit of gaslighting was the beginning of her trying to destroy my confidence in my own sanity. She tried to put doubt in my mind that she wasn't saying things. I knew she was. Then she tried saying that because I was hearing things that I might be turning schizophrenic. I could tell then it was a nasty fucking game she was playing. Something was definitely amiss. There were exterior forces at work. I was suspicious right away as soon as she mentioned the illness. She tried to force me on medication. She was a ruthless tramp. Fucking hell! What did I do to her? I thought she was possibly working for the pharmaceutical companies. Trying to shut me up. She confirmed she was on the hospital's side one night we were out on a date. She said when we were out bowling "I am for the hospital!" laughing. She did it in front of people, waiting for a reaction. I didn't give her one and I said nothing but I was very aware she was playing the ruthless cunt. This book is going to expose everything. The big pharma drugs she was trying to put me on fuck with your body and your mind. I was trying to avoid being on them. It was very difficult around Letterkenny with all the gaslighting to stay sane. They have a mafia mentality, and I was persona non grata. The drugs affect patients so badly. I wouldn't take the medication for her. It caused friction between her and me and made me think I will never get married because my wife would have the power to section me. FYI I'm not bipolar. Fuck off, you CUNT!!!

She was enjoying playing the Doctor. She had smuggled some medication home and was trying to administer it to me. Oh, what a thrill these nurses get from playing doctor. They are so fucking boring and sycophantic to Dublin nurses. My case for elation in Donegal in

2006 was based on my first admission to St. Pats mental asylum in Dublin. You will read about that in-depth and make up your own mind.

The female nurses always flirted with me in the Dublin mental asylum, and they did it in Letterkenny too for years. It stopped for no reason. The well was poisoned by someone!!! I think it was the men. The Bipolar elation case Letterkenny mental asylum built was bullshit, and the Doctor, Doctor Comet who made the diagnosis created a massive headache for me. It was only by the grace of an alien oligarchy that I was helped through every little fucking problem that arose from the diagnosis. I have to admit it has been good for research!

Riverdance's kids thought she was fucked in the head. I overheard them talking downstairs one day. One of them said, "Does he not know mum is sick?" She was a psychopath to me. It didn't really put me off her though, and I did fuck her in her uniform one evening, a fantasy of mine. All those nurses flirting with me day and night in the asylum put a horn on me that lasted in my wank bank for years.

She had just come back from work. I asked her to leave her uniform on and pulled her down on the bed. I was already naked. I laid her back. She looked so fucking frigid. She knew she was doing wrong AND I knew it excited her. I could see the spark in her eyes! I pulled her trousers and her panties down. She said quietly, "this is so wrong....". I laughed and spread her legs. I stuck my cock up deep inside her. It was a smooth operation. She looked like she was scared of being caught. I fucked her as gently as I could and came with a gratifying smile on my face a few quick moments later.

She told me another day after that, that one of her female colleagues asked her was she having a fling? She said she had to admit it. She couldn't hide it. She was sitting in the hallway of the asylum in a daze. She was waiting to go into a meeting and she couldn't help thinking about the sex we'd had the night before. She said it had to be the most erotic sex she'd ever had! I gave her multiple orgasms. I was lying beside her fucking her in the scissor position. A favourite of mine. It lasted about an hour. She looked so fucking exhausted afterwards. I laughed to myself and thought another satisfied customer!! She got mad with me and said "I bet I could be any woman!!" And I said "No, you bring out the best in me!!" She did not believe me lol. Her colleague knew by her flustered appearance that something was going on. She said she was orgasming as she was sitting there. And that her knickers were soaking wet. I laughed. It had been pretty hot! It got me going again and we fucked all that evening too.

I was sleeping with the enemy too, two of my fantasies fulfilled. We were like under-cover agents in a battle. I think she was trying to kill me. She nearly drove the car off the road on the way to Belfast airport when we were going on holiday to Malta. I managed to grab the wheel and stop her. She was working under-cover for something! Strange things were happening in Malta too. She had people following us. I figured out she was in some kind of underworld fraternity.

We shagged on the balcony one afternoon in our hotel during the day and made a sex tape. The builders on the next building a couple of floors up, about 30 feet away were wolf whistling and videoing it. There were about 10 of them, and they were all looking down laughing. They were giving me the thumbs up. I smiled and waved up at them, putting on a show. She said the strangest thing when I came. "Now I have a tape!" She said. She always seemed to be setting me up for blackmail.

We'd met in Letterkenny asylum two years previous and fulfilled our flirtations when I turned up at her hostel. It was definitely a fantasy of hers! She told me Scissorhands had stayed in her little hostel a couple of months before me. I believe that's when the two of them set up the conspiracy against me. I reckoned in my not unfounded paranoid theory that they planned if I ever turned up on Riverdance's doorstep they would put their plan in motion and destroy me. There are not that many hostel's in Letterkenny. It was bound to happen.

I did turn up, and Riverdance and I fucked like bunnies for months. I doubt if that was ever in Scissorhands's plan!

I thought about leaving, but the sex was fucking brilliant! I was homeless too, so I thought I would play along. I thought I would pump her for information. I was fucking her for the rent as well so it was a pretty sweet deal.

I also thought it would make for a witty anecdote, like the time I said "I have to cum in your mouth, Riverdance!" when we were in

Belfast on a weekend break. On the Saturday morning, we were so horny, we didn't give a fuck that the kids were in the next room! She wanted me to wank off as she watched. She was fucking purring. I could feel her fucking pussy getting soaking wet. I was about to cum when one of the kids squealed in the other room. Riverdance jumped up on top of the bed. I was about to explode. She went to run out of the room but I shouted "Riverdance! I have to cum in your mouth!" I made it sound like it was imperative. She was so confused and in a tizzy because of the kids that she just put her mouth over my cock and took the cum. It was very funny. She was in such a panic. I laughed my head off when she left.

I thought if I stayed with her for a while as well, I could get an inside scoop on the psychiatric world from her perspective. I told her about the gaslighting by the nurses in Letterkenny mental asylum, and she laughed. She confirmed with a superior sadistic smile that they did do the things that I'd experienced. It was common knowledge amongst them. It was all the confirmation I needed. Nurses were narrating what patients are doing like eating dinner "Juan is eating his spuds!" looking straight at us. We were the only ones there, me and another guy and I knew if I asked why she was saying that, she would deny it. They were tormenting me. "I'm going to infiltrate his life and ruin it!" said a male nurse with his back turned to me and me the only one in canteen. They were all doing the same thing, it was vicious.

I was using the asylum as a place to stay because I was homeless so in their mind's I was taking up a bed. They were bullying me to make my time as hard as possible. Riverdance said they often do that. She thought it was funny. It's a trade secret. She told me not to tell anyone. She said the nurses are always stealing the medication in there as well. IT'S NOT A TRADE SECRET NOW YOU CUNT! They were playing on the fact the general public would not believe a person with a mental health condition!!!

I believe the seedy plan that Scissorhands and Riverdance had was to blackmail me over the paedophilia situation she was trying to create. Riverdance was trying to entice me with it, or she was fucking trying to land me in Dundrum. I told her about my book, and she just thought millions of pounds! I could see her brain in overdrive when I explained what I was writing. How dumb is she not to think I would not write about her? She put the plan in motion and started gaslighting me a few weeks into us sleeping with one another. She was trying to manipulate me. I don't think so! The brainwashing with her sexual deviance was both erotica and paedophilia.

She started the paedophilia when she said in the kitchen, "another couple of weeks, and you'll be in Simon's bed, and I'll be in Angel's bed!". Simon was her 8-year-old son that she was trying to make gay. He was always hanging out with his mum and angel. I think he just liked the attention. Riverdance was trying to encourage him to be gay. She was trying to get me to have sexual relations with him. It was fucking twisted. Again, she said this with her back turned to me. I let it go. I thought I need to get somewhere else to stay. I rumbled everything when she was on the phone one afternoon while we were lying in bed. I could hear Scissorhands voice on the other end of the line and I could tell by the way she was talking it was Scissorhands. I figured it out it was me they were on about, Riverdance thought she was talking in code. She was a dumb criminal! She was looking at me and laughing. And whatever Scissorhands said to Riverdance, Riverdance said, looking at me "ok" "I'll leave him alone!" and had a sadistic smile on her face. She smiled cruelly at me. It confirmed they had a plan. It was straight after she tried to get me shagging her kids. FUCKING JESUS!

She told me paedophilia and incest is rife around Letterkenny. She used to say things like abused people have the best sex. I had to agree. I've had a lot of ladies that have been raped and abused and the sex was out of this world! She was grooming me for paedophilia, or so it seemed. I wondered was she already at it? She said the kids were raised to be aware. I hadn't the foggiest what she was on about. I now think it was paedophilia speak. It was a weird fucking atmosphere before I got the hell out of there. When my paranoia became real life, and I got the confirmation from her phone call with Scissorhands, I thought it's time to skedaddle.

Luckily enough around this time, Riverdance had got me a place to stay in her friend, a transvestite's, hostel just over the road from her.

Riverdance said she needed some space. I felt so sorry for the kids, but I didn't know who would believe me if I told. I only hoped it would surface at their school if it was happening. It was a terrible bad time. I knew it was nearly over with Riverdance. I moved into her friend, Ariadne's hostel. The minute I moved in; Ariadne had an eye for me. I think Riverdance had set me up. I figured out on the first night there that Riverdance had set me up for a sexual encounter with Ariadne because he came into my room that night with his long hair and the fly on his jeans down and said, "come on then". I gave him my politest turndown and prayed to alien he didn't kick me out. I was enjoying my time away from Riverdance in the other hostel. Ariadne was constantly hitting on me though. He wanted me to shag him up the ass. He tried enticing me with a story about him and Riverdance. Trying to turn me on! He told me they had sex with one another. He said Riverdance loved his boobs. I came up with a brainwave on how to get Ariadne satisfied. I put him onto a hooker nearby and he spent 250 euros getting the whole nine yards done on him. He got a dildo up the ass and said it was fucking brilliant. I laughed my head off. He was a bit of craic.

When I split up with Riverdance, I left in a blaze of glory. It happened when I thought she gave a punter a blowjob. He pretended she did. I beat seven colours of shite of him and slashed his fucking tires. The Gardai got wind of it and sent a van to take me to the Letterkenny mental asylum. It was Doctor Comet who saw me. Doctor Noir was off. Doctor Comet and I go back a long way and he even told me that I could be issued with a clean bill of health. So. I'm working hard to get it! He understood my plight as soon as I explained it and let me go. I was only in the asylum for about an hour. It was first thing in the morning. I left Riverdance, forgot about Scissorhands and worked on this book for the rest of the year living in that hostel.

This book is about me, a nobody in the world of celebrity - an adventurer. I did worry about telling all my secrets. After all, it's normally celebrities who write autobiographies. I love a good story, especially if it makes a difference. I believe life is about creating memories. I've always looked for excitement in my life. I love my joie de vivre. Spirit of life. I never had Bipolar. I don't even believe in it. I believe it's all emotions.

Drink and drugs fuck your emotions up. My insight comes from 20 years of experience at the front line. And as for the family folks, kids cause pressure, causing depression. Elation and depression are happiness and sadness. They are normal human feelings. Even in the extreme. Medication destroys your brain.

While drunk in 2003, I pretended to have Bipolar to get off with breaking a window in a 5-Star hotel in Dublin's city centre. I threw a brick through the window from the street and I pretended to have Bipolar so I wouldn't get a criminal record. I believe I am covered from being arrested for the same crime twice in writing this book by double jeopardy. I have already been done for drunk and disorderly for it! I faked the illness so I could continue to get employment after the charge, hassle free. INSANE!!! I know!! If I hadn't pretended, my life would have been fucking excellent. I convinced the admissions Doctor in St. Pats mental asylum that I needed help. I now want that Doctor to come forward and speak on my behalf. I want her to tell the truth, that she believed there was nothing wrong with me in the first place. My father was forcing the issue. It was his idea.

I'd heard of Bipolar from a girl I met named Flo, so I knew the symptoms of elation – easy as I thought! I can pretend that! I can do two months in the asylum standing on my head – it'll be fun! I'd seen the movies. I was also a writer and thought maybe I could write about it one day and maybe I could change a few things for the patients in there for the better. Change the system from the inside out! Flo had told me terrible abuse stories of what occurred in there! Pourquoi pas (why not)?!! I thought!! I changed my mind after 1 day in the hospital. I refused the medication on the first day and they raised the ante on the second, forcing me. They said I wouldn't get out. It was frightening. I no longer had control of my freedom. I was being forced to take medication. I realized some of the ramifications of my faking it – it was too late! I couldn't get out. I pleaded with the nurses to get me out, saying I'm voluntary, but the nurse said "you might be voluntary, but the Doctor has put a barring order on you! You can't leave!" They were keeping me in! And, on top of that, my assigned Doctor, Doctor Lucky (Lucky I didn't kill him!), convinced my Father I was Bipolar. The very thing I was pretending to have. It was my own fault, but I had told the truth 1 day after they put the pressure on me, to my Dad. I told him I'd pretended in admissions but he didn't believe a word that I said to him. He did not believe that I'd pretended. He thought there was something wrong anyway because of the fucking bullshit rumours of my travels in the weeks previous, which I write about in this book. The rumours had travelled home to Donegal. My Dad was my point of contact with the rest of my family as we both were in Dublin, and my family all hail from Donegal. His slant on the whole fiasco was how the rest of my family found out. They believed I was Bipolar too, and in 20 years, they have been going over and back between my father and me deciding if I'm Bipolar or not. It's been a fucking eventful to say the least. I lost my whole family. This book, my soberness and my continued success in life is to prove to them, once and for all, that I am telling the truth about pretending to have Bipolar to gain admission and that there was nothing ever wrong with me! Everyone just wanted me to accept it!!! Who the hell wants to end up stigmatized to death with mental illness for life when there is nothing wrong with you?!! Is it any wonder I have fought my corner all these years, saying I am of sound mind! I risk losing employment publishing this book! I just hope everyone reading it, especially future employers (because it's going to come out eventually, this world is a small place!), believe I am telling the truth throughout. Please, people! If you've ever thought about pretending to have a mental illness to get into a mental asylum, please don't! You will come out with an illness that will be hard to shake. Guaranteed! It's not worth it! I lost everything.

My Father died, believing he was right in his actions towards me, regarding me being mentally ill. His actions were fatal. His disbelief of me ruined my life. He was such a stubborn old cunt. He knew I was ok but by backing down he would ruin his reputation. He'd gone from the man who drove his eldest son to run away to sea, to the man that was going to sort his son's life out. What a fucking idiot of a man! He was embarrassed by his actions in later life, I believe. My fake Bipolar diagnosis and subsequent diagnosis of paranoid Schizophrenia (because I told Doctor Noir about the gaslighting and he said I had persecutory delusions! WHAT A DICKHEAD?!!!), changed the way my Father looked at me and treated me. I lost all my independence, and I was treated as an inferior within the family. What I said was no longer believed and I was no longer looked at as being the head of the family. I am the eldest, and the dynamics were fucked. My brother, James, who was 15 years old when this went down and is ten years my junior, took over as head of the family in later years. He was a good little kid. He did piss-takingly tell my mother that I had broken down crying in our sitting room after my near fatal car crash that you will read about. The take-over by my little brother was demoralizing to go through. My brother got left my father's entire estate. 26 acres and two houses. I'd been taught to take it over since I was a child. It's not much, it is only farm land, but it was a responsibility he gave to me when I was seven years old. He told me if he ever died, I was to look after the family, that I was the head. I've never forgotten it and still take it seriously to this day, even though things panned out as they did. The estate was promised to me for years but so fuck! It's done now. I'll make my own estate. My Father asked me for a loan of 20,000 euros when I got a car crash claim in 2006 to finish the renovations on my Grandmother's house, his home house. He made a semi-detached out of it. He said it's going to be yours one day anyway to get the money out of me. I was very reluctant to give him so much money. I believed him and gave him the money, but I never got the money back or the house!! I only got money back from my dad when he died. The money thing doesn't bother me now. He left me 13 grands in his will. I'll put it to good use and just to make him turn in his grave I'll spend the money on publicizing this book on how he ruined my life!!! Lol. I'd asked my Father 8 years before he died what was happening to the land we own when he died because I noticed a change in his attitude towards James and I. James did not speak to my Father for years because my Dad slept with his girlfriend's mother. Talk about Jeremy Kyle or Jerry Springer!!! James only started talking to him again I reckon because he would have been cut out of the will. I am annoyed by my brother's actions regarding my Father telling him he would be left everything. He could have said "no, that is Juan's inheritance!" That's what I would have said. Or, seeing as it was a semi-detached house and I was homeless he could have said "give Juan one of the houses!" Fucking hell!!! I am very, very, very pissed off about not getting a house. My sister got a house and my brother got two houses. My Father had begun to treat my younger brother as the eldest when he'd obviously decided to leave everything to him. It was weird. Treating him like the elder?!! Fuck did that piss me off! When my Father told me, he was leaving it to James that one night in 2013, it was a hard pill to swallow. The injustice of it all. But in time I got over it. It wasn't the monetary value. It was the status of James being the senior in my Fathers eyes because of the Bipolar condition I was supposed to have. My Father told me that me being Bipolar was the reason he changed his will. It made me bitter against him. I don't get depression, but that brought me down. I got over it, and it's all in the past now. I wish there had never been doubt thrown on me. I can see the flicker of doubt in James's eyes sometimes when I'm telling him something ludicrous that happened to me. My father died in August 2020. His death was the only closure I got with him. Sad to say, but I felt relief the friction was over. The faking being mentally ill really ruined our relationship, my relationship with my family and my life. I do not take medication even though it was forced upon me. In my parent's eyes at the time, the diagnosis, even though it wasn't the truth, explained all my bad behaviour in all the years previous but I've always known that those shenanigans were always caused by drinking alcohol. My parents believed Doctor Lucky and every other Doctor who built their cases over the years on Doctor Lucky's original bullshit diagnosis! This is the true story of my life. As you will gather, I've always been a bit wild! It doesn't mean I'm mentally ill!!!!

HOME LIFE

I was born in Derry in Altnagelvin hospital on April 11th, 1978. My Mother, Marian, was a nurse in Altnagelvin at the time and my Father, Juan Snr, was a ships pilot on the river Foyle. He navigated ships up and down the river Foyle.

I had a great childhood growing up in Carrowtrasna, in Donegal. Or Shrove as most people know the area as. My sister and I, Margaret, who is two years younger, were big buddies all the way through our childhood growing up there. We had our odd little fight but nothing compared to the scream she yelled at me when I was explaining to her the story of how my first admission to St. Pats mental asylum in Dublin came about not long after I got out. I was trying to set the record straight. My father had lied so much. We were driving down from Derry and in the middle of me explaining she screamed "YOU'RE BIPOLAR AND THAT'S IT!!!" It was all I needed to know that I could never have the same relationship with her again.

I attended Greencastle national school from the age of 4 to the age of 11. When I was ten my younger brother James was born, and it was like having a new toy for my sister and I. It felt to us like we were his parents as well. It was fun!

I remember one time when James was about one year old. Margaret and I were playing with him in my bedroom. We had one of those old wind-up phones that you used to contact the operator with. The game was simple. We gave James the plug of the phone to hold. The metal end was electro-conductive when you wound the handle. We placed him in the middle of the room and extended the lead away from him. He sat there smiling with the plug in his hand. We giggled with excitement. We wound it up and gave him an electric shock. He started crying but didn't let go. We made him laugh, pulling faces, then when he giggled, we done it again. It was hilarious.

I was a little reprobate growing up. I really lived free range. I roamed the countryside. I first got drunk on my 13th birthday but I had my first beer when I was 8 with Barry McCann. We found a tin of Tennants lager along the side of the road. Joie de vivre. I can still remember Barry's eyes light up when he said let's drink it.

On my 13th birthday, I was left in charge of a house full of food and drink by our neighbours with Kiltboy (I'll introduce you to him in the chapter W.A.B.C), my sister, and two of my cousins from Derry. The adults all went to the pub. It was fucking hilarious!

It was a wedding reception in a little house in Asabrick. The next townland across from Carrowtrasna. We had a massive food fight, the minute the parents walked out the door. It was funny. We all had loads of alcohol and ran about like edjits! We got it all cleaned up before the adults arrived home. It was a close call! The next morning my Father asked me had I been drinking. I don't know how he figured it out, maybe he smelled it, but he asked me why I did it? Then he said just before I answered "were you just trying it to see what it was like?" I agreed "yes!" I didn't know what else to say. He said "ok, just don't tell your mother". Then he asked was Margaret drinking too? I said no, lying. I knew I'd be in the shit if he found out!

I had a great group of friends during my teenage years. We had lots of wild experiences together.

I attended Carndonagh community school in Donegal. It was the biggest secondary school in the country at the time. At the time of my attending, it had around 2000 pupils and over a hundred teachers. I had a good time there. I fought like an animal for the first couple of weeks in first year, even giving a Second year a black eye one morning in the library because he was trying to bully me. Myself and Munhall were studying for an exam first thing and this little CUNT from Moville wouldn't stop kicking the back of my chair. I told him to stop BUT he did not do it. So, I walloped him and sent him flying over the table. I had a killer punch even when I was 12. I got a little fame in the school for fighting, but I thought no fucking way am I going through secondary school the way I went through national school with everyone wanting to fight me. So, I hung up my gloves. I wanted to concentrate on my studies. I thought leave that to the other fucking assholes who enjoyed the notoriety. There were a few dickheads from Glengad, that followed me around, kicking at my heels, trying to get me to fight but I never did. They were from second year. I never gave them the satisfaction.

I didn't have another fight until 3rd year. Eamon, the other 3rd year I kicked the shit out of, was an asshole and a bully anyway. It all originated out of an engineering project. Eamon had been rumoured to have used a lot of pullies for his crane project. He said that he'd heard that I was spreading the rumour that there were no pullies for anyone else. When he challenged me, I told him I did not spread rumours and I never would. Cathal, the red-haired wonder, was winding him up to fight. Grant was his Muff personal ass-licker. He was a little numb-nutted boy with limited intelligence. Eamon took off his leather coat. He fancied himself as a bit of a hardman. Then he asked me did I want a slap? I asked "who's going to give it?" He then took off his watch. I made a joke of him saying "Are you going to do a strip tease or hit me?!" He went fucking nuts at this! I knew he would. I knew if he swung at me first, he would be totally in the wrong. A stupid schoolyard rule but a good one to know! I knew I would have the law of the teachers on my side. The teachers always asked after a fight, "who threw the first punch?" He threw the first punch and I kicked his hairy hole around that classroom. There was blood all over the walls where I punched him on the lips and nose. When the fight was over, he was bleeding from every orifice. I gave him a proper ass-fucking!!! The principle called us up to his office. He was an ex-Dublin Gaelic footballer and a tough nut. I always admired him. He asked me in first. I told him Eamon said "do you want a slap?" And he said "good enough! He started it!!" He said,

"Send him in!". Eamon, the 3 trees weasel, came in and the first thing he said, the snivelling little CUNT, was "this isn't the first time he's been in trouble!!!" He was such a fucking little weasel. The principle said "it doesn't matter!", and said "did you ask him did he want a slap?" He said "yeah, but it was just a figure of speech!". He was not very bright for an honour's student. The principle left him crying. He was 3rd year for god sake! What a fucking baby?!! He was reprimanded severely with all the blood pouring out of him. It was really satisfying!!!!!

My 4th year Math's teacher got very angry with me one day because I was dragging my heels buying the Math's book. He'd reminded me a few times. I was duking in to my mates' book until I remembered to buy it. The teacher was a bit of an asshole and he had a spite at me for beating up Eamon in 3rd year. They were from the same area and Eamon was one of his favourite students. The teacher was very strict and full of pomp. He blew up and said "You'll never amount to anything!". Fuck you, you midget little cunt. I am a Superyachting Captain and soon to be a fucking multi-billion pounds selling author. Jesus Christ it was honours math's, of course I'll amount to something!!!

I was working every evening in our bar that we had bought when I was 15 years old. My dad had bought it on a whim. My mother had sent him out for a carton of milk, and he met the owner putting a for sale sign up and struck a deal. My mother was not impressed! The work in the bar was arduous during the school year. It took priority.

When we bought the bar, it was fun and terrible working there. As I grew up working there, the pressure from my father became unbearable. He was a fucking tyrant. It was bloody impossible to maintain the work load he was putting on me. When I was 16, I fucking flipped one day during an argument with him in the bar about something stupid I'd forgotten to do. I ran off leaving him in the bar and nearly topped myself. It was lonely. I had nobody. I ran on my own to the cliffs in Shrove about half a mile away. Crying my eyes out all the way. I climbed around the bottom of the cliffs until I saw a cliff face, I knew I couldn't scale and started climbing. I thought I would fall off before the top, and it would all be over —no more pain. The rock face was about 150 feet high. I climbed most of the way up when suddenly the rocks became loose under my feet and fell to the ground. I thought, uh-oh, I don't want to bloody die! I had nearly gotten to the top. I was a better climber than I thought! I changed my mind and climbed down carefully. I thought ruefully. I hope I don't fall now after changing my mind. I had a little laugh to myself. It was a juxtaposition situation. I was so glad to get to the bottom. I thought I am never giving someone that power over me again. It was around then that I started writing. I wanted to vent my frustrations. It worked, baby, and now I'm an author. Funny how things work out! My dad thought writing was one step back to the asylum for me - as you will read. He was such an old fuddy duddy after the false diagnosis of bipolar.

The bar was really affecting my studies in 4th and 5th year of secondary school. I lost interest and I didn't know what I wanted to do with my life. In 5th year I thought about the army and going to the air corps but the pay for the army was not great and I failed my interview for the air corps. I had aspirations of being an Astronaut pilot. The aliens said I would have been an awesome pilot. I told my father that I'd failed the pilot interview when I came out and he said put it down to experience. I said experience is what you get, when you don't get what you want. He laughed and said, "where did you hear that? That's a good one!"

It was fucking diabolical working in the bar when I hit 18. I wanted to be out partying with my mates. Instead I was cooped up like Cinderella. I asked my Dad could I run it when I was 19, but he bloody laughed at me. I was fed up with him walking in after piloting and ruining all the systems we had in place. I was already running it. I did not see the difference with him putting me in charge. I had so many great ideas. I was really enjoying working there then but I thought fuck this and thought I'm getting out of here. When we sold the pub, I was 24, my Dad went through a mid-life crisis. I was away at sea for most of it. He really took an interest in my life again. It was so over-bearing. I preferred his half-assed parenting better. He was a bit of a wild man when I was growing up. He liked to piss it up with the best of them! It definitely rubbed off on me. James, my brother, had a completely different up-bringing. He was a decade younger than me. My Dad put on this responsible adult visage when he was talking to James. I took notice of it. It was a bit weird for me. I thought my Dad was trying to right the wrongs he'd made with me. He brought me up with a wicked sense of humour. Both him and his brother my uncle Charlie made me a comedian before the age of 7!!! They were always telling me dirty jokes, then explaining them to me when I didn't get the joke. They went down a treat in the playground. I paid no attention to the way my Dad was bringing James up. Not until he fucking started beating down on me with it. It was like he had taken excitement completely out of his life. He'd lost his Joie de vivre. He'd had a complete attitude adjustment and because I wouldn't play along with it, he fucking blackballed me in the family.

I remember one time the bar was being cleaned by me before opening. I was doing my very best. My Dad came back and asked me had I cleaned out the ashes on the fire place. I said I had. He checked and saw some ashes still left in the fire place. He went fucking bananas. I said it was only a couple. He said don't get smart with me. I said I wasn't. He went fucking mental. He lashed out at me, smacking me in the face with a bin liner full of frozen kebabs. It bust my lip. He fucking cracked then and broke down crying. The pressure in the bar was unbelievable.

My opportunity for escaping him at 19 came after talking to a lecturer, Bill Kavanagh, from the fishery college in Greencastle. I'd been idling at the Tech in Derry, doing an Electronics course I didn't want to do. It was only after speaking to him that I got a bit of focus. He used to come into our bar on a Friday for a pint on his way home. He told me about the Seamanship course in Cork IT that I could apply for just using my Junior certificate – 3rd year qualifications in my secondary school. I had done very well in these in honours level. 6 B's and two D's. I'd told him I'd done terrible in the leaving cert.

I put it to my father one day in the bar that I wanted to go to sea. He said "if that's what you want, then I'm 100% behind you!" He said to me before my first trip away to sea "You have to be like your Grandfather" I said "What do you mean?" He said "Your Grandfather O'Donnell…" he said to me said "Be the hard prick or the soft pussy but remember the hard prick fucks the soft pussy every time!!" He told me that those sentiments were in our family for over a century. His father, my grandfather told him those words when he was going away to sea as well. I have passed those words onto my nephew Leo, my sister Margaret's son. He is going on to be the first Chief Engineer in our sea going family. I'm really proud of him. He's only 13 now and he has made the decision of his young life. He will be a millionaire in his own right. Sarah, his younger sister and my goddaughter will hopefully be a psychologist. She is a little scamp. I love her to bits. You can tell she has a really bright mind on her. I thought what my father told me was good advice and never ever let anyone walk over me. In hindsight, by going to sea I was really pulling the wool over his eyes to get away from him. I felt so beat down living there. As I said my father had been to sea for years before my birth, as had my Grandfather, great-Grandfather, great-great Grandfather, some of my uncles, and extended family. It was in the blood. We had over a hundred and fifty years of tradition at sea and a hundred years tradition of pilots on the River Foyle in my Father's side of the family. I had voiced my interest at going to sea when I was very young but my father had put me off the idea of going away. He said you didn't get to see the world anymore. It was a crap job for nowadays. Ships have quick turnarounds and no time in port anymore. I still wanted to shag my way around the earth!!! He he. I had always harboured the idea of being a ships pilot like him.

I felt a little guilt at leaving the rest of my family to run the bar but I wanted to go to sea. But as much as the bar was terrible to work in, there was a lot of fun times! I had a lot of sex when I was young because of it. I loved older women and they loved me. I was like Charlie in the chocolate factory with women, booze and cigs.

The pub years were also my most formative years growing up. My dad said it was the best psychology lesson you could get.

Before going to Cork to do my Seamanship course, I'd been doing the electronic and electrical engineering HND course in the Tech in Derry. It wasn't really grasping me. I was fed up to the teeth with it. I spent most of my time playing snooker with my mate Mac Sea from Greencastle. Mac Sea was a couple of years below me doing a GNVQ on the same subject. He's now an electronic engineer in Holland. You can read a WhatsApp conversation between us on my website for this book, iCon. The aliens reveal their existence to him in it. I'm not sure he believes in them…

I wasn't interested in doing the HND and only did it because the grades I got from leaving cert – my school final exams were fucking shit mate. I repeated the leaving certificate, and got worse the second time. The results were not as good as they could have been had I studied. The bar had a massive impact. I was told to study in the bar by my father. It was annoying. I couldn't concentrate, unlike the blonde who stared at the orange juice carton because it said to concentrate on the side of it.

My jokes and stories come from thought by association.

19 was a good age for me soccer wise though. I scored a goal from the half-way line against Illies in a league match one Sunday, extremely hungover a bit like George Best! I knew with my energy levels; I couldn't chase down the goalie one on one. I was just inside their half, but he was off his line. I was fubared (fucked up beyond all recognition!) so I blasted it over him. I reckon my Grandfather on my Mother's McLaughlin's side of the family, who played for the Republic of Ireland and Cork City in the 1930's even though he was from Derry, would've been proud.

As you will see, I went on to become a Captain in Superyachting and a Chief mate in the Merchant Navy.

The following are a few select stories so you can get to know me better before I fully tell you how I got the diagnosis of bipolar. That way you can see, they were just trying to tame me.

BULLY ME?!!

When I was 10 years of age, I was bullied at school by older kids called Big Berndan & Berndan rubber ass. There were a few other bullies but they do not merit a mention. Berndan rubber ass was called rubber ass because of his big rubber lips. Rubber ass, rubber lips!!! Rubber ass used to bully me incessantly, but I always got him back. I put chewing gum in his hair one time. It was hilarious. He had to have it cut out!!! It wasn't as bad as when Big Berndan was bullying me, I couldn't sleep with that. It was affecting my school work every day. I was afraid to snitch on him because of schoolyard protocol. NO TOUTS. Touts will be executed. It was soul-destroying. As I said, I had a couple of bullies growing up in Greencastle school, but Big Berndan was the biggest asshole of the lot of them. He was intimidating me every morning on the bus and laughing at my confidence being dulled. He had just moved house further down towards Shrove, because his old house in Poundtown was being renovated, so he had to get our bus to school. He normally walked. He did not like my popularity and started bullying me not long after he started riding our bus.

I was a bubbly child. I was a bit of a wild kid and a ring-leader. We had a gang of boys in our class that used to hang out every lunchbreak. Damo and I used to lead the battalion. We sat beside each other in class causing mayhem. Our gang took on the older kids and had running battles with them. It was LOTS of fun. Big Berndan, the bully on the bus, was two years older than me and the biggest CUNT in school. He was even taller than the principle. I wasn't able to fight him off because of his size. He was a fucking massive DICK. I was younger than the rest of my class so I was a little smaller. Berndan used this against me. I had started school a little earlier than most people in my class. He was really getting me down. I was putting up with it, but it was destroying me.

After about a month, my dad came into my room one night after I'd gone to bed.

He asked me about it. He asked if I wanted him to do anything to help. He didn't want to shame me in front of the school. I had a bit of a rep. I was a rapscallion and a really good fighter in my year. But I always got good grades. I figured if I did my schoolwork, the teacher couldn't get angry with me lol. I told him I would deal with it myself. He said, "you better do it soon, or I'm going to his parents!" He left, and I lay awake brainstorming. I thought, how I can make this Berndan stop? He was way too big for me to fight. The only thing I thought I could do was scare him with something. I'd been bought a pair of nail clippers from Mallorca by my Auntie Margaret from Derry, and it had a knife on it. I thought fuck yeah. I'm going to scare the shit out of him with that! I'll put it to his throat the next time he jumps on my knee. The nail clipper's blade didn't look that scary, but the bottle opener looked like a pirate's knife, way scarier. Why are they like pirates' knives? They just ARrrr!!! A bit of 10 years old humour for you! I went to sleep with a smile on my face.

I wrote the poem, Axe no questions, Tell no lies, years later while thinking back to my playground years. I remember thinking the first lines of the poem from the memory of when I was about 10. I was looking around the playground at the time. It was then that I really realized what politics really was. Everybody was vying for attention and trying to be the star of the show. Then as I grew older and watched politicians avoid answering direct questions on TV. It angered me. I watched them as a young boy, probably around 10, on TV using evasive techniques as my Father explained to me, that that's what they were, and it pissed me of. I asked him why the politician wouldn't just answer the question. He just laughed and said, "that's the way they work." When

I was about 16, I asked him more about politics, and I said I thought about joining a political party. I asked him how it worked? He explained they have an idea and a party line. Which meant if you had your own ideas and didn't agree with their ideal, you still had to go along with it. I thought fuck that. I edited the poem in 2019 after listening to side speaking (gaslighting or underground talk) from the general public in Letterkenny. Side speaking is a jailbird technique. The criminals would say something to wind the prison guard up. The prison guard would react and ask what did they say? And the jailbird would deny saying anything. When the jailbird would say it, they wouldn't look in their targets direction and say it loud enough for them to hear it. I'd had enough. I refer in the poem to Donegal's spirit mountain - Errigal. It's a source of pride to Letterkenny and the Donegal people all over. The Japanese wanted to buy it years ago for a couple of billion dollars. It's full of the rock quartz, and the Japs wanted to make spectacle lenses out of it. They were denied. The bullying in Letterkenny bothered me, but I thought fuck them. I was drinking a lot, and I think they wanted me out of town. They are doing the same in Rathmullan. The little town beside the beach, 20 minutes by car from Letterkenny, that I am living now as I rewrite this book. WELL FUCK THEM!!! I ain't going anywhere until I make a good few quid!!!!! The Follower's party I refer to in the poem is Sinn Fein.

'06/19

Axe no questions. Tell no lies.

The politics of power,
have always caught my eye,
from the schoolyard as a kid,
to watching grown men, lie.
The moment it was defined for me,
what politics really was,
the belief in a change for the better,
caused a stirring in my clause.

The purple shroud of mystery,
that's worn with so much pride,
is just a scam to block the damn,
so, every lamb can hide.
Out in the open,
where we all can see,
is where they stand upon the tree,
branches supporting,
to the roots in the ground,
how long will they stand there?
When is the axe found?
Chipping away with every mistake,
We'll whip up the wind that'll make the bow break.
It's the safety net then,
that's formed through opinion,
deciding if their fate,
feels like a minion.
Correctness or not,
conversations are forgotten,
but insults intended,
fester until they're rotten,
only if you let them,
and I wouldn't bet on them,
deceived is to be believed,
in their follower's party,
pick on the loner,
then laugh at him heartily,
everyone leads,
they're all at the back,
no-one at the front,
they're all screaming attack,
the passion and wealth,
and no bloody stealth,
no training,
all feigning,

staggered Jesus's,
reigning,
squashed and moshed,
their trundled hopes joshed,
by parties greater,
and out of the dome,
the little squirrels that naw,
in the damned of their town,
they won't stop it,
'til they cop it,
they want everyone down,
not only to their level,
but below the floorboards,
buried in a soul,
of a bastard's putrid holes,
just like theirs,
the strong of us taking the toll,
they sit back,
armchair rebels,
taxi driver mirror practicing,
for when they meet the real deal,
and show how they feel,
Ooohh, I'm so scared,
You fuck wits are nasty,
In numbers, you're strong,
All trying to be rasty,
Smoking the weed,
A whole town on one man,
Oh, you all so brave,
Well, watch me fuck you' all up when I behave the knave,
Excited,
Delighted,
I will be,
To pull down your Errigal, Letterkenny,
And sell the scree,

47

The japs will love it,
You can sycophantically suck their eye,
And when I leave town,
You 'all can carry on playing I-Spy,
incestuous ideas and behaviour,
of an insular fold,
festering flies,
as in the market place you dwell,
(Nietzsche had it right!!!)
The faithful fabric of society,
they are about to fell,
they know no better,
from their intellect,
With them in charge,
the world would be wrecked!

Big Berndan, my very own bully, was two classes ahead of me. His younger brother kidneypunch, was in my class, and we were always at odds with one another. I punched him in the kidney when we had a gang fight one lunchtime, and he has had trouble with it ever since. I learned it from my Daddy. There was a split in the camp in our class. There were 18 boys, and 4 of them were on his side. We had our gang of about ten desperados. I always found kidneypunch sly. He used to look shiftily from the corner of his eye at you. Maybe he was waiting for another punch!!! LOL. My first experience of definite shifty men. He played football every lunchtime while we desperados fought and caused general mayhem.

Before my dad discovered it, Big Berndan would sit in my lap and jump up and down, squashing me, on every morning for a month. He was showing me he was king of the bus and stealing my essence. I had my seat a few seats from the back, and I wouldn't move. He used to sit in the middle seat at the back with his legs spread open. Totally aggressive. He would do the jumping up and down routine for a few seconds and embarrass me, then walk laughing to his kingdom at the back of the bus. It was about a couple of miles to the school, where he got on, but his was the last stop. I thought it was an eternity when I pulled the knife on him. He would shout, "ALRIGHT JUAN, ALRIGHT?!!" laughing cruelly as he jumped up and down.

When my father gave me an ultimatum, I decided to stand up to Berndan. The knife was my only hope!

I was learning karate from my dad in Moville but it didn't do me any good in this situation.

The nail clippers were lying beside my bed. I picked them up and hatched my plan. The plan was I'd wait until he sat down on top of me and I'd put the knife to his throat. He had the same routine every morning, so I knew what to do. I thought I would threaten him to leave me alone.

The next morning, I got up, put the clippers in my pocket with the blade out, and went with my sister Margaret to get the bus at the top of our drive. I never told Margaret my plan, I knew she'd talk me out of it. But I didn't want to spoil the surprise either!

We got on the bus, and my mate, Wobbly's little brother William, who was about seven years old, was sitting halfway down the bus on the left, piped up, "what are you going to do today when Berndan gets on?!" he was laughing, it was fun watching his superior get beat up on. He was really enjoying it. I brandished the knife and he started laughing. I did it without the driver seeing. I said, "Berndan won't be bothering me today!" They were all impressed and very excited. I sat down in my usual seat. Berndan got on with his kid brother kidneypunch a little later up the road. I stared at Berndan as he walked down the aisle towards me. He had an evil grin on his mug. He was staring right at me. I'm sure many people know who have been bullied recognize it. As he approached, I tightened my grip on the clippers in my pocket. The hooked blade was out, and I felt comfortable. He jumped in on top of me, and I chickened out. I was afraid of his reaction. He was fucking HUGE compared to me. William shouted "WHAT ABOUT THE KNIFE JUAN???!!!" It steeled me up, and I thought, no way am I losing face. I pulled it out and held it to Berndan's throat. Berndan was facing away from me. I said, "Move, and you're fucking dead!!!" He said "touch me with that, and you're dead!" I got aggressive with him then. I pulled the blade deeper in against his throat...I could feel him wilt. He practically shat himself! The driver saw what was happening. He never stopped Berndan beating up on me. I don't know why? The school had heard about the bullying, but no one did anything. The driver sped up. There were no other kids to pick up. He drove the bus like he stole it. He was a good driver, but I think he opened the door to let the clutch out. The driver was shouting for me to let him go. I wouldn't let him go until we got to the school and I was safe. I held on for fear of what would happen if I did let the big whore go!

When we arrived, the school was informed. A couple of teachers came out and broke it up. When they arrived, and I felt I was safe, I let him go. We both got summoned to the Principals office. The Head Principal was off that day, so we were dealing with the Vice-Principal, Miss Polly, my class-mate and friend Paddy's mother. Berndan and I were standing beside one another in the office in front of her. I remember thinking this is such an uneven fight. I thought it was ridiculous. I was looking up at him in the office. He was such a posing CUNT!!! Polly was chastising me for bringing a knife into school. She was threatening expulsion when I stood up against her. I said, "You all knew I was getting bullied, but you never did anything about it, so I did it myself". She stopped chastising me and that was the end of it. Back to our classes. I was KING of the SCHOOL!!!

W.A.B.C

I remember when I was ten years old as well, my friend Kiltboy from Barrhead, Scotland, used to come over with his family every summer and stay with their old Uncle Vincent for about six weeks. When he was here, we were inseparable. He'd arrive down at my house before we'd even have breakfast! He'd get his breakfast with us, and that was us for the day! Off exploring the fields around us, building huts in the bushes, and basically living like the Indians did...feathers, not dots!

My mother used to whistle loudly to us when it was dinner time. She'd use her finger and thumb for a screeching whistle. I could never do it. We could hear it from a few fields away. She was a pretty cool Mum. When I was really young, she taught me how to throw stones. It's the reason why I'm such a crack shot today!

One day, Kiltboy and I were playing up behind the house of my old uncle Jimmy. There was an old car rusting away to shit. We decided to break the windscreen of the car with large stones from a nearby stone wall, it took a lot of effort but we managed it in the end.

Beside where we were playing was an old caravan that was being used as a Pirate radio station. It was broadcasting out over our area and beyond. It was called W.A.B.C. When you went into the caravan, the walls in the foyer, I suppose you could call it, were covered in the signatures of people who had visited and had put their music requests on.

So, we asked the DJ could we write our names up on the walls too, to which the DJ replied "yeah, go ahead but be quiet." The studio was in the next room. The caravan was tiny. We were having fun but I noticed Kiltboy was writing his name over the top of everyone else's. He was such a bad boy. He was laughing his head off when he was doing it! I knew it was wrong and I also knew the DJ wouldn't be happy but I didn't say anything. A few seconds later, the DJ came out furious because we were making so much noise, then he saw the wall and went fucking mental...

"Get out ta fuck" he says, "and don't come back! Ye's aren't allowed within 100 yards of this station!"

So, we duly left, a little pissed off at ourselves at being given out to, but we walked away and formulated a plan of getting him back. We stood about 20 yards, or so we figured the distance to be, then began pelting the tin caravan with stones from our black widow slingshots knowing you could hear the rattle and ping inside. That'll really piss him off we thought. He came out again and chased us away. He was cursing like a trooper this time!

We ran a little way down the hill, then sat down on the edge of the road on the grassy verge and thought that was funny but fuck him, he can't chase us away from one of our favourite playgrounds! Who was he?? A stranger telling us what to do!! We shouldn't have been pelting the caravan with stones or doing the writing over other names, but it was innocent enough to start with, so we thought of another plan to get him back.

I knew that my old uncle Jimmy had a rifle that he always kept beside him as he sat at the fire watching TV and drinking whiskey!! I thought if we could get the gun, we could point it at the DJ and scare the crap out of him. Jimmy had a reputation in the area as a very smart man. I knew that I had to be really cool. He was in his 60's at this stage and he could be a bit impatient.

I knew that in one of the rooms in his house that he'd built for himself, was a room he called his laboratory. There were bits of old engines and other paraphernalia lying about. So, the plan was that I would go up to Uncle Jimmy's house, knock on the door and ask to see his lab. While he was showing me, Kiltboy would nip in and take his gun. So, we did this, and even with Uncle Jimmy's bewilderment at me looking to see his lab, the plan worked!

While I was in looking at the lab, we'd agreed the signal would be for Kiltboy to look in the window with a thumbs up, but instead, the smartass did it by showing me the gun when Jimmy wasn't looking. I'd diverted Jimmy's attention away from the window by asking to see something away from it. I thanked Jimmy and left the house. The house was only 30 yards from the station. I went around the corner of the house to Kiltboy.

We were ecstatic. The plan worked, but then we had to decide who got to point the gun!! We were fighting over it, both of us holding it and pulling it over and back and it loaded!! When Kiltboy shouted quietly "You know Karate, you kick the door in!!!" I knew he was playing games with my head. Trying to stroke my ego. I was a pretty switched on kid. So was he, the little scoundrel. But I decided to do what he suggested.

We went over to the station, and I went in first with Kiltboy close behind me...then, on the count of three, I kicked the door in, breaking the latch, then I jumped to the side. Kiltboy jumped in front of the open door and pointed the gun at the DJ and screamed at him, "FREEZE YA BASTARD!!" in his thick Glaswegian accent...the DJ screamed "HOLY SHIT!!!" We took off running. I shouted we need to put the gun back! We got to Uncle Jimmy's house, then repeated what we'd done before only in reverse...I knocked the door again. This time I told him that there was something in his laboratory that I wanted to see again and that I didn't get a good look at the last time....as I said he could be a bit impatient at the best of times, especially with kids, but he humoured me and let me in. Kiltboy put the gun back.

I left the house, and that was it we high-fived and got the hell out of dodge.

5

ARCTIC SUN

....

On the summer of my 17th year on this planet, I got a berth on a 26m twin-rigging trawler called the Arctic sun. I was the youngest on the boat at 17. I'd had serious thoughts about joining the Merchant Navy around this time too, even though my father was putting me off. I thought by seeing if I could handle being away at sea on a fishing boat, it might give me an idea how the Merchant Navy would be. As it turned out, I loved it.

They decided to give me a go at hatch man after I pulled a fast one on my neighbor. They said I'd make a good hatch man because I had a strong build. The hatch, in layman terms, is the isolated room in the bottom of the boat that is kept at minus 6 degrees to keep the fish fresh by freezing them. My job was to help the other hatch man to grade, ice, and stack the fish boxes full of fish. I also had to keep a record of how many and the location of each type of fish. Great I thought the most physical job on the boat. That'll toughen me up, I thought. I loved hard work. It is great for the body and mind.

Before we joined, Colin, my neighbor, the other crew member was giving me a lift to the pier to join the boat. I asked Colin could he cook shortly after I got in to the car for the drive to the boat. I was leading the conversation. I knew that on fishing boats the last man on cooks! He said, "yeah we hold dinner parties at college "Can you cook?" He asked. "No!" I said, "I'd burn water!" (lying!!!). He regaled me about his cooking the whole way there. When we landed, it was the first thing they asked. "Which one of you is cooking?" I knew the protocol. It was funny. Colin had to cook and do the work on deck as well! He was sick as a dog too. Seasick! Man did he give me a dirty look!! He figured out my topic of conversation on the ride over right away!!

This day a crew member, Paddy Joe, and I were down in the hatch working. There was a problem with the conveyor belt. The belt that took the fish down from the deck above. The working deck was below the main deck (there were three decks) and it housed the conveyor, it was where the fish were gutted and thrown on to the conveyor. The fish were gutted by four other fishermen on the working deck, as I said it was a twin rigger (two nets), and the Skipper piloted the boat as we hashed. We were a crew of seven. The other deck crew threw the gutted fish on the conveyor at one end of the boat, which then travelled forward the length of the boat and down into the hatch where we iced them and stacked them below as they fell through the funnel at the end of the belt. We had an awaiting fish box set up on the table to catch them as they fell. Then another two fish boxes on the table that were for grading small and medium Haddock into. The large Haddock had another box sitting down on the deck, as did every other type of fish that came down.

Paddy Joe, to all intents and purposes, was a character. He had the reputation as being daft as a brush and crazy as hell with a drink in him. And even without it! He was strong as a bull with the bad temper to match but a likeable character at the same time. The whole crew were sitting chatting in the crew mess one afternoon, a couple of days after Colin and I had joined. Paddy Joe was fairly new to the crew as well. Everyone started quizzing Paddy Joe about the stories they'd heard about him. We'd heard so many that we were trying to find out which ones were true? He was reluctant at first to talk about it, but then it got wilder and wilder! He stabbed his brother in the side with the broken coke bottle that he had smashed on the bed side locker because his brother would not move over in the bed. They shared a bed, and Paddy Joe came back full of drink one night and lost his temper because of his brother's ignorance! We'd also heard when he was a kid (he was 27 at this stage) that he had tied his father to their tractor on a hill when his father wasn't looking and let off the handbrake. The tractor nearly dragged his father to his death! He wouldn't tell us if that one was true or not. He was good craic.

So, there he was, Paddy Joe, at the sorting table and in charge, as I was a greenhorn. There was a fault in the conveyor and the pressure of it was getting to him. The conveyor wouldn't respond to the wandering lead controls in the hatch. The stop/start button wouldn't operate. It had to be operated from the next deck above and was either on full or off, with no start/stop. He started to panic every time there was a flood of fish, they would scatter all over the deck, and he would do things like shout profanities and punch himself in the head. I was laughing into myself. I thought, this guy is big and mental. But I didn't want him to know I was laughing at him! I didn't want that temper directed at me! The rest of the crew had told me about his insane strength, so I had respect for him but watching this was SO funny. The fish were spilling everywhere. He screamed at me to break some ice which was caked in piles in the lockers. We took it from port. He just had to unload the pressure and he done it by screaming at me!

As we used up the ice, the various lockers were used to stash fish boxes in after. I broke some ice for the fresh boxes, then stood and watched him again until some more boxes needed stacking. He was really starting to lose it. So, I said, "Give me a go! I know I'm new but I'll give it a try". "No!" he shouted, "you're too green!" So, I said, "well, if I can't do it you can take over again," so he gave in and gave me a go. I knew I could do it even before I asked. I'd been watching him intently, and I had learned what he was doing. We caught up with the back log within 10 minutes, and it was flowing nicely. The boxes were getting stacked by Paddy Joe, and I was doing the grading of the fish. The other guys on the boat had pre-warned me to watch him and keep him working because without thinking, he would slow down and he would also watch you break your back trying to lift something without helping because he seemed to think everyone was as strong as himself. They said don't be afraid to ask for help. He's a good guy. He'll be only more than happy to help you lift things. As things slowed down a bit, the conveyor was still running, but only a few fish were coming down. Paddy Joe just stood there daydreaming, looking idly at me. I was slowly grading the fish, and without thinking, I half flicked him in the balls, jokingly, and told him to break some ice. He just looked at me. Then he said with a big wild grin on his face, "do you wanna play with this?!!" I looked him dead in the eye and said, "Aye, go on ahead, I have a pair of gloves on... I'll get nothing on my hands!!" laughing back at him. "I will, you know!" he said threateningly jokingly. I said, "go on ahead." He'd already started taking off the shoulder straps of his oilskin bottoms. As I worked away. He was dressed in a t-shirt and oil skin bottoms whereas I had the full regalia on, oil-skin top, bottoms, and wooly hat, crazy cunt, so he was. He continued saying "I will, you know!" So, I said, "go for it!" As he was taking his bottoms down, I surreptitiously reached for a monkfish under my right arm with my left hand, but I thought that might take the tip of his cock off! Have you ever seen the teeth on those Monkfish fuckers?!!! I grabbed a large Haddock instead. As he took his cock out, I smacked the fish across the tip of his cock with a whack!!! "OUCH!!" he screamed, nearly falling on his knees. He started complaining as he stood up straight, as I howled laughing and carried on working. He started laughing too, shouting "you bastard!!" He put his cock away and pulled up his bottoms, then he rubbed his crotch, looking at me, saying, "aw Juan, it's all sticky now!!" He shook his leg and pulled his bottoms out at the crotch, laughing!

6

CORK COUNTY COURTHOUSE ROOF

....

I left the course I was doing in Derry and started the Seamanship course in college in Cork. I'd passed the interview to get in to the Seamanship course handy enough. There were 16 of us in the class. The main lecturer told us that there was a 50% drop out for the course and one of us would die. We all looked around at one another wondering who it would be to kick the bucket? It was actually pretty funny in a morbid kind of way! We had a good group of people in that class. I was 19. It was a 6-week induction course for my Officer of the watch unlimited. We were all a bit wild. Even the lecturers were a bit of craic. One lecturer, who was always a bit more hospitable after 10 O'clock morning break, because as we figured out, he'd had a drink! We could smell the whiskey off his breath!! He was in his 70's. He told us one day that we would be spending a long time away from our families and friends. He dropped a hint that we would not get any sex for a while. He said "That's known as an Irish man's toothache, and the cure for an Irish man's toothache, is a big black mamma and a bottle of rum!" It had everybody in the class laughing!!

One night, not long after we started, a couple of my friends and I, Fergus from Mayo, and Ronan from County Clare went out for the night in Cork city. We'd had a good old night in a few of the pubs we used to frequent. We went to a nightclub and when it was over, we started to walk back home to Bishopstown. As we were walking down Washington Street, I noticed a hoarding around the bottom and scaffolding around the Cork county court house, the second highest building in Cork city. Ronan noticed where I was looking and just laughed. We both knew what the other was thinking – let's climb it. We climbed up onto an electrical box then up the outside of the scaffolding to the top.

When we got to the top, we climbed in through the scaffolding net and onto the roof of the courthouse. As we stepped onto the roof there was a short buzzing sound. Ronan thought it might be an alarm, but I was like, "Nah!! What do you think they would have an alarm up here at the top of the building for?" Silly enough, both of us agreed with the reasoning.

We stood up and began walking around the top of the court house. The nah nah song was out at the time, and we were singing it down to Fergus the Mayo maestro... "Naahnaaahnaaaahnaaaaah...nah nah naah nah naaah!!!" He was shouting back up, "Fuck you!!" You bastards, I can't get up there!! With my fucking knee!!" In his thick Mayo accent!! He'd hurt an old injury earlier from me jumping on his back in the nightclub. He shouted up for us to throw him down a lighter. He had a cigarette that he wanted to light, so we started flicking matches down at him, laughing. The next thing we saw was the tower crane beside the building. Again, Ronan and I looked at each other. That, was going to be the next climb, but lucky enough, the gardai came along. We could have killed ourselves. We must have been making too much noise. The Gardai were alerted. It could have been the alarm! The gardai began looking up, and shining torch lights up at the building. We could see the light passing the top edge of the building just above our heads. We were ducked down behind the 3-foot peripheral wall and only glanced a look down.

The light shone above our heads. I made bunny ears above Ronan's head. "Stop!" he said. It was pretty tense. As we sat there waiting, the gardai suddenly disappeared. We looked down again. There was no noise, no garda, no maestro...no one. We thought right, the coast is clear. We started climbing down but Ronan was just back from New York where he had been working on the building sites so climbing scaffolding was second nature to him. He was just bouncing down it. I was climbing down it as fast as I could. We were pretty drunk at the time but still compos mentis. I got half way down and suddenly, I heard Ronan shouting loudly, "FUCK!!!"

The gardai were shouting, "You're caught, you're caught…stay there!!" They'd been hiding!!

I was half way down. I glanced down at the fracas, saw what was going on and stuck my head in through the green sheeting that was covering the outside of the scaffolding. It ran all around the outside of the scaffolding. Ronan said the next day, laughing, that when he looked up, as they shone the torch up at me that I looked like an ostrich burying its head in the sand.

A Garda shouted up to me, "Get down out of there, we can see ye!" I looked around, and I could see their lights shining on my ass so I climbed on down. I got to the top of the hoarding, but as I climbed down, I went down inside the hoarding by accident. I should have stepped off onto the top edge of it. The older male guard went crazy and pulled me up by the collar. I shouted "Right!! I'm coming, I'm coming. I'm just trying to get out of here!!" He let me go, and I climbed up. He said, "What're your names?" Ronan gave me a dirty look when I said "Juan O'Donnell". He said after, I should have lied. He told the truth as well because I gave my real name. I tried hitting on the ban garda (female cop). There was only two Guards. She was quite attractive. She laughed in spite of herself!

We were walking away across the road when Fergus pulled up quickly in a cab and shouted, "C'mon lads!!! Jump in!!!" We ran over the road singing, "Naah…Naaah…Naaaahnaaaaah…nah nah naah nah naaah!!! Under our breath. We jumped in and went back home! It was so much fun!!!

MERCHANT NAVY DAYS

I finished the 6-week college phase of my course. And not long after that incident on the court house roof, I was 26 days in to my first trip at sea when I got in trouble again! I was still aged 19, when it happened. I joined a ship in England somewhere. I can't remember now off hand where it was as my discharge book was stolen in later years as you will read later in the chapter Lost in France, so I have no reference to look back on. When I arrived at the ship, it was all new to me. I phoned home and told my parents I'd arrived. I told them I'd got there safely and everything was fine.

It was all good. There was a lot to learn. It was on an oil tanker, so I'd all the valves to learn, all the pipes and where all the pipes and everything went. I had another deck cadet there to help me, so it was fine.

We had no nights ashore, then 26 days into the trip, we got a chance to go up the road in a place called Immingham in Hull. The other cadet was from there, so he said he would show me around. That it was his town and that he had a lot of friends there. We both went ashore. The ship was leaving at 6 O'clock the next morning, so we had to be back before then. In to the town we went! He took me around a few different bars. We checked out the local talent, then went to a night club, and hooked up with all his mates. We got pretty rowdy…and pretty drunk!

I got lost from him inside, so I left the night club looking for him, thinking maybe he was outside it somewhere. When I left the night club, I couldn't find him anywhere. And whenever I went to go back in to the night club the bouncer said "No." "C'mon, man let me in. I'm looking for my mate!" I said. He said no and the cunt kicked me in the shins and said, "You're not coming in". I thought, fuck you!! And turned and left.

I got a taxi back from Hull to the oil refinery where the ship was, but because I didn't have a shore pass, they wouldn't let me in. I was trying everything to convince them who I was and to let me in. I told them, I knew where the boat was, I could see the big smoke stack, the chimney. I knew the ship was on the other side. I told them which berth the ship was on, but they still wouldn't let me in. I said, "That's fine, ok.", and walked off.

I walked down the side of the perimeter fence still on the main road. The oil refinery was in the middle of nowhere, it was well out of the town. It was just all grassy fields around it. I walked along the fence about 150 feet. I looked around and saw that they went back into their hut. It was getting daylight. I was worried about missing my boat. I looked at the fence thinking, it was high…maybe 10 feet tall, but I thought I could scale it even in my state. I started climbing up and got to the top. Then, as I was trying to pull myself over it, one of the spikes at the top went through my thumb. There I was, hanging by my thumb, holding on to the fence. Only using my feet and my other hand to hold me up. I was gripping the fence with my feet to take the weight off my thumb. It was a lot of work to stop my thumb from ripping. The two security guards came out a few seconds later and shouted, "WHAT ARE YOU AT?!!"

"I'm just trying to get in…" I shouted back.

They said, "We told you. You're not getting in." They said get down but I told them I was stuck and they laughed. They were pretty light-hearted about it. One of them came over, and I stood on his shoulders. Then, I pulled my thumb out of the spike. It didn't hurt as much coming out as it did going in! They took me over and into their little office hut, got out their first aid kit, and bandaged up my thumb. I asked, "Now can I get in?" "No!" they said, "You're still not getting in!!" and put me outside again!!! I was like fuck sakes. There I was, standing outside thinking, I am going to get in trouble if I don't get back to the boat before we sail. I thought fucking hell – my first cunting trip!!!

I thought to myself - I'll just take a walk down here, down the side of the main road, the road that was parallel to the refinery. They went back to their hut. I didn't say to them where I was going. When I got to the end of the fence, about 200 yards from the entrance, I could see the river. The field beside the refinery was full of sunflowers, so I thought I could walk through the field down to the river, then go around the fence at the water and get into the vessel that way. As I stepped into the field, I could see the flowers were all higher than me. I had to walk through them and jump up to see what direction I was going, but there were drills in the earth too, so I couldn't run too fast otherwise, I'd trip over them and fall.

I had to run a little, with the sunflowers hitting me in the head, then stop, jump up to see where I was going, then run another bit! I kept thinking of the joke my uncle Seamus from Derry, had told me as a kid about how the midget tribe in Africa got their name the "wheredafuckarewe's"...they got it because as they walked through the tall grassy plains when they were hunting, they had to keep jumping up and down to find out where they were going!!!

As I neared the end of the field, coming close to the water, there was a bit of a clearing in the sunflowers. It put me in mind of a moat. It was an inlet from the main Humber River, and it ran alongside the oil refinery fence. I looked at the wire fence. I could see my ship through it on the other side. I went to walk into the water, but my feet sank into the silt all the way up to my knees. As I tried to lift my foot, my shoe came off, and I had to dig for it. The silt was very deep and dangerous. I looked at myself after I finished digging. I was covered in silt and mud. I got my shoe and putting it on; I thought – right! The best thing to do here is lie down and swim across the little moat. It was only about 30 feet across, so I just lay down on my front and swam across it but it was the same thing when I got to the other side. I pushed my hands down, testing it, and when I did, they sank. I sank up to my shoulders. I was lying in the plank position. I panicked a little bit, but I'd seen a show called London's Burning years before, a TV programme about firemen in London. And in an episode, how they had saved people by spreading out their hoses and filling them with water, then spreading their weight and sliding along the mud to save the people in the mudflats. I started doing that. I spread my weight out and started shimmying my way over the mud and up onto the bank on the other side. It worked!!! It probably saved my life. I stood up and thoughtfully looked at the fence. I could see a sign on it saying 40,000 volts – Danger!!! I knew I couldn't touch that!

I could see as I was looking at the river, with the ship and the fence on my right that the fence ran right down into the River Humber. I thought, "Well, there is no electricity going into the water at the river!" I ran down the banking, got to the edge, and dived into the river, then swam around the fence. I was up on the other side in a couple of seconds. I ran across the banking and suddenly, two torch lights were shining at me. It was the two security guards again. Both of them had torches. They were shining them at me. I just put my hands up as they were shouting "STOP!!! STOP!!!" They saw it was me and they started laughing again. They said, "We knew it was you. We told you! You can't get in. You're not allowed." They said they'd called off the police and the ambulance that were called automatically when the alarm was tripped. They had called them off when they realized it was me. They'd thought they had an intruder, then they saw it was me. They then said, "Right, we'll let you in, but you gotta tell your Captain when you get back!" "You look like the swamp thing!" and started laughing. They said "We saw you on the CCTV" so I said, "Is there any way you can erase it?" I was young at 19 …and a bit of a wild man. They said, "No. We've got to show our boss, so what you do is go back and tell your Captain as soon as you go back on board." I said, "Right, Ok, Ok…" I just agreed with them. I went back to the ship. The ship was brand new, only a year old. Everything onboard was clean and spick and span on it. I walked on, covered in mud, onto the deck, went into the accommodation, and climbed the stairs up to my cabin. There was mud everywhere. There was a trail behind me.

When I went into my cabin, and stepped into the shower with my clothes on to wash the mud off. I thought in that moment, "How the hell am I going to tell anybody about this?" I washed and got cleaned up, and as I did, it was time for stations. Stations are what's called when it's time to let go of the ropes and leave the port or enter the port and tie up. The Filipino deckhands had cleaned up the mud after me so I wouldn't get in trouble. They were good like that. Good crews look out for one another. I went out on deck, but the Deckhand said, look, you're still too drunk. Get off the deck because it's too dangerous. I said, "Ok," because I had tripped and fallen. I went back in and went to bed.

Later on, that morning I went up for my watch onto the bridge, and the Captain was like, "SOoo!!! D'ye have a good night last night?!!" I said, "Yeah, Captain it wasn't bad."

He said, "Ah, yeah, yeah!!!". He was pretty jovial. The time was ten o clock in the morning. "Anything to tell me?" he asked. I said, "No, no, nothing I can really think of." Then he said, "What about that?" brandishing a letter!!! He gave me the letter to look at. It was a letter from BP (British Petroleum), and it said... One of his crew members had breached the security of the refinery, and if the crew member wasn't dealt with sufficiently that the ship would lose the million-pound charter... so he said, "Guess which one of you is going? You or the ship?" and I said, "Yeah, I guess it's me then." "Yes!" he said." "Right answer!". "What's going to happen is you're going to write me a full report of what happened. It has to be sent to the office. Then after that, you are going to go to a disciplinary hearing in Liverpool". Head Office! So that's what happened. It was a couple of days passage to the next port.

In that time, he had me strip the varnish off the deck inside of the bridge (wheelhouse) then re-varnish it. He had me polish all the brass on the window frames of the bridge. There were 26 windows on the bridge. I counted every one of them, it took me fucking ages. He was laughing non-stop at me. So were the other Officers. He worked me basically to the bone until we got there. I knew I'd done wrong, and as long as I wasn't getting the sack, I didn't mind. It was a punishment I didn't mind doing. The rest of the Officers were slagging me off, saying I was running along the refinery banking shouting, "Ulster says NO!!!" And I said, "Well, I wouldn't be shouting that!" and that kept them laughing. It was good banter, and it relieved the pressure I felt under. That was good fun, but it was dangerous what I'd done.

When we got to the end of the passage and into the next port, the Captain said, "You have to make your own way." I told him I had no money, so he had to give me a travel cheque for my journey to Liverpool. He was a little pissed off at that. I thought it was funny.

When I got there, the company had put me up in a Seaman's mission, lodgings for Merchant seamen. That night I took the report that I had written out, I thought the best thing to do was to take the report and learn it. I didn't want to be left where I couldn't answer any questions in the hearing. I was so used to being in trouble! I got the report, it was one page long, and I wrote out possible questions and answers on another page. Everything that I could think of that they could ask. I'd ask myself one question, then the follow-up question until they petered out, and I had no more questions to ask myself. Or questions that they could throw at me that I could not answer. I learned all of them off or as near as dammit. I had it clear in my head what I wanted to do and how to lead the hearing.

After that, I decided I'd have a few pints of Guinness to help me sleep. The Captain had given me some money. I went down to the mission bar, and there I met an old guy whom I told the story of why I was there. I told him about the hearing. He was a salty old sea dog, and he chatted about getting the channels. The channels happen when you are going home after a long voyage. He said "when you are going out of the channel destined for a long voyage and you tell a joke, you might get a bit of a laugh but when you tell the same joke coming in the channel to the port after the long voyage is over, everyone is giddy and everyone is in hysterics laughing at the same joke". The giddiness is called the channels from the days of the old tramper's when men signed on for a year or two and they were returning to their home port after the long voyage.

Anyway, I went to the disciplinary hearing the next morning. I was sat outside the office with my rucksack when one of the secretaries came in. Quite an attractive young lady. She said, "Oh, you're early". "No point being late for a bollocking," I said. She looked a bit shocked and said, "I suppose not," She walked on in. Oops, I thought! I better watch the language.

I was summoned in a few minutes later. There were three men sitting in front of me. They were each introduced by the man in the middle. There was Captain Barry Greggs, the training manager for all the cadets. Then there was Bill Pottiger, who was the personnel manager and then 3rd in charge of the fleet, Captain Ballbag who was leading the show. Captain Ballbag grilled me, and it was intense. He could not catch me out on anything. So intense, in fact, to the point where I told him to "Fuck off," for bringing my family's name into question. He had nothing else to throw at me because I was so well prepared. He'd insulted my family tradition of piloting saying "you and your family of pilots! You're just using this company to get your license and become a pilot!!!" It cooled after he left. I said I was glad the grilling was over, but Bill Pottiger said, "No Juan. It's just the beginning. We still have to go through the rest of the report."

We went through it, and I did the exact same thing that had flustered Captain Ballbag. I answered all the questions the way I had prepared. The remaining two men realized I was just scared of missing the ship. I had breached the security of the compound but it was my first trip at sea, and they understood the reasons for my panic, if not my actions. I did risk my life doing it, but to me, it was all under control. I wasn't that drunk; I was drunk but not stupidly drunk. As one of my lecturers put it "God looks after young children and drunk sailors!" Obviously, I could still function, and I can remember everything that happened, so I wasn't that bad. Bill Pottiger said they were going to send me home, but because it was my first offense, they said they would give me a chance. I would join another ship after a brief period at home. What they were doing at the time felt like the worst punishment they could have given me after sacking me. They were sending me home to my father, and I knew he wasn't going to be a happy camper. I asked them could they not just send me straight to another boat? They had a chuckle and said "Why do you not want to go home?" I said not really. They had a laugh. They knew my father was going to crucify me.

It was because of all the effort both my parents had made to get me there. I only had about 15 months to get 12 months sea time in before the final college phase. I had lost a lot of months at the beginning of my time because I'd had an ulcer on top of my foot that I'd sustained at college when I was playing indoor football. I received a blister, then let it get infected by wearing dirty socks and going on the beer. There was a lot of effort to get me there, and it was my first trip. My Father had been with the same company, and some of my other family had been with the company too, so it was a big let down.

The training manager had said after the hearing, phone your father. I gave him a call. We had the pub at the time, and I knew if he wasn't piloting, he'd have been there, and because it was so early in the morning, then he probably wouldn't be up. He had probably had a very late night because it was summer time. Hence, it was probably 5 or 6 in the morning before he finished in the pub. It was a very busy pub in the summer time. He answered the phone, and I said "Daddy, I have to come home." "Why?" he said. "I just got sacked" I said, and he said "Right, what time are you getting in?" and "Where?" and that was it. That was all he said, he put the phone down but I kept talking to stop myself being embarrassed, saying "Ok, alright, I'll see you then. Bye!" and put down the phone. I don't know if they twigged it or not. I had pretended as if everything was alright, but it wasn't. I went home and spent nearly two weeks cleaning every little bit of our family pub. I was doing every single job that needed doing from morning to evening then tending the bar in the evening. It was alright after a while; I was used to the work but the impending sense of doom there was when I was not working and I was at our family home was much more unbearable. We lived separately from the bar. I knew it was to be expected as I had let everyone down.

After that, I got a phone call to say I was going back to sea and I was to join another boat. When my father heard its name, he started laughing because whenever I told him the Captain was Robert Day (known as the prince of darkness, I later found out!!!) he said, "Is Robert Day still going?". He said "Ask Harbour Harry about him!" Harbour Harry was a distant relative of ours who'd sailed with Robert Day years before. One night, Harbour Harry was in the bar, and I asked him did he remember him? He said, "That bastard... is he still alive?" I said "Aye why? He is going to be my new Captain." He said "Wait until I tell you about him!" POD (Prince of darkness) came up to the bridge at night when Harbour Harry was on watch and turned off the navigation lights unbeknownst to him. Then he disappeared. He returned again 10 minutes later and gave Harbour Harry hell for not having the nav lights on! He shouted "Mr. Mate, how come those Nav lights are off?!! Are you not paying attention to this watch?" Harbour Harry was laughing when he was telling me the story. He said he's an old cunt..

I joined the boat anyway. I wasn't too worried. I was just so happy to get another chance. I loved being at sea. I was a little worried but more apprehensive than anything. I thought he couldn't be that bad. My dad said when I joined, I was either going to be his blue-eyed boy or his whipping boy. No in-between.

I joined the boat this day, putting my bag down in the passageway when I was called up to the bridge. I went up, and the Captain was there, the second mate, the chief engineer, and the personnel representative from the office. There were 5 of us on the bridge. It was a tiny bridge compared to the other ship that I had just been on. My father said to me before joining "that's what you get for messing! You have gone from the pride of the fleet to an old rust bucket!"

A grilling on the bridge of the new ship started from the company representative, they used to call him clip board. He always had one with him. He said "Well now, I see you got your boots cleaned!" They all started laughing. I didn't get what he meant; I didn't understand the joke. I asked him what he meant, and he said, "You got your boots cleaned...the mud... the mud. You got the mud off your boots!!" and everyone started laughing even more, and I was like, "Yeah, yeah, I got the boots cleaned." Knowing I had to stand there and take it, but the alternative of getting sacked was a lot worse. Then he said "So where are you from anyway?" and I said "Near Derry" and he said "Where is that near?" and I said "It's near Greencastle" then I said "Yeah a place called Shrove" and he said "Where is that near?" I started getting the picture of what he was driving at. Most people wouldn't have known it, but I did. I said, "Moville," and he said, "Ah yes, yes Moville, yes." I'd had this before within the company from another racist shipmate. "Moville, yes, we had a ship sunk there one time by the IRA," "Yes, I remember that well...." he said as if it was my fault!!! I said sticking up for myself, "Yeah, we were dredging coal up for months afterwards." Everyone roared laughing at him, he did not like that at all. Luckily for me, the Captain saw his discomfort and stepped in, saying, "Right Juan, come on, let's go, let's go!!" Grilling over! And we left the bridge.

The Captain told me to follow him down to his office. I said, "Ok" and followed him down. He closed the office door and he said "Do you smoke?" I thought no, not really but just starting...when in Rome... so I said "Yeah I smoke,". He gave me one. I was sitting there having a cigarette and he sat back. He says, "Sooo, tell me what happened..." so I started telling the story just like I have been telling you. After a minute, he says, "No, no, no, skip to the part where you told Captain Ballbag to FUCK OFF!!!!" "Haw haw haw haw!!!!" he said laughing and he said "I never liked the man!!!"

SO that was it!!! I was his BLUE-EYED BOY!!!

8

AM I GAY?!!

I was on another ship called the Rosethorn about 7 months later. I was still a cadet. It was a cargo ship, so we spent a little more time in port. Often getting weekends in. It gave us time to get up to some shenanigans. It was great fun being in the cities after always being miles out of town at the oil refineries on the Tankers.

One of the Deckhands was an ex-British soldier. His nickname was MT or Empty. He told me a Chief Officer on another boat had called him bungalow because he had nothing upstairs. He had a great sense of humour. We got on like a house on fire. We were in Manchester this weekend and having a bit of time off, we decided to go ashore for a few beers. It was a normal night out. We were in a bar having a couple of scoops, and he spied three pretty young girls. He asked me to use my charm and chat them up. I thought I would have a bit of craic with him and said, "no, your turn!" He said, "no, you're brilliant at it!" I laughed and took the compliment. I'd done pretty well on the loving front since I'd been onboard. I'd slept with a couple of women. One naughty little girl in Liverpool sticks out in my mind. She was from Ellesmere port. There were tons of good-looking women in Liverpool. It was one of our regular ports. We got the eye from a ton of women there.

Meanwhile, back in Manchester, I decided to try on my charm. MT and I went over to their table. I asked the ladies could they tell me where a good bar and nightclub was in the city. It was an ice breaker

I used all the time. It was just so they could hear my accent. That was the real ice-breaker. It's got to be the easiest way in ever. I love having the Donegal accent! I said we'd never been here before. The first thing they asked was where we were from. It was the usual question when they heard me speak. MT loved it. It got us in every time. "Ireland!" I said. "He's from Doncaster!" "Oh, what are you doing here?" the good-looking blonde one said. "We're in on a ship." "Oh nice," she said. She said, "You need to go to the gay village." I said, "We're not gay!" They all started laughing. "No! It's not like that!" she said. "Everybody goes there!" "Oh, right." I said, "Thanks!" "Do you mind if we join you?" I asked. "We're just leaving," she said, "We might see you down the gay village later". "Ok," I said. She'd made our minds up!

They left, and we drank our drinks and did the same. We were laughing and joking walking down the street when we noticed a big pink neon light of the statue of liberty with a limp wrist hanging from the side of a building. "Let's go in there!" MT said. I was a bit hesitant, then I thought, "fuck it" "aye why not?! A bit of craic!" We went up the stairs into the bar. We opened the door not knowing what to expect. As soon as we walked in, we were hit with a wave of sexual energy. It was like a fucking tsunami! Really weird. All these guys dressed as a woman ran at us. It was surreal. There were about 20 of them. They all surrounded us, and all they were asking was, "Suck your dick?" They were pulling at us to take us to the toilets. It was fucking mental. They were all over us. MT said before I could even think, "Yeah, awrite!" laughing his head off. He was a proper head banger. He walked off with two of them, arm in arm. I told them, "no thanks!" laughing and walked to the bar.

A tranny at the bar that looked more like a woman than any of them was a bit less forceful with me said, "I'll suck you off in the toilets!" He was really effeminate and he talked really girly. It really looked like a woman. He was thin and had boobs. I was a little horned up at the thought of it and thought I wouldn't mind an orgasm. I was a little bit tipsy and thought fuck it! I said "Ok." There was music playing on the big screen television. It was the George Michael song "Let's go outside…" It was kind of fitting. When the drinks in, the wits out!!! That's my excuse, and I'm sticking to it.

I was being bullied onboard the Rosethorn as well. It had been going on for a couple of weeks. The Chief mate from the Isle of Man was asking me every morning where his blowjob was to wake him up? It wasn't funny after a couple of days. It was wearing me down. He was making all sorts homosexual jibes at me. I was starting to question my own sexuality. I know a lot of men do that. It is very normal. I'd had a lot of women, but the constant berating made me doubt myself. So, now faced with this opportunity, I thought, why not find out? I went downstairs to the toilets and went into a cubicle with him. He was in a skimpy little outfit. Skirt, high heels, and a black wig. I took out my cock, and he got down on his knees on the floor and started sucking. I thought, this is WRONG!!! I was hard, but I couldn't cum. It didn't do it for me mentally. I knew he was a man. The fact my cock was hard was normal. A vibrating bus would make me horny! I thought fuck it! I just wanted to cum! He was sucking for all he was worth. He was wanking me off too but I still couldn't cum. So, I thought I'll shag him up the ass like a woman, doggy style. I asked him could I shag him up the ass, I thought it was more like fucking a woman. He was fucking delighted. "Really?!" he said. "Yeah, why not?" I said. Thinking I would cum quick. He got his knickers off and told me he'd had the operation to get his balls cut off. He showed me where the operation took place. I thought this guy is really set on being a woman. FUCK is that dedication! He told me it cost him 10 thousand pounds. I thought, you crazy cunt! He said they tucked the penis up inside. "Ok," he said, "fuck me!" bending over. I said "can we not do it in the front? Are you on your period or what?!" I was in denial, trying to tell myself it was a woman. My conscience was really getting to me. He didn't play along. He said loudly, "I'M A MAN!" in a deep voice. "Ok!", "ok!" I said, chilling him out. I was set on orgasming!

He bent over, and I tried sticking my cock up his ass. It wouldn't go in. I gave him a quick pump or two. Then stopped. I got a friction burn on the helmet of my cock. I'd heard of the leper saying to the prostitute keep the tip. I thought I might catch AIDS but I didn't develop the flu like symptoms in the following weeks so I knew I didn't catch it but it was worrying times for me in those weeks. I got tested after just in case. He didn't seem to care about sexually transmitted diseases. My cock wouldn't go into him without any lube. I never thought of spit. I wasn't that au fait with anal sex! I had a crisis of conscience and thought there's no fucking way I'm gay. I felt so stupid and stopped. I wanted to cum but thought, "nah this isn't for me!" I'm not even Bisexual, I'm trisexual (try anything once!"). He was very disappointed.

We went back upstairs, and when we got to the bar he ran in and shouted to everybody "HE SHAGGED ME, HE SHAGGED ME!!!" He was running about, and everybody was slapping his outstretched hand, cheering him on. I was so embarrassed, but it was kind of funny. MT came over to me laughing and said, "I had two of them sucking my cock in the toilets" "It was fucking brilliant!" he said. I got a little jealous and asked the transvestite and his mate beside him at the bar would they suck my cock together. He looked disgusted and said, "NOooo!!!" I never thought about it, but there could have been shit on my cock!

A little while later and unbeknownst to me, MT got in an argument with some of them, and they threw him out. I was at the bar getting a drink when it happened. I came back with my drink, and one of them said, "Your mates an ASSHOLE!!!" They had locked him out. I said I better go out and sort things out, but the tranny at the door with the long green hair, red lipstick, and black beard said, "finish your drink!" "He'll be alright!" "You're alright!" He was a bit of a hard case. I had another couple of sips and said, "must go!" He opened the door, and I went out onto the street. As I crossed to the other side, I heard screams and looked back. As I looked I could see three men in mini-skirts and fluorescent coloured wigs beating the shit out of someone on the ground about 20 feet away. They were kicking and hitting him with their stilettos. They were trying to kill him. I thought, "FUCKING HELL!!! THAT'S MT!!!" I took off at a gallop.

I ran straight in with my head down and cracked one of them square on the face. He dropped like a ton of shit. I punched the next one knocking him down too, then I swung around with my elbow catching the last one on the face as well. I made sure he went down as well. They were all nursing their wounds as I picked MT up and shouted. "COME ON YOU CUNT!!!" I looked back at the bar and saw all the tranny's emptying onto the street!! We ran to the end of the road. About 50 yards distance. There were cops pulled up half way down the road. I don't know why they were there but I so happy to see them. We ran behind them for safety. I'd heard stories how violent transvestites could be!!! As we got behind the cops, the tranny's that chased after us arrived on our heels. They were held back by the cops. Other trannies from the bar were running down the street squealing their heads off. They were running in their bare feet with their stilettos raised above their heads in their hands, ready to kill. It was a sight to behold. It was fucking hilarious looking! The two police cars had blocked the bottom of the street. They were between us and the tranny brigade. The tranny brigade was going fucking mental!! They were all kept back by the cops. They were screaming at the cops and threatening us. The cops had their backs to us. So, unbeknownst to the cops, I blew the tranny's some kisses to wind them up even more. It was fucking HIL-AR-IOUS! They screamed blue fucking murder at us!!! The cops looked back to see why they were getting so annoyed, but I had stopped and pretended I hadn't done anything. We went on about our night. The Gay village is a weird fucking place.

I was on the Rosethorn for 5 months in total. It was a long and interesting trip. I joined a Tanker called Stellaman after that. The English Captain was a bit of a wild man. He loved going ashore in Hamburg, Germany. It was the only place he would go on shore leave. I'd never been there before. The boat went there every 3 weeks. We were on a permanent run. It was something to look forward to. The Captain asked me one day on watch, not long after I joined, had I ever been to the Reeperbahn in Hamburg? I said "no". He said "have you never been with a lady of the night?" laughing. I told him I hadn't. He said "ah! A cherryboy!!!" The other sailor on watch started laughing. A cherryboy is a sailor who has never been with a prostitute. "We'll have to fix that!" he said. "The Captain pays for the cherryboy!" he said. "We'll go up the road when we get there!" I was really looking forward to it after he said it.

We arrived in Hamburg and 4 of us got a taxi into the city. We went straight to Herbert Strasse. The Captain said to me as soon as we walked through the barrier that blocked the normal women and under 18's, "go ask her how much it is?" He was pointing over to this gorgeous black-haired bombshell in the window. I was a little nervous but I went over. She opened the window as I approached. "Hi!" I said. "Hi!" She said. "How are you? My name is Olivia" she said with a sexy glint in her eye. "How much is it?" I asked. "100 marks" she said. "No rough stuff. No fucking in the ass!" I was a little bit shocked and had a laugh to myself but I really wanted to be with her. She looked really dirty and had a great seductive smile on her. I said "just one second!" and went back over to the Captain and other crew men to tell them what she'd said. They all started laughing when I told them. The Captain said "right c'mon! You never go with the first one you meet. There's tons to choose from!" "Let's get a beer!" he said. I was so disappointed. I thought I really had a connection with her. Lol.

We went into a bar on the red-light district street and I had my first Jägermeister. It was long before it became popular worldwide. I was told by the Second mate before we went ashore not to get the Captain drinking them. He warned me saying "once he starts those, he doesn't stop!" I thought it was funny and bought him one as soon as we got into the bar. He said "now young man! It is tradition when you buy a Jägermeister here, that you buy everyone at the bar counter one!" I thought, thank fuck I have enough money and bought the 7 of us sitting around the bar a Jager. The Captain bought another few rounds of it, getting well into the groove of things. The second mate looked a little worried! We moved on to another bar, I was still thinking about Olivia. The Captain was leading the way.

He took us into another bar and as the 4 of us walked in this woman kissed me on the cheek! I never thought anything of it! I thought fucking hell! I'm not even in the door and she's all over me. We took a cubicle seat and my kiss-o-gram went back to the bar. She was wearing a tight black and white dress. She had long blonde hair and was very attractive. She was looking over in my direction. The Captain and the two lads started egging me on. There were saying "look at that! He's only in the door and he's scored already!!" The Captain was winding it up even more saying "she is really into you!" The lady was giving me serious eyes, then after a few seconds, she walked over to our table and pointed to my cigarettes. I signalled her to go ahead. Have one. She took one out. Then in the deepest male voice you have ever heard said "could I ave a light please?" I nearly crapped myself. The 3 guys all burst out laughing. They had taken me into a transvestite bar. The Captain was in stitches. They'd known all along!! The tranny could tell I wasn't interested and went back to the bar. They said "you have to be careful here! There are ways of telling men from women but you really have to watch yourself in places like this. They do such a good job nowadays with sex changes." It was way more professional than Manchester. The Captain said they file down the Adams apple but the way to tell when you are checking them out is by the size of their hands and their calf muscles. "The shoulder's is another good indicator" the Captain said. I was taking it all in.

We left there and went to the Captain's favourite place in St. Pauli, the area which the red-light district that we were in is called. It was a hotel converted into a massive brothel with all the Asian women you could think of. There was about 50 women. The other two crew went for a beer in the bar beside it and the Captain and I went in. He took me right to the top floor. The very first girl was a beautiful Filipina girl. He said "We'll start here and look at every one of them. It's your first time so we have to get you a good one!" All the women were sitting on bar stools at the entrance to the rooms. I was really taken by the Filipina girl. The Captain noticed this and said "remember what I told you about not going with the first one you see!"

We walked all 5 floors but none of them were as good looking as the first one. He said when we got to the end "you want to go with that first fucking one you seen. Don't you?!" "Yeah". I said, a little bit embarrassed. "Right!" he said and gave me the money. I went back up to the Filipina and went in. She stripped off and told me to lie down on top of the bed. She put the condom on me then lay back. I fucked her as gently as I could. I asked her about herself as I was fucking her. I felt a little guilty. She said she sent money home to her family in the

Philippines. I felt a little bit better when I got to know her. I only had 30 minutes with her. I was trying my best but I couldn't cum because of all the alcohol I'd taken. It has always been a bit of problem of mine. I often thought it was more of a gift though because I could last longer without cuming. I told Jamima this when we were hanging out but once again, she tried to run me down. I told her I could last for hours when I was drinking. She said "how boring?!" "I prefer men to cum after 10 or 15 minutes" she said. She was just being a bitch I thought. It is not the case when you are giving them multiple orgasms. 10 or 15 minutes is nowhere near enough time. Each to their own. Let her carry on.

My time was nearly up with the Filipina girl and I hadn't cum. I was really pissed off. My first time was special because I'd never been with an Asian girl before but I wanted to finish in a blaze of glory. She gave me a few more minutes. Then there was a knock at the door. She was told to hurry up. She gave me another couple of minutes and finally I came. The Captain was happy for me and we went back to the boat.

Skipper Strasse in Antwerp, Belgium was another interesting time for me. And Rotterdam also. I went alone to these places just for the thrill of seeing it and of course the ladies. I loved the history of all the old sailor haunts. They were famous in the underground.

The next time we were back in Hamburg on Stellaman I went into the Reeperbahn on my own. I was looking really good. I'd lost all my puppy fat. I was training every day on that ship. I was walking past a line of 7 hookers that afternoon. As I walked past, each one of them stepped out and said "looking for business?" I said no to each of them. They stepped back into their line after I said no. I'd had a few beers and was in a giddy mood. As soon as I got to the end of the line, I turned around and pretended I'd decided to go the other direction. They all stepped out again asking me the same thing. I refused each one of them without laughing. I thought it was hilarious. I got to the end and turned again. I walked back past them again and they all stepped out again. I caught the eye of one of the women and she could see I was only having a laugh. She looked like a bit of craic. She started laughing her head off and said in English "He is having fun with us!" The other's started laughing. I said I was. I also thought she was very sexy. The Captain had warned me to stay away from the street girls. He said they're dangerous. They'd rob you but she was really reasonable at 30 marks for a blowjob so I told her "ok, let's go!" We went across the street so I could get money out of the bank machine, then she took me up to hotel type apartment. I lay on the bed and she put the condom on with her mouth and started sucking me off. It wasn't doing anything for me because of the alcohol. I said to her to look into my eyes and I'd masturbate. It always turned me on a million times better than anything when a woman looked erotically into my eyes. I came in a minute! She asked for her money and as a joke I said "Why do I have to pay you? I did it all myself!" She went fucking crazy. She screamed at me "YOU WILL FUCKING PAY ME!!!" and ran out of the room before I could tell her I was joking!!! She came back with her pimp. He had a gun and he pointed it at me. He said "you will pay the lady!" I said "of course! I explained I was only joking! I left, feeling pretty fucking alive with excitement. I was buzzing off all the red-light atmosphere. It was right up my street. I was looking forward to getting back to college with all these stories.

CORK MAN STABBED
FOR CIGARETTE

I arrived back to college after our 18 months sea service. All of us were a bit more worldly. I was 21. TC, my mate from Galway was living with me. We were constantly drinking; it was a great laugh! One night we were coming home from a nightclub in Cork with a bunch of girlfriends that we had. As we were walking past the Beamish brewery outside a well-known Cork nightclub on the little bridge leading up to Barrick street, a guy came up to me and asked for a cigarette. My Dad had told me how to handle this situation. "Don't give them a in!" He'd said. I didn't like the guys approach either. He was very aggressive, so I told him I didn't smoke. I had a pack in my pocket. I was with one girl ahead of TC by about 30 feet, and he was with the other friend of ours, Martina.

The young dickhead, after asking me, went back to TC and Martina. I could see two girls sitting on the wall of the bridge watching and laughing at him in action. It was obvious to me; he was showing off to them. As I was looking back, he asked Martina, for a cigarette and she gave him one, and I thought No! Martina don't open the door for him! I was looking back to make sure they were ok as I continued to walk. I could see the young dickhead put the ciggy behind his ear and ask for another one saying "my auld doll smokes too." The girls on the bridge wall were pissing themselves laughing at him. He was really turning it on for them!

Martina was a little fazed by this, but TC told the guy to fuck off because he'd already got one. The guy threw a punch around the back of Martina's head, punching TC on the jaw. He knocked him down, out cold. I ran back and thumped the cunt on the jaw as well. He fell too. I got TC up but the guy got up again. We started fighting. I threw a load of punches and knocked him down again. As he was lying on the ground on his face, TC picked up his head and held it like I was about to kick a 2 pointer at Rugby. He shouted "GO SHAM! KICK HIM! KICK HIM!" I felt a little guilty about kicking him a full kick on the face. I thought I might kill him. So, I gave him a glancing kick with the outside of my right foot. I think I might have broken his jaw. I was backing away when I tripped on the curb and fell backwards. Our woman had gone to the other side of the bridge. I rolled back up on to my feet really quickly. As I did, I felt a thump on the top of my head. I thought the cunt had punched me. I couldn't believe he had got up again so quickly. I thought he must be on Cocaine or something, he was wired, I didn't know what he was on! But he was pumped up on something! I looked at him and saw the knife in his right hand. I hadn't realized but he'd had the knife in his hand the whole time. I had slashes on either side of my head, luckily enough not that deep. He screamed at me "C'MON BOY!!! I'LL SLIT YA!!!" I thought now we have a fight! I looked around. I could hear and see four of his friends coming with bottles. They were shouting to him. I thought fuck this, I am well out numbered. The guy didn't attack, and I walked quickly, backing away to the other side of the road, keeping my eyes on him. When I reached the other side of the small road, our girls screamed and said, you're bleeding. I hadn't realized it, but it wasn't a punch to the top of my head, the fucker had stabbed me, the blade ricocheted down the side of my head, and I was bleeding heavily. Lucky the blade didn't penetrate. I would have died!!! At this, I flipped!! I completely lost my temper.

I was about to go at all of them. I was screaming now too, shouting "C'MON YOU CUNTS!!!" …frantically looking for a tin can along the side of the street, that I could tear open and slash him with. I was very angry but the four guys around the man remained calm and held him back. The fucking dickhead was still bouncing around shouting and trying to get at me from the other side of the road. They were saying to me, "no trouble...no trouble!" They walked away with him.

The girls, TC, and I walked up to the taxi rank to where we were originally going. The girls were saying "you need an ambulance" to me. I was sitting on the taxi ranks outside window ledge smoking a cigarette when the ambulance arrived about 10 minutes later, but when it did, I said, "I'm not going to the hospital, I'll be grand!" Martina said "look at the window behind your head!" I looked around, and there was a trail of blood on the window pane from where I had turned my head. It was spurting out! I stubbed the cigarette out and got in. They put a patch on my head.

When we got to the hospital, I was shown to a bed and waited for the doctor. TC had been slashed in the arm too, so he got treated for that. He said he got it when he went to block one of the strikes that were coming at me and that he'd saved my life, so we were even! I laughed at this. He was fucking knocked out the cunt! Just kidding! I don't want to ruin his street cred.

Martina was crying at my bed with her head down on the covers beside me. I was rubbing her head when I saw TC looking in. I smiled and winked at him pointing down at Martina with my eyes. I was really looking to get with Martina for a long time. She was really cute! This seemed to me as the perfect opportunity...the sympathy vote!! (And I did get with her! Not long after this. OMG My new girlfriend Briona (whom you'll read about) walked in on us when we were shagging! It was right at the start of Briona and I's relationship so I thought she would get over it and she did. Martina was one of her best mates. Share and share alike I thought!). TC laughed quietly shaking his head and walked away, back to the waiting room.

When the doctor arrived, he looked pretty young, and seeing him come at me with the needle and thread, I said, "Where do you practice anyway... on drunk people like me?!!!"" "No," he replied. Startled but amused. I was just having a laugh. "They have dummies with rubber scalps for that!!" he said. I let him stitch me up. 10 stitches from the top of my head down to just above the top of my left ear. After I was stitched up the gardai came in and took a quick statement and my address. They said they would be around in the morning to take a full statement of the night's events.

We all went home. TC and I went back to our house in Bishopstown on the outskirts of the city. There were 5 of us in the house, and 4 of us were all in the same class in college.

The next morning, TC and I woke early and started with a couple of beers to avoid the hangover, so by 11 O'clock, we were well on our way again. Ronan was living with us too. He stayed home from college too for the beer! The 3 of us had taken the day off because of what happened. Ronan had stayed home too for the craic, but Donny went into college, and Niall had gone to work. They were all mad as fuck in their own right. The detective arrived alone, and I showed her into the kitchen. I thought I recognized her but couldn't quite place her. It was only then it hit me she was ban garda at the court house when Ronan and I had scaled it from the Court house roof chapter. I knew I remembered her from somewhere. I could see the flicker of recognition in her eyes too but she did not mention so I let it go.

She sat down at the head of the table in the kitchen. TC and I sat opposite each other. Ronan stayed in the other room.

We started with the statement. TC and I had other ideas about how this statement was going to go. We had already decided that we didn't want the guy to be caught. We thought we had given him a proper beating. And although he had done what he did, we thought that fair was fair. We had other reasons too. Read on. We were worried about the beating we gave him but we found out the next day from another garda that this didn't matter because it was self-defense.

The detective began with "what did he look like?" So, a little bit drunk, I said, quoting from the movies and cop shows, "he was male Caucasian between 5'9" and 5'11" with brown hair between 19 and 23...." "Great..." she says, "...any distinguishing features?" writing intently. I kicked TC underneath the table and said, winking at him that "he had massive ears!" "Oh good," she said. "He looked like Dumbo," I said. (She had told us that his description would be going in the Evening

Echo. The Cork city evening newspaper, so I thought, why not have our own justice and get his friends to slag him off if he boasted to them about what he had done. We'd made Crime-line on the TV too. TC's father had asked him on the phone later on that week. Did he hear about it? And he said, "Ahhh yeah…. that was us!!" His father was devastated.)

She said, "I can't write that…. what about large protruding ears??" "Yeah!" I said, "that'll do." Then it was TC's turn! He told her the man "was wearing a Liverpool top, but it was the away top, the beige one." "This is great," she said, "we'll need you both in to look at CCTV footage tomorrow. This will really help us find him." She left. Pretty happy with what we had given her.

We drank on, then the next day we went to the Bridewell police station in Cork city to watch the CCTV. We'd had a few drinks before we went in. We were in the darkened room watching the 9 TV screens, and I fell asleep! I must have dozed off for a few seconds, but TC was blocking the line of sight of the guard in there with us, so he didn't see me. I woke up when TC shouted, that's him there!! He said later, "you bastard, you could doze. I had to stay awake because the guard was beside me!!" TC had spotted the asshole walking in and out of the shot. I shouted too "yeah, that's him!!" "Good," they said, and that was it. We went on the batter after that. Drinking all over town. Me with the big fanny pad on top of my head, and bandages strapped around my chin holding it in place, and TC with the bandage on his arm.

We did a pub crawl, and every bar we went into, the barkeep would ask what happened to my head. We'd say, "did you hear about the stabbing last night?" they'd say, "yeah," and we'd say that was us and that we got attacked. They threw us up a free drink in some of the bars we went into. It was good craic, but we went home after and waited for the newspaper. The newspaper came out that evening, and it had the front-page headline "Cork man stabbed for a cigarette". I'd told the guards I wanted the fact that I was from Donegal to be hidden because I felt if these hooligans knew where I was from and if he was caught and I fingered him in court, then I wouldn't feel safe in Cork again. That I'd always be watching my back every time I'm out for the night. It read the "Gardai were on the lookout for a youth between 19 and 23 with large protruding ears…" just as I'd said in the description…we were all in stitches…me literally!

That was it until Martina read it!! She came up to our house and gave out hell to me saying, "What the hell are you doing? You can't lie, in a statement" and I said "We weren't really lying, just bending the truth a little!" She said, "That's it, I'm going to tell them the truth! What if he does it to someone else?!!" I could see her point, but I said it's my head, and I didn't really want him caught for the simple reason that his friends could attack us again. Also, the large protruding ears slagging in the newspaper was enough revenge for me along with the beating he got.

A few days later, the detectives landed on our doorstep again. I answered the door, and the female detective who had taken the statement said, "we've had conflicting evidence and reason to believe that you lied on your statement. You told us that your assailant had large protruding ears…"so I answered, "all I can say is that they were bigger than mine!" They had no reply to that apart from the point of asking, "do you not want him caught?" to which I said "no, I don't," and I explained to them the above reasons. They were very accommodating about the whole thing, and that was it.

A couple of years later, at a house party in Cork with my girlfriend Briona, when I was sporting a shaven head, a guy seeing the scar asked me what happened, and I told him the story. He said he knew the guy that had done it. He had met him through friends that he no longer hung out with. I asked him did the guy get grief over what was written in the newspaper, and he started laughing. He said that all the guys mates called him Dumbo after it. I was pleased the nickname stuck but now as I write this, I want that asshole DONE for attempted murder. It's a cold case, over 20 years old!!! That piece of dog do is going to prison. If you know him…tell him he fights like little girl! Any leads, please tell the Garda Siochana in CORK!

10

CAR CRASH

S hortly after I got stabbed in the head, I met my girlfriend who was to be my future wife. I met her on a night out with all the kitchen staff from the Cork University hospital. There was 15 women and me! They were laying it on thick for the local men in the nightclub we were in. All 15 women were coming on to me. It was hil-ar-ious! I picked Briona and shagged her that same night. She was working in the kitchen staff too. She was a little bit weird. I thought she was fun and a really good-looking girl. We shagged non-stop for a couple of months. I went back to sea for 6 months to finish my sea time for my final college phase. I was going out with Briona for that whole year, six months of which I'd spent at sea as a cadet. I came home and went back to college in September. Then in March, I took her with me, up to meet my family in Donegal. I was looking forward to showing her off to my friends. She was a young stunner! We spent a great weekend together enjoying St. Patricks day parade in Moville. Our float for our bar The Drunken Duck was a rush job. It consisted of a picnic bench, flags and loads of beer, sitting on a trailer. Sure, what more do you need? Ceol agus craic! (music and fun!).

When the weekend was over, we got ready to make our way back down to college in Cork again. Mickey decided to extend the weekend a little. Mickey whom we were getting the lift with said that by leaving in the early hours of Monday morning, we'd have more time at home.

He said we could drive down through the night and make college early on the Monday morning. Mickey was a friend of my fathers from years before. He was in the same class as me in college. My father and he used to fish salmon together, and an early memory of mine was one day I was allowed to go with them on the 30ft half-decker. Kids weren't normally allowed, in case they jinxed it, very superstitious bunch!

We got the net caught in the screw (the Salmon net is fouled around the propeller), and Mickey volunteered to have a rope tied around him and dive in as the others held him. He cut the net free. I don't think he could swim. That gained my respect anyway, and I never forgot it. So, I always found Mickey a kindred spirit. I trusted him and never thought much more about the drive down. I'd had a few beers in our bar because we were leaving at 3 am and I thought to myself I could get a sleep on the journey.

When we were about to leave. Briona said she had a bad feeling and was very disconcerted about getting into the car. We left anyway, and in just under an hour, I started feeling sleepy and drifted off. The next thing I remember is waking up and saying "AH FUCK" as the car was sliding. The straight road ahead moved over and back in my view out of the windscreen as Mickey tried to regain control. Then "BAM!" we hit the crash barrier along the side of the road on the right "BOOM!" I was knocked out! I remember waking up inside the car upside down and Mickey trying to say something to me, but I couldn't hear because of the radio. I tried to turn the radio down, but as I turned the knob, I turned the volume up instead. We were upside down with Kylie Minogue singing "I should be so lucky...."

Blaring on the radio. A weird moment because loud music was not at all fitting for the scene that was before me. As I found out later, Mickey's legs had been severed off on one and so badly damaged on the other that they had to amputate it later. He also had a punctured lung.

Briona was in the back seat, so I couldn't get to her or see her injury at the time. I knew I had to do something when I came to. The side impact on the barrier on my side had knocked me out. We could tell from the car after the crash that the barrier had gone through the car like a knife. It had entered the back-left door where Briona had been sitting, leaving a torpedo-like hole in the door. The crash barrier had hit her leg, almost severing it (it looked like a leg of lamb with the bone in the middle when I saw it later), cut my seatbelt and my seat in half. (I'm speculating here, but it seems plausible enough reasoning that the crash barrier hit my hand because I put my hand down to check if I was wearing my seatbelt just before we struck). It cut the gear stick off ploughing into Mickey's feet in the foot well, severing his legs. The car then flipped over backwards because we'd spun around and were hitting it in reverse, then flipped over, almost catapulted by the barrier and down a small embankment, landing on the soft moss in a field beside the road. As we travelled through the air, the barrier had come straight out again, so we'd narrowly missed death, not once, but twice. Briona was calling me, and Mickey was trying to keep it together. I knew he was in pain; I could hear it in his voice, but he was also trying to remain calm. What a man! Briona was in pain also, but she was also keeping calm. What a woman! I was the only one who didn't seem that badly hurt. Mickey said, "you need to get help". I told him I would go now, but when I tried the door beside me, it wouldn't open.

We then tried Mickey's side. Although there was a concrete post against it, between the both of us, pushing on the door, we managed to push it open and get it ajar so I could climb up through and outside. Once there, I went around the back to the trunk to get my phone in my bag. I knew I had to act quickly, but when I opened the trunk, all the luggage fell out, so I rummaged around quickly in the trunk light. I found my red bag, took my phone out then in the light from the interior of the trunk I looked at the fingers of my right hand. The middle finger looked like a Twix bar with all the chocolate taken off and was just as thin. It was de-gloved, as they call it in medical terms. I tried the phone, no signal. Fuck!!! I thought, I've to go and get help but I didn't want to leave. The car was hissing, and in that crazy moment, I thought I don't want to leave, if this car blows up, I want to die with the woman I love.

It was only fleeting. A more logical thought took over. My back has sore, but I didn't overthink it. I told Mickey and Briona that I was going to get help. I climbed back up over the barrier, up the embankment, and back onto the road. I looked, and in the distance, I could see the lights of two houses, they were about 400 yards away. I started to run on the road but immediately slipped and smacked my hands down on the road. It was sore as hell. The road was that slippy. There's a lot of accidents on that stretch of road for some reason. I found this out later, and it explained why the people in the houses didn't panic when I got to them. I also felt it was my approach in talking to them.

I ran along the grass verge towards the houses to avoid slipping. I got to the houses, and I thought to myself, remain calm and avoid the confusion panic creates. I knocked on their door without panic, loud enough for them to hear me. A woman answered, and I explained we were in a bad car crash along the road somewhere and we needed help. She said she'd phone an ambulance, and it was okay, she'd get her husband. She told me to go next door and rouse them too. I thought she was fobbing me off at first, then I realised that she was just telling me that they would help also. I was a bit shook. I knocked on the second door, telling them I'd been to the first door, and they'd said to knock here and that I needed help. The two men came out onto the street, and to this day, I'm eternally grateful. One had a flashlight, and as soon as they emerged and I knew help was on the way, I collapsed. It must have been the adrenaline that was keeping me going because I'd broken four bones in my back. The Doctor called them fishbones. That was the pain. The men said, "are you alright?" and helped me to my feet. They said, "C'mon, you'll be ok, we need to find that car!". I said I was ok and let's go. We half ran, half walked because of my back, to the spot where I thought it was but I couldn't see the car. Luckily because they were locals, they knew where the crash barrier should be. The sight that faced me stays with me to this day. We climbed down. Briona had crawled out of the back-door window. It had been smashed in the crash but her leg was still trapped inside. We clambered around the other side of the car. One of the guys shone his flashlight in. I saw Briona's leg. Part of it was hanging off, and I could see the bone in the middle. They kept Mickey alert and conscious by talking to him and telling him help was on the way. I climbed around to Briona and lay down beside her, wrapping her head up with my body in the foetal position, wrapping myself around her. I'd heard somewhere that you can feed life into someone in doing this and help them survive. I froze stiff in this position until the emergency services arrived.

At this point, I didn't know. But Mickey had also reached the services from his car phone. Some composure on him to do that in the situation. The ambulance arrived, lifted me on a stretcher, and slowly straightened me out. The fire service cut Mickey and Briona out. We all went to the hospital. I heard afterwards that Mickey had 16 pints of blood through him and had his second leg amputated in hospital. But more power to him, he was up and walking on his new legs and back to a new job within 11 months. His eldest son thanked me for saving his life. That meant a lot to me. Briona, on the other hand, had trouble and pain every day with her leg. They put a pin in and screwed it together, but it kept breaking and wouldn't knit.

We spent two weeks in a Dublin hospital. I had a skin graft done on my fingers and a plate strapped to my back. They'd taken a piece of skin from my right thigh, removing it like they'd peeled a potato, they'd explained. There was nothing they could do for my back but strap support to it and for me to have plenty of bed rest. I healed up rapidly and came on leaps and bounds with my physio, practicing and pushing the movement of my middle finger every day even though it hurt like crazy. Briona and I were very much in love so on the 10th of March, my father's birthday, while lying on my bed, I came up with the idea of marrying her. I thought about all the pros and cons and whether it was a kneejerk reaction but I felt it was all so real, so I went ahead with it. I went to the room where her bed was and asked her to marry me. She nearly died with shock! "What?" she said. "Marry me!!" I said, half going down on one knee. "OK!!!" she said, giggling. "What will Mammy think?!!" she said. I said we'd run it by her when we got out.

We spent a lot of time together during those 2 weeks. One of the nurses thought it was bit unhealthy, but we were happy, so what odds. We got out, and Briona's mother collected her and took her home. I went home to Donegal for a couple of weeks, but I was determined to go back to college to finish out. I informed the college of the crash, and my head lecturer said I could come back the following year because of the time I'd missed and what I'd been through, but I said no. I told him

I wanted to come back and finish that year. He was really impressed. I thought my life was down there, with Briona and doing my course. I wanted to stay on the roll I was on. So, to keep in tune, I asked one of my relatives, who was the principal of the National Fishery Training College, Ireland in Greencastle, my next town over, for some tuition before the Easter break and during the Cork college Easter break. I studied in my own time. I knew I hadn't missed that much time really. I got great tuition in the Fishery college. In this time also, I came up with the idea of how to ask Briona's mother for her daughter's hand in marriage. Bishop Daily from Derry, a man whom I admired, had written a book detailing his life. I knew he said mass in the Hospice everyday where my mother and my late auntie had both battled their cancer, so there was a good chance my plan would work. My mother had survived. Although she contracted lymphedema and has a badly swollen leg, a side effect of the surgery to combat the cancer. So, I bought his book, and as coincidence would have it, my mother was in the hospice receiving treatment. One day I was visiting her, Father Daily, as he was then, having finished his bishop term, was going out to the carpark and I saw him leave. I took my chance and called him. He stopped and I asked him to sign the book to Briona's mother. I said could you write "You're only getting this book if you give the right answer!!" He looked shocked and said "I am not putting that down!!" lol. He had no craic in him. I said just sign it then, which he did, and I thanked him. I went back down to Dublin shortly after this, armed with the book and balls galore, feeling this was a brilliant idea. Her mother couldn't say no! Briona was at a check-up in the hospital. I met up with her and her mother to journey back down to where they lived in the Tipperary.

Briona, her mum, and I were driving down to Tip when her mother suggested we go for something to eat. She was so thoughtful! She said she knew a lovely bar & restaurant. This was it, a nice place to ask for her daughter's hand in marriage, it was memorable and a place her mother liked. We stopped and went in. Briona was sitting beside her mum. I excused myself, saying I'd left something in the car I needed, asking her mother for the car keys. I brought the book back in and sat opposite them, telling her mum I had a present for her, but whether she got it or not depended on her answer. She started to laugh asking, "what's this?" So, I asked her the question. "Is it OK to ask for Briona's hand in marriage?"

"WHAT?!!!" She exclaimed.

I have to say it here now. Thinking back, I was on a high from surviving the whole car crash thing because, as far as I was concerned, I'd done a heroic act. I'd got out and got help, and whether a good thing or not, the drama of it all had brought Briona and I closer. I was way too young to be getting married. Marriage is antiquated anyway.

Her mother said "yes!" and told her whole family. There were big celebrations. I passed my exams eventually. I failed a load of them but had the idea that all I had to do was keep repeating them until I passed everything. It worked! I did my orals exam in Dublin and the examiner recommended to me that I go and get my Chief mate/Master's right away. He said he was really impressed with me!

I got a job on the Granuaile for a couple of weeks after I qualified. It was my first job as an Officer. It was enough experience of working on a Supply type ship to get me started in the North Sea.

I got a job working, a month on, month off on a supply vessel to the oilrigs in Aberdeen. My mate TC was working there as well. He was on another Supply ship. He once asked me if I ever had sexual relations with any of the hookers that are always down by the docks at the end of the night, when you're on the piss?!! I said no but he started laughing and said have you not even thought about it? I said I had not but not long after that conversation I got an offer of "Tenner a suck! 20 a fuck!" on my way home. It was one of the hookers TC was on about. She was not bad looking. I had a few quid left on me so I thought, why the fuck not? I took the "20 a fuck" and did her doggy style up a dark alley. She hiked up her skirt and bent over, putting her hands flat on the ground just like fanjita did many years later. It was a bit bloody scary but I braved it anyway. Those hookers have balls of steel!!!

It was my first real position as a 2nd officer, and I was relishing it. The driving experience I was getting of the vessel was awesome, but there was this tinge I was getting, and I was starting to feel awful. The longer I spent in the dark nights and bad weather, the worse the feeling got. I was drinking non-stop, practically every day when I was on my month off. I went down and further down, blaming everything and everyone around me until I could see no outs but change my situation. We'd sold our family bar at the time also which had a profound effect on me because it had been my home practically for the previous nine years. I'd had a vision of running it on my time off but I wasn't ready to take it over when my father decided to sell. He offered it to me for 70k but he wanted to remain overall manager even when I bought it off him, but I thought fuck that!!! It was one of the reasons I'd run away to sea in the first place. I couldn't work under him. It was lucky in hindsight, that I didn't take it over, due to the downturn in the economy.

I was flying out of Belfast every time I went back to work in Aberdeen. I'd come home, spend a few days with my family, three weeks with Briona, then the last couple of days with my family before flying out again. I was travelling the country on buses and trains to do it. I never thought to buy a car!!! I was so fucking wound up with Briona's leg. It was a fucking terrible nightmare. We fell so out of love.

My mate, Wobbly said, "Your problem is you don't know whether you're coming or going." He was right, but I was having problems with the other Second mate and the Chief mate on the boat in Aberdeen as well.

I wasn't happy there and definitely needed a change. They had started to bully me. They were laughing at my expense. They were slagging me off when I was on the bridge. It was really awful. It brought back memories of the final stage of my cadetship. I had 6 months to get 6 months sea time in. I had to split my sea time between two vessels. 3 months on each and not go home for a breather because of the ulcer I'd had on my foot. All that lost time. When I joined the first ship, I was met by the asshole of a Chief mate. He was the worst bloody Chief mate I have ever sailed with. He never stopped blowing his own trumpet. He was steady undermining the Captain. He had just completed his Master Mariners and thought he was a brain surgeon. He was trying to ruin my confidence. He tried at every turn to embarrass me. He would shout at me in front of pilots and other shore people and give me dogs abuse if

I slipped up on anything. It was the most torturous couple of months I had had since going to sea. Briona was on the other end of the phone for me but I felt like fucking killing the cunt. I held back because of Briona. She said "Why spoil your entire cadetship because of one asshole?! You only have a few months left to complete your training." I left it alone.

He left that ship and I thought I'd seen the last of him. I called my mate Donny from college a few weeks after he left. Donny was doing his training with the same company. I'd told him about the Chief mate, when he started pushing me around. I was joining Donny's ship after I left the ship I was on. We were switching places. Donny said when I called him "You're not going to like this but the new Chief mate on here is him as well!!". I could not fucking believe it. Another couple of months of torture, I thought. How the fuck am I going to deal with this? It was all that was in my mind. I thought I would end up throwing the guy over the side. He was fucking evil.

It came time to join the new ship for my final 3 months. I was joining in Plymouth docks. I got a taxi from the B & B to the port. It was a bit of a journey through the city so I struck up a conversation with the driver. He was ex-British Royal Navy. I told him my problem with the Chief mate and he offered me some good advice! He said the way they dealt with that in the Royal Navy is beat the living shit out of them when no-one is watching. He said "you'll know when the time is right!" He was a really good man.

I joined the ship and the first thing I did was go to the bridge and meet the new Captain. He took me to his Day room and said "I have been told you are having trouble with our new Chief mate". I said "Yes. He is a complete asshole!" He said Donny had told him. He said "Do not worry. I am putting you both on opposite watches. You will hardly meet him." I thanked him. Everything went smoothly for about 2 weeks. Then, we were in Belfast to discharge a cargo. I was supposed to be getting some leave to go home for the night. This did not materialize because of rioting in the city. It was marching season. I was so fucked off. I was standing first thing in the morning at the railing of the ship after a long night watch, looking out over the mountains towards home thinking it would have been nice to go home, when the asshole Chief mate came out on deck. He snapped at me right away. He said "What the fuck are you doing standing there doing nothing?!" It was the first time I had stopped fucking moving in hours. I was having a little breather. I went fucking crazy. I grabbed him by the collar with both hands and held him out over the railings. He fucking shit himself! I looked up the deck to see if anyone was watching but the deck crew who'd been watching, all turned their backs. I was so delighted. Everyone had my back. I screamed into his face. "IF YOU EVER FUCKING TALK TO ME LIKE THAT AGAIN…I WILL THROW YOU OVER THE FUCKING SIDE!!!" He was so frightened. He was a scrawny, unfit 40-year-old. I was 21 and strong as an Ox. We came to an agreement! I pulled him back in and pushed him down the deck. I walked straight up to the Captain and told him I had just had a fallen out with him. The Captain said worriedly "You did not hit him, did you?!" "No" I said. "OK!" he said, "We will deal with it later!" It was all smoothed over and I got no more grief from him.

It was a bit different in the North Sea. The Captain was a bit arrogant. There wasn't as big of a crew. The Chief mate was an ex-cop and had a real big ego on him. He was a smarmy smart ass. The Second mate wasn't that bad but he took my cabin after my first trip. I arrived back from leave and he was making himself comfortable in it. We joined on the same day. I said "What the hell are you doing? This is my cabin." He said "Well, it's mine now!" He was twice my age so, he thought he could throw his weight about. That cabin was way more comfortable for sleeping in because the bunk was thwart ship, meaning it went from port to starboard, instead of going from forward to aft like every other bunk on the boat. The ship rolled a lot in the bad weather. The Second mate that took my cabin was a bit of an over grown oaf. I just got on with it and took the other Officer's cabin. It was the beginning of the downward spiral for me on board. They ganged up on me and I was trying my best to work around it. I was on watch with the Captain so I stayed out of their way. The Chief mate and other Second mate were on watch together.

I wrote this poem called 'The Squall' at the time that all the things were going against me on board.…remember you can read more of my poetry if you buy my poetry book 'Anonymous in the town that talks' available on Amazon!....Just sayin'....

23/11/03

The Squall

Lying in limbo, books on the shelf,
more interest in learning about my inner self,
my sense of direction is like a confused Sea and swell,
look good on the outside,
but all is not well,
self-confidence, motivation, single-mindedness, and goal,
are lost at present, and it's damaging my soul,
from all the right moves and brimming with zest,
a lust for life that was a "no-contest,"
they're simmering beneath,
just waiting to shine,
but I need a stage that is rightfully mine,
a stage that's not handed to me but earned through time,
with respect, hard work, and being straight down the line,
above all else to thine own self be true, is a statement I've held close,
but not always adhered to,
playing the wide boy, games that aren't mine,
taking measurement from other's is surely a sign,
I've not strayed far, but far enough to hurt,
the ones closest to me and especially myself,
paranoia, self-doubt, states alien to me,
they aren't readily apparent, only a few can see,
as a young boy, a teenager, and now a man,
was, still is, a belief of greatness in my destiny's hand,
my character is strong, maybe not as vocal as some,
but my spirits not broken,
and they've far from won.
My time to shines not arrived,

but it will come,
I just hope I see it,
and I've not let it past,
Was it our bar?
Was that my last?
That is not my belief,
but can't help the what if's,
it sounds like back tracking,
a severe quavering of decision,
that was once so stiff,
I'll miss the attention and being the star of the show,
something I crave but at least I know,
now for a substitute,
that earns equal respect,
no begrudging of success or eternal regrets,
don't listen to others, to thine own self be true,
sail by your own compass like you were taught to do.
Fuck'em!!!
aye
Fuck'em!!!
The bullies did not ruin me!!!

Everything was wearing me down though. The bullying and the fact that I had fallen out of love with Briona. Had I stopped using drink to help cheer me up, who knows? Even then, I felt there was a deeper disconnection with her. She was acting the cunt! She was always undermining me in front of her family and friends. I didn't feel right for her, and I began to feel drained around her. She was also pulling the piss out of me about my confidence. She said I was really big headed. She was a bit fucking childish if you ask me. She was really fucking jealous of my confidence. She used to sweat buckets in public out of sheer nerves. It was so embarrassing but I never pulled the piss once. I used to cringe.

I felt guilt about wanting to break up with her because of her injury. How could I leave her after all we'd been through? I stuck it out for over a year after the crash, but I was perpetually down and trying not to show it. There's only one option I could see, and that was a change of environment. I phoned a number for another company in the same game who were headhunting people to crew their vessels in West Africa and got an interview. This immediately gave me a buzz. I knew Africa would be a new lease of life for me. I'd been in these situations before where I was down, then the situation would change and I'd be ok again. It's bloody human. When I look back at it, I think I hit a high after the car crash happened. After all, I was the hero. I'd got out and got help. Then I hit a low with all the drinking and piss taking from Briona. I came back up again in Africa as you will read. The car crash definitely caused me trauma. The relationship with my father was like human suppression also. He'd force his point on me and hammer me when I didn't agree with him. He was a bit of a tyrant.

11

A NEW BEGINNING

....

I went for my Second mate's interview in Scotland. I landed the job, no worries. Great I thought, a new job, doing what I loved, and in the African sun! I was looking forward to the adventure. I thought this will be a new lease of life after the shit time I'd had in the North Sea. I joined a vessel called William C. Hightower. It was going well from the minute I stepped onboard!!!

But then, I received an email from Briona outlining my drinking and everything I'd done bad during my leave. She broke the only rule I'd left her. I told her do not put anything in an email that could hurt my career because they were all routed through the new companies office, in Aberdeen. We'd had a fight before I left. I thought she might do something stupid and she bloody did. My warning didn't stop her. She let me have it, both barrels. I was livid and, in my head, I finished with her. It was the catalyst I needed, and it was a turning point in my life!

I was so fucking happy. I couldn't wait to sample the delights of the Dark continent. I'd never been with a black woman before. It was a joyous moment for me. I will NEVER be tied to only ONE woman ever in my life. I plan to have 3 women. They will all know the rules of engagement. LOL.

I was ecstatic. The millstone that was the relationship had been lifted off me. I began to chat better with my shipmates and enjoy my work and life more again. My shore leave was a lot more fun too!

In one instance, we went ashore in this little Island of Malabo in the Gulf of Guinea. I went for a few beers with my colleagues, but as often as not, it was more than a few beers. The rest of the crew went back gradually to the ship, but I decided to stay for a few more beers and get a look around. We were told not to venture further than the bars around the docks, but as always, my adventurous and curious side got the better of me, and I wanted to explore. It was the middle of the day, and I'd been around the block, so I thought, "what's the worst that can happen?!!" "You could get shot. That's the worst that could happen!" they told me later. So, off I went rambling around the dirt tracks that were the main streets through the town. It was really entertaining.

I walked into a bar I noticed, and the first thing I met was an empty step. There was a step down into the bar. I tripped and fell head first, running headlong into a table sitting in the centre of the small bar. I smashed the glasses on the table with my face, receiving a deep gash on my chin. The man behind the bar and some of the customers helped me up! They knew before they asked, that I was from one of the ships down in the harbour. They helped me back to the boat. I'd an arm over both of them, and when we got to the boat, they would not hand me over. I was a terrible sight, pissed out of my head with blood all down the front of my shirt. They asked the captain who was down on the deck, for $30 to cover the damage. I got in trouble for that. The Captain paid the money there, and then and the guys threw me back to him. I got a written warning the next day for that!

Things moved along pretty nicely after that. We didn't get ashore for a few weeks, then we got a night off. The 2nd engineer Ryan and I decided to take in a bit more of the Island. We'd had a few beers in the local bar at the end of the quay that had become our local, and after meeting a few of the local 'women', we decided to venture further. We went to an all-black nightclub, and it's safe to say we were nearly the only white people there. We had a whale of a time! The crowd of nightclubbers that were dancing there, did the hokey-cokey around us on the dance floor. Ryan and I were in the middle dancing to the music. It was really fun!

Then we met this guy at the bar who was from Glasgow. He'd been there for a few months on a shore-based contract working on land but still with ties to the ships so we had something in common and he was good craic. He offered us a lift home. We got into his 4x4 with me in the passenger seat and Ryan in the back with a few of the local women. The car was over loaded so one of the local ladies, jumped into the front seat along with me, sitting on my knee. We started getting cosy in the darkness on the way home. I dropped my hand and started to fondle her pussy! Rubbing her clitoris for all it was worth! She was really enjoying it. She was grinding erotically on my cock at the same time. I was so fucking horny!

When we got to her stop, she asked me to come with her. I asked my driver mate what he thought I should do?!! He was a bit older, so I thought a bit wiser! He said, "it's up to you!" so, with some trepidation I went. The excitement took over and I was no longer worried. It was going to be my first time with a black woman. I'd always heard the saying "once you go black, you never look back!" We walked through what could only be described as breeze block building, ground level with no glass in the windows. There were people sleeping side by side on pieces of cardboard, and we had to step over them to get where we were going. She raised her finger to her lips, signalling "Shh" as we did. It was a bit nerve-wracking, but I was more excited about what was going to happen. She opened the door and turned on the light. In we walked to what looked like a one-bedroom cell. There were two windows, and neither of them had glass, and both had bars in them. We began getting frisky and getting down to it. She stripped naked. Her big bosom was heaving. I could tell she wanted to be fucked doggy style like a fucking slut! She lay back on her back and I slid my cock deep inside her. I fucked her for a couple of seconds then she rolled over on top of me. She smiled down at me, then she did the muscle clench with her pussy around my cock. She was smiling erotically at me as she did it! I was told it's unique to black woman. My mate Jamima was so fucking jealous of this story and said all women can clench their pussy but I haven't had one since that can do it like my Malabo beauty. The Chief mate on the boat told me that a black woman had more clench than a white woman. I really enjoyed my first black experience with her. She said to me as she clenched, "te gusta?" (you like in Spanish.) "Me gusta!" I said laughing. She had a fucking gorgeous body on her. The bed was terrible. It was just a mattress on the ground. I'd had never experienced such animal excitement. We lay and chatted broken English afterwards. I asked her did she think my dick was big? I'd heard stories about black men's cock's being large so I thought she would be a good judge. She smiled and said "Medium!" I laughed and said "good enough for me!" That's big in white man's world!!

Next thing she got a phone call. She stopped playing with my cock and took the call. I didn't understand anything of what was said. My Spanish was ok but they were talking so quickly. We fumbled through what had to be said. She told that she had to go but she would be back in one hour. I did not ask her where she was going or for what? But I guessed her to be a lady of the night. She left me to lie there naked on the bed. An hour, I thought, that's nothing. She'll be back in no time. Twenty minutes in, and I had different ideas. I started to panic when I saw the daylight appearing through the windows. I got dressed. It was getting lighter and lighter outside! It happened so quickly in that part of the world! When the sun came up, it was like someone is turning a light-switch on. I decided to leave. I tried to open the door but discovered the door had three locks that all had to be opened from the outside with a key. I really panicked then. First of all, I looked for something to screw off the locks. She didn't even have coat hangers. Nothing metal at all. I sat down, facing the door, placing my feet on the wall, either side of the door and tried pulling the door open by putting my fingers underneath it. I was trying to break the locks. A fruitless operation, to say the least. I sobered up pretty fast here, and panic-stricken, I began to scream.

"LET ME OUT!" "LET ME OUT!"

It fell on deaf ears. Then an old guy, old by the sound of his voice, spoke to me through the door. He only spoke Spanish so he was no good! I lay back on the bed flummoxed and all the while thinking I'm going to be late for work, but there was nothing to do but wait. After a short bit of time, I heard her voice outside the door talking to what sounded like the old guy's voice who had come to my aid. The door opened, and in came the black lady of the night! She came straight into my face in a bad temper. I was sat on the edge of the bed. She said, "Problema?" "Que problema?" What's the problem? Why are you screaming she was getting at? I was sitting on the bed fully clothed and she was standing pointing her finger into my face. Her expressions were typically African and dramatic. "Why you scream? She said "You think I try to kill you?" she said smiling seductively.

"No, no, no", I said, feeling brave again knowing that I now had a way to get out there. She said "Jiggy Jiggy?!! One more time?!!" Pointing to the bed again. I checked the time on her phone. So, knowing that I still had time before work, I said, why not? So, we fell to it again. I fucked her doggy style and came to thunderous applause in my head. LOL. She said afterwards. "I be your wife!" and gave me her phone number. I laughed into myself and thought "no fucking chance!" I didn't want to be tied to any woman. The phone number was only 4 digits. It made me realize how small the Island was. That made me laugh too. I heard afterwards from a shipmate when I told him the story, that lots of Sailors kept local women as their wives as well as having one at home! I thanked her for her number and she called me a cab. The cab was there in a couple of minutes. It pomped and as I was leaving, I said goodbye to her at her bedroom door, but she said "no, no!" "I go with you! It's not safe!"

As we got out of the building there was a group of guys sitting outside drinking local hooch from canisters. One of them was holding a gun in his left hand and tapping his right with it. They were staring angrily at me. I looked at them as I walked towards the cab, and said, "AWRITE?!!!" cool as you like and still a little drunk!!! I was never as glad to get into a taxi! And I got back in time for work, so it wasn't a bad night.

12

IGNORAMUS

The rest of the trip was going smoothly, but there was an incident involving the new Chief mate who seemed a little highly strung. He had really high blood pressure, judging by red glow of his cheeks! Maybe an alcohol problem too? He had joined after I'd been there for a month or so. We were on watch together. He said, he knew my mate from college, Ronan, and didn't like him. It put me off the man right away! I was a bit stupid doing that. Ronan and I have since fallen out. He's very arrogant.

One day, we were at a drillship delivering the cargo from our boat to theirs, and we were using the DP equipment, which is dynamic positioning. In other words, a laser pod from the top of the bridge shoots out a steady stream in a fan-like motion hitting reflectors positioned at intervals on the installation that you are working on. These beams, once reflected, go back through a computer giving distances. You basically drive every rudder and every propulsion system from a console using a computer screen. Anyway, this Chief mate and I weren't having the best relationship.

He was still pissed off after I came back a little late from being ashore in the pub one night. I had asked him while we were working, "Do you mind if I do all the driving to and from all the installations?" "No bother," he said. I thought he looked a bit relieved; I didn't know why? I wondered was it the advanced nature of the ship?

We were working at this drillship off Ghana. He was working on the DP system which he had told me, he had already done the course in, so I had to leave it to him. He was a bit up himself about it, to be honest. Then all of a sudden, as we were working, the ship started surging towards the drillship. I'd had this happen to me before, but I left it to him. I watched our vessel get closer and closer to the drill ship, but I knew the limit at which we could still get out of the situation. He began panicking, but I still said nothing, not looking at him, just staring at the ships closing in, waiting for him to call for help. Then he suddenly crapped himself and started shouting "stop it quick! Do you know how to stop it?!" I asked him did he want my help? Dragging it out for a little more pressure on his part, and pleasure on my part! "YEAH!!!", he shouted panicking even more. I hit the button "present position" on the console. A procedure that has been tried and tested. I knew the machine's capabilities, so it was all in hand. It brought the vessel back to the safe position when you first switched over from manual to DP, a safe distance off. That'll teach him a lesson, I thought! There was a whirr as the engines increased, surging us back to safety. The relief on the Chief mate was audible. He walked off the boat when we reached the shore again, blaming the boat going to Nigeria, saying that this isn't what he signed up for, telling us that it was too dangerous. I think that DP incident shook his nerves too! His loss, we had a great time.

13

NIGERIA

....

We sailed the William C. Hightower to Nigeria. When we arrived, I had never seen so many customs and excise onboard one ship. The army with guns were lined from our bridge to the end of the gangway – no exaggeration. They were all drunk and high. The corruption was unreal, but so was the craic! One night, the Ship's agent arranged for a few of us from the crew to go to this bar in the jungle area called Papa's bush bar near Onne, where we were docked. 5 of us crammed into an old beat up Mercedes and having a few beers in us already, we shouted for the driver to drive faster! The more we shouted, the more he laughed and the faster he went! There were speed bumps on the main road to slow the locals down. They were crazy drivers. We were bouncing around inside the car, laughing all the way. We got to the bar, and the minute we stepped out, it was like we were famous. The women surrounded us. 15 -20 women with their hands all over us. Looking for money was my first thought, but then I realised it was just to turn us on! The rest of the guys were getting the same treatment. The ladies were looking to get picked to hang out with. We went into the bar and had our bottles of extra strength Guinness, and we were told that the biggest brewery for Guinness in the world was in Africa and it was just up the road. The alcohol content was 7% a bottle, and needless to say, they loved the Irish. We had a great night. We were dancing and drinking the night away.

After a short time there, each of the other guys from the crew had settled with a woman to talk to and buy drinks for, which was the routine there. I continued dancing and not picking any woman in particular, until the 'Maître D' amusedly said to me, "you must pick a girl!!" I just laughed and said, "I can't choose even one since they're all so nice". She started smiling!! I picked a woman and sat and had a drink with her. I wanted to have sex with her but the Maître D' said it was not that kind of bar. It was a good night and I had a lot of fun. It wasn't a brothel, just a bar and you coupled up for the companionship and to be happy.

When we were in Onne I had a little criminal adventure. There was paint onboard that was not needed. I decided to sell it for beer money. We had run out of cash. The boat didn't carry any money because of pirates. This other new Chief mate was drinking and I had arranged with a local gangster to meet me at a certain time. I told him I'd have the paint ready for him. He agreed. I organised for Ryan the 2nd Engineer to keep the new Chief mate occupied with our last few dollars. I was drinking with them too. When it got to the designated time, I went to the paint locker and retrieved a stack of paint tins. I put them in a couple of heavy duty shopping bags. I went to the dock and the gangster was waiting. I got the money and went back drinking. The Chief mate had not got a clue. It was a bit of craic!!

I got off the boat shortly after this. We were leaving Nigeria and going to Ghana. My trip was over when we reached Ghana.

14

AIRPORT IN GHANA

So, it was 2003, I was 25, single and having the time of my life again. I was on a good ship, the William C. Hightower, in West Africa, and I was feeling the buzz of the new job. I loved being on the boat and if you listen to the bullshit that the Doctors feed you, I was manic! High! The truth was, I was actually just brimming with confidence again and delighted to be a free agent once again! The relationship with Briona had been detrimental to my well-being. I was feeling very good about myself because of the success of the trip and the driving experience that I had received. I'd gotten over the car crash. That had me down for over a year. So fuck your analysis Doctor Lucky. I was not manic, I was over excited to be in the prime of my life with a great job and body to die for. It was the best condition I had ever been in. I'd been running around in the African sun onboard the ship when there was no cargo onboard. It took a lot of energy.

When I left the boat after the first trip, I went with two of the deckhands, both Portuguese. In Merchant terms, they were called AB's – Able bodied seamen. There was Miguel, whom I wasn't getting on with, and the other one, Sergio, who I was getting on well with. The former had a problem with me. When we were onboard, he would argue with everything I told him to do. He couldn't take an order from someone younger than him, even though I was telling him the right thing to do. He was ex-military navy. He would find problems with everything I said. There was a lot of friction between us, but I let it go whenever we left the boat. He didn't seem to want to do so. He didn't want to speak to me!!

Before we left the boat, Sergio and I were up on the bridge of the ship on watch and thinking about what delights we were going to eat when we got off the boat. Sergio was saying, "I want a steak…I want to have prawn salads," and I said, "we will get lobster", and we will do this and that. It was fun. Having a laugh and getting excited about getting off the ship after two and a half months.

When we got ashore in Ghana, we arrived at a decrepit enough-looking hotel. The beds were lying unmade like someone had just got out of them. It made me think about the cleanliness of the joint. But what the hell, we were in Africa. Let's live it up! They didn't have anything we wanted on our imaginary menus when we were fantasizing on the boat, but they pulled out all the stops for us when we said we wanted steak. One of the staff asked us to give him twenty minutes and ran off. We sat for a while and had a couple of beers. Nothing wrong with the cooking on board, by the way! We just wanted to celebrate a bit.

After a while, he came back with our steaks and we had a great dinner. We then waited for our driver to come and collect us to go to the airport.

On our way to the airport, we stopped at a Customs house. It was a small building on the outskirts of the town. One of the guys there tried to sell us some blood diamonds. He told us where they were from. I was very wary of it. He took them out and held them open in his hand for us to see. I was a bit tipsy at this stage. I picked one up, but because of absurdity of it all and also because of beer in me and the laughing (I was joking with him), I knocked his open hand, holding the diamonds, dropping some of them on the ground. We had to get down on our hands and knees to look for them on the tiled floor. We found them, but he wasn't a happy camper. We had no money to pay for them, and we didn't want them anyway. He accepted some of the blame for dropping them, so he let it go.

We arrived at the airport about 5 in the evening. We went in, checked our bags, and went to the bar. But to our dismay, the bar was closed, and the plane was due to leave at 11.30 that night. So, we had a lot of time to kill.

There was going to be no drinking before we got on the plane, but I had other ideas.

I had no cash, but I had my Visa gold card. I went in to the duty free shop, and thinking my way around the problem, I came up with a solution. I figured they couldn't stop us drinking our own booze. I was able to cater for the 14 other guys from another ship, that happened to be the American drillship that we were tending to as the supply vessel. We met them when we got there.

The duty-free shop's drink was all so cheap. It was like two dollars for a bottle of brandy and $1 for African Cream, which I thought was a very decent price! There was rum, whiskey, vodka, everything you wanted for 1 and 2 dollars. I was like a kid in a candy store, there was everything I could want. I took a bottle of this, and a couple bottles of that. Because of the leopard skin print on the bottle of the African Cream, I took it as a souvenir, along with a bottle of whiskey for my dad and a bottle of brandy for myself, and a chocolate bar just in case I needed something to eat! The girl at the counter was a gorgeous Ghanaian girl, very cute, and she said, "You must spend $20 to use the visa card". I said "holy shit, that's a lot of drinks!" She laughed flirtingly. I walked around, picking booze-up trying to cater for everyone's tastes in my head until I got up to the $20 mark. She flirted with me a little bit more, laughing at what I was doing, but then she said, "You cannot take those on the flight," and I said, "Oh well, we will see. We are going to drink most of them here anyway if we can." She laughed again at this.

I went back out to the bar area, where they were all sitting. We got cups and had a drink – the whole lot of us, much to the delight of all the sailors there. All the while, the airport security was oblivious to it all. It was fun. We were all sitting, chatting, and getting to know one another. When it was time to go aboard the flight, we were all pretty pissed. When we were leaving to go through customs and the final passport check, I put the remains of the swag in a plastic shopping bag, about 5 bottles in total.

Our hold luggage had already been checked through. I took my shopping bag along with my shoulder bag with my documents in it. I always keep these separate from hold luggage as carry on – much safer in case your baggage is lost. I then headed for the final check through along with everyone else. The older Portuguese gentleman, my nemesis, Miguel wanted nothing to do with me because I was carrying the booze. He wouldn't even stand beside me because he thought I was drawing to much attention by breaking the rules but Sergio the other Portuguese guy just laughed at me. I was testing, to see if I could get away with smuggling them.

As we were going through customs, I thought right, out in the open for all to see, I acted casual. I thought, I'll just pretend that I'm not carrying anything unusual so they might not check it. We were walking through the customs and I put the plastic bag down and handed the customs man the nap-sack, the document bag. They searched through it and said, "Ok, go ahead". I just put the document bag back on my back, and lifted up the bag with the bottles in it again, making sure they didn't clink. It just looked like a present, and I walked through. Second customs, the exact same thing, and to my delight, we went out to the bus carrying us to the aircraft. We, my two ship mates and I, along with some of the American crew, were on the first bus out so when we arrived there, we were first in the queue to get on the plane.

We were standing there, and I was the first person to go up.

I stepped up onto the gangway up to the plane when there was a clink from the bag as it hit my leg! I thought, "aww shit!" The ground staff lady looked at me and said, "have you got bottles in that bag?" I said "yeah", she asked if it was alcohol and I said "yeah." Then she said those dreaded words, "have you been drinking sir?" I said, "yeah I have been drinking but not a lot". She said, "I think you might be too drunk to get on this flight. Let me see the bag". I showed her the bag and in it were the bottles of brandy, whiskey, and African cream. She took a look and said, "You cannot take those with you ". I said, "they are just present's. Here you can have them if you want!" She said, "no, no, we have to get you off the plane, you have been drinking and I think you are too drunk." I said, "half of the people in the plane have been drinking!", "it's not just me!" I said. "I'm not drunk or anything." I asked her, "do you have an alcohol test where I could blow in to the bag?" To which she replied, "no," but she said she would ask the Captain if I could fly. I waited as she walked up the gangway steps. I could see after a few seconds, the Captain looking out his window down at us. She returned and said "no," "we are going to have to get you escorted back to the main building."

The American guys from the other ship had been tending, started arguing then, shouting at her "let him on, let him on". As I was out on a limb, I quietened them down telling them I would handle it, meanwhile thinking, don't abuse her, it'll get worse.

I said "it's alright guys, I can deal with it." So that was it, no going home for me. I was livid. She radioed for an escort from another bus, and in the meantime, while I was waiting, there were more and more buses arriving and the queue was getting longer and longer. People were getting very irate as they were waiting for the situation to resolve, and more and more of them arrived to board the plane. The ground staff got another bus for me, and as the bus came out, I saw two armed soldiers in it – two guys with assault rifles waiting to take me back to the main building. I told them that I wanted to see the manager, and when we arrived back at the main building, they took me up to see the manager. I still had the bag of booze with me. There was an armed guard at the door. I was standing there waiting and waiting for what seemed like an eternity. It was only minutes, but I couldn't control my temper at the injustice of getting kicked off the plane. So, I burst in, and as I did, I saw the manager, just sitting there at his desk facing the door, taking a big slurp of his coffee. This enraged me even more, and I said, "What you're too busy to see me but you have time for a cup of coffee?!!!". As I did, the armed guard that was standing at the door, put his gun to the back of my head and shouted, "STOP!" The manager put up his hand to the soldier and said "no, no, it's ok!!!". The soldier relaxed and took the gun away. I could have been shot. The manager said, "Come in. We can talk". I sat down, and we talked.

If it hadn't been trying to make Briona's graduation, I wouldn't have been too bothered about it. He took me into the other room where his personal computer was and asked me where I was going and what I was doing, and he said, "Right, ok, we will see what we can do. We can't get you on another flight tonight since there is no other flight tonight so you are just going to have to wait here." I asked to be put up in a hotel, but there was none available. He said, I just had to wait at the airport.

I went back into the main part of the airport and into the departure lounge where I could wait with my shoulder bag and a shopping bag full of drinks. By this time, it was about 1 am, so I hadn't much else to do except sleep, or at least you would think so. I knew with all that alcohol; it wouldn't be long before I found a partner in crime. I spied a back packer around my age and went over to talk to him. It turned out he had been touring around and was quite partial to a late-night beverage.

We sat all night and chatted, hopes and dreams and so on, and every so often, the cleaner guys would walk past, so I gave them a bottle too, thinking they would take it home with them but they didn't. They got livelier and livelier. Some of them had even started singing. They were drinking on the job. You wouldn't get away with that over in Ireland, I thought, but here it looked to be the norm! They were giving me high fives!!

The next morning, I was able to walk through security without being checked because I got to meet all of them as well. They didn't keep checking my passport every time I went from one area to the next. But I did drink too much of the booze. I was poisoned from it the next morning. I was rotten, I got sick so many times. I was sitting outside the toilet. I had a really bad hangover. I got through that, and then that afternoon, I went to the check-in desk to see if I could get into the club lounge, just to see if I could get bumped up. The staff lady said no. But then she said, dress better, and we will see what we can do. I had my Hawaiian shirt on. Caribbean style shirt, colourful green. I put on a more formal shirt and cleaned up (well, I was pretty clean anyway). She said she was going to seat me at the emergency exit door, so there would be lots of room but no drinking!

Finally, I got on the plane, and I was sitting beside a guy from Togo. He was a good companion. We laughed. He didn't drink and I told him I wasn't allowed to drink on the plane so whenever the trolley came around, I got a soft drink. I'd told him the story of why I wasn't allowed to drink, and Chief Stewardesses came and told me the same thing. She was quite forceful. So, whenever she went away, he ordered a small bottle of wine from the trolley and gave it to me. I thanked him. He was a really nice guy. He was on his way to Alabama to go to study in college. I hope I meet him again some day.

15

GRADUATION

After I arrived back in Ireland, I went to Cork and went straight to a hotel. I didn't see Briona because she had things to do with finishing college, so I went shopping and bought some new clothes. I have to say, I was feeling pretty good. It was just after a fantastic trip. I was fit. I was tanned and I had money.

Briona and I met up that night when I went to a bar and met with all her college mates, some of whom I knew. I had all my photographs developed, and I brought them with me and showed them to them. One of them asked if I should be showing Briona the pictures (there was a group photo with one of the local ladies grabbing my balls!) I told him that they were alright. I was only having a bit of craic in them.

Briona was going home the next day after her graduation, but her brothers offered me to go sailing, so I did and we had a good time but the worst (and best, depending on what way you looked at it!) was yet to come.

16

BREAK UP WITH BRIONA

I arrived back home to Tipperary with Briona's brothers. It was great to see Briona's mum. Things were going ok between Briona and I but I still wanted to break up, I just needed the opportunity. The opportunity arose the next night when we were going out to the local pub. It was going to be a late night at the pub because it was summer so Briona warned me if I got drunk like I had been getting drunk, she would break up with me. Perfect, I thought and pissed it up with her brother's and sister's and locals. I was singing and star of the show, something she hated. When we got back to her mum's, I went to bed but I felt like getting sick and ran to the bathroom. I spewed before I got to the toilet and it sprayed all over the carpet and walls. The rest went down the toilet. Briona came in, and although she didn't get angry and shout at me, (as her mum was in bed!) I knew she was fuming. She said she would clean it up and speak to me in the morning. The next day I got up hungover. Briona was pretty quiet. Then around lunchtime she called me outside. I went out and she handed me back the engagement ring and said "I told you I would do this; I don't want to marry you!" I took the ring back, delighted my plan had worked. I felt, at the time, this was the best way of us breaking up. I thought if I broke it off, she would have been crushed and it would have shattered her confidence, which was bad at the best of times. She would now have the bragging rights!!

I was on an immediate high after that, along with the high I felt after coming back from Africa, tanned, fit, and now newly single!

The next day, I high-tailed it home on the bus to Donegal! I got home delighted it had worked and relieved that I was no longer in the relationship, while a little guilty for going about it in the way I did. Even back then, she said I had a problem with my drinking, but I wasn't ready to accept it. I have not got a problem. I love to drink. It's so relaxing. I have not time for AA or any of that crap. I believe that people can restrict their drinking on their own, that's what I do and I've done it all my life. I arrived back home to a frosty response, to say the least, from my parents. The first question my Dad asked me was, "what did you do?" "Nothing," I said. "Yeah, right!" was his response. They were right, but at that stage, I didn't care. I felt free for the first time in a year. I'd been thinking about it for a while but hadn't the balls to do it because her leg was so badly damaged in the car crash.

After falling out with my parents, I talked to my friend Munhall who said he was going back to Dublin to work. He was a Civil Engineer. I said I would go with him to get away for a break because of the hassle I was getting from my parents. I told my parents I was going away for a few days. I had 8 weeks paid leave from work so I was a free agent. I felt so fucking free!!!

When we got to Dublin, Munhall and I went out for the night and danced the night away with a couple of Norwegian girls we met. The next day he went to work.

After he went to work, I opened my first can of beer of the day. It was 8 am. I had phoned another friend the day before, Roger, and we agreed to meet in a café in Rathmines that morning. I went to the café and while I was sitting there having a coffee reading the newspaper, a woman came in and sat at the next table with her back to me. She struck up a match to light a cigarette. I was drawn to her right away. She was very attractive. I decided to have a little fun with her, so I feigned a cough because of her smoking. I coughed a couple of times, and she shook the match out and looked around at me. I concentrated on the newspaper and did not look at her. She lit another one, and I coughed more violently this time. She turned around again, this time asking if I minded if she smoked. I told her, "Do what you want. It's not my café" and smiled. She knew I was having her on with the coughing and she asked if I did mind if she joined me. "Free country", I said grinning. She laughed again and sat at my table. She told me her name was Flo. We had coffee and chatted, and she told me she worked across the road at her younger brother's mortgage company. We chatted for a short while and I told her I was going flying with my mate Roger Little. He was picking me up at the café. She said her brother learned to fly at the centre we were going to as well. Roger arrived and in a bit of a fluster said it was too windy for flying but we could go sailing. I introduced him to Flo and she was suitably impressed. She asked "what kind of lifestyle do you lead?" "Can't go flying so you go sailing instead?" I laughed and Roger said "wanna come?" She said she would have to ask her brother. We left for Rogers house with the agreement that she would call me to see if she was coming or not. She phoned a short while later and said her brother didn't think it was a good idea to go sailing with two complete strangers. I asked her out on a date instead that night to which she agreed to straight away. Roger and I went sailing, then that night Flo and I met up and I went back to her apartment. That began a love affair that lasted two weeks. But I genuinely felt love for her. I proposed to her after a week, and she said yes. But she said we had to keep it quiet until her parents got used to us being a couple first.

When she felt the relationship was getting serious after the first few day's she told me she had something important to tell me. She said she had been diagnosed Bipolar but she didn't believe in her diagnosis. She asked me did I know what bipolar was? I told her I'd never heard of it. She asked had I ever heard of manic/depressive? I said I had. She said it's the new name for it. She told me she'd been admitted to St. Pats mental asylum with anorexia, a condition she has developed after being raped while walking through a park early one evening when she was 19 years old. She was 32 at this stage. A few years older than me but I did not care. She said she ended up being diagnosed with bipolar because she fought so hard with the nurses to do her exercises when she was in there and that they said her temper was ferocious because she had Bipolar. When she was describing Bipolar, I laughed and said, "after hearing the symptoms, it sounds like I have it too!" "No, you don't," she said. "There's a lot more to it than doing mad shit and having a few highs and lows," but it whet my appetite, and when she described the injustices, she was subjected to from some of the doctors and nurses, it made me very angry. She said she knew she didn't have bipolar, but it was near impossible to disprove, the symptoms are so wide ranging. She said she had a mountain of doctors and nurses to fight in the 15 years before I met her. She also told me a good thing to remember in her opinion if I ever needed it, if you get in trouble with the law, it's better to have a mental record than a criminal record. She said if you go looking for a job, a company can check up your criminal record but they cannot check your mental record. Little did I know, but this planted the seed that set me on my journey. I also felt if I got admitted to sort the pharmaceuticals out, I could withstand these bullies. I've been fighting them all my life. The aliens have told me that I was always going to do this mission.

I laughed at the stories of her escapades in and out of hospitals. She said the women there were all very promiscuous. "You'd love it!!!" she said. I told her I'd love to go into one to see what it's like. "No! You wouldn't!!" she said, "because once you get caught up in the system, it's near impossible to get out of!!!" (if only I had of listened!). The aliens have told me in this year 2023 that my hospital admission was preordained. They have planned everything from my birth. I was going in to take on pharmaceuticals and the doctors. My mission as King of Pachsion, which is what I used to be, was to end mental illness. I chose myself for the mission to earth when the idea was founded among the elders of Pachsion. They killed me painlessly and they put my spirit of the King that I was into my mother's womb on earth when I was conceived. I also found out from Flo that the health insurance companies only covered you for 8 weeks in a private hospital, and the treatment for an illness was 8 weeks. You weren't treated in 3 or 5 weeks. It was eight weeks. It was tailored to suit and get the maximum for both to profit. After 8 weeks, you had to pay, and an admission in St. Pats for 8 weeks was 26,500 euro. Corruption?! I think so.

After a couple of weeks of me not leaving the apartment much, we wore thin on each other. She told me she needed her own space for a while. I was a bit disappointed but understood.

I phoned TC, my mate from college that was in the stabbing incident. He was in town. We met up at a bar near Rathfarnham, where Flo lived, at 10.30 in the morning. We drank all day, catching up, and I explained to him that I'd broken up with Flo, saying she told me she needed space. He smiled and said "she'll take you back". We drank all day until closing time that evening then, when TC was about to leave, I said so "can I go back with you?" He said, "No sham" in his Tuam slang. He said Anna, his partner, would go nuts because of the way we acted around each other when we were drunk. Rowdy as hell. I said I'd be quiet. He said no and he said Flo would take me back in. I acquiesced. I decided to get some chips and walk home to Flo's.

When I was in the chip shop, I tried having a bit of banter with the elder Dublin guy serving behind the counter. Me being a culchie from Donegal and him being a Dublin Jackeen. (humourous slang Irish terms for country and city people). And with the difference in prices in cities compared to the country, especially the Capital, I hit him with, "How come the price of chips down here is more expensive than in Donegal?" "Are your potatoes more expensive?" He kind of smirked, and I laughed and got my chips, and left. There were a few other customer's in but I paid no attention to them. I looked around to see if they were laughing too.

As I walked along the road, I got to a darkened area which was between the two main built up areas. I must have been well wasted not to have noticed their approach or oblivious and thinking of home when this tall 6" 4' well-built guy steps in front of me quickly on the footpath —stopping me in my tracks. He said, "Eh ya Nordin cunt! (Northern cunt – always friction between northerners and southerners) What's your problem?!" It was the same guys from the chip shop. I immediately took in my surroundings. There were 3 of them, but I fancied my chances. I'd go for the big one in front of me first. I had one asshole to my left and one behind me. I concentrated on the one addressing me and said humourously, "my problem?" and I put my hand to both my cheeks, one after the other, stabbing at them with a chip saying, "my problem is I can't get my chips into my mouth!" I did this to diffuse the situation. It didn't work! The guy behind me punched me on the back of the head right behind the left ear saying, "ya cheeky cunt!" As he did, I saw my chance and used the momentum and the distraction to drop my bag of chips and jump up and grab the big fucker by both ears, and head butt him on the nose. As he went down, I continued to nut him. Then I sat on his groin, I went into a frenzy of nutting him 3 or 4 times on the nose as he lay on the ground. The other two assholes were trying to stop me.

It was like that scene in the movie Gangs of New York, where Daniel Day Lewis is headbutting Leonardo Di Caprio in the face as he lies on the table, in the theatre in front of everyone. I wondered did I inspire that?!! It happened a good few years before Gangs of New York!

There was blood everywhere. I nearly fucking killed the cunt!!! He was staying down. No more auld shite outta him. Now for the other two. I started screaming at the top of my voice for adrenaline and to alert anyone near who could help "Agghhhh!!!" "Agghhhh!!!" I screamed. I turned, and side-swept the one behind me with a kick as I lay on the ground. He nearly fell. He was reaching for my pocket as I did this, obviously after my money! Not too much thought of his bro! I'm not sure now but in the heat of battle, I may have broken a finger or two of his, as he reached for my money. The other one had run off in fear, as did the remaining guy when I broke his fingers, I heard him squeal!

I stood up, and in what seemed like an instant, the gardai and the ambulance were there. Someone must have heard my screaming and phoned it in. The big fucker was lying out cold. One of the ambulance men came to me. "Are you alright?" he said." I'm fine," I said. He said, "You've got blood on your face." I said, "it's not mine". He said, "you're going to have to come to the hospital with us to get checked out." I said, "I'm not waiting in casualty for 5 hours just for you to tell me I've got a sore head in the morning. I know why I'll have a sore head. I've drinking since 10.30 this morning!!!". At that, the gardai who had pulled up on the other side of the road called me over. They asked me what happened, and I explained that I'd been attacked. As I pointed over to the guy on the floor, I could see the ambulance guys were using smelling salts to bring him around. I shouted over to them, "There's no point using smelling salts! "He's got no NOSE!!!" I thought it was funny at the time. "SHhhh!!!" The Guard said, "you can't be saying that!!!" I laughed. "You shouldn't be walking around here at this time of night. It's very dangerous!" he said. I decided to throw a bit of levity into even more and wind them up "Why?" I asked. "Are you not doing your jobs?" "Eh?!"" He didn't acknowledge it and instead said, "you should get a taxi". I asked "are you going to give me the money for a taxi?" "Look" he said "just go home". I decided to have a bit of craic with him, and said, "any chance of a lift?" He said, "You're not in Donegal now!" So, I decided to manipulate him. "Well, it's true what the Guards up at home say about the Guards down here!" It stopped him in his tracks. "What's that?" he said. "You're inhospitable and unwelcoming!" I said. "Get into the back of that car!" he said gruffly opening the door. I thought it might work! I told my Brussel sprouts joke then when we took off. "What has female pubic hair and Brussel sprouts got in common? You just brush'em aside and keep on eating!" That had them laughing!

They gave me a lift back to Flo's housing estate, which wasn't far. I asked them not to pull over in front of the house. To stop short in case she seen the Garda car. I told them I didn't want to get in trouble with her. They stopped short. The one I had been jesting with, had the passenger window down so as I got out and closed the back door, I reached into my pocket and pulled out a fiver handing it to him. I said, "Thanks, guys!" Smiling. He laughed saying "get out of here ye cheeky cunt! I laughed and so did they. I struck out for Flo's thinking of my approach and how I was going to get in. I knew I had blood on my face, so I decided to play the sympathy card. I went to the patio doors at the back where her bedroom was and knocked. She pulled back the curtains. She was standing up. She opened the door and I said, "Hi" feigning beat up. "What happened you?! she said. Sympathetic straight away. "I was jumped" I said. There's blood on your face she said. "It's not mine". I told her. She let me in and we had the make-up sex. She was well impressed when I told her the story. We went for breakfast the next morning with her younger brother who owned the mortgage company, and his wife. They were really nice people and they were very impressed with my reactions when I related the story to them. Flo and I, stayed together for another few days after but she decided we needed to end it. She wanted her own space.

A BREAK IN FLO

I went on the rampage around Dublin after breaking up with Flo, drinking and partying hard! Day and night! I was really enjoying myself. And contrary to the reports back to my parents about this period – I took no hard drugs. I took a couple of puffs of a joint or two but that was it.

So, there I was in a bar off O'Connell Street, having a pint of Guinness. It was quiet, and a girl sitting behind me at one of the tables came up and ordered a drink. She sat back down to what looked like college books. I heard her French accent, and it intrigued me. I've always had a soft spot for the French accent on a woman, it sounds so erotic. I gave a knowing wink to the barman, signalling I was going to chance my arm with her, he just laughed. I took my drink and went down to her table. "Hello" I said. And asked did she mind if I joined her. She smiled back and said, "No, sit down". I sat down, and she told me she was an au pair over here in Ireland studying psychology. "Hmmm" I thought. You've got my attention already. I loved people who had anything to do with mind analysis. I loved to play with them analysing everything. Another reason that took me into the asylum!!! Even if they don't analyse, you always get a good argument out of them. I like their intellect.

As I said, it's another reason I went into the asylum. I wanted to pit myself against other sharp minds within the staff, especially the Psychiatrists. Without sounding arrogant, I see myself as very intelligent. The aliens have told me that I am a genius and the smartest man on the planet. They have told me that all humans are of average intelligence compared to me. I wondered if that was true when they told me but they answered in my head straight away and said all earthlings are not very smart compared to me lol. I've been told by lots of humans all of my life by lots of different people; male and female of all ages that I'm intelligent, so to fight all the Psychiatrists, for me at that age, on the crusade I was on, in Flo's honour as you will see, was the ultimate!

Pity about it, fucking up my life, but if I make a Zillion dollars out of the book and movies and show patients to whom this has happened too, that you can overcome a misdiagnosis and not let it ruin your life completely, then I believe it'll all be worth it. I'd love a clean bill of health for the sake of my sanity and no longer have doubt about everything I say when it sounds out of the ordinary to people close to me. They have to understand that I don't have an ordinary life. These things are happening to me because I'm in the public eye. Strange things happen to me because of the life I've led and the stranger people I've met.

The French chick and I spent the day and the rest of the night together. She didn't drink much, and neither did I, when I was with her. We hit her favourite club and I eventually walked her back to Beaumont in Dublin, obviously thinking I would get lucky but obviously not in her eyes! She kissed me goodnight on the cheek outside her house and said she couldn't invite anyone in because she was staying with a family.

It was daylight at this stage, and I'd nowhere else to go. So, I said goodbye and started walking, thinking I'd make my way back into the city centre. Then two minutes from her house, I spotted a familiar sign from a window business at home on the side of a van. I couldn't believe it. I checked the registration, and it said "DL," I thought "Up Donegal!" "Yes!" I thought. I know these guys. There is bound to be somebody I know from my hometown in the house. I knew a friend and neighbour of mine, Kevin, worked for them. I knocked on the door a couple of times. I knew it was around 6 am so they'd probably be getting up soon enough. I'd had my phone stolen a few days before, and, in all honesty,

I felt a freedom at not being able to be contacted. I kept on knocking until I got a response.

A guy I didn't recognise answered the door. I told him who I was and where I was from and asked him if my neighbour Kevin was staying there? He said he was and told me to come in. He showed me the couch. Sweet, I thought, but I was still too alive to sleep. I sat there thinking of the events that had just happened, waiting until they all got up. An old adversary from my national school days, Kidneypunch, (you read about him and his older brother Berndan – the bully – in the chapter 'Bully me?!!') whom I told you I never got on with was in charge of the house.

If I'm honest with myself, when we were kids in national school, I admired him begrudgingly because he was good at sports and all the girls liked him. So, I was definitely a little jealous of him too. That was all water under the bridge now.

There were eight of them staying in the house all working for the same company. Kidneypunch told me I could stay and get some rest for a couple of hours but I couldn't stay with them for any length of time because it was company policy. I told him I understood and didn't mind and definitely didn't hold it against him. He apologized for not being able to let me stay many times over when I'd meet him on a night out at home for many years after it because I ended up in the mental asylum a couple of weeks after that. He told me he believed there was nothing wrong with me because he met me around that time, and he saw for himself I was A-Okay!

He used to say when we met, if only he had let me stay, maybe it would have panned out differently. I always told him not to worry because I did not blame him, for me not being able to stay. It was the rules. I appreciate him saying I definitely wasn't mentally ill when he met me. Our meeting was only a couple of short weeks before the admission so there was no fucking way there was anything wrong with me!!! There are many more people who met me around that time and they say the same, I was dead on! My father got bad advice to have me checked out because of the stories he'd heard of my wild behaviour around Dublin and beyond. If he had met me in college or when I was away at sea, he'd have thought it was par for the course! Those were wild times, but the stories never got home. Holy shit, if he'd heard them, I'd have never got out!!! You'll read quite a few of them in this book!

I always told Kidneypunch when we met on our nights out – that he was under orders and I understood. When he told me the rules, I told him I was just happy to get a couple of hours at the time, collect my thoughts and be on my way.

I loved rambling. When Kidneypunch and the crew were leaving, Kidneypunch said, pull the door after you. Kevin, my neighbour told me that my cousin Ronan was in the city working and I should go and visit him. He said he might be able to put me up for the night. He gave me Ronan's number and left. I chilled out there in their house, got a Chinese meal and some beer and watched the entire series of Billy Connolly's World Tour of Oz. I thought it was brilliant. It really inspired me to keep on rambling. I thought at the time, I'm going to write about these adventures one day! I've always wanted to write my tales down and publish a book ever since I started my career at sea and really began my adult adventures. So, this book has been a pipe dream for over 20 years! It's great to finally realize it. Furthermore, if it becomes a bestseller, wins the Pulitzer, made into movies, makes me a lot of millions but ULTIMATELY it gets me a clean bill of health in the world's eyes, especially the world of mental health, then it's really doing its job!!! I hope it's not too wild and you end up believing the Psychiatrists!! Back to Billy Connolly...In a way, I emulate him in my style of telling jokes and stories. I branch off but come back to the point of the story.

I left there having watched all of the Billy Connolly show and went for a few pints in town. I tried contacting Ronan. I got him eventually after a few failed attempts, and he gave me the address. It was late when I got there, about 11 o'clock or so. I knocked anyway, hoping there was still someone up. His roommate, an American guy, opened the door. Pat was his name. We sat down and he told me he was over in Ireland working on a science fiction book he was writing. He told me he was working in the Guinness brewery factory as a security guard. He told me I could go in and use his name and get in for free. I availed of this free pass mercilessly over the next couple of weeks, even giving a tour to two Aussie guys at one point. The two Aussie guys were in a pub and I got talking to them. I asked them had they been in the Guinness brewery yet? They said they hadn't. I said I could get them in for free. They took me up on the offer and we went to it. We got in free using Pat's pass. I took them passed the bullshit right up to the Gravity bar at the top. We got our free pints and there was no seats. We sat down at the window slightly blocked off from the rest of the bar. We were chatting when I overheard two Americans asking one another could you smoke in here. They were wondering if there was a ban. I had a brainwave for a bit of fun. I said to the two Aussie guys, watch this. I had already noticed the floor staff lady was the same old battle axe that had been on one other day I was in. She was very sharp. I lit a cigarette and started puffing on it. I really looked like I was really enjoying it. The two American ladies said right away. I knew you could smoke in here. They both lit up. I stubbed mine out and sat back winking at the Aussie guys. They were stifling laughs. I was doing the same. I knew what was coming. All of a sudden, the battle axe spotted them and came thundering over screaming "YOU CAN'T SMOKE IN HERE!!!" I bust out laughing. So did the other guys. They said sorry. Then she went crazy. She insulted them. She said "You Americans come over here and think you own the place. Well you'll not get away with that!!!"

Back to the story, Pat and I sat and chatted, and he told me his girlfriend had died in the Twin Towers, poor girl, and in a way, he was over in Ireland to get away from it all.

We talked about his book and different sci-fi books we were interested in until it became evident, Ronan wasn't getting up. He'd to go to work at six so he didn't get up, lazy bollocks, I thought ha! Just kidding!!

I asked Pat, did he want to go for a pint? He said "no man, my problem is once I start, I can't stop." "Ha-ha!" I exclaimed, "You're in good company." He said, "I only have 100 euros and that is to last me a while!" "We'll figure it out," I said.

Away we went into the night talking books and about events in our lives. I found him a good guy to go drinking with. I thought he was the soundest American I'd ever met. We got a few pints here, a few pints there and had great craic all night, until we found ourselves looking for an early house at seven in the morning. I told him I knew of one close by, so we walked over to the place. It was a lovely summer morning. Great time for a pint, and to keep the party rolling was my ethos at the time! And still IS!!! 24- hour PUBS!!! The aliens have told me there will be 24 hour pubs worldwide in a few years time.

The bouncers on the door of the early house had other ideas when we got there. I think they recognised me from some time before, maybe a little paranoia, either way, we weren't getting in. I asked why we couldn't get in, and they said, "look, you wouldn't like it. There's no one in there anyway". After arguing for a second or two, trying to get in, we said fuck it and left. We walked around the corner heading to another one I knew of, but as we were passing up the side of the building, I glanced in through one of the coloured glass windows, and to my shock and horror, the place was packed. The lying bastards! I said to Pat to hang on a minute and knocked on one of the small square windows. I'd come up with a plan. There were four, what looked like young students revelling in their boldness, sitting there. So, I thought, they'd be up for it! I knocked on the window to get their attention, then pointed to the side door, and motioned for them to open it. They started laughing, and the one I was looking at gave me the fingers. It pissed me right off. I drew back and smashed my fist in through the window and gave him the fingers right back! I still laugh at the shock on that student's face. I then drew my hand slowly back out, careful not to cut the veins on my wrist, but as I did, I sliced my thumb between the first and second joint on the topside of my right hand. After I retrieved my hand, I said in through the broken glass then, "I hope you enjoy your pints, there's probably glass in them now!" I started laughing, but the bouncers had other ideas. They came running up the side street towards us. I stuck my thumb in my mouth and began sucking the blood, and as they reached us, I sprayed the blood from my mouth at them and screamed, "DO YOU'S WANT TO BLEED TOO?!!" It stopped them in their tracks. Then they tried to tell us to leave but in a narky kind of way. I was pretty pissed off and sobering up. I said, "you don't own the footpath!

And anyway, think of all the people getting in while you're here arguing with me!!". They left bruised but not beaten. We still didn't get in!

Pat and I parted company, and I rambled around Dublin for another while. Meeting so many lovely people and getting over two breakups and a car crash too.

I was in Bruxelles pub on Grafton Street this night not long after that. I was having a good time. It came to the end of the night, and although I was tirelessly trying to pick up women, they were having none of it. The old Donegal accent wasn't working. It might have had something to do with my dancing outlandish and being a little bit crazy. My plan was to pick up a woman and stay in her place – simple enough. It didn't work, I hope it does now!!

Out I went, onto the street wondering where in the hell am, I going to stay? I didn't fancy walking around all night. Not on my own anyway. Boring! Then suddenly, there it was, a plan, a genius solution opened up in front of me. The Holy Grail! The 5-star Hotel, my mate TC, had told me about in all its glory. TC said he'd met with Anna his girlfriend and all their parents there. He said it was very well-to-do, and it was kind of unknown to the general public. A five-star hideaway of sorts in the centre of Dublin.

I walked over, and to my delight, the front doors were open. I dandered in, thinking up my game plan. I decided to try and blag it to see if they'd give me a room key. A bit stupid really! As I approached the desk, I saw that there was one guy in his penguin suit behind the desk. And as soon as he opened his mouth, I laughed inwardly, his accent was French, and he was little. I'm going to have fun here, I thought. The first thing I said was "Room 101," thinking "English 101". He said in his petite French accent, "we do not ave a room 101". "Oh," I said, "sorry, can I start again?" I played on the drunkenness a bit. He asked me was I staying at the hotel, and I cut him off...asking could I have a room for the night, pulling out the gold card. I used it to the hilt, it got me into places and treated differently, and I knew it would, my father had one. I knew what the glint of the card could do.

Unfortunately, this time, it did not work! He said, "We are completely full". "You must leave now!" he said. I argued for a second saying, "if

I had been some drunken star on the Raz coming in at all hours, I'm sure I'd be treated differently!" At this stage, he was out and around the counter, to enforce his point. "You must leave!" he said getting irate and put his hand on my shoulder. Instantly I thought, yes! A way in. I fell onto the ground and started screaming, "assault, get the guards!" He began to panic, as you would. Then out of the late-night bar came the night manager. He shouted at Piers, we'll call him, "what's going on?" Over my shouts, the night manager asked, "What did you do?" "Nutting, all I did was ask him to leave," Piers, the concierge replied. "Assault, assault, call the guards," I screamed as I continued lying on the ground. "Did you touch him?" the manager asked heatedly. "Yes, but I only put my hand on his arm!" "I told you never to touch anyone," the manager said. I knew this was the law. I'd heard of it somewhere before —another one of those urban legends. I stood up as the manager was bollocking him and said, "hold on, and hold on". "No need for the guards", "I'll let it go if you give me a room for the night!". The manager took one look at me and said "out!!!" laughing to himself. I asked him where he was from, and he said "Limerick." Cunning bunch, I thought and laughed. He knew I was on the blag. Little Piers didn't know what the joke was. Silly little CUNT.

Out I went, out the front door, thinking where the fuck am, I going to stay now? I was just outside the hotel's front door, which had a large glass front facing the street, when I heard them locking all the doors. The doorman who must have been on a break had returned, and he was helping Piers get all locked up. I turned and grinned, thinking that'll not happen again. It was kind of funny. The concierge Piers was now looking at me along with the doorman. As I looked back, the cheeky little fucker of a Piers gave me the finger. I couldn't believe it! I just thought insult to injury. Here I am with nowhere to stay, and this wee bollix is giving me the finger. A wave of inspiration came over me. I looked around and up at the second story of the building at the big window to the right of the front door. It was the biggest window I could see. I reckoned it to be a dining room. I got out my door key and jimmied out one of the crazy paving stones of the pedestrian area I was standing on. I knew they were imbedded in the sand. I took the brick in my hand. I looked up again at the window I was going to throw it at, weighing the brick in my hand. It was going to be a tough throw, but I was well able for it. There were two people sitting under it, a guy and a girl. I asked them to move, they saw the brick in my hand, and at a good guess, and they knew my intentions. I smiled over at the two buckos, who'd locked themselves in, then pointed up at the window like Babe Ruth, the American baseball player used to do, when he said he was going to hit a home run! Then with as much force as I could muster, I hurled the brick. It hit the window 'THUMP!' without breaking it, and it fell where the two people had been sitting, lucky they moved! The two-hotel staff looked on stunned! I held up my index finger to them and signalled them to "wait 1 minute!". I walked the 30 feet or so over and picked up the brick, and casually returned to the same spot from where I had thrown it before. I had time for a second throw. They had double-locked themselves in. From the priceless expressions on their faces I could see they were flabbergasted and too stunned to move and stop me. This time I ran a few paces towards the window and threw the brick with all my might. It went through. SMASH!

I turned around to face the concierge Piers and the doorman in the hotel again and gave them the finger back. I was in hysterics. It felt good to get my own back. The shock on their faces was brilliant. Then I legged it! I ran out past Bruxelles on my left and up to the right, back onto Grafton Street. I slowed to a jog then walked, thinking that was fun and quite satisfying too. To my amazement, I heard a shout from behind me. "ARRETER, ARRETER" "Stop" - "Stop!" I looked around and there he was in all his glory. The little concierge running, with his coat tails flapping, straight at me. I started to laugh and ran again. What a sight, I thought. He caught up with me in no time. I couldn't run with the laughter. He tripped my heels from behind. I fell. As I was falling forward, I remembered a blood blister I had on my right hand, so I burst that off the ground as I hit. I rubbed it all over my face before I turned over. Once again, he started panicking. "Merde, merde" (Shit, shit). There were drunken revellers everywhere, another reason why I'd slowed down. As soon as I started screaming, they surrounded him! He had me pinned to the ground. "WHAT THE FUCK ARE YE AT?"

they started shouting at him. And when he opened his mouth, and they heard his accent, all I heard was, "you French fuck! Coming over here taking our jobs". "Leave him the fuck alone." At this point, I had to intervene. It was getting a bit heavy, and to be honest, he didn't look like he could handle it. I was just lying there, not fighting back, glad of the rest, thinking up my next move. So, I stood up, pushed them back a bit, and said I was alright, no harm done, it was just a blood blister, showing them my hand and told them that I was taking the piss. They laughed. The little concierge held on to my sleeve and told me the gardai had been called. He took me over to one of the alcoves of a shop front on Grafton street and said go in there as he guarded the entrance. I was laughing at the hilarity of it but I played along. I could have run away. Next thing everyone who'd been watching started shouting, "Why don't you run away?" "Look at the size of him!!!" "I've nowhere to stay," I said. "At least I'll get a cell for the night" I replied. I got a laugh for that comment as well! The gardai were in no hurry, it seemed. It felt like an age waiting for them, and it looked to me like they were surprised to see me when they arrived. It turned out the bucko was from Belgium; he was a nice enough sort when we got talking. We were waiting about 20 minutes before they arrived. When they did, I got into the Garda car and immediately started to rant again about the assault, telling them to get me away from him. "Pretentious pricks!" I said. They didn't know what to think. I could tell by their faces. Piers tried to state his case over my ranting, but I kept talking over him. Eventually, after a few seconds or so, the Garda told me to shut up ta fuck! Telling Piers, they'd handle it. Then they drove off with me in the car. As they drove to the police station, I tried my old and tested routine of levity in this situation to break the tension in the car. I told a joke or two. It didn't work. Hmmm, tough crowd, I thought.... I asked them, were they playing bad cop/bad cop? None of my patter worked. We arrived at the Garda station. They put me straight in the holding cell. There was one other guy in there when I went in. He was a small skinny type, a bit younger than me.

He was sitting in the corner on the single bunk of the dark cell. "Alright," I said. Then when I saw the blood on his face and I asked, "what happened to you?" "You'll find out when Robocop comes in," he said. We chatted for a minute. Next thing the door swung open, and in walked a young garda around the same age as me rolling up his sleeves. Obviously, ready for action. He meant business the way he was standing. I stood when he entered. He said "you must be the funny guy?!" "That must make you the 'tough guy' then," I said.

"Why?" What if I am?" he said, pushing me on the chest.

"Did you do that to him?" I asked.

"What if I did? What are you going to do about it?!!" he said, pushing me on the chest again. I said, "Push me one more time, and you'll find out!" He pushed me again, and as he did, I trapped his hand on my chest, (a technique I learned in Jiu-Jitsu(traditional)). I leaned forward, so he'd no other option but to lean forward, closer to me too. Then I grabbed him by the tie and collar and balls, picked him up, and slammed him down on the ground on his back. I'd a lot of strength back then! I jumped up on his chest with both feet and started singing at the top of my voice. "THESE BOOT WERE MADE FOR WALKING AND THAT'S JUST WHAT THEY'LL DO!!!....." Right away, through the door of the cell, two guards came running in and knocked me to the floor. I put my back in the corner between the bunk and the wall, throwing my legs up (another defensive technique I'd learned from somewhere) as they started kicking and screaming at me so I started screaming back at them, "C'MON YOU MUTHAFUCKAS!!! IS THAT ALL YOU'VE GOT??!!!" They kicked my legs to pieces, but the rest of me was grand. A third younger garda, that came in after the other two, started shouting, "stop it, stop it! You're going to kill him". They backed off, spitting at me and still trying to throw kicks as they were being dragged back. I'd hurt some egos with that stunt!!! They left, and so did the good garda. I sat back up on the bed with the help of my new mate. He asked me, "Are you alright?" Then he says, "WHAT the fuck did you do that for?" in his inner-city Dublin drawl, laughing. "Fuck'em,", I said. Then he goes off on one kicking the cell door shouting, "FUCK YOU'S!!!" He sat down after a moment. Calming down then he said, "Have ye a light?"

"Yeah," I said, "but I've no smokes."

"I didn't say cigarette," he said, pulling out a joint from the top pocket of his shirt.

"Ha ha ha," I started laughing. "Fuck yeah," I said. "Here we go." I thought.

We sat and smoked and stifled our laughter. He was a good guy. All of a sudden, the hatch from the office into the cell opened up. They must have heard the giggles! The smoke just billowed into the light of the office. "WHAT THE FUCK?!!" the garda who opened it shouted. Next thing the cell door opened again, and in they came.

"Stand up! HAND'S AGAINST THE WALL!!!", they were shouting.

"WHERE'S THE DRUGS?!!!" they screamed.

"Up in smoke," I said laughing. My mate laughed too. We both received a dig in our ribs from a fist for my smart remark. They left cursing, finding nothing, and closed the door behind them. It was high five-time for the lad and me. We'd a good laugh. We chatted for an age then I told him I was outta there. He said, "You won't get out until 6 am" so I said, "watch this!!!" I knocked on the hatch, and it opened.

"What?" said the guard.

"Look," I said, "I've never been in this situation before." "What time is the breakfast in the morning?" I asked.

"Shut up ta fuck and sit down," he said, slamming the hatch.

My cellmate laughed, but I wasn't finished yet. I left it a couple of seconds then knocked again. Asking him this time to make my eggs 'over easy' with one sugar in my tea. He cracked, saying, "What the fuck do you think this is?" "He thinks he's in a fucking Hotel!" I could hear him saying to the others as he slammed the hatch closed. There was a rattle of keys at the door. It was the younger good garda. He says "you're outta here!".

"Good luck," I said to your man. I gave him a knowing wink, and he just laughed and said, "See ya later." The guard closed the cell door. I wasn't finished; I asked the good garda, "did he have a smoke?" He says under his breath, "you're pushing it now." "I don't smoke," he said.

Time to push the boat out, I thought, and have a little fun. "What about the rest of the guys?" I said.

"I'm not asking them!" he said.

"Do you want me to ask? "I said, reaching for the office door.

"No!" he said, pulling me back.

"I'll ask," he says. In he went then and all I heard was "cheeky CUNT!!!... some boy him!!" Then out he came out with three fags. Score! I thought! He opened the front door and said, "on ye go."

"Go where?" I said. "Where are we anyway?"

"Adelaide Road," he said. "There's a hostel next door. If you knock, they'll let you in".

"Cheers," I said.

"Good luck," he said.

18

ADELAIDE ROAD

I left and went the few doors up. I saw the door of the hostel and knocked. A few seconds past and after knocking a few times, the door opened. The guy hadn't even bothered to open his eyes. He just turned around and walked back to his bed. I went inside and closed the door quietly behind me. It seemed like a nice enough place from what I could see, not that I cared too much at that stage. I just needed a place to rest for a while. The sitting room was on the left as I went in the door, so I went in and turned on the TV. Not much on to watch as usual, but I sat down anyway. Then I spotted some cornflakes and spied a fridge. I got up and checked and "yip! Milk." "I'm sorted," I thought. I poured myself some cornflakes and milk, then sat down and waited for the world to arise once more. It'd been a while since I had some sleep at this stage. A couple of days, I figured, but I still wasn't tired. There was too much going on.

The first of the people got up in the morning. Some of them were going to work, and others were just getting up to face the day. Most were on holidays. I said "hello" to them. Then the guy who ran the place was about so I went to meet him in his office. A nice affable kind of guy. He was a writer too, soon to be a very famous one after we met, he wrote a number one and I can't help thinking in some way I inspired it. He also told me he was a famous singer that I'd heard of brother as well. He'd written a historical book on Inishowen, where I'm from. I couldn't believe the coincidence. It was the first of many, I found. He astounded me with his knowledge of my home. I told him I'd seen his sister at the Eminem concert in Fairyhouse, which I'd gone to with Flo during the couple of weeks we were together. I'm proud of the fact that I got Flo into Eminem. She loved the song 'The Way I Am', a favourite of mine too.

I booked for a couple of nights, not knowing how long I was going to stay. Then I met this guy called Paddy who was staying there. I'd great craic with him. He was working as a security guard in a local store, and we hit it off right away. He used to be in the army, but he got kicked out for playing a prank on a guy. He left a manhole cover open for another soldier to fall into, and the guy got badly hurt. He still regretted it when I met him, even though it happened 3 or 4 years before. I'd met him in the evening after I'd been around a few bars. I got barred from a bar close by as well. The barman there was a bit of a dick. I didn't do anything at all. He'd said I'd too much drink then just said you're barred and wouldn't give a reason... asshole! I was suffering from sleep deprivation at this stage as well. I'd no routine, but I was having a blast, loving it; the feeling of relief being single and no stress was surreal.

I went to the gay bar this night. Use the back entrance, they prefer it! My mate TC once again put me on to it. When we were in college, he'd told me his brother Dan was gay, and he'd been in it one night with him. He told me it was full of chicks. Definitely untapped. So, in I went. It seemed pretty casual. Normal enough. Good mix of people. Not much out of the ordinary apart from the stage where everybody was dancing. I got to get up on that, I thought. The stage that is!

I ordered a Bulmer's and casually began to mix. I still had a bandage on my thumb from when I'd cut it, putting it through the window. It was done like a strap up my wrist. When Pat and I had left the scene after smashing the window with my fist at the early house bar. Pat told me that I needed to go to hospital to get it looked at. I'd spotted a building site, and thinking on my feet I said to him, I know a quicker way. I had other ideas. They're bound to carry a medic, I'd said, directing his attention to the building site. I went across the road to it, and lucky enough, the first person I showed my thumb to said, come in here, and I'll patch you up. He'd it done in minutes, and I was back on the Raz!

Anyway, this guy said to me back in this club that I needed to change the bandage.

"What?" I said.

"Your bandage. It's looking worse for wear".

"Oh," I said.

"I'm a doctor," he said, "can I buy you a drink?"

"I'm not gay," I said. He started laughing.

"It's just a drink," he said.

"That's how it starts," I said. "I'll just get that out of the way!" I said, laughing too. I told him the story of what happened to my thumb, and we'd a good laugh. I really wanted to dance, I told him, looking up at the stage. "Just do it", he said. "Yeah, fuck it," I said. Watching them all lined up facing front, it was like they were putting on a show. It looked like fun! I left him and went up the side of the stage and made my way to the front, centre stage behind the main guy show boating. I started dancing, copying his moves. I could see people laughing in the crowd. He could see them laughing as well because he looked back at me to see what they were laughing at, but I looked away and danced differently. He turned back, facing the crowd again indifferent. I went back at it, exaggerating everything he did. I was making fun of him, obviously! He looked around again, and this time, he spoke to me. He shouted over the music, "are you copying me?" He was a big guy, and he looked kinda pissed off, so I said, "Yeah, man. I was just trying to learn your moves," feigning submissive. He started laughing. Phew, he believed me! I thought. He said, "C'mon, out to the front." So, the two of us were dancing along with the rest of the troop behind us. Funny as fuck and great craic. Some guy! A lot of them had their shirts off so I thought why the fuck not?!!! I wriggled my way back to where the bouncer was standing at the steps up onto the stage at the side and asked him was it ok to take my shirt off? "Go ahead," he said. "You can do anything you want in here!" I laughed and took it off, throwing it beside where he was standing. Then I made my way back to the front, where the main guy was leading them. The big guy started laughing when he saw me with my shirt off, then after a few more seconds of dancing, he said, "I'll leave ye to it. You have the stage!" I carried on dancing for a while, loving it. Then I saw them from the stage. Slow-motion kissing in the throng of the people. On the other side of the bar from the stage. Two beautiful women. I love this place, I thought. That was me and my dancing, though. I had to be part of this. I left the stage, grabbed my shirt, threw it over my shoulder, and went down, and eased myself up behind them. I tried ordering a drink, but it was more to get the girl's attention more than anything. I tried looking exasperated. They broke away from their kiss, and the one on the right noticed me first. It was hard not to, and I'd a shaved head with my shirt off. The one on the left said she'd get the barman's attention.

"What do you want?" the one on the left asked.

"Bulmer's," I said, and she turned towards the bar.

The other one sitting on the barstool, turned and put her legs either side of me and rubbed my chest. "I saw you on the dance floor," she said. "You were good!"

"Thanks!" I said. Rather chuffed. "I saw you too," I said and smirked.

"You's were good too". She smiled provocatively then started kissing me.

"Whoa," I said but not too loudly as to alert her friend. I pulled back a bit.

"What about your friend?" I said.

"She won't mind," she said. We carried on kissing. Then the friend turned around and joined in. "Ha-ha," I thought. This isn't happening. This is cool as fuck.

"Hold on a minute," I said. I stopped and pulled back a bit. "Does everybody see this?" I said to the people standing nearby. I could see they all were watching when I broke from kissing them both. "I want the camera footage for this," I bellowed, pointing up at the security cameras. I couldn't believe it, I started laughing, and they smiled, so I went back to kissing them both. I spent some time with them, all night in the club in fact. We were in the upstairs area of the club chatting until I couldn't hold my piss anymore. I did not want to break the atmosphere. I told them I'd to go to the little boy's room. They laughed; I went. On the way back, I passed two guys who stopped me and asked, "What do you have that we don't?" pointing at the women.

"A ten-inch cock" I replied, slapping my leg smiling. I'd been asked that one time before at home in a nightclub in Donegal, the week after my 21st birthday party in the club, and that answer caused a riot. The man who asked me ended up with his throat cut. I did it by accident. I punched him after receiving a blow on the head from his friend. I had a bottle in my hand. It smashed and slit his throat. He wasn't that bad though. Superficial wound. 25 now when this happened. I still hadn't learned. But they just laughed, it didn't bother them. More cosmopolitan in Dublin, I presumed. I went back to my women. They were getting ready to leave. "Are we going?" I said. "We are but I don't know about you," one of them said, laughing. "Fuck" I said. I knew I shouldn't have left, I thought. Then I laughed admirably and said, "Goodnight, it's been fun." "Goodnight," they said, and that was it, no threesome, it would have been my first, the holy grail to all men if they're honest! Ah well, back to the drawing board. Out I went into the night, still buzzing from the night's antics, if not a little disappointed. I got back to the hostel and had some rest. I was well knackered and well ready for it.

I woke in the morning and decided to catch a tour of Dublin. I took the open-top bus tour, which is a great way to see the city, any city. I'd great fun meeting new people and visiting a few of the cities more obscure taverns. Basically, I did a pub tour in between the sights. I was well on the way when I came back to the hostel and full of chat. It was gonna take a lot of booze to put me out. I got talking to Paddy again from Kerry, the security guard. We went for a few beers, but he told me he'd court in the morning so he couldn't go too mad. I didn't want to stop, so he said he was going home to bed but seeing I was undoubtedly going to stay up, he asked me to give him a call in the morning so he wouldn't be late.

He'd to be there at the Four Courts at 10am.

"No, bother," I told him, and on I went out for the night.

It was pretty uneventful. I wandered around a few bars on the pull but not trying too hard. I kinda wanted to be on my own but in a crowd. Strange feeling, but it didn't keep me out of the strip bars on Leeson Street. My first trip there of many. It almost became a pilgrimage at the end of the night. I came home empty-handed that night too, but still mindful that I'd to get Paddy up in the morning.

I was bored and restless when I set foot back in the hostel mainly because I had no one to play with! I smirked as I hatched a plan for some fun. I decided to wake Paddy up early. I went down to his room. There were three other people in the same room. He was on the bottom bunk of one of the four beds. I turned the light on and said, "Quick, Paddy, get up, get up.

You're late!" and threw him his clothes.

"Fuck" he says. Waking up in a panic. "C'mon, you need to hurry". I said. He put his clothes on, and I rushed him up the stairs. He opened the front door. Then he turned around and said, "You bastard," laughing half relieved. It was still pitch black. I broke my balls laughing. "What time is it?" he said. I told him it was only 5 am. "C'mon, I said you're up now. We may as well do something." I told him I'd come with him for a bit of support. I'd been wearing the same clothes for about a week now, but I'd been washing, so I looked respectable enough.

He told me there was a brothel nearby, and it had done him out of 60 euros. They'd taken him in, taken his money, he got no sex, and then they kicked him out again. "Let's go!" I said. "We'll get your money back". "Yeah," he said. "Why not? They owe you!!" I said. We had plenty of time before the court. We began walking and eventually found the house. I started knocking on the door. There was no answer. So (not proud of this, but...) I began running and back spin-kicking at the door. A pretty powerful kick if you can do it right. Still no answer. "Let's kick it in," I said. "No," he said, "Fuck sake, leave it." "Fuck them. They owe you the money!" I said. "They must have bolts all around the door," I said. No matter how hard I kicked, it wouldn't budge. It was solid. I'm sure they heard us, though. I picked up a rock and tossed it through one of the top windows.

"That'll cost them 60 euro at least", I said.

"Yeah," he said and laughed.

We ran off. We got a bit away and slowed down to a walk again and made our way slowly into the town centre. It was about 09.30hrs when we were passing a Centra shop, and I said, "What about some wine. It'll calm your nerves".

"Yes," he said. "Fuck it!"

I could see the glint in his eyes, joie de vivre, I thought my kinda man, just how I was feeling. We bought the wine, a bottle each. We were lucky they served us. It is normally half ten before they serve alcohol. Then we found a quiet street beside the Bank of Ireland and drank it up. I checked the time. We had to get going so I told Paddy I'd thought of a plan to get him off with the charge or at least get it reduced.

We arrived at the courthouse nicely buzzing! Paddy was nice and calm after the wine. There was a right rabble of people there, all looking edgy, not knowing what was coming next. There was nervous laughter as always, but this one suave lawyer stood out. He was tall and slender with a big head of grey hair, and looked like he could have played a solicitor on stage. When he turned around after someone spoke to him, he did it as though he permanently wore an invisible gown. There was a big swoosh as he turned. Time to make a few friends, I thought, so I got his attention (as he was speaking to everyone) and told him the joke, "what has a woman and a tornado got in common?" I asked. "What?" he asked. Already laughing, "They're wet and noisy when they come, and take your house and car when they go." He laughed, and he told one of his own. It escapes me now. But we were making friends. This was good. Then I had a moment of inspiration!

"Paddy, you're my brother!" I said.

"What?" said Paddy.

I took him aside and said, "Look, do everything exactly as I say, and anything I do or say, go with it!"

"OK", he said.

"Good man", I thought. I knew I could count on him. Man, after my own heart.

We went inside, where we met his solicitor. I had a solicitor friend and he told me that they all talked to each other deciding the outcome of cases before they were heard. Judges to solicitors, solicitors to cops, and so on. So how you dealt with every one of them counted. Mannerly and convincing was always best. His solicitor, John, began to advise him, telling him to plead guilty, apologise, take the fine and he believed the sentence would be suspended. At this point, I cut in. We were outside the door of the courtroom inside the building, but we had relative privacy. People were coming and going through the door as we stood in the hall. I spoke to the solicitor John straight and said, "Did he tell you he split up from his girlfriend?"

"No," said John.

"Well, he did. He's always bottling this stuff up. That's what gets him in all this trouble. That's the reason I'm here".

"Sorry, who are you?" asked John.

"I'm his brother". I was a couple of years older than Paddy. I couldn't believe John never copped on I had a Donegal accent, and Paddy was from Kerry, but I had it covered anyway. I was going to tell him we sent Paddy away to school in Kerry when he was young because he was always a bit of a handful. Amazing what some people will believe! Anyway, I carried on, "he's been having problems since the break-up." I told him. Then I bollocked Paddy in front of John for causing all the hassle. He broke down and muttered an apology.

Ha! Oscars, please!

"This change's everything," John said, "Leave it with me."

He disappeared into the courtroom doing what I hoped he would. Talk to the judge. Paddy and I grinned at each other. Not out of the woods yet, but it was a good start.

The last thing Paddy said to me when we were going into the courtroom was "don't make me laugh when I'm up on the stand", and I have to say, I thought about it but it was too serious a time.

"OK," said John, full of bluster this time as he came out of the court room door. "Come in and take a seat. You probably won't be called until the second half but have a seat and wait anyway, and it looks better". I was feeling confident!!

We were sitting apart. Paddy, two rows in front, when I started getting fidgety. It can be pretty mind-numbing in there if there are no interesting cases, so I started talking to the young fella in front of me who was chained to a guard. I asked him his story. He said he'd been lifted for joyriding and spent some time in prison. Then when they let him out of jail, he'd no way home, so he nicked a car to get home!

I said, "I bet if they had given you a fiver for a taxi, you wouldn't have done it?"

"FUCKIN RIGH'!!!…." he said loudly. "Shhh," the Garda he was chained to said. Telling him to turn around. Funny, I had a point but he shouldn't have been joyriding.

I went for a smoke break and stood outside. There were a lot of guards in the courtroom. All of them as it turns out! I wandered over to the prefabricated building with the Garda emblem on it. A mini police station on the grounds. I knocked on the door walking in, saying, "helloooo…..!!!". I was going to ask them some stupid question or other if there was anyone in there to cover my ass for being in there. I was only checking if there was anyone there or not. Curiosity was getting the better of me, and I was hungry for more craic! I walked on in, and there was no one there. I closed the door behind me. What a buzz! What sort of secret info was lying in here, I wondered? It was just one room. I sifted through the documents on various desks. There was nothing much of interest. I decided to leave and as I did, I spied a baseball hat on the coat rack on the way out. So red it was almost glowing at me. It said "Big" on it in white writing, and it was crying out for me to wear it back into the courtroom. Ha! I stuck it on backward, and struck out for the courthouse a few feet away and went back in. I wore it backwards into the courtroom. I wondered which garda it belonged to and would he or she say anything. They all saw me coming in, but no one said a thing. The only thing that was said to me, in a hushed voice, was, "Take the hat off, respect the courtroom". I duly apologised, taking it off, holding the laughter in. I sat down, and immediately for something to do, I asked the Garda who was sitting on one of the side benches running along the wall close to me, for some paper. I saw his briefcase. I already had a pen. I'd been doing some writing. The poems were flowing out of me. Not all great, but they were rhyming and getting better. He was only too happy to oblige. I thought I'd made a friend for life! LOL. I began to write, and it obviously caught the judge's attention because he became more deliberate in what he was saying. Possibly because he may have thought I was taking notes. I don't know this for sure. I remember some of what he said. He seemed pretty fair and lenient when it boiled down to it. (Little did I know I'd be up in front of him a couple of short months later). He was lenient, especially when it came to dealing with Paddy. When Paddy was up on the stand, he didn't look at me once. I'm not surprised, he wasn't taking any chances!! I did not mind. I wanted him to get off with the charge! When his case was seen, the Judge addressed the court.

"Now new light has been thrown on this case," the Judge said. "This young man has been through what can only be described as a tough time. That is his personal business, and we won't go into it in court. But..." he said, "due to his service to his country..." His army service he was referring to. "And even in his present circumstances, I think he is a fine upstanding young man. 80 euro fine, and I hope everything works out for you."

"Thank you, judge," he said, learning the lingo from those who'd gone before him.

Outside we celebrated. "Yes!!" he said. He was punching the sky! We were delighted.

"Remember the deal," I said, "If I got you off with it, you have to take me the whole day on the beer!"

"Yeah!" he says. "C'mon!!" We went straight to the bar around the corner to see what badness we could get up to. I knew it would be a solicitor's haunt.

There were a few lawyers in there, but not much craic, and no one was biting from our law-breaking chat. We played a few games of pool. Then off to the Guinness brewery that Pat, the American, worked at, my new local. I told Paddy I could get us in for free. I used Pat's free pass. We went upstairs, straight through the museum bit and up to the Gravity Bar at the top.

Two free pints but more if you become a local and they recognised you. We ordered our free pints, and what better way to celebrate than a beautiful view of the city.

Paddy phoned his parents; the relief was obvious; the tension had been palpable for them. He put me on to them, and they thanked me. He's a good fucking guy and still is, I'm sure. Hopefully, I'll meet him again if he reads this. The same goes for the other people I mention that I met and became friends with. There are so many people I would love to meet again.

CARLOW

A fter we decided to give each other space and end it, Flo and I never had sex again! It doesn't mean I wouldn't like to still!!! Mores a pity, we were like rabbits for those two weeks. She had a great body and was really adventurous in bed apart from when I kneeled over her and came on her face like a porn star. She'd agreed to it, it turned her on. I knelt over her face, as she looked up submissively, and wanked off over her mouth and cheeks. She was so aroused as she played with her cunt. But when I came, a bit went in her eye. She yelled. I laughed. She said it stung! And sat up. "Probably the salt…" she said. Like I said – smart lady! Her expression when I came on her face was that of degradation. She was silent after she yelled. I could tell from her expression that she felt degraded. I asked her what was wrong and did she feel degraded? Because that's what the expression looked like. She said she did a bit. I gave her a hug and we fucked some more. I tested the move out on Fanjita, many years later, she said she felt the same, no dirt in them! Ha! I enjoyed it immensely both times!

Around the time of the break up, I got talking to my friend Jim Kearney from college. He told me that his sister had a 21st birthday in Carlow. It was only a bus ride from Dublin, so I decided I would go and visit him. I didn't want to go home because I was still pissed off at my parents, and I really didn't want the party to stop. I was having too good a time. I got on a bus to Carlow but as it turned out, I arrived a day late. I went into a big pub there where Kearney used to work as a barman. I had dinner, and I got talking to them and asked them about Jim. They said he wasn't there, and that he was away. Shit! I thought.

I gave the head barman a bit of grief there. I was only having a bit of craic, but he wasn't taking it that way. He had a bit of an attitude that I didn't like. I was taking the piss a bit. The staff thought he was an asshole anyway. They told me that as soon as he'd left! I had a good enough time with them, chatting and that. I left there and went to another bar and was kind of dancing a bit erratically. It was fun weirding them out!!! After that, I went to the next bar, then the next bar, and then I went into another bar and the barman said, you're barred. I said "how come?" He said, "Look, we have had word that you have been travelling around town from bar to bar, and you're just barred. We don't have to give you a reason". I went to another bar, and the barman there, said the same thing I was told in the other bar. I was told the other barmen were phoning ahead, saying that I had to be barred. It was alright. I found a drink somewhere, and I ended up looking for a nightclub that night. I didn't find one. I had nowhere to stay, so I got into a taxi and asked the taxi driver did he know of anywhere I could stay? He said yes and took me to a hotel he knew.

I booked in and paid, then had a Bulmer's and sat on my own peacefully in the hotel bar. No mental illness!!! No elation, fuck you psychiatrists…It was time to chill and sleep a bit, so I went to my room and had a lovely sleep. I woke up in the morning hungover with the telephone beside the bed ringing off the hook. I answered the phone, and the lady said, "Morning, time to leave. It's checkout time". I had a pint of cider beside me on the night stand, so I drank it and freshened up for the day. I had already paid my bill so I went outside and waited at the side of the road where I'd been told I could catch a bus to Dublin.

I had read a book while at sea in Africa a couple of months before this. The author told the story of traveling around the south of Ireland drinking. That was his idea for a book. He drank his way around Ireland in his 60's. I thought fuck that! I'm doing it in my 20's! Way more fun!!! His golden rule was never to pass a bar with his name above it! It inspired me to do the same. I thought if an Irish/English man in his 60's had that much fun in Ireland doing it, what kind of fun would a full-blooded Irish man of 25 have doing it? More I reckoned! And I was right!!! Maybe I could write a book of my own, I thought at the time. What you are reading is the result of many inspirations.

I saw a bus coming, but I was on the wrong side of the road. I hailed it. It stopped, and I asked the driver where he was going? "Kilkenny," he said. Ah!! I thought. Kilkenny, I have never been to Kilkenny before. I had always heard good stories about it. I'd heard about the comedy festival and how it was very musical and always thought it sounded like there was a good air to it, so I thought there and then, why not? I'll go. I'm free, I've got money...pourquoi pas? It was exactly what I wanted to do, continue rambling!!! I wanted to ramble around and do a bit more of travelling. I knew I had time. It was another 3 or 4 weeks before I had to go back to work. I got on the bus, and after 15 minutes, I lit up a cigarette, had a few puffs. I knew I wasn't allowed! I was hitting on the girl across the aisle. I had about half the cigarette smoked when the driver stopped. As soon as he stopped, I put it out. He turned and stood up. He walked up the aisle a bit, and shouted up the bus, "If I catch whoever is smoking on this bus, they are off!" Nobody told it was me. I didn't own up!!! The girl sitting opposite me, started laughing quietly. She turned to me and said with a grin of "you're a bad boy!" I laughed and thought fucking shagtastic! Lol. The bus driver continued to drive. She said "how are you doing?" "Not too bad!" I said, laughing. She told me her name was Lilly and asked what I was up to? I told her that I was on my way to Kilkenny for a look around. I told her I had no real plans. I said that I was off on leave from the Merchant Navy and I'd another few week's leave left. She asked me if I had ever been to Thomastown. "No," I answered, she said, "It's a great night out on a Monday night." She told me a bar I should try saying that she worked there. I said, "fair enough, I'll see you there!" I got off the bus in Thomastown and went looking for another bar. I didn't want to get to Lilly's bar too early. I had a pint or two in the other bar I found, then I went looking for her bar. The town isn't that big, so it was easy to find. When I went into her bar, the music was pumping. Everyone was up on the tables dancing. There was a great vibe in it. It was great craic. I bought a drink, and I was standing at the bar just getting into the atmosphere with everybody dancing and singing when the barman came out, turned the music down, and shouted, "Everybody SHUT UP!" The place went silent!! Then he threw a pint of water out from behind the bar at everyone laughing, saying he was only joking, then pumped the music up again! Everyone was laughing and cheering. This is brilliant, I thought!

I thought I would get into it even more, so I jumped up on top of the table with the locals and joined in. I didn't know anyone, and I couldn't see Lilly. She obviously hadn't started work yet. I was dancing away on top of the table, then I thought, coup d'état, to get down even one more step with them, I grabbed the Kilkenny flag with my teeth that was pinned up on the ceiling and swung down off the table. Everyone stopped laughing, singing, and dancing around me. Ooops! I thought, too far!!! They all stared at me with the flag in my mouth! Too much I thought. It wasn't a protest at Kilkenny or anything!! I just pulled the flag down! It is only a joke, and I had swung off the table with it between my teeth. I apologized to everyone around me. Awkward! I thought I'll take my leave for a while and wait till Lilly comes on. I may be in for a shag tonight, I thought. Lilly was cute.

I walked out the back to the beer garden outside, and I thought I would have a cigarette, let things cool off! I was having a cigarette, but I could smell dope in the corner, but I thought, nah, I won't intrude, plus I didn't really smoke dope at that time. An odd puff of marijuana here and there was the height of my drug-taking up to that age. We got random drug tests in the company I worked for, as is the norm for most Merchant Navy companies these days, so I never bothered with any drugs, although if I'm honest, they always intrigued me. I did think I was missing out hence the experimentation in later years when I wasn't a sea for a while.

A few people came out of the bar into the beer garden, a group of guys and girls. They stood close by me, about 6 of them. They started trying to kick this swinging flowerpot. It was about 3 feet long, and about 4 and a 1/2 feet off the ground. It was a hanging basket. They just wanted to see if they could get their foot that high. So, I said to them, here, give me a go. So, they stepped back a bit, and I jumped up and came down on it with an axe kick. Splitting the pot in two with my heel. They were like, WHOA! When I think back, it wasn't a nice thing to do in the bar, but that's what happened.

I thought it was funny at the time, and then as soon as I had done it, I thought, no that's not funny. Mainly because I didn't get a laugh. It left a bit of a mess, and there was silence and looks of disgust from the group. They walked off. I was standing there having another cigarette when the barman came out and said, "That's it, you are out of here!!!". When I asked why? He said that the group of guys and girls had told him that I had broken that basket. I thought, you ratting bastards. What did they tell for? I left and went out of the bar. It was about 9 pm and I thought, where the hell am, I going to go now? I had nowhere to stay, so I continued walking along the street, going out of town looking for a B&B, when I met this guy walking down the street. I stopped him, said hello, and asked him if there is any accommodation in town? I said that I was looking for a B&B, and did he know of anywhere? He said there was nowhere in Thomastown at this time of night, but he could give me a couch for the night if I was really stuck. I said thanks very much. He took me up to his house that he shared with his mother and showed me the couch. He asked if I was hungry. I said I was so he made me a sandwich. Afterwards he says "do you smoke? Sure, we'll share a joint and then go down to the town". He said he knew a great bar down there. It was great craic. I asked which bar it was, half guessing already. He told me the name. I said I couldn't go there because I was barred. He asked how I was barred, and he started to laugh, saying "sure you're only here!!" I told him I'd had a bit of an incident earlier where they barred me for breaking the flowerpot. He said, "ah, you will be alright. It's not that big of a deal. You can come down; I will get you in". I thought, right, OK. We had the joint, and he showed me where the key to get back into the house if I got back before him. We walked down towards the pub. When we got there, he said for me to wait outside and he'd find out the score. He came out a minute later and said, "Jesus, what did you do? They hate you in there. You must have done something bad". I said, "no, not really." I did pull the Kilkenny flag down, but I was just trying to join in on the show. I told him again that I broke a flowerpot too, so he said he would bring me out a drink. He brought me out a bottle of Bulmer's, then he went back inside for a couple of drinks. He told me to wait outside, he wouldn't be that long, and that we would head back up to the house. He stayed longer than I thought, I'd have probably done the same because of the craic that was going on in the pub. He brought me out another drink. The door into the bar was locked from the inside, I could hear the click when he was coming in and out, but I could also see the curtains were twitching. I could see girls looking out. So, I thought, I'll put on a show again.

When the curtain twitching girls were watching, I started singing a song at the top of my voice. One I'd learned before I left home, 16 ton... *Some people say a man is made out of mud. A poor man is made out of muscle and blood. Muscle and blood, skin and bone, a mind that's weak and a back that's strong...* It's an old one but Johnny Cash made it famous again around that time. I watched it sung live by ZZ top a few years ago in Fort Lauderdale, Florida, after crossing the Atlantic on the yacht Passion. They had wing-suiting, which is on my to-do list, on video screens behind the singers. I was drunk as hell and stoned on 'Gorilla'. It was a great stress relief after the crossing.

Anywho, I was singing the song, and the girls were looking out laughing. I poured a little of the bottle of Bulmer's over my head, going, "aghh!!..." Shaking my head over, and back with a big grin and crazy eye's. They closed the curtain again giggling – and judging from their expressions, they thought I was nuts, exactly the thought I was going for! Ha! I was only putting it on! I was having the craic! I walked off leaving my new mate inside, and began walking up the street, back to his house. I was kind of lambasting everything I saw at the top of my voice. There was nobody there. I was just letting off steam, drunk, saying things about the town businesses and how they got the name and stuff like that. The signs above certain businesses giving way to inspiration. I was walking up the street looking for his house. Then, I saw this house with a big garden up a hill, and I heard music coming from it, or I *thought* I heard music coming from it. I walked up the driveway and knocked on the door, but there was no answer. The lights were on in the hallway and downstairs. I knocked again but there was still no answer. I tried opening the door and it was open! I walked in slowly shouting, "hello, hello, anybody home?" Goldilocks style. I called again but there was no answer so I walked on into the kitchen. I spied a pizza box as soon as I walked in. Oh! Nice! I thought. I wondered if there was anything in it. When I opened it, there was 3 slices left. I thought to myself, well I am a little hungry, so I sat down and pulled a bit of pizza off and ate it. I looked across, and there was a wine rack, so I thought, well I am a little thirsty...... so I took a bottle of red wine from the rack, red is my favourite wine, and opened it and sat and had a little feast to myself. After I drank the bottle of wine and had all the pizza, I grabbed another bottle of red wine, opened it, and thought I wouldn't mind a lie down. Thinking if anyone came back, I'd explain it all away, and I'd be grand. I'd improvise! I went upstairs, still calling out to see if there was anyone maybe sleeping but there was no one home. So, I lay down on one of two beds in the room facing the stairs so I could see anyone coming up the stairs. I thought when the people who owned the house came back, I would be able to make friends with them by using a little charm...that was not to be!! As it turned out!! I lay there just relaxing, drinking from my bottle of wine, when I heard the front door opening and people chatting. As I was listening, I could hear footsteps coming up the stairs and thought, this is it! Time to turn on the charm and have the excuses ready! I stood up and walked out the door. When the girl who was climbing the stairs got to the top of the landing, I couldn't believe my eyes...and neither could she.... she started to scream as soon she saw me. She was one of the girls from the bar who'd had gotten me kicked out and all her friends. Guys and girls. I walked out of the room casually as you like and said "hi! "and told her, "I think I have the wrong house"...she was screaming at the top of her voice to her guy friends," IT'S HIM!!!...IT'S HIM!!!" I told her to calm down and that I was leaving, but she was scared shitless...which in a way, I'm not surprised, but there was no malice intended. It was just one of life's coincidences!!

I walked down the stairs as they were all screaming at me. Apart from this one grey haired guy, that didn't really fit being there, I walked past him on the way down the stairs. He just smiled and shook his head.

He seemed to know I meant no harm, and I was only having a bit of craic. One of the guys went to make a move for me at the bottom of the stairs, but I told him, "don't even think about it!!" He pulled back!! I walked out the front door and down the drive, as casual as you like. They started shouting to another party reveller coming up the drive, "Get him!!! Get him!!!" I started to run, and in my best Rugby moves, I dodged past the fucker coming up, running on down to the gate. They didn't give chase.

As I got out onto the main street again, I slowed down to a walk and started wondering where my new friend's house was, and as if by some miracle, I walked a few more paces, and there it was. I was never so happy to discover somewhere to stay and couldn't believe how the night had unfolded.

I was in St. Pats Mental Asylum the following year and met a nurse from Thomastown there. I told him I'd been in Thomastown the year before and I told him what I did at that house. I figured it must have been famous because of his reaction. I was laughing. He said angrily to me, "yeah! Well, you won't be doing it again! They got two Doberman dogs after that!" He was an asshole! I thought, so you've heard of me?!! And laughed again. I said, "I don't want to do it again!" Shutting him right down!!! Some of them nurses are fucking ARSEHOLES!" No fuck-ing sense of humour!

KILKENNY

The next morning, I left my new mate's house and I walked into Thomastown feeling I'd had enough of the craic here. I had decided to go back into Dublin. As I was waiting for the bus, I met Lilly again. I was horn mad again! Lol. She asked me what happened the night before? We never met up. I filled her in, much to her amusement. She and her friend were driving into Kilkenny for a court date, and they offered me a lift, so I made the decision and decided to go on to Kilkenny. When we got there, we arranged to meet up after their hearing for a few drinks, but the pub they had said to meet in had been closed for some time, so I didn't see them again after that.... unfortunately, nice women.

I booked into a B&B type small hotel in the centre of town, then went exploring. I had a couple of drinks here and there, and then I found this pub that had a stage out the back in another room behind the bar. There were only a few people in, but the guy that I met at the bar said he was a band manager. I was having a drink with him when I told him I enjoyed singing and I had a song that I loved to sing everywhere I went —16 ton. I told him I had learned it off before I'd left home on this journey of discovery, which is what it was and it had turned out to be. "C'mon..." he said, "there's a stage out back... show me what you've got!!!" We went into the room behind the bar, and there was a Russian guy just finishing up playing his electric guitar. As he got down, I jumped up and took the mic, and started singing. The

Russian was about to put his guitar away when he heard the start off notes I began with. He had this look on his face that said I have to get in on this, so he jumped back up on stage and began playing the tune I was singing...*some people say a man is made out of mud*....I sang it well enough I thought, and got a clap from the few people that were there. As I was leaving the bar, I asked the Russian guy did he want to go for a drink but he said he didn't drink and he was only there for the music. It made me think about my drinking.

Off I went to find another bar and then another and then crashed for the night in my hotel room. I did the same the next day, getting to know the people who owned the bar that was attached to the B&B. I remember I was suffering badly from indigestion. One of their Family gave me a blast of heart medication spray for the acid. He had it because the heart-attack tablets gave him chronic acid, and it worked a treat... nice people there, and I was having a laugh with them.

Then later that day, I went into another bar because I could hear the music coming from it and ordered a drink. The musicians were awesome, and the bar was packed. Then in between songs, I went up to the guy singing and asked him could I sing a song? He said not during their set but that they were having an interval in a few minutes and that the stage was all mine. They stopped for a break, and I went over, took the mic, and said I was going to sing a song called "16 ton." I sang the song for all I was worth, along with all the actions I'd put into it and I got a clap from everyone in the bar at the end which I was well pleased with!

After I finished, I went over to the bar again where my drink was sitting, and this guy turned around to me and said "very well sung, young man!" "Thanks!" I said. He asked me what I did for a living, and I told him I was in the Merchant Navy and I was just visiting Kilkenny for a few days. He said he was a movie director himself and he lived in a wealthy part of Dublin. He said, "I'll tell you a funny story..." He said, "you'll never guess who I had in my house the other day?" "Who?" I said. "Daniel Day Lewis!!" he said. I said, "Who?!! I've never heard of him". He looked shocked and tapped his wife beside him and said "this young man has never heard of Daniel day Lewis!!"...she half laughed too in disbelief then I said to him "Nah I'm only joking of course I've heard of Daniel Day Lewis"....to which the director replied..."WOW!!! You're good!!!" He said, "You've been discovered!! Here's my number!" giving me his business card. It happened just like that!!! It was a bit surreal. Being discovered for Hollywood. Every performer's dream!!!

I was a little bit drunk but I thought this is a chance of a lifetime. He said "When you're done doing whatever it is you are doing, give me a call!".

I told him I would, then excused myself from their company and sat down at a table with two young American dudes. They were sitting down at a table listening to the music. It turned out they were both musicians. I did not want to bleed the director dry! I sat with the musicians anyway, Kilkenny seemed to be a mecca for them. The younger of the two was watching the guitar player play so he could learn the tune he said.

We hit it off and they invited me back to their campsite, I suggested we get some booze. I told them about the drink Buckfast, so we got a bottle of that and a few beers and went back to their tent. They were from San Francisco and no two finer gentlemen you could meet. We sat and chatted, and a Belgium friend of theirs from a few tents over came and sat with us. He was French-speaking and taught me a few swear words in French that I still remember to this day. Speaking phonetically (I also made up a term for my learning of phonographically, where I remember everything everybody says). I remembered "toedacue" meaning asshole, using the mnemonics of a picture of a guy with a pool cue stuck up his ass and "Va tu fait futra!" which means go fuck yourself. I'd like to say in all my time in France I have never had to use them. Great people! Then he told me my brain was like a sponge, and he thought I had ADHD!!! He told me other stuff in French too, and it amazed him how quickly I was learning.

French was one of my best subjects at school so I had an advantage.

I got a 'B' in honours French at Junior certificate level, so I had a good basis for learning it. In fact, I got 6 'B's and two 'D's like I said earlier. Spanish, Engineering (favourite subject), Technical drawing, Science, Irish all 'B's and English and Math two 'D's which is funny considering I am writing this book. Although it was all honours apart from Irish. That was pass level. I am self-taught in English. Leaving cert was not so good. Like I said earlier in the book, I did my Leaving certificate twice and got worse the second time!

I know our pub we bought threw a spanner in the works for me. My Father blames drinking and women, but I know the truth! One memory is of my dad making me study my Maths in the bar. We used to work shifts, and he said when I complained that I had to do my homework over there and he said that there'd be no-one in. When I complained, saying I needed the right environment, he scoffed at me in his self-humouring way. Had it been now where I can learn anywhere it might have been a different story. So, I can see it from his point of view now. He thought I was just trying to get out of work back then. It sticks out in my mind because I thought at the time, this is never going to work. I wasn't wrong. After my junior cert, which was on the year we bought the bar, I slowly lost all interest in everything except those subjects that came easy to me. The bar was great craic but my studies suffered.

I haven't done too badly in life even though the bar affected me, and I learned a lot of life in those years behind the bar. It was funny that the Belgium guy had said I had ADHD. When I was wrongfully admitted to hospital after this siege, I told the Doctor, Doctor Lucky (whom you'll meet later) what he said. I thought it was funny. Doctor Lucky said, no, you have Bipolar. Jesus wept!! I was only trying to get off with a charge!!! It was fucking ridiculous how they could diagnose so quick. You'll understand my predicament when you read it. I was right of course; I do not have bipolar nor do I have ADHD. I don't have any mental illness, but Jesus, do they try and convince you in those places! He also said, when he was trying to convince me, "your intelligence raises 10% when you're manic". I believed my intelligence was increasing but that was all the info I was getting. I knew he was trying to sell it to me, and I know they still use that tactic of bullshitting people about their intelligence being in abundance today.

Another one of Lucky's coercive tactics was telling me a lot of the Hollywood stars have it. Hoping I would accept it and stop arguing with him. I knew he had the final decision and my father's ear, so I needed it over turned and still do. It has fucked up my life. I want a clean bill of health which, like I've said but no harm reiterating it, is the reason for this book.

I KNOW I AM NOT BIPOLAR!!!!!

I know from the Alien race that Bipolar doesn't even exist. They have told me that there is no mental illness on planet earth. It is all made up by doctors to sell medication. The elation is happiness that comes is from attention. You don't need psychotropic drugs for life. They destroy your body and mind. Nor do you need ignorant people thinking they know better than you, and continuously telling you to calm down because they heard you're Bipolar. They barred me from nearly every pub in Letterkenny and Moville for having too much fun. The Gardai arrested me on a few drunk and disorderly charges then made up a ton of false charges, just for being drunk in a public place. Wankers of Guards! The Gardai really bullied me in Letterkenny. They made up those loads of charges, just to get me in jail, which didn't work. The judge was very wary of them. I fit in Letterkenny people, in the bars of the rest of the world. Moville you are a wart on the bollocks of time. LOL.

Anyway, the three guys and I sat and drank in that campsite, and sang and chatted at their tent. The young guy who'd been learning by watching the guitarist in the pub started playing the song he'd heard, and I could not believe how he did it. It turned out they were both at a music college in the States and were likely to make it big if things went their way. We went on out that night and I pretended I was Australian for a bit of craic to try and pick up some woman and have a laugh with the two Yanks. We went to the big local night club and paid to get in. I had no other cash on me but I had my visa, and they were on a shoestring, so I told them I would buy them a few pints. They said it was no problem. They were fine but I said not to worry about it "you'll get me back some time", "it's a long road that has no turns" I said. I went up to the bar and ordered 3 Guinness. When it came time to pay, I asked the barman, "did they take card"...He said "no," so I asked could I see the head barman (all this in an Australian accent), to which he complied. The head barman came over, and I presented my Visa gold card, and he said not to worry that he'd make an exception. Glint! I told him we would only have a few pints. He said not to worry, so we danced the night away.

It got to the end of the night and we were all outside with some other people we met. I started singing some Irish songs and one of the girls I'd met inside earlier said I thought you were from Australia...I'd forgotten the accent! I was like...."ahhh.... I was only playing about!!"... she thought it was funny but I didn't get anywhere with her so it was home to the B&B to some cornflakes and milk with my two new buddies then they went to their campsite and I went to bed.

I woke up the next morning, still a little pissed as I had been for days at this stage and went down for the cure...a bloody Mary or two should do the trick.... I thought my clothes were smelling a bit, as I'd been wearing them for days. I went back to my room in my tipsy drunken state and thought why not shower with them on! That way, I could kill two birds with one stone! So, that's what I did. I stepped into the shower only taking off my boots and got soaped up. I was smiling to myself at what a great idea. I washed my clothes and rinsed them off, rung them out, then put them back on. I thought to myself, they'll air dry in no time.

The only thing was I had no deodorant, so I left the B&B after getting dressed and went to find a supermarket. I was walking on Main Street when I spied a local store. I went in and straight to the hygiene section. I picked up a can of deodorant and sprayed it under both armpits and over the rest of me then put it back. I wanted no luggage and didn't want to waste money on something I would leave behind me (and I thought it was funny!!!), I have to say I loved Kilkenny, and I will definitely go back there for the comedy festival some time. Maybe do a bit of stand-up telling these stories!

I was rambling from one pub to the other after that when I met this guy who was in his 50's and he told me he was a bit of a local celebrity. He said he had his own comedy show there. He'd approached me when he heard me telling jokes in the bar, I was in. We teamed up and went on the lash...he was leading the way as he knew all the bars to go into and have a bit of fun telling our jokes. Things petered out after a while, he kind of bored me. So, I went back to my B&B and had a sleep. I got up refreshed and the next morning, I got the bus for Dublin. I knew it was time to go home. I checked for the Directors number and discovered I'd fucking lost it. It was such a disappointment. Jesus has drink had a serious adverse effect on my life! Hollywood is calling me!!

1ˢᵀ ADMISSION – ST. PATS MENTAL ASYLUM

When I got back to Dublin, I booked into a hotel in Temple Bar. I didn't think much of that. The carpets were sticky as hell. It made me think about the cleanliness of the rest of it! I thought, it must get a lot of abuse with stag do's and things like that. I went down to the bar where friends of mine were bouncers. Half my old Rugby team from secondary school were all bouncing in Dublin's Temple Bar around that time, but they weren't working that day. We'd won the Donegal secondary schools title twice when I was in 4ᵗʰ and 5ᵗʰ year of secondary school. I was playing scrum half. I loved that position. Lots of action.

I was standing at the bar and saw these two gorgeous looking blonde girls, and I thought, I'll go over and talk to them. It turned out they were two Aussie birds. I told them a joke about Kiwi's (if they had been kiwi's, the joke would have been about Aussies!!! – Always goes down well!). I was going out on a limb a bit, it was a bit crude, but I thought they could handle it! The joke went, "what lubrication do Kiwi's use for shagging sheep?" "What?" they asked in unison, already laughing! "Sheep Shit!" I said. This got them tuned right in to my wavelength right away!!! I could tell they were both in to me. I was thinking threesome immediately!! They were stunning and had a great sense of humour. Nice combo, I thought. I always look for a sense of humour in all my women. It is the most important thing in life. We laughed together for a short while until there was an interruption that changed my life. If it hadn't happened, I'd have possibly had a threesome with the two hot chicks and been away home to Donegal. I would have gone back to sea, and none of what you are about to read would have transpired. There would be no bestseller! And my life would not be in tatters.

An old friend of mine, Mossy, who was down there bouncing, shouted to me from the bar. "Hey Juan!" I'd caught his eye as I was talking to the two girls. I thought "fuck it anyway!" I excused myself from the two women telling them I'd be back. I went over to where he was sitting. It was painful to leave the two girls, but I didn't want to be ignorant to him. I hadn't seen him since college a few years back, when we used to share a bus to Derry Tech. "Juan, what's the craic?" he asked when I went over. I said, "Jesus Mossy, how's it going? I'm not doing too bad. I heard you were down here." He bought me a pint and we chatted. Just as my pint arrived, he excused himself to go out and make a phone call. Little did I know at the time it was all subterfuge. I had no idea what he was up to! I was so pissed off at not having a threesome. I'd heard Aussie chicks were filthy in bed and I'd wanted to find out first hand!!! I forgive him. He was just doing what he thought was right.

Jesus, the bullshit that surrounded my story! Chinese fucking whispers. I was 25 years old, leave me the fuck alone. My Dad was a total control freak. My brother and sister did not have to put up with the same crap that I did. I thought all this after the wrongful admission. I had to tell each person who mentioned it, individually, the story of how I faked Bipolar to get into the asylum, it wore me thin. I was a grown man and knew my own mind, so what if I went partying and shagging around for a few weeks?!!!

Mossy landed back in anyway and said, "Sorry about that!" Telling me nothing about what he was doing. Really underhanded. We carried on talking, catching up on each other's lives, when his phone buzzed again, it was about 20 minutes after the first phone call he'd made. He excused himself to go outside again and take it. When he came back in this time, he said to me "there's someone outside wants to see you".

I asked who it was. And he said go out and see. To my disbelief when I went out, it was my Dad! "What are you doing here?" I asked.

As it turned out, Mossy had rung a friend of ours who in turn rang my Da. My Dad had been down in Dublin looking for me along with my uncle, his brother. He was staying in Dun Laoghaire in a hotel. He was also visiting my auntie, my uncle's wife, who was in the hospital getting a liver transplant. She was one of my biggest supporters in all this. She never believed I had Bipolar and believed my story of faking it to get in to the asylum.

After getting over the shock of seeing my Dad, we went over and sat down by the Bank of Ireland in the square in Temple Bar. I felt the relationship bond back with him again, it kind of made me tearful. I welled up for a second. My emotions getting the better of me. My Dad and I were best friends, and the whole rift because of the break-up with Briona had taken its toll on me. He asked, was I alright? I said that I was grand. Then I said, "Daddy do you know what the problem is?" "What?" he asked. "I'm a genius!" I said, "And nobody knows it!" He was standing up beside me. I was sitting on the step. He put his hand on my shoulder and said, "No Juan, son, you are not a genius." I had to laugh at that. Thanks, Da, I thought, for bursting my bubble and bringing me back to Earth, but I did feel that I was really bright and that I was a wasted talent. I was a little drunk. I thought at the time, I didn't know what I wanted to do with my life because of the recent events. I had met a lot of people with influence over the previous few weeks. I had strong ideas of acting in Hollywood after meeting the Director in Kilkenny. I had thoughts of going to acting school. I knew all the drinking and partying had to come to an end. I was wasting my time with it. I'd wanted to be an astronaut when I was younger. It was the adventurer in me, and going to sea was my substitute.

My goal of being Captain was realised in Superyachts. I spent a week as Captain then got the sack for drinking for the whole week that I was in charge. It was on a yacht called Anedigmi. The Captain that sacked me was the regular Captain. He told me not to tell anyone because it would really affect my career so I've kept it quiet until now. I hope this book does so well that I can buy my own 60-metre Superyacht. The aliens have told me this is going to happen. They advised me to move to Sint Maarten in the Caribbean and buy a mansion. They have said as well to buy a mansion in L.A. Right on Hollywood. That way when I go into acting, I can live there while I'm working. They told me to have 3 wives but do not marry. Just call them my wives. One will be from Australia, one from Germany and one from Spain. I love these countries and the women are stunning in all three. I will hold interviews for the position as my wife when I'm a Billionaire. I will sail my yacht to the 3 countries and meet as many women as is possible. I will be not one bit put off if there is no interest. I will have 3 women from these countries anyway. I am going to be travelling around with my comedy act so all the women that come to the show will have a good sense of humour and not be to stuck up as to tell me to fuck off. I will get my women. I am going to have 6 children with them. 2 per woman. The Spanish lady will not be a Catholic asshole. She will be a new age Spaniard. The German woman will be out and out intelligent. They are so bloody smart. The Aussie woman will have a real sense of fun about her. This will be the perfect mix for a good life. They will love to party as much as me. They will all have a GSOH (good sense of humour) and love taking drugs. I will have a brilliant time with them before we settle into parenthood. We will all travel the world on the yacht. I will have a foursome in bed every night. Lol. I cannot wait.

So anyway, my father and I are mending bridges, and he said, "I think you should see someone." I said, "What do you mean?" He said, "Well, I think you should see a Doctor". "What like a Psychiatrist?" I asked. "I don't feel like seeing a Doctor," I said. Then I told him "I don't want to see a Doctor." "I'm alright!" I said. "There is nothing wrong with me." I was heeding the advice Flo had told me a few weeks previous. But he said, "No, look you broke that window in the hotel". I replied, "Oh you heard about that? Yeah but they wouldn't let me stay...", "It was a bit over the top," I said. He said, "Yeah, well we need to sort it out. It will probably help your case with the gardai if you see a Doctor and get a letter to say you weren't in your right state of mind." "Where is the Doctor?" I asked. "St. Pats mental asylum" he said. OK, I thought. That's Flo's hospital. I agreed then thinking, fuck it, I'm going to have some fun! The aliens told me just this year, 2023, that they are responsible for that idea. They told me that they orchestrated my thinking to agree to the doctor taking a look at me. They said it was my mission. That was why I was on earth. They killed their King under his instructions with a mild lethal injection. Not so evil as to fuck up his mind as he passed away like they do on earth. They put him to death and transported his spirit to earth and put it into my mother Marian's womb when I was conceived. She was a dynamite nurse and could look out for me all through my childhood. So many things to look out for on earth!! So many illnesses. The King of Pachsion decided the mission to earth was so dangerous that he could not choose anyone else for it. He said to his people "I am doing this mission to earth for the greater good of humanity on earth. They are our brethren. They are only in their infancy. We are the most evolved people in the universe. We have to help!" They hate psychotropic medication and they absolutely detest psychiatry and psychiatric nurses!!

Fuck alcohol anyway, if I hadn't had those half dozen pints before my Da and I had met, I doubt I would have come up with the idea of going in. Lol. Now I know the truth. All this writing is funny to read with the aliens talking to me now. They have really opened up my eyes to the Universe in the last year. They are talking to me all the time. They speak to me from the minute I wake up, to the second I go to sleep. They are in my dreams. They speak to me while I am sleeping. They have told me that I am evolving every day that I am alive now. That I am the most evolved human being on the planet. I thought in hindsight before I heard the truth from the aliens that I might have come up with the idea of going in, but I wouldn't have followed through. I thought to myself with the drink taken, if I do this, if I go and see a Doctor and I pretend to have Bipolar, which I had heard about from Flo, she is not to blame for any of my capers, I had just heard about it from her, I might get off with the charge. I remembered her telling me that prospective employers can see your criminal record but they cannot see your mental record. I thought, what if I pretend to have Bipolar and I get admitted to a hospital and plead insanity in court? It could work! Flo had told me lots of stories about the woman being very promiscuous, "All the women are very promiscuous" she'd said. She had whet my appetite. She had good times in there as well, she made her own fun. The doctors and nurse bullied the shit out of her. I was fucking fuming at it. I so wanted revenge on them. It was the real reason I went in. To fucking sort them evil fucking assholes out. I also thought that maybe I would have a bit of craic in there. I suppose I had a bit of heartache with her too, but we were still friends, and she came and visited me whenever I went into the hospital. I didn't tell her what I was up to because I knew she would be pissed off. I knew she wouldn't have agreed with my decision because of the hardship she has had to endure. I definitely have a case of PTSD from being in these places over the years. They fucking destroyed my very being. The bullying that I received in later years when the doctors and nurses figured out I was on a mission to overturn my diagnosis was fucking brutal. I believed while I was in there that the places were bugged. It was a common thought amongst the patients. Everybody thought the little square unit on the ceiling in every room was a listening device. The nurses said it was for the bleepers they wear. Nobody believed them. The patients were all paranoid.

I agreed with my Dad to see a Doctor but deep down I did not feel comfortable with the idea of it. But I thought if I get a mental record for being Bipolar and not a criminal record for breaking the window, which was a bit extreme – the extent that I went to - then things would work out for me. Looking back, if I had just taken the broken window rap, life would've been ok.

I went to see my auntie after that. The one who had the treatment for her liver in the hospital. We stayed in my Dad and Uncle's hotel in Dun Laoghaire. As it happened, my mate Paddy, if you remember his mum Miss Polly from the chapter W.A.B.C from national school was at his insurance companies' team-building exercise there. Coincidence or what?!! We hit the drink big time. He was such a wild man as well. I never overthought about going to meet a Doctor. My Father was in a good mood with me because I'd agreed to see the Doctor and he had given me a free reign drinking. I reckoned at the time; he was just keeping me sweet. Keeping me liquored up! I knew he was glad I was distracted and not thinking about the Doctor's meeting because he let me drink right up to the time of going into the asylum without complaining about it. It was fun with Paddy and his colleagues. We had lots of drinks and a laugh all night. We were letting off fire extinguishers in the hotel and shit like that.

I flew back up home to see my mother before meeting the Doctor. I was happy to be back in the family realm. When I look back now, I was on a high because I'd been living the high life for weeks and loving it! They talk about the 'Jesus Condition', whenever you are in a manic state. I just felt happy. Whenever I drank, I felt elated, so I know it was not a manic state. I was drunk and elated from it, but who doesn't get that way?!!! My creative juices were flowing. I was exuberant, not Bipolar. With all my plans for books and movies of my recent weeks and my life at sea, I felt like I was going to be famous. I still do! I felt I was on the cusp of being famous at that time, no wonder I was on a high! When I got back to Donegal, my mum thought I was off my bap altogether. All I wanted to do was drink! She thought I was crazy! I was drinking all day and enjoying the summer sunshine! It was completely not the norm, but I was on holidays from the sea! That was where my head was at. I remember giving the dog some of my Guinness to drink. I put it in an ashtray, and he began drinking it. He kept chewing stones from the garden then dropping them into the ashtray. Not long after that, he had to have an operation to get the stones out of his stomach, but I don't think it was me because of me! I hope! I just think it was a coincidence.

I flew back down to Dublin after a couple of days at home and stayed in the same hotel near Dun Laoghaire again with my Dad and uncle. I was still a little broken-hearted because of Flo! There were a lot of things going on and my emotions were on fire. The fact that I was back friends with my father was all that I needed at the time. I enjoyed being out at night. So, I went out the night before seeing the doctor. I felt the city's vibe but it was kind of worn out at that stage. I was partied out! I didn't however want to be cooped up in a hotel room. I was released when I was in and around Dublin city, and I could do whatever I wanted. When I came back to the hotel after my night, as you will read, I got some wine at the late-night bar, drank it, relaxed and went to sleep.

The next morning before we went to see the Doctor, I wanted to go shopping. I decided I had to get some new clothes first. My father was treating me, so we went to a hairdresser in the city centre near Grafton Street that I knew and got a shave. It was one of those Turkish shaves with hot towels and cutthroat razors. They actually brought us drinks; well, my father didn't drink it, but I had a brandy while getting it done. It was all very nice. It was star treatment, very cool!

We left there and walked up Grafton Street. My father said I was like a destroyer ship walking up the street. I just saw people moving away. I didn't know what they were thinking. I was just on a mission to get some new clothes...I felt free! Some people say that I felt like I owned the city, but I didn't really. I just felt free. I felt at home there. We got to the shopping centre at the top of Grafton Street.

As I write this, (2016!), I just felt the spirits in my mind suggesting "your roots are in Donegal!" and I just saw roots coming out of my feet and planting. The San Pedro I took in 2006 has left me hallucinating since. The hallucinations don't interfere with my daily life. They are very rare now and I just ignore them. They are translucent and only last a split second.

Anyway, I got the clothes. I thought for a bit of craic I would sign my old jeans and tell the shop keeper I was going to be famous. I played them for a joke. I kept a straight face and I signed my jeans with a black marker pen that he gave me. I gave the old jeans to the shop keeper and said, "Keep them because I'm going to be famous soon!" and he went "yeah right" (I doubt if he ever kept them! lol). I'd gotten trousers that Briona had suggested I buy years before, corduroy type, purple trousers. They were a little bit extroverted. Briona is an artist and she is a very good one. Eyes are her specialty. The most difficult of all to paint. All the clothes I purchased were very extrovert. I got a nice bright purple Timberland shirt as well. The pants and shirt matched but did not really go with my old brown Docker boots. I didn't want to ditch my boots however. We'd done a lot of miles together. They gave me a lot of comfort. They had a good spring in them, and they were the best boots

I'd ever had, so I kept them on. I had a Walkman which my brother gave to me on my brief spell to Donegal. It was a cool Walkman, sports edition. It was waterproof, which suited me. Shockproof too! Very much needed!! I was listening to Eminem. Number 18 on the album "Till I collapse," which was my favorite song on the Eminem show album. I was listening to that song the night before when I was walking up Leeson's street on my way to a strip club. I much prefer brothel's any day! I hate all the teasing at strip shows lol. When I went in to the strip club, I bought a Bulmer's at the bar. After a few minutes, I got talking to one of the dancers. She was curious as to what I was listening too. She asked "what are you listening to?" I said "Eminem!". "Oh!" She said. "I love Eminem!" I let her have a listen. We were getting cozy when next thing two security men came out and took her away. I was getting too close to her. They came out from in back. I had just learned from her the word "Isveikata," which meant 'cheers' or "bless you" in Lithuanian. How I remembered it was an anagram of a 'visa card.' When she left, I went up on stage and danced on the pole. I got asked to leave for that. I left the strip club and went home. That's when I got the wine. The late-night bar was just closing up when I arrived at the hotel. I went to bed and went to sleep. Something not possible if you are fucking elated. And do not give me the bullshit about self-medicating with alcohol. It is a relaxant not a bloody psychotropic poison.

The next morning my Dad took me shopping, like I said, then we went to the asylum. He said, when we woke up "right, we are going to go and see the Doctor today." I got him to take me shopping. I was prolonging it a bit. I was a bit nervous of going to the asylum.

We went to the asylum, and while we were waiting to be seen, I wanted a cigarette. We went outside and stood at the main door. I was listening to Eminem, having a cigarette when I saw some people approaching to enter the building. I started singing out loud, "I think my Dad's gone crazy!" this is the final song on the Eminem album. My Dad was laughing, and they were laughing awkwardly too. I just seen the whole thing as a big joke.

We went in and met the admissions Doctor. She began the analysis by saying I have a question sheet that I am going to ask you a series of questions from. Is this ok? I said yes. I'd been through one of these before when I was aged 23 for drinking, and I knew the answers to give to get the score or result I wanted so I could lie if I wanted too. I decided I would answer these questions truthfully. I did not want to be there. I had backed out of going into the asylum at this stage. I thought it wasn't a good idea. The Doctor asked, Had I been sleeping rough? Had I excess energy? Was I not sleeping well? Had I been promiscuous? The last one I answered as much as I could!!

I answered all the questions truthfully and as I figured would happen, she said at the end "I think everything's alright with Juan, there doesn't seem to be a problem." My father lost his cool at that point. He said in a loud and irate voice, "there's obviously something wrong with him! Look at him! Look at him," He said exasperated.

I was dressed in all the clothes that he'd bought me. I was looking a little extroverted BUT I was not mentally fucking ill.

My father pulled out his phone and left the room in anger. I thought fuck, he is angry at me again. I changed my mind about going into the asylum again because of his reaction. I didn't want to disappoint him. It was a terrible decision when I look back on it but I was still young and wanted to cur favour with him. I knew what he went out of the room for, he was going to try to pull strings to get me admitted. But I figured, it really depended on me. If I said I was fine, they would have just said, that's fine, go on ahead! I should have gone home and gone back to work. And contrary to what my father spread throughout my family and the community; I had not gone over my time for going back to my job at sea. He tried to make out I was totally deluded at the time of the admission. He fucking lied through his teeth!!! He told so many lies back then to make himself look good. We fucking argued about that one. I told him I could prove it but he fucking dismissed everything I said. He was such a cunt to me when the whole diagnosis came about! He thought he was the fucking man around me! I knew I'd put his nose out of joint when I came back from Africa. I was brimming with confidence. He hadn't ever, seen me like that! I'd only been like that when he wasn't around. I'd been away from home for years!!! The rest of the community can take note of that as well.

As soon as he left the room, and I'd had the change of heart about the admission, I decided to play the mental patient card. I knew from Flo, one of the symptoms of Bipolar was rapid speech. So, as soon as the door closed, I turned to the Doctor, and I said rapidly, "sorry doctor, I didn't know what to say when my father was there, but I have been sleeping rough, and I have been doing everything that you said on there, and I'm really, really sorry…..".

She said, "shhh, calm down, it's ok, it's ok". "You're fine". "We'll look after you" My father came back in and she said "Mr. O'Donnell, I have spoken to Juan on his own, and we are going to admit him. I do think he does have a problem and he need's our help….". "We will let him in." My father was so relieved. I felt fucking weird. I did not know what to expect. I was completely fucking sane. The doctor opened the door beside her desk in the small admissions room, and it mysteriously led into the ICU (Intensive care unit). It freaked me out when I looked in but I went with it. My Dad's plan had worked. He'd wanted me admitted all along. I took in my surroundings and went for a cigarette. I held no aspirations of what to expect.

The next day there was an interview arranged with my Doctor. I called him Lucky. They asked where I would like to hold it, so I suggested we have it in the smoke room. He came into the smoke room to do the interview looking the quintessential Psychiatrist, his hair, his glasses, and even the way he held the clipboard and crossed his legs. I thought, here we go, this is my chance to ask the questions I wanted to ask. He was the same doctor that Flo had! I remembered his name from when she told me. She had told me terrible stories about him, so I was already primed and ready to let fly at him. He was the evil cunt that was killing people with ECT!!! He began by saying that the symptoms I had were indicative of Bipolar syndrome and what I was experiencing was something called mania. I lit on him straight away. I said, "How can you pigeon hole me like that?!!" You have spoken to me for less than a minute. You know nothing about me, my personality, my sense of humour, any of my life or experiences before this…. you know nothing about me!" "How do you know?" I said. "I can tell by the pressure in your speech". I said" that's bullshit!". I disagreed with his diagnosis of

Bipolar even though I had faked its symptoms, so you could say it was my own fault, and I was arguing for no reason, but I just wanted to give him shit because of what Flo had told me about how easy it was to get labelled Bipolar. I said to him "the pressure in my speech is from the anger I feel about this diagnosis". It was understandable, I thought. I replied "I have just come off a boat as well, where I had regained my confidence after a terrible car crash and where I was giving orders to people, one of whom didn't like getting orders from me, so I had to be forceful with him, so the pressure was coming from that also." I told him I was an authoritative figure, and you could hear it in my voice. He turned to my father and uncle, who were sitting there, listening and said, "this interview is terminated." "Why?" my Father asked. He replied, "because I feel threatened..." so I looked at him dead in the eye and said, "what do you mean??? I haven't even hit ye yet!!" He jumped up with his clipboard saying, "that's it!" and practically scurried out of the room.

After he left, I sat down and broke my balls laughing!! I thought Flo would have been proud of me!!! My father said, "what are you laughing at, you're in here for 8 weeks, you better make it easy on yourself! Go get him back!" I reluctantly agreed with him and said "ok," and went out the door after the doctor. I caught up with him as he walked angrily up the corridor. He didn't slow down as I spoke to him, obviously angry (or scared, ha!). I said to him, as he walked on, in the best acting I had with a softly spoken submissive voice, "Doctor, I'm really sorry. Look, it's my first time in one of these places, and I obviously need your help, so will you come back and finish the interview?" He stopped and looked at me. This time it was his turn to look me in the eye, but his reason was to see if I was lying or not. He obviously thought I had given him his stripes back because he straightened his back up and said "ok" and walked back to the room with me behind him. He had such an arrogant air about him. He walked back in to the smoke room and facing my father and uncle, said, "after speaking to Juan, I'm willing to take him on." What he didn't see was me behind him, pretending to hold his shoulders from behind and gyrating my hips in and out as if I was giving him a serious ass fucking!!! My uncle smothered a laugh. I couldn't see my father, but as the shrink turned around to look at me to see what my uncle was laughing at, I acted timidly again, which was what he was obviously looking for, so he was none the wiser. Lol.

After my two days of being there, and them forcing me to take medication, to which I wouldn't agree to at first because I knew I didn't need it, I decided I didn't want to stay and told the truth about faking it in the admissions. None of the staff believed me. The head nurse said laughing, "that's what they all say!" What a head fuck! They told me I had no option and that I couldn't get out. I was at their mercy! I said I was there as a voluntary patient, so I should be able to leave whenever I wanted to which they replied, you might be voluntary but the Doctor has put a holding bar on you, so you can't leave. I asked how that was voluntary, and they said that's the way it is. I was being forced to take the medication. I was livid. I wanted a second opinion. They wouldn't believe my story of how I had pretended to have Bipolar to get in there. I got the second opinion I asked for, but the Doctor that came in looked like he was on the verge of retiring, half asleep, it was the middle of the day! He looked bored and like he didn't give a shit. He was there because he'd been told to do it. He listened then as I spoke rapidly about how I had come to be there. I spoke quickly because I felt I had limited time with the guy, so I was trying to fit everything in about the situation but rapid speech is also a symptom of bipolar, so you cannot win. The symptoms are so wide ranging. It could cover everyone I knew. It was impossible to argue with, but I tried. At the end of the second opinion, the doctor said, "you may have been pretending but you do actually have it!" I said, "how do you know?" He said, "rapid speech"! I said, "I knew I only had limited time to tell you, and that was the reason for that!!!" He dismissed me. The whole thing is a total mind fuck. That was it. I was stuck there for 8 weeks in that hospital. After that, I thought you want to see mental, then I'll show you mental! That was when I began the play acting, I'd seen in the movies on how to wind the staff all up, especially the hard case nurses.

Some of them were real bitches and would verbally attack you any chance they got. I re-enacted things from movies like "One Flew Over the Cuckoo's Nest" and any other movie where people were incarcerated and being held against their will. "What about Bob?" and "Patch" were two of my favourite comedy's about mental health. I felt like I was carrying on Patch Adams's work. Patch Adams is a hero of mine!! I rebelled.

Because of my rebellious attitude I became an object of desire to two young females there. They thought I was a bit of craic. Kena and Fran. Kena was 17 and she was in with anorexia. I thought she had a great little body on her! Fran was 16 and a little bit naughtier than Kena. She was in for a suicide attempt. I was 25 so there wasn't THAT big an age gap!! I told Kena in the TV room out of earshot of the nurses that I was going to escape. I said that I didn't want to stay there, and she was like, "no! don't, don't! They'll only bring you back in. You'll make it worse for yourself!" I told her I wouldn't.

She told me she was receiving ECT. I said I thought that ECT was antiquated and barbaric. I said, I thought that they didn't do it anymore. And especially not for something like anorexia. She said she hated it but she said that she couldn't do anything about it because she was under 18 so it was her parents' call. She said that Doctor Lucky, who was in charge of it, had manipulated her parents into thinking it would work, and she had no say in it. He was a proper killer. I told her I would write about it one day and get the law changed!!! It has since changed. You must agree to it now. They can not force you.

We were sitting in the TV room a couple of days later, and I was telling her a few stories of my escapades. She was having a right old laugh. Then she said that I wouldn't see her for two days because she was going for her ECT and general anesthetic. So, she would be sluggish and spending the day in bed, and on the next day, she would be recovering from the general anesthetic, she received every time she was zapped. You are only meant to receive a couple of those general anesthetics in your lifetime! When the two days passed, she came back, and I was sitting in the TV room again. She came in and sat down beside me. She looked very down in the dumps, so I thought I would cheer her up with a few witty anecdotes. I began telling her a story when I realized I had already told her it so I stopped and said "I've already told you that!" but she said, "don't worry, I won't remember you telling it anyway. The ECT fucks up your short-term memory". She was smiling at her own gag, and I did laugh too, but I thought is that this is fucking terrible and it should not be used anymore.

We became very close friends, Kena, Fran, and I in that first week. We were all in our Pyjamas all day long, so the hormones were raging between the three of us. Fran had the dirtiest look in her eye for me for that whole week but she was only 16. I would love if it had of been like what the aliens are planning for earth. No age of consent. I thought I would get hung if I went near her! Kena was so horny too. We were turning each other on big time!!! Kena was not legal age but near as damn it lol! They were both so bloody horny for me. We were in the TV room one day. There was no-one around. It was near the end of the first week, when Kena suggested we go to Fran's room for a bit of relief for me. She said it was Fran's idea. She was so fucking excited!!! Fran was smiling at me with a dirty look in her eye as Kena told me their idea. They were horned up to the last.

Kena said Fran would keep watch at the bedroom door while her and I went into the bathroom and got it on. Fran's room was at the top of the corridor so it was last to be checked by the nurses on the 15 minutes suicide room check. I said "Let's fucking go!" I'd been fantasizing about something like this for the whole week. I'd been as saucy with them as I could and they had reciprocated. I had really put the work in, on getting into those Pj's of theirs! We went to Fran's room. Kena took me into the bathroom. I pulled down my trouser bottoms. My cock was already erect! She grabbed it and started wanking me off. We kissed passionately as she did it. It was so erotic. I was fulfilling my fantasy. One I'd had since Flo had told me about the joint. Kena stopped after stroking me 5 or 6 times. I could tell she wasn't very experienced. It was an even bigger turn on. One of her first lol. I said to her could we do it doggy style over the toilet? She had a great body on her. I wanted to hold onto that ass and ride her rotten. Man did she bring out a sweat in me! Phew! Those little breasts were so pert. She said no. She didn't want to get caught. She opened the door and Fran was looking at me with my cock standing to attention. I could see she was turned on looking at me. She had such a horny look in her eye as she looked at my throbbing cock. She said to Kena "you have plenty of time!" I wanted to ride Fran, there and then. Kena could have watched! But that was it. I was left with blue balls. An orgasm of a lifetime in my sack! We went back to the TV room. Our hormones were still fucking raging. The girls were giggling. I said to the them I have to get this orgasm out! They laughed at me. I said "I'll be back in a few minutes. I'm going to my room for a wank!" They laughed again. I'd loved to have brought both of them with me! They were horny as fuck!

I went straight to my room and closed the bedroom door. I got under the covers in case a nurse walked in. It was only the afternoon. As I was lying there, bottoms down, getting ready for the wank of a lifetime, a beautiful-looking blonde nurse came in to see if I was ok. She made me even hornier. She was from Poland and extremely pretty. She asked me what I was doing in bed? I said just resting. Then I asked her what the Polish word for wank was. She said "Coinyabeta" and left the room smiling with a naughty glint in her eye. I think she knew why I was in the bed! Jesus, I was loving this place now. She closed the door after her, and me and Pamela and her 5 sisters fucked hard! I thought of Kena and Fran naked playing with me. It didn't take me long to cum!

I wrote this poem (after cleaning up first!!!) afterward. I laugh now when I think of it.

Coinyabeta
The pleasures of wanking

It's a solitary game,
something like patience,
but if you work too hard,
you'll end up a patient,
It's a fierce boring job,
but someone's got to do it,
a wank's not for Christmas.
It's for the rest of your life,
and you'll have to go solo,

till you find a girl or a wife,
wank with your left,
wank with your right,
be ambidextrous,
and let yourself take flight,
for when you get good,
you learn self-control,
restraint and delivery,
no matter the toll,
so, practice your moves,
let those fingers find their grooves,
like a pianist and his piano,
how funny it is they go together,
if only this feeling could last
Forever!

I've lived out quite a few of my sexual fantasies throughout my lifetime. I feel very lucky in this regard. I have a great sense of fulfillment among all men!

My rebelling continued throughout that week. Doctor Lucky had had enough of it, and called my father into the asylum. My Dad brought my younger sister in along with him to the meeting. Doctor Lucky began by saying, "we are having trouble suppressing Juan," to which my father replied, "Surely you mean help him, Doctor?" The Doctor was quick to reply. It should have been a big red flag to my father. He should have known I was telling the truth. "Yes" said the doctor, "sorry, help him. But the medication isn't working!!!". This was because I was fighting it and the system for all I was worth, nothing else. Doctor Lucky, who was in charge of ECT in the hospital, said their last option was ECT. Had my father not reacted the way he did I could have been taken out of the realm of life. He has done it to so many people. He fucking hated me! My sister said my father said no to it and that he nearly attacked the Doctor for suggesting it. I feel at this point my father should have believed my plight to get out of there. I told my father the truth of what I did in the admissions, when he was outside the room,

I told him about faking it, but he wouldn't believe that I could put on that good an act. He believed with Doctor Lucky's analysis. Jesus wept but I didn't know how dangerous a fire I was playing with. I thought I was only having the craic. I could have had my brain fried and all my memories deleted. They could have left me in a vegetative state for life! What a cunt of a doctor! My sister said when she explained to me in my room in the ICU after the meeting "Juan, you better calm down, or they are going to give you ECT." I asked what do you mean ECT me? She said she'd just been in a meeting with my Dad and the Doctor, telling me the story, and said, you better calm down, or they are going to electrocute you! That was it, I ended the play acting.

Doctor Lucky was testing out medications on me to see which best suited me, which angered me to fuck and still does because there was nothing wrong with me in the first place!! It was experimentation for him. He prescribed this medicine after a couple of days in there of refusing it all. It was called Serenace, and it was in liquid form. I only took it because Fran and Kena told me that it's best not to fight the Doctors all the time because it would just make my time in there all the more difficult. I decided to go with the flow and get the fuck out of there any way I could. I took it and went in and sat down in the TV room.

I was sitting with Kena watching TV chatting when my head started turning to the left all the time. I couldn't control it. It was like a muscle spasm. Kena said you better go to the nurse's station quick. She said I was more than likely having an allergic reaction to the medication. By the time I went to the nurse's station, which was only seconds away, my throat had swollen up, and I was finding it difficult to breathe. My body, arms, and legs, were all twisting over to the left. The Female Doctor on duty said for me to run to my bed and lie face down quickly, so I did. I was coughing and gasping for breath. It was fucking frightening. She said "pull down your bottoms!!!" She gave me an injection on my ass, which had no effect! She gave me a second one, and I could feel the relief instantly of being able to breathe again. It was like a chemical castration. I've met other patients in later years that had the same reaction to it and I suspected they gave it to unruly patients to calm them down. The patients that I met that it had happened to were all live wires. The swelling in my throat eased, but I began to get sick. The Doctor handed me a small waste bin that was beside my bed, and I vomited into it. It wasn't a very nice experience. Scary, in fact, it made me frightened as to what these medications were doing to my brain. When I stopped vomiting, the Doctor asked me how I felt, and I told her, "it felt like I half-swallowed a Viagra!!" She didn't get the joke. I was rubbing my throat. The guy, Pat, in the next bed started laughing and saying "he's got a stiff neck!!!" I said, "You got it in one." She half laughed, but I wasn't happy. I asked her why it had happened, and she said that it was a side effect and that 90% of people are fine with it, so I asked what about the other 10%?!!

After that, things went pretty smooth, I still felt trapped and couldn't wait to get out of there.

One of the female nurses even hit on me on that first admission. She was on the evening staff. She gave a male nurse her number for me, and got him to ask me to give her a call when I got out. She was standing at the end of the hall, smiling down at me when he asked me. She looked really pretty. I looked up the hallway to her and smiled. I said to him I definitely would, taking her number. I thought, she is risking her job, the crazy bitch. Good for a fuck though! These women knew there was not a fucking thing wrong with me! They are all crazy bitches.

I knew completely without doubt, that I wasn't Bipolar. Although, I'd pretended to have it, to get into the asylum. I felt the feeling of being trapped in there was insurmountable. JESUS CHRIST, IT WAS SO FUCKING SCARY!!!

The head nurse, Paula, came to me this morning while still in the ICU and told me there was a seminar in the auditorium on Bipolar. She thought it would do me good to go along. She thought maybe I'd learn something. I did go along but it was to my detriment. For when my Father and others latched onto what I learned, they used it against me! My father just could not be wrong for keeping me locked up! Paula, the nurse, thought I might get some of this fabled insight they talk about. Basically, insight is where you agree with the Doctors analysis, as fucking if?!!

I got some insight, alright but not what they were expecting. I thought when she told me about the seminar, what is the point? I know I'm not Bipolar. I went along anyway. Paula was nice, and like she said, it was an hour out of the ICU in the big auditorium and a break from the normal routine. I walked to the auditorium and sat half way up and to the right. There was a lot of people there. Practically, full capacity. About 150 people. The head of the hospital was giving the seminar.

The seminar began, and about 10 mins into it, the speaker mentioned Unipolar down, where people only get depressed. I raised my hand. I could see he didn't want to answer. He ignored me until I started clicking my fingers. I wasn't going to be ignored! I had a little inward laugh to myself as well. I could see that you didn't really ask questions, but I wanted to be heard and ask my question, so I kept it raised and clicked my fingers until he answered. "Yes??" he said, pointing up at me. I asked him, "if you can have Unipolar down, could you have only unipolar up??" "Yes"," he said. He said that this was possible. He drew a circle on the white board where he was describing things and put a 1% segment in it. He said then, that only one percent of Bipolar people were Unipolar up. Where they only get the elation. He looked like he was making it up. You could feel the stupidity in the room. Everyone being duped. It made me laugh. I thought now for a bit of fun with the doctors and nurses in the ICU. I had a bit of ammo to go back to them with. On an unfortunate note, I told my Dad the story of unipolar up as a joke anecdote. He thought fucking hell, Juan is unipolar up! He doesn't get depression. He tried spreading the story to people. Just because it sounded exotic. He was fucking living off the mental illness diagnosis. There was nothing exciting going on in his life after he sold our pub so he ploughed all his attention into me, making me as sick as fucking possible. He fucking hated me for arguing with him about it and he was so fucking nasty to me when I did. He loved the attention he was getting off other parents. He'd become the go to man about mental illness in Moville. He lived off the attention until he died. He had no fucking status after the pub was sold and the piloting was kaput by Harbour Harry. The argument with the Harbour in Derry that made him retire early. My old man was such a stubborn cunt. But alas, Harbour Harry, you put my old father in an early grave. 68 is very young, he died of a broken heart. The pilot tradition has been in our family for over 100 years, you sickening cunt!

My Dad tried to manipulate me into saying I was unipolar up because he had told so many people already. I thought "Dad, I am way too smart for you to manipulate me with that one!" I argued with him and told him "I told you the unipolar up anecdote as a joke!!" He went bright red. I thought you, stupid old decrepit cunt. He was ruining my life as a bit of a pastime for himself. He had nothing else going on. He really enjoyed talking superior to the Doctors about me. Always talking over my head when I was in their company. I'm sure a lot of patients will understand what I am talking about. I've seen it happen many times with other patients too.

In one instance, in Doctor Lucky's office, when I was down in St. Pats in Dublin for a check-up appointment after I got out, my Dad sat party to Doctor Lucky abusing me! I was on medication that affected your balance physically so Doctor Lucky asked me to walk to his office door from his desk so he could see the effect. I got up from my chair where I was sitting beside my Dad and walked to the door. As I turned to walk back, Doctor Lucky exclaimed "Head still held high!" I could tell by the way he said it, he was giving me shit! He was on about my confidence. Confidence which he and my father were both trying to ruin on me. They hated that I saw myself as their superior. I was way more intelligent than them both! My father never said a thing when the doctor exclaimed it. It really fucking flattened me. I knew then, both cunts were on my case. I knew from my Dad's treatment of me after that, that he was trying to flatten my confidence as well. I had confidence in myself and they were forcing me to take the medication so they would be seen to be right of their treatment of me in the eyes of the world. There was a lot of mixed opinions in the community at home. The people with a bit of sauvignon in them agreed with my dear old da and the people with a bit of savvy in them knew that this whole fucking thing came about because of the car crash I was in with Briona. I'd gone a little wild because I'd come back from the dead! With Briona out of the picture I was able to sow my wild oats throughout the Republic of Ireland!!! I was blowing off steam you sickening nonce's!!!

It was black and white with my father. No changing his mind, and he never did. I was Bipolar in his eyes, and that was it!

We argued about it until the day he died. I didn't even cry at his funeral or his death at all. About seven years before his death, like I talked about already, when he told me he had cut me out of his will, I wished him dead, and, in a way, he was dead to me from then on in. I had to cut him off emotionally. He was killing me. He was a killer as well. Something I always admired in him!!! The death he was bringing was causing me so much pain! Two killer's that have come to the end. They will keep going until one of them dies! It was me or my Dad!!! I knew it wasn't going to be me. I never looked at him the same way again after leaving the inheritance to my brother James. It was destroying me the way he was treating me. The pain he put me through was unbearable. He wasn't a father figure to me after the diagnosis. He was a disciplinarian and a tyrant. They told him he could section me (put me in hospital by law) after the first admission, and he wielded the threat like a big stick.

It sounds so not much of a big deal, but try going through all those admissions you cunt!!! As far as he was concerned, I was back under his rule and he was enjoying it! If he could get me on the disability allowance, which is what he was pushing for, he could retire from ever caring about me. After years of fighting on my part, I got back to sea. If I had of listened to him, my life would have gone down the shitter. It happens to so many kids. I am about to put an end to it. Especially in America. They are destroying children for generations to come. Holy fuck! How could a 5-year-old kid not be boisterous!!! The aliens love America. They have been watching you since the first white people got there. They knew it would be brilliant. America is such a great country to live in.

I had paid a visit to my father in Carrowtrasna in 2013. That night my Dad and I talked in the car, after he left me back up to my flat in Moville. He sounded like he was looking for excuses to leave all of his estate to James and sure, who gave a shit about a mental patient? My fake illness of Bipolar was his way of doing it. He said me being Bipolar was why he left it all to James. He took advantage of me with a house as well. I bought when I was 22. I don't remember exactly how he sold it. I was told by a solicitor that I must have given him the power of attorney. My head has been so screwed up with medication and manipulation that I don't remember it. He sold the house when I was going through a hospital admission in Sligo mental asylum in 2006. You will read about that later. I'd bought the house for 202,000 euros. He gave me the deposit of 20,000 to buy it at the time. I was to pay the deposit back to him in full. After the sale in 2006, he told me it was sold for 160,000 euro, and that I'd lost money on it. I found out the truth in 2018 from the estate agent who sold it, that the house was sold for 254,000 euro and he kept the profit. Devious cunt! When I told him, I was getting lawyers involved to retrieve the money, he said arrogantly he would see me in court. He was such a self-righteous cunt. I let it go. I had nobody else to rely on. I needed his fucking help. I was over a barrel and he knew it. He was so fucking cuntish to me. My brother James thinks I am writing this novel to blacken my father's name.

That is so wrong. I am writing it to get a clean bill of health and dispel the lies that my father told. The house sale was a lot of money to me in 2018. I was stuck in a hostel in arse loving Letter-fucking-kenny. My Dad owed me 30 thousand! Not to be sniffed at.

He helped me out with a few grand, after we made amends about the house sale, to get my Merchant Navy courses done and keep my ticket alive. It was the least he could do! He told everybody that he did this. So much for "What's mine is yours!" A fucking lying cunt of a statement he made when he thought I was going to make millions on this book! He was making sure I would give him some money!!

As I said, he left me that 13 grands in his will, so we're all square now, I guess! That night when he told me he was leaving his land to James, it brought back the memory of 2006 when he told me I could no longer follow in his footsteps and become a ship's pilot on the river Foyle because he believed I was Bipolar. It was fucking gut wrenching for me. He had to recommend me for the position, and he wasn't willing to do that. The power he had in the pilots was taken away from him by the Harbour of Derry and he went fucking do-lally! I thought, about fucking time, you're not that powerful! I felt so relieved that if I wasn't going to become a pilot, then nobody could become pilot lol just kidding!! The little monopoly he had created was taken down. I was a legitimate candidate for pilot. I had more than enough experience. I eventually got over it and thought the take down was a little bit of justice for me. He wasn't as omnipotent as he thought. I did punch the wall beside my bed that night in 2013 when I thought of what he had taken away from me by cutting me out of his will. I put a fucking dent in the plaster. I'd wished it was his head.

Anyhow, I went back to the ICU after the seminar, and Paula asked how I got on? I told her that if I was anything, I was Uni-polar up. She immediately disagreed with me and said, "no you're not. You're Bipolar." I was so fucking angry at this. I asked her, "how in the hell do you know anything about me after the short time I am in here? I don't get depression!!". I took her to task and said "I'm getting loaded down with shit because of the problems this whole fucking diagnosis is causing, and practically ruining my fucking life, but that's not depression. It's a series of issues that need remedying, and when they are remedied, the feeling lifts...the end!" She didn't know what to say!!!

The morning after the seminar, the word had spread that I was saying I was Unipolar up. A junior doctor, one of Dr. Lucky's understudies, came into my room and pulled up a chair. I was sitting up in bed.

She asked in a really light-hearted way, as she sat down "So Juan, are you bipolar today?" It was a running joke at the time. I replied "no, if anything I'm Uni-polar up!" ...I was just fucking with them; I knew there was nothing wrong with me. She said, "what? You mean you don't go down??" So, I leaned forward towards her and smiled and said provocatively, "Well, only if you ask me too!!!!" She went bright red and put her clipboard up to her face to hide her embarrassment. She stood up quickly and said, "I think we have talked enough for today.... I will see you tomorrow!!" She laughed as she left the room. Another little fan!

I went through the routine of going through each of the stages for getting out of there. The ICU (3 weeks), second stage ICU (1 week) then the final stage upstairs where they gave you your clothes back (4 weeks).

After I got out of the asylum, my plan was to go back to work at sea. I wanted off the medication, but my parents and would not believe that I had faked the illness. They were so fierce with me about taking the meds. It was the most harrowing time of my life. I had nobody to turn to. My sister was a fucking tyrant as well. Like I said in the chapter Home life, she yelled at me. She was the closest friend I had growing up. I confided so much in her. It was so bloody scary. I had to keep my focus. The medication was so strong. I thought it would fuck up my whole life.

I had told no one my plan for pleading insanity in court for breaking the window. The plan worked. I did not get done for vandalism. So, I was actually pretty happy about that. "Now to get off the drugs and back to work", I thought, "I only have my parents to convince!" I knew that the doctors in Dublin had hundreds of patients, they wouldn't be worried about one madman from Donegal slipping through the net. The fight with my parents became the most bitter war of my whole bloody life.

The plan of pleading insanity in court was the biggest thing I had ever faked. I was always on the wrong side of the law growing up. I was permanently outside the teacher's staff room when I was a schoolkid. This was an extension to that mischievous nature.

I told my friends at home what I had done to get off with the charge in Dublin. They laughed and called me a crazy bastard! Some of them did not believe me. They wanted to believe my Dad because they were licking his fucking anus! Sycophantic cunts!!!

When I was up in court for breaking the window in the hotel, the judge read the letter from the asylum. It was given to him by my solicitor. The letter I had gone to all the trouble of getting to say I was mad. It worked in my favour and the judge was lenient. So were the guards. My father was talking to them as well. I got pretty famous throughout the Dublin Gardai because of my rapscallion time in the city before the admission.

Since I got out in 2003, it has been a permanent fight with my parents about taking the medication. My Dad is dead now, as I keep telling you, but my Mum, still believes the fucking lies my father told her. She is my only source of friction now. She will not admit she was wrong to lock me up! Viva Las Vegas. I AM PROVING EVERYBODY

WRONG!!!!! My brother and my sister are a little easier to talk to about it. I will have a relationship with them eventually.

I got an outpatients appointment for a second opinion on the Bipolar diagnosis, to see one of the most eminent Psychiatrists in Ireland in 2009. He was bloody famous. It was in Dublin. My father was excited when I told him about it. I wasn't too fucking bothered. I'd practically given up all hope of meeting a doctor who would see the truth, that I was telling, at that stage. My father had heard about him. My father was so fucking into the whole bullshit of intelligence being the reason for my diagnosis of Bipolar. He was living a lie. I knew he doubted himself about my diagnosis. I could see it in his eyes when we talked. He would never admit it. He was living off the reflected glory of the intelligence propaganda. Lots of patient's families do it. Big Pharma and doctors play on it. It is one of the biggest myths going that all mental patients are geniuses. If that was true then all the patients would be millionaires. He wanted to meet this famous Doctor. He was getting off on rubbing shoulders with them all!!! Not one thought of my feelings at all. I was devastated by the whole bipolar fiasco. We were in his new house in Carrowtrasna. He was so full of himself in his new surroundings. He had no sympathy for my argument. I was so fucking down trodden and brow beaten by him. My brother did not see any of it. My Dad was a house devil, street angel. He would never do anything to harm his public reputation. He never said anything to me in front of my brother. He asked how I was getting to Dublin for the appointment. I said, I was going by bus. He said, I'll drive you down. I told him no. I didn't want to be near him for any length of time. He was making my skin crawl. At the time, he was loving being in the limelight in the community for mental health issues. There were so many people in the community licking his fucking ass! It was a mind fuck for me. I had faked the Bipolar!!! I had nothing but distraught times because of all the attention he was getting. Everyone that believed him, hated my guts. I was always telling the story of how the diagnosis came about, contrary to him. And my father was undermining me all the fucking time. He had no prior. I was the only criminal in the family. He was loving it. He was a bit of a gangster. I wanted to shy away from that life, although it always intrigued me. Probably the reason I got into Yachting. Lol. Lots of gangsterism in that. I had a fucking brilliant time. I met loads of them. They looked after me. I really appreciated it and I will repay the debt.

But I had to keep my father on side. So, I decided to accept his offer. I thought eventually that we'd patch things up when I got the decision over turned. I thought he would believe, whoever in power, that told him the truth that I wasn't mentally ill.

We drove to Dublin and it was amicable enough but the whole thing was grating on me. The relationship between us was so false.

We arrived at the Doctor's office. My Father waited in the waiting room when I went in for my appointment. I told the old Doctor my story. He listened intently to my entire script. I was so exhausted telling it, at this stage. I didn't hold out any hope of him believing me. It nearly exasperated me telling it. I finished the story and at the end I asked him what did he think? He said "I don't think you're Bipolar either." I was so relieved. I could not wait to tell my father.

I left the doctor's office with a massive feeling of joy. Finally, I thought. Someone with a bit of cop on. My father came down from the waiting room and we went out to the car. We got into the car and the first thing he asked me was "what did he say?" I give it to him without any sugar coating. I said "he doesn't believe I am Bipolar either!" My father got his angry face on him and said in his most evil voice "he is full of shit!!!" I nearly laughed in his face. I thought you fucking stubborn, half-witted old cunt!! Who the fuck is your superior?!! That was the end of it. My father would not believe anyone. That is the end of anyone telling me that I am bipolar. I was told by the most eminent psychiatrist in the country that I wasn't bipolar. So, if you do not believe him, how bloody stupid are you?

My fight continued and the old Psychiatrist's opinion was argued against again in 2020 by another bloody evil excuse for a man. This parasite was a psychologist who preyed on criminals and thought he was a man of the world because he done work in prisons. He wore it like a badge of honour. He even stared me into submission in one of our meetings. Total silence for nearly 10 seconds. I knew the clientele he was used to dealing with were thick as pig shit and I thought to myself when he stared me out "you, useless piece of human excrement. I only spoke to break the silence because you have my doctor's ear and I want out of here". I was in Letterkenny asylum at the time. That psychologist has a neck on him. My God has he got some balls. I'd fucking kill him in the real world for dissent like that. I felt like breaking every bloody bone in his scrawny little grey-haired body. Throwing his weight around like that. How's that for a fucking crim, you, dickwad?!! I asked him when I broke the silence, what the staring match was about? He fucking lied through his teeth like he was talking to some below par intelligence criminal saying "I am not playing games with you. I wasn't staring you out at all!". Lying cunt!!! He quizzed me on my history when he was put in charge of my case. I told him I'd faked Bipolar in 2003 in St. Pats in Dublin and all he did was fucking argue with me about it. He made me feel like I had no fucking way out of anything else but a diagnosis of paranoid schizophrenia. The diagnosis that Doctor Noir had put on me because I complained about the gaslighting I was receiving in Letterkenny. The gaslighting that he wouldn't believe is happening!!! The kids are even at it. Good luck finding a life outside Letterkenny kids. You are doomed to misery. It was another trumped up, bullshit diagnosis. That psychologist was so far up Doctor Noir's fucking arsehole, it was painful to be part of. They are a law onto themselves, just like every asylum on the planet. I am now revealing the truth of all the manipulation that goes on in the asylum of Letterkenny. Sligo and Dublin asylum's too. The psychologist was telling me to just settle for the diagnosis. He was trying to be my friend. Another coercive technique. I've seen them all. I told him about the old eminent psychiatrist who gave me a clean bill of health in 2009. He asked me how long the appraisal was and I said about 5 minutes. It felt very short. And he said that the old psychiatrist was wrong. I asked "how can you argue with him? He's the most eminent psychiatrist in Ireland?!!!" The psychologist replied in the most condescending, arrogant way with "the appraisal was too short!" I thought you fucking cunt. They could not be wrong!!! Dismissing a Doctor like that! This, is the arrogance I have been fighting for 20 long hateful, demoralizing years. I want that eminent psychiatrist to speak for me again only this time I want him to tell the world. I want and I feel I need someone of his capacity to put it to bed once and for all THAT I AM NOT MENTALLY ILL.

My life was torrid after getting out of that asylum after that first admission in 2003. I could hardly string a sentence together because of the medication. It was fucking over-powering. The Dublin Doctor had drugged me up so much, I was comatose. I was on a ton of lithium. All I could do was sit and veg. It wasn't me. All my friends knew it was wrong but they couldn't do anything to help me. I remember this time vividly. My brain was working in a different capacity. It was like I was watching my life in progress but not able to participate. The medication that they are feeding patients is fucking destroying lives all over the planet. If it hadn't been for my fight against everyone, I'd have been in that state and on those drugs for the rest of my life. It was like a chemical lobotomy.

Not long after I got out in 2003, the period became longer between appointments with Doctor Lucky in St. Pats in Dublin. The drug I told you, that I was on, that affected the motor skills in the brain ruining your balance physically speaking inspired me to go steel erecting. I was so determined to beat the pharmaceuticals hold over me that I went steel erecting with my friend's company in Donegal. I did this for a couple of months. I worked up on the heights, fighting that medication for all I was worth. I could not wait to tell the evil arrogant Doctor Lucky in St. Pats, stick that in your pipe and smoke it! He was trying to destroy me. We had become serious adversaries. He and my father had allied up to bring me to my knees. They wanted my confidence obliterated but I would not lie down and curl up in a ball which the Doctor's and the system do to so many people.

A year later, I got the opportunity to go on a tall ship called the Jeanie Johnston. I'd fought with my parents so hard that we came to an agreement. They said that as long as nothing went wrong, they wouldn't break my balls about having to take the medication. I got off the medication!!! I felt so good after a few months off it. Things went really smooth for me. I thought I had my life back and I could put the whole nightmare behind me. That was not to be...

22

FRIGGIN' ON THE RIGGIN' ON THE JEANIE JOHNSTON

So, the following year after my first admission, it was 2004, my father was getting ready to take a ship up the Foyle to Derry. I was sitting in our sitting room, watching television when I saw a Tall ship sailing slowly up the river past our house which faces the River. I guessed my father was taking the boat in. I shouted to him in the other room "what's the name of the boat?", he shouted back, "The Jeanie Johnston."

I had read in the newspaper a couple of days before that the Jeanie Johnston was doing a round Ireland cruise as part of a cross-border initiative teaching young protestant and catholic people from the different divides how to sail. I thought that's pretty interesting! So, I asked my dad was he taking it up? He said yes. I asked him if I could go with him for the run, and he said yes.

We got aboard and the crew there were all young and really good humored. I was standing with my father and the captain, when I took the opportunity to ask the captain if he had any jobs going as a second mate on the boat? He said, he just might do! He said that they were going to Belfast after their trip to Derry, but when they returned to

Derry in a couple of weeks, he would see then. He said, he could almost guarantee there would be.

I went off to make the two of them coffees and meet the crew. When I was in the galley, I bumped into the Chief mate, Jer, who knew a friend of mine from home that went to college in Cork, Ireland, where I studied my navigation. We hit it off immediately, and I told him I'd asked the Captain for a job as a second mate. He was really encouraging and said he hoped I got it! After that, I met the rest of the crew, and they were great craic too...I couldn't wait to get the job with them.

I went home that evening then the next day I was asked by a crab boat captain did I want to do a trip crab fishing? He said they were a man short. So, in the two weeks that I was waiting for the Jeanie Johnston to return, I went crab fishing for ten days on the crabber. I have to say crab fishing is the toughest physical job I have ever done and the most dangerous! The crew were a great laugh, though, and the time went quickly.

I joined the Jeanie Johnston replica famine ship in Derry soon after that, and as it happened, my father was taking it out. There were three pilots, so it was kind of potluck on who the pilot was going to be as they worked on a rotation system. It just happened to be his turn. It did make it all the sweeter for me. As he was disembarking at the mouth of the river Foyle, I was climbing up the rigging and I shouted to him, "look! After all those years of you telling me not to climb. I'm getting paid to do it!" He laughed and waved goodbye to me, then I was off on my adventure.

We went to Killybegs first, after Derry, and had a nice weekend there. I learned as much as I could onboard, on the trip around, it was in a very short time. I did it because I would have to teach the paying passengers who came on how to sail the square-rigger. It was really fun teaching everyone, and I loved climbing the rigging and setting the sails.

I ended up sharing a cabin with a girl called Scruff, and after a long hard day in the first week onboard, we had a little romantic interlude. I asked her to massage my shoulders because I had a pain in them, which she did, then I told her I would massage hers, and that was how it started!! I leaned in and kissed her when I was massaging her shoulders.

She kissed me back and she was immediately turned on. I could see it in her eyes!! I laid her back and pulled her shorts and panties down. We had the cabin to ourselves. I slowly eased my cock inside her. She was a bit nervous. She was only 19, and I being 26, I was a bit more experienced. She told me she hadn't had that many partners. I took it easy with her, slowly penetrating her in and out, kissing her lips, and pushing my cock deep inside her. She still had her t-shirt on. I thought she was a little embarrassed of her body. She was carrying a little weight. I did not care. After a few seconds, I thought I would spice things up a little. I pulled out my cock. Her pussy was dripping wet. I lay beside her, cock erect, and asked her to suck my cock. She did not want to. I asked, her why not? I said to her that I feel it's a very important part of the sexual experience. Oral from both partners. I had the girlfriend I spoke about earlier a few years later, Fanjita, who wanted me to lick her out so she could orgasm every night. She said I orgasmed, so why couldn't she? I couldn't argue with that reasoning because I knew where it would lead if I said no, no sex for a while until the argument had calmed down. It had happened before! Licking her out became a bit of a chore unless we did a 69er which was good, she was great at sucking my cock while I fingered her and licked her clitoris, but she normally wanted cunnilingus on its own, so she could concentrate. She pointed to all her erogenous zones for me to kiss on the way down to her pussy, starting with her face lips, then I was to kiss her breasts on certain points slowly licking and sucking each nipple, then kiss and lick her naval, caress and kiss the inside her of her thighs with my tongue then finally licking her pussy lips and parting them with my fingers and finding her clitoris with my tongue. Then she wanted me to run my tongue over and back her clitoris until she came. She said flicking the clitoris over and back instead of up and down sent little shocks up her body making her orgasm quicker. I had it down to a few minutes by the time we finished two years later. I was fed up doing it every night but how I managed to persevere was the thought that "this is great training for every other girl I would ever be with" I knew I wouldn't stay with her. It was the most toxic relationship I have ever been in. The shagging was the only thing going for it. She wanted sex three times a day for two years, so did I. She was a hornball but a terrible person the more I experienced of her. She was psychotic, the dangerous one's always are the best sex. The pussy eating method works. I've tested the routine on many women, and I always get them off! After two years at the front line, I'm an expert.

Scruff told me she had never given a blowjob before. She was nervous. The light was on and I was watching her intently. I told her not to worry I'd show her how I liked it. She sat up on the bed and looked rather hesitant and shy as she was about to put her lips around my cock. It was a real turn-on. It felt virginal! I lay back on the bunk. She pulled her hair back from her face and proceeded to lick the tip of my cock. She smiled nervously up at me. I could tell she was feeling good in herself. A bit of excitement! She put my whole member inside her mouth. It went in deep. I could feel the juices in her mouth fill and swirl around my cock. She wasn't long picking it up. I showed her how to wank me off as she sucked. It felt really good. Another one of my fantasies was fulfilled. To have sex with a girl on a ship while I was working! It was a wet dream of mine as a cadet with Fishers. I used to pray when I was doing my training, that the company would send me on a ship with a female cadet so I could shag her!!! There were a lot of lonely nights around then but the ships had a lot of porn! There were a few female cadets in our company and I'd heard sex stories from my other sailor mates about them. I'd heard other tales about sex with female cadets in other companies as well from close mates. It made me so horny!! I loved being at sea! Shagtastic!!

I exploded in Scruff's mouth after a minute, I was so turned on. She wasn't expecting it and gagged. I told her to swallow, but she wasn't ready for that! She ran out the cabin door and into the head (toilet on a ship) and threw up. I could hear her getting sick. It kind of spoiled the moment, I have to say!!! LOL. She was very embarrassed when she came back. That has happened to a couple of women in my time, and they've always been embarrassed, just swallow! If the dove is the bird of peace! What is the bird of love?.....The swallow!!!

I had a Lithuanian girlfriend, Erika, who preferred sucking my cock to having sex. She enjoyed the sex too but she loved drinking my juices! She was very attractive and had a great body on her. She had massive boobs as well. I often thought women should have a boob at the back for dancing! The space between a woman's tits and her pussy is called a waist because there is room for at least another pair of boobs there lol. I'm all for the woman's movement…I hate when they just lie there!!! I think she was a hooker in the old country. She was so fucking awesome at giving blowjobs. I used to think her love for my cum was the reason she was so good at giving them but she was a hooker for sure. I found out in later years that this is true. She wasn't getting ready to spit it out into a cup beside the bed or run to the toilet to spit it out! She drank it down with lust in her eyes….Grrrr!!! What a sexy fucking bitch! I didn't feel guilty asking for one because she enjoyed pleasuring me so much. She also knew I'd return the favour. Spitting is ok, but ladies learn to swallow. It's a sign of maturity and will improve your sex life. I read recently too, it's good for the womb when it comes to conceiving, so there is medical data to support my advice on swallowing! You need continuity when making love —no stops and starts. Everything goes is my motto. That way, you become enthralled in each other. Throw away your inhibitions, live out your fantasies. For example, I always ask a new girlfriend if she is up for a threesome with another woman. You'd be shocked to learn that nearly all the girlfriends I have been with, would! And not only that, they have had fantasies about other women. Threesomes are divine!

Spitting the cum out always makes me think of the joke, 'What is the difference between love, true love, and a show-off?' "Spits, swallows, and gargles!" Erika and I got on great, and her blowjob technique has never ever been surpassed. That includes the 30 or so hookers from all over the world that I've been with in my life and they have sucked SOME cock!!! Erika sucked and wanked my cock in tandem, and it was like intuition when I was going to cum. She made the experience exhilarating! She would swallow every single drop, sucking my penis until I got the shivers up my spine at the end. It was brilliant! I have never forgotten her. It means a lot to us men for a woman to swallow, after all, it's like drinking your cunny juice. We don't mind! Quid pro quo! Scruff and I snuggled after that. I told her not to be embarrassed for getting sick. It was her first time giving a blowjob. I told her she'd done well and she'd get used to it!

One problem did arise after the first week there. If only I had just stuck to having lots of sex with Scruff instead. It was the alcohol!!! I also thought if only I had stuck to my theory of having lots of sex partners and shagged all the passengers instead of drinking, I would have come out on top!!! I firmly believe that you can have one partner or multiple partners, who cares? Lots of sex is safer than alcohol any day for me and much more fun! I could have had Scruff on a steep sexy learning curve all day long and left the beer alone! I could have ended up Captain on there too. Some of the higher powers there involved in management had told me so. They said, keep your nose clean, you've been earmarked to be Captain here, such was my positive impact on the crew and guests BUT I drank! I was really good at my job and interacting with guests, but my drinking let me down!

I've worked on Superyachts since 2007 as you will read and I got sacked a load of times. 10 different sackings from yachts in total. Nearly all the sackings were alcohol-related. I've learned my lesson! I plan to own a Superyacht. It's a great quality of life. There's a lovely social side to it, and I love all the women that work there. All really dead on. I also believe that yachting crews should not be allowed to let their romantic impulses go to waste, a little bit of flirting makes the world go around. I don't agree with putting a restriction on crew getting frisky with each other. The restriction affects their work. I think it can be dealt with like adults. A lot of crew, meet their life partners at work. I should have gone into yachting at 22 when I qualified. I'd have been a Captain of a yacht by now and married to a stunner. I recommend Superyachts to any young sailors, male or female. The Merchant Navy is great as well.

Anyway, back to the Jeanie Johnston Tallship. I started sleeping in, and the work and drink weren't mixing.

I never thought once about what my father had said about what happens if things go wrong. If I hadn't drank, there would never have been a second admission. The Captain who gave me the job told me that I had better watch myself. He said the new chief mate was out for my blood!! I thanked him. So, in Galway the eventuality happened, I more or less got sacked, the new chief mate, Plodfoot (The Bosun named him that because his daddy was a garda), gave me an ultimatum after we all slept in. He'd said before he sacked me "NO more sleeping in!" Then I did! He cornered me in the Bosun's locker on the bow and said I could either stay with no pay or leave now, so I thought, well, I love this job too much to leave, so I'll stay with no pay, plus I thought to myself, he couldn't tell me what to do anymore as I wasn't paid as crew. I carried on as normal. One day while we were in Galway, a Galway journalist was on board. I thought, for the craic, I'll get her a free trip on board. So, I orchestrated for the journalist who was called Kirsten, to get on a trip for free. Each trip was 300 euros. Even though Dick, the other second mate was trying it on with her. It didn't work! He was 25 and in the year behind me in Cork, so we didn't know one another until we sailed with each other. But we were competing with each other. I'm not sure he liked me that much, after all, all the women fancied me!!! We did have some good craic onboard. We used to check the new manifest before the passengers would arrive to see what ages the chicks were. Then fight over them when they got there! It was great craic! One solicitor I kissed was really pretty. I'd scoped her out before she arrived then charmed the knickers off her!! Although when I won them, he didn't always take it too well. He tried his best to vie for Kirsten's attention this time and failed. He was definitely the jealous sort. We were both trying to get our names in the paper for the craic. How I got her on board was I told her to go and say to our PR manager, who was onboard at the time, talking to other guests, that if he gave her a free trip, she would write a glowing article about it. She was a bit shy about it, but I told her exactly what to say. I knew him and I knew it would work!

She asked him, and he agreed. She was really happy with me for pushing her. We also had a little thing going on, but once again, Dick, was sniffing about too. Kirsten and I hit it off and had a brief affair a few months later (with no touching!!!) when I went down to stay with her in Galway. I think she was in the marrying mood and was taking it slow! I wasn't ready for marriage. I never want to get married. It is out of date. Men and women should have multiple partners throughout their lives. Children can stay with their mother. It is in the stars!!! The aliens have decreed it. I do not believe in any religion! They have dictated for too long on this planet. GOD does not exist!

During Kirsten's few days trip with us, she really enjoyed herself and even mentioned Dick and I in the article. We got a good buzz out of that. Dick and I were even competing over who got the biggest shout-out in the article when it was published!

We left Galway and soon arrived in Fenit, County Kerry. There was a bit of Hollywood waiting for us there. The movie actress Maureen O'Hara came on board, the day after we arrived. She was in her 80's but really elegant and still a looker for her age, I would! I got talking to one of her nieces, Ellen, who was really sound. We were resting in the stern of the boat, talking, while some of the other crew were showing Maureen and her entourage around. Ellen asked me what age had I started working at sea? So, I told her my first time working at sea was Salmon fishing on the River Foyle in Donegal. I told her it was a baptism of fire, and I was 13 at the time. I said that a lot of the young boys where I lived went through it during the summer when the salmon season was on.

She asked me the age-old question that every sailor gets from a girl. Do you ever get sea sick?" Which isn't tiresome if you have the right answer. I used one from my friend John from home who is in the Air sea rescue. He said "if you're sea sick, eat oranges. It's the only thing that tastes the same coming up as it does going down!" She laughed at that.

I told her no, I didn't get sea sick but I had a funny story of a friend of mine, Paddy, my mate, was getting sea-sick on his first day on my uncle Jimmy's (from W.A.B.C fame) half-decker. Trickey, my other friend, and I were laughing at Paddy, when some of the sick that was going over the side blew up and hit Trickey in the face and went into his mouth as he laughed! He then wretched over the side immediately, leaving me in stitches! It's was really funny, I told her, both of them getting sick and Uncle Jimmy giving out. She laughed at this and said, "C'mon, you really have to meet aunt Maureen!!" She took me by the hand to meet her aunt. Maureen was halfway up the deck with some of our crew and the entourage as Ellen held my hand and shouted up the deck to her saying, "Aunt Maureen, this is Juan O'Donnell and he's from Donegal.". Maureen stopped in her tracks, looked down the boat from 20 feet away, and said to me loudly, "oh you Donegal lads, are all so very handsome, aren't you's??!" to which in my head I was thinking of saying, "the hell I am!!!" like John Wayne used to say in the movies, the actor she is famous for acting with in the 'Quiet man' but I didn't, - much to my regret. I think she would have found it funny! I said "thank you!!" Ellen and I parted company, but I could tell I could've shagged her. I was like a pussy magnet on that boat. It was the most sexually satisfying three weeks of my sea-going career! One of the reasons I went to sea was to get laid until my knob fell off! Ha! I used to read the dictionary when I was younger. I read it all the time. And while I was a cadet, I came across the word 'Licentious'. I thought it described me to a 'T'! It means 'promiscuous and unprincipled in sexual matter's'. Licentious to thrill! I laughed and thought, I'm a licentious kinda guy!!!

A word of note, Sailors make the best partners for loving. We shag our way around the world on a very sexual learning curve. We are experts in bed! And even as you land dwellers imagine our lives to be, you cannot imagine how free we feel to be out on the open ocean. We have very wild tales when we come back to land lubber life. We are the aliens of the human race. We are very different from you land dwellers. Land dwellers tend to exaggerate their stories. We have no need!! So, learn a lesson from our ancestors of the sea, do not exaggerate when you are recounting a tale. It will be found out and you will be a laughing stock.

We took new passengers on in Fenit and I was getting along really well with them even though I'd been unofficially sacked.

The new Captain joined in Fenit as well. I did not take to him. We were a few days at sea with the new passengers but by the time I got to Dingle, I'd had enough of the new Captain and the new Chief mate. They both seemed arrogant to me. I'd lost the buzz and I wanted off. After a couple of days in Dingle I told the Captain I wanted off. He said to me "why not take a couple of weeks off and come back to us?" I told him no. I said I wanted my discharge book back, and I wanted off there and then. The story got twisted by the time my father found out. He'd heard I got the sack off the boat, not that I'd walked off and immediately thought I'd gone high (elated with Bipolar) again. The Captain and Chief mate were trying to save face. I was fucking popular as fuck!!! Doctor Lucky had told him these highs normally happen in the summer, so my Dad was primed and ready. He told my father that bipolar people had no insight into when they were sick. He said once they get a sniff of the high, they go crazy and don't to come back down again. They need medicated. It is so fucking imbecilic. It was the biggest horseshit ever.

So, before all that happened, there was more fun to be had in Dingle. Read on! I couldn't wait! I'd heard loads of stories over the years about the craic there. I was really excited and loving the crew and the job to bits even though I knew it was nearly at an end.

23

WALKING ON CARS

We arrived in Dingle after that. We tied up and set up the museum inside the accommodation for the paying public the next day. The next day as I was mingling with the visitors, I spotted onboard was the most beautiful girl I thought I had ever seen in real life. She was absolutely stunning! Sallow skin and black hair. Mediterranean looking. As I looked, Dick, the other Second mate, caught my attention! He'd spotted her too, and he was the same distance away from her as me, 15 feet or so. I raced across the deck to her. He had been talking to some members of the public, and it slowed him down. By the time he got to her, I'd made my introduction. I put my hand out to her and welcomed her onboard just as he got to her. He tried to butt in, introducing himself, but I asked her where she was from and when she said Spain, I was thrilled, I put my Junior certificate Spanish to work. It was the reason I'd learned it so well in the first place – for the chicks! Dick was livid. I turned to him and winked an imperceptible gratifying smirk without her seeing. I asked her about herself, got her phone number and a date that night, all in Espanol. I wasn't fluent but she was really enjoying my attempts at it. Fair play to Dick when I turned on my Spanish charm, he walked off and left me to it. I think he knew he'd been beaten! He didn't cock block me even though I'd been getting all the tail since I'd come onboard and it was really putting his nose out of joint! Lesbian sex can get ugly too. I've heard the cock block equivalent for a lesbian is called a beaver dam!

Scruff had told me it was Dick's job to romance all the ladies before I arrived. It was really fucking him off. She wasn't jealous at all of my insatiable appetite for the fairer sex, which was lucky because I didn't give a fuck! Good healthy competition was what Dick needed, and I was giving it to him! Ha! The Mediterranean looking girl was called Nuria. She told me she was in Kerry for the summer. She was teaching horse riding to kids in a town close by called Ventry, and from what I gathered later, she was lusted after by every hot-blooded man in town. I arranged to meet her that night at the one and only nightclub. Dick had to concede I'd done well. Five o' clock came, and I said to Scruff I was going for a pint before dinner, so I went up to a pub in town.... really cool pub. I wasn't too fussed in having a relationship with Scruff onboard, and it wasn't that I didn't give a fuck. I was just having too much fun being single. It would've closed down all my options, and at that time, I felt like studley! I was a kid in a sweetie store with all the cute female passengers.

I shagged one of them and was caught by the Plodfoot, in the morning in one of the other crew bunks much to his disgust. It happened on the first night there. He didn't know what to do! He pulled back the curtain to the bunk in the morning, not expecting to see me. I was lying naked on top of my Chemical engineer passenger chick, Niamh, really sexy girl, smart too. She fought for my attention with Kirsten, the journalist, the night before. Niamh won; she was way saucier. It's all in the eyes, and hers were saying I'm going to ravish you. That she did, all night long. And as he pulled back the curtain, I was just penetrating her with my cock, sliding it in slowly for maximum pleasure, licking her nipples as I did, Plodfoot looked like he could have killed me. I was watching the smile of pleasure on her face and saying good morning to her, kissing her lips when he interrupted me, hollering, 'ARE YOU UP??!!" I pumped my lady friend with my cock, she gasped, and I turned my face to him and said to him with a smile – "I am now!!!" He yanked the curtain closed again with a face like thunder. It was totally against the rules, but I was no longer employed by him, so he couldn't say a damn thing! I laughed my heart out, so did she. Then she said, "you're bad!" She also asked would I get into trouble, but I told her I'd been sacked, and he no longer had any jurisdiction over me. I was loving it, taking full advantage of the situation. She went down on me. I was so fucking horny. She sucked my balls and drank my cum and I got up like a God! I was a nightmare for Officers I didn't get along with. I got loads of snogs off lady passengers over the three weeks and a good few of their phone numbers. One lady said when I gave her one of my t-shirts in my cabin "Is this genuine Juan smell??!!!" I laughed and said "yeah!" She was delighted and sniffed it deep. I knew she wanted to shag there and then but we only had minutes in my cabin. It was all very quick. We had a quick snog and that was it. I told her I would visit when I was off on leave. She said her mum fancied me too. I laughed and said I'd see what I could manage! They all wanted me to visit them when I was off. No wonder I was on a high, so would my Dad have been if it had been him!

With my date with Nuria very much to the forefront of my mind, I ventured into Dingle on my own to celebrate a little and meet the locals before dinner. After all, I was a celebrity. So why not take full advantage of my newfound fame! Hehe! I had planned on coming back to the boat to get ready for my hot date that night, but the damned thirst took over! The old shoe shop for a pub that had been recommended to me was a lot of craic! I had a few pints and got talking to some of the locals, and then as the night wore on, we started singing and telling jokes and having a great laugh. It was about 11 pm, and I went outside for a cigarette. I was talking to two of the local guys who were smoking and drinking outside too when one of them asked me to sing them a song. He'd listened to me inside and was enjoying them. I was like, "naw... .naw" and they were like, "go on, go on," so I was like "yeah, alright," so I started to sing out in the middle of the small side street outside the pub. There was a little church on the other side of the street, across from the pub, but the street was quiet.

As I was singing, a car came down the street and started sounding its horn really aggressively...I thought, Jesus, no need for all the pomping.... I'll move. Then a flash of brilliance came into my head, or so I thought at the time (very sorry about this!) I'll do a Hollywood style...I'll run up the car and down the other side. It'll be a bit of craic – showing off to the lads! So, as the car came down the street still pomping, I ran up and onto the bonnet, but as I went to jump onto the roof, my foot slipped on the bonnet, and my knee went into the windscreen, cracking it. The driver stopped the car and jumped out, but instead of some ignorant man as I thought it must be, it was an angry woman instead!!

She began calling for the guards, but I pleaded with her, while still standing up on the bonnet, looking down at her, "please don't call the guards. I'm bound over to the peace!!!" I said. She said, "I don't care!!" "Call the guards!!" I was bound over to the peace from the breaking the window in the hotel incident the year before. She was shouting. I said, "I'll pay for the damage; I have the money, just please don't call the guards!!" The two lads that were there had started laughing and shouted, "run JUAN!! RUN!!!" I jumped off the bonnet and ran down the street and around the corner and into the first pub I saw on the left. I calmed my breathing down and went up to the bar ordering a Carlsberg. Not wanting to draw attention! I got the pint and calming down, having half the pint drunk, a few minutes passed, I thought I wouldn't mind a cigarette, so I went outside. I lit a cigarette and as I was standing there, a Garda car pulled up with the front passenger window down. It was such good timing lol. The guard in the passenger seat said annoyedly, "get into the back of that car!" and I said, "what for??! What did I do??" At that, he stepped out, opened the back door, and said, "how many other fuckers d'ye think are going around this town tonight with a Donegal top and cutoff jeans on?? Eh??" I had to concede on that one, so in I got.

I told them the run over the car was an accident, and I tried a bit of humour which they responded to quite well. I told them I was off the Jeanie Johnston, and it went a long way with them. They were taking it easy on me. When we got to the Garda station, they didn't even put me in a cell. We just sat in their open office and talked. They asked me about myself, and I told them the story about the windscreen again and the reason I done it. I tried turning on the old charm too, telling them that I was a famous singer from Donegal's third cousin, Daniel O'Donnell, and that I didn't care if they thought he was gay or what they thought of him. After all, he did a lot for charity, helping the poor in Romania! They said "no, no, no, we don't think that at all about him, we really like him!" It worked a charm!!!

I met Daniel O'Donnell a couple of years back while unjustly incarcerated in Letterkenny Mental Asylum again, here in Donegal and told him the story. He laughed and said, "Did ye get off?" I said I did. "Good man!" He said, laughing as he was walking away.

I shouted after him could I put him in my book and he shouted back, "NO BOTHER!!!"

The guards believed me. So, I said to them, well you know, the boat I'm working on is very high profile, and it would look really bad for the boat if I got arrested...I was trying every angle I could think of. The aliens were giving me inspiration. They have told me that now... The guard said then, after keeping me for half an hour or so, "if we let you go now, will you go straight back to the boat?" I replied, "yes, of course!" "And you'll pay for the window and apologize again?" I said, "definitely!" so they let me go. But I had other plans. I knew that I would have to walk past the only night club there and I had the hot date with Nuria that night. I left the Garda station and walked down the street. When I got as far as the night club, I went to walk in, but an elderly bouncer, late 60's I figured, stopped me. He was very ignorant about it, too, I felt. "You're not getting in!" he said. "Why not?!" I asked, shocked. I could see my dreams of bedding Nuria fade away in front of my very eyes! He said, "You are not getting in dressed like that!" I pleaded with him in a friendly way, saying I just had to meet a gorgeous woman and I would bring her straight back out! But he wasn't entertaining me at all. He was an arse!

I said one of the bouncers could come with me, but he'd dug his heels in, and he wouldn't budge! There was a massive queue outside the door, and they were all watching. I tried her on the phone, and after ringing out a few times, she answered. I told her I was outside. She said she would come out and meet me. A few seconds later, the entrance door to the nightclub opened, and to me, it was like a scene from a movie, this stunning girl with her long dark hair blowing back in the wind as she walked out the door towards me. She came straight up to me, into my arms, and kissed me on the lips! Maybe some people may say what I was about to do was uncalled for, but I turned around to the auld bouncer and said, "it must be terrible to be old!!!!" I know I'll be old too someday but fuck him!!!

I asked Nuria to come back and see my boat, and she said she would love to, but the friend she had with her was not liking the idea. She had come out the door too, much to my dismay! I don't know what her problem was. Jealous, I presumed by the nasty look in her eyes. We walked down the street. Nuria, her third wheel friend, and myself. We stopped and I got a burger. I was starving but her friend was not liking me at all, and I could see she was trying to get her hooks into Nuria and take her home. I could feel a change in Nuria towards me when I got back from buying the burger. She was all over me beforehand, then whatever the tinker girl had said to her when I left them alone had cooled her. Lesson learned! If I was in this situation again....starve!

We walked on down the street until we got to the bridge at the corner, we were holding hands, but her friend was a hanging out of her ass. There were dozens of people who'd been in the few bars standing there chatting, and more were pouring out onto the street. It was Nuria's turn off to go home. I was straight ahead down to the docks. As I tried every persuasive technique, I could muster to get her to come back to the boat alone, two young lads worse the wear with the drink, came up to us and started serenading Nuria with compliments. They told her she was the most gorgeous girl in Dingle. They asked me was I with her. When I said I was, laughing at their performance (They really turned it on for her), they shook my hand, telling me I was the luckiest man in Ireland. They took notice of my Donegal top then and took the piss a bit saying, I'd come all the way down from Donegal to steal the nicest girl in town. They were a bit of craic! When they left, I tried convincing Nuria to come back and spend the night on the boat with me. If she had been alone it was a cert, but her friend was causing major ructions, and I couldn't get rid of her!

As we stood there talking, the Garda car pulled up. They stopped in the middle of the street, in front of everyone and signalled to me, to come over to them. Nuria asked me, what was it about? I shrugged, telling her I didn't know. But I'd be back in a minute, I told her. I went over. I saw it was the same guard who had picked me up earlier. He said, "I thought I told you to go straight back to the boat! And I said, "I know but look at that!!!" I said, pointing at Nuria. "How could I not go and meet her?!!" I asked him. I told him I had the pleasure of a date with her that night!! I said, "c'mon, cut me some slack!!" He said, "right then," then pointed his thumb into the back and said, "tell that man in there a joke." I looked over his shoulder into the back and saw what looked to me like the Commodore of the Gardai with all his medals and stripes. He was looking at me with a bit of craic in his eyes, but I knew I needed to impress him, if I did, I was on a winner, so I told old faithful, I said "what do female pubic hair and Brussel sprouts have in common??" And he says "what?" I said, "you just brush'em aside and keep on eating!!!" They all started laughing and said, "go on, get out of here!!" When I went back, things had definitely chilled with Nuria... her friend had got her hooks in good and deep! She had changed her mind about coming back to the boat. No matter how hard I tried, there was no taking her back. So that was it! I went home alone!! Nuria was GORGEOUS!!! I LOVE SPAIN!!!

The next morning, we were having a Mass said on the boat. The top of one of the superstructures storage boxes was turned into an altar. During the Mass, which was being said to about three hundred people or more, including an Irish rugby player and a TD, we were told, so I had a good audience, I thought, I came up with a plan for a bit of a joke. I thought at the time that it was good enough to be taken seriously too. All of us, the whole crew, were in uniform and standing in a line relative according to rank facing the dock. I walked up the seaward side of the boat to the wheelhouse and went inside. I quickly but very neatly wrote out a poem that I had written about seeing a pilot whale on the journey there. I had regaled the passengers with it, and it had gone down really well. Now for a grander audience, I thought. I folded it up neatly and went back outside. I reached up to the top of the superstructure where the two priests were standing and tapped one of the two priests on the ankle, the one who wasn't saying the mass, and handed him the poem. I went back to my position. I could feel the Captain's eyes burning into me as I walked past him and stood in my place again. I didn't look at him. The other crew were quietly asking what I had done, but I told them to wait. Everyone was stifling their laughs.

As the mass came to an end, the priest opened the piece of paper handed to him by the other priest, then began with what I'd exactly written on the piece of paper....He started with "and now a poem... by Juan O'Donnell...the bosun's mate(I was actually 2nd Officer, just standing in) of the Jeanie Johnston..." the crew giggled out loud this time. The Captain was furious from the expression on his face. However, people clapped at the end of it, and I was quite pleased.

As soon as the Mass was over, the dignitaries came down the gangway and on board, so, the Captain didn't have the chance to chastise me. They were shaking all our hands and covering my ass when it came to the rugby player, and in front of the Captain, I asked him what he thought of my poem, and he said, "I really liked it, it was really good!" That was enough for me and obviously the Captain, too, because he never said a word.

The next day I decided I wanted to leave. I'd really had enough of the Captain, although I had let by-gone's be by-gone's with Plodfoot after the initial sacking had calmed down. His wife, who had come on board, was really nice. It softened me up. I more or less threw in the towel, and I went to a supermarket and got a bottle of Buckfast. Then I went to sit by the water's edge and had a drink.

I had told Dave the Bosun I wanted off, and they were in contact with my father. Everyone thought I had gone off the rails, but I just needed some head space. I was of the same mind I am now! Dave the Bosun and his Swedish girlfriend, Freda, were leaving to go off on some leave so I went with them. The idea was that I would meet my father when they left me to Dublin but not before we went to the South Pole bar in Annascaul once owned by one of my heroes Tom Crean, the famous Irish adventurer from there, who became one of my heroes after I read his book. I was in the pub and spying their T-shirts, I asked the barman if I wrote them a poem about Tom Crean, would he give a T-shirt? He yeah one of the normal ones. I said I want a polo necked one and he said they are only for staff. I gave him the poem anyway. I can't really remember the poem now but I said quoting an old bosun from Fishers "Tom Crean was hard as nails on the outside, but on the inside, he was one big spike". That made them laugh. Another one the same old bosun told me when I was going ashore as a cadet. He said "If it smells like fish, that's the dish. If it smells like cologne, leave it alone." He was a character.

We stayed in the house of a friend of Dave and Freda's in Macroom in Cork after that for the night, having a lovely meal and some wine. The next morning, I woke up before anyone else. And gasping for a cigarette and, after a search in the house, came up empty-handed, I decided to go into town for some. I walked outside to a beautiful morning and I did not know which way to go to town. I walked to the gate and thought left or right and thought I'd just go right. It looked like the best option. I was walking along when I noticed the road swept from where I was standing, around to the right in a large semi-circle then back to straight ahead again so I thought to myself, being from the country and used to walking through fields with animals in it, I'd take a short-cut and walk as the crow flies. I was still a bit tipsy!!! I climbed over the fence and began walking towards the other side of the field, cutting out the loop. As I did, the cows in the field followed me. I noticed glancing over to a house on my right that the curtains were twitching and that the people inside were watching me. I thought to myself, I'll have a bit of craic here. I stood still in the middle of the field and let the cows surround me in a semi-circle like a farmer would if he was feeding them. Then figuring the people were watching, I started to bless the cows! Making the sign of the cross with my right hand and wearing a solemn expression on my face, like a priest would do saying Mass.

The curtain twitcher's were about 30 yards away, so I knew they had a clear view of me. After a few seconds, the cows became a bit aggressive. They started jumping on top of one another. It started to get dangerous, and I thought I was going to get trampled. I started to run for what looked like a deep drain or ditch that had been dug in the field with all the cows running after me. And knowing it was too big for them to follow, I jumped over quickly. One of them actually tried jumping it when I jumped! Luckily it didn't break anything. I climbed out of the field, and a Garda car pulled up with only a Ban Garda behind the wheel. She asked me would I mind getting in? I said "what for?" She said "strange behaviour" in her lovely Cork lilt...I said, "that's hardly a charge!" I told her for the craic, I'd get in if she put the cuffs on me and roughed me up a little!! She laughed and pushed me over in the back seat. She was a little flirt! The guards in the station were good craic as well! It was all very relaxed. They left the cell door open and got me a chicken dinner with spuds and gravy while they were waiting to let me go. I had no phone or number for Dave and Freda. I was there a couple of hours when a switched-on Dave turned up. I asked him how he knew where I was. He said, laughing that if he was looking for me, he thought the Garda station would be the first place he'd look!!

We left there and went to Dublin and met my father at an agreed location. I was feeling fine now as I remember back. I was ready for home, but as I stepped into the car, my father said, "You know where you're going now?!" In hindsight, I should have argued that there was no need for another admission. I'd just gotten drunk. I was fine! He was such a dictator. He had been told lies about my behavior on board the vessel and had acted accordingly. It was a joke! The Doctors had disillusioned him. I was not fucking elated. There is NO SUCH THING!!! It is bullshit. If I wasn't so hell-bent on changing the system in the asylum from the inside out, the one-man crusade I was on, all because of what Flo had told me, I would've put up a fight. I really didn't want to go back to St. Pats Mental Asylum again. I'd had enough the first time but I had no money or job now, so I was at his mercy. I also thought of the pros and cons of going in again. I knew I'd have more craic and meet new women. So, I thought to myself, it'll be another little adventure. Fuck it! I thought and didn't argue.

24

2ND ADMISSION – ST. PATS 2 – THE SEROQUEL

When I went in the second time, I was greeted by Paula again, the lovely nurse who was the head nurse in there whom I knew from before in the ICU. My father said when we went in, "look who I have for you!!!" and she jokingly threw her eyes up in the air and said "Aw no!!! Not again!" I laughed. My father was enjoying the comradery with the staff. He enjoyed being in charge of my life again. It was SO fucking demoralizing. I do not wish it on anybody. All patients go through something similar. I thought I would play along with them and not complain. I had nobody in the entire world to help me. It was so fucking scary but I knew it would come to an end eventually. The aliens have told me I had so much resilience. They were always with me. They put ideas in my head for the fun I had when I was in there.

My father left me in Paula's hands, and as I knew my way about, I went to the smoke room. I still had my shades on that I'd been wearing on the Jeanie Johnston, so I was looking very summery as I smoked. There was one other guy in there. I'll call him Harold. He was sitting with his feet up across the chairs. I introduced myself, but he didn't speak, so I left well enough alone. Then after 5 minutes of smoking in

212

silence, he turned to me and said, "What's been going on in the last 20 years?!!" I asked him, "why?" He told me that he'd been in a very bad car crash with his wife and two kids, and they had died in the crash. He said he had no memory since. I felt gutted for the guy, so I told him a few things then I came up with a solution. I told him I would help him out by getting a history book from my mum, and he could read what's been going on. So that's what I did. I asked to make a phone call later and got my mum to bring in the book. He was very solitary, so I didn't speak much to him. Then when my mother brought the book in the next day, I gave it to him, and he said, "what's this for?" We were in the smoke room again, and we were the only two in it. I told him that the day before he'd asked me about the history of the last 20 years and my mother had brought a book in as a present for him. It turned out he had schizophrenia, and he was only joking. I couldn't believe it. He was so convincing. It turned out he played these games all the time with people, and I wondered did he have Schizophrenia at all or did they have it all wrong!! He was just a piss taker and played on the diagnosis?!!

Or does Schizophrenia even exist?!!! Now, in the year 2023, the aliens have told me that there is no Schizophrenia. It is just the spirit world communicating with the living world. I am able to talk with the dead. They try all the time to communicate with me but the aliens stop them and tell them to get bent!! You don't need medication, narcotics or alcohol for this to relieve these symptoms. It is all made up. The drugs are useless. They are just sedatory. They do not relieve any anxiety. They just leave you tired and wanting to lie down. That is the whole idea behind them. Then you eat and get fat. That causes depression. There are millions of earthlings with the gift of speaking to the dead. Psychiatry is fucking ludicrous. They put you on medication for hearing voices. They then tell you just to ignore the voices. The medication does absolutely nothing to abate them. All you have to do to stop the voices of the dead is tell them in your head to FUCK RIGHT OFF!!! Do not say it out loud. Say it in to yourself. You will feel them leaving you and if you are as evolved as Juan, you will see them leaving as well. We are talking through Juan. He has us in his head 24/7. So, don't think it strange when we refer to him.

Another thing that bothers me, the psychiatrists try to prevent the use of narcotics as a relaxant. I believe all narcotics should be used and legal. The aliens are going to make this a reality in a couple of years time. Drugs will be legal in every country on the planet. It will solve all the problems of a lot of crime. And it won't be a stage by stage process. They will be legalized in a matter of days. The reason they won't do it in a matter of days at the moment is because it will put law providing people out of work! There is a world evolution coming. We will teach kids the dangers of overindulgence in narcotics from a young age but teach them how to use drugs too and if they decide to do it, then we will let them use. They are going to do it anyway!

Harold, as it turns out, was really good craic when I got to know him and very intelligent. He really opened up to me, and so much so that his parents were asking me about him when he wasn't around. They were obviously worried, and he didn't talk to anyone else. He never spoke to his parents. He told me that. He was playing games with them. I saw lots of kids do this with their parents. He was really well-read and a lot of fun but a definite fucking game player. He played the cool cat all the time, and as it turned out, he was only 23 just three years younger than me, and I believed he had a wife and kids. I thought he looked a bit young for that!

One evening, Harold and I, were sitting in the hallway resting area which consisted of a recess in the corridor with 3 tables in a line at the patio windows that led out to the small garden and 4 chairs at each table. The patio doors were all locked in the evening and only open when they decided it was playtime!

While we were sitting there, I asked Harold if he wanted to have a bit of craic? He said, "aye, why not?" "What do you have in mind?" I told him to watch this.... I went up to the nurse's station just a little way up the hallway and stood at the desk. The night staff had been on for a couple of hours, so it was late and dark. The corridor had been darkened down for the evening. When the nurses came out of their room from whatever they were doing to find out what I wanted, I asked for a cup of tea. The male nurse said, "no, you're not getting any tea at this time of night." "You're going to bed soon" he said. I went back to my seat with Harold, and he said, "what are you doing? You know they won't give you tea at this time!" "Watch and see!" I said. Thirty seconds later, I went up again and asked for a cup of tea again. I got the same response, but this time, I argued saying, "why can't I have a cup of tea? It's only a bloody cup of tea...!" The nurse said, "no!" So, I went back to my seat and waited a minute this time. Harold could see what I was at...I was winding them up!

I had caught the same two male nurses, one of them was even from Donegal, a couple of nights before, breaking the sleeping tablet Dolmen into my largactyl liquid medication because I had refused to take the sleeping tablet. I tried to get them done for malpractice. I wrote a letter, putting it through the proper channels to the head of the hospital, the Unipolar asshole!!! I never found out what happened. They say there's law there, but there's none.

I went up for the last time and asked for my tea again. This time they got angry and said strongly, "no, you're not getting a cup of tea. You're going to bed soon, I told you!!" I started throwing a pretend tantrum! I ran down to where Harold was sitting and jumped up on top of the table. I started running from one table to the other screaming, "I WANT A CUP OF TEA! WHAT'S WRONG WITH A FUCKING CUP OF TEA?!!! The nurses and doctors came out of the woodwork. There must have been about eight staff in total standing there watching with trepidation. Not all were worried, though. The female nurses who were good craic and knew me had smiles on their faces. I saw one of the nurses smirking as I jumped down about 5 feet back from their line. She could see by the smile and the glint in my eye showing I was only carrying on. They were the ones who were horning me up inside. I wondered where they hired for that reason? The doctor who had pleaded with me to get down jumped back along with all the rest of them when I jumped down. I laughed, loving the control I had. I was enjoying scaring these little arseholes.

One of the other Doctors, an Indian-looking man, was preparing an injection. I knew what it was... It was a tranquilizer. He said, "Juan please remain calm". He then said "Juan, will you take this injection". I asked, "what is it?" He said, "it's just a sedative that will knock you out and give you a good night's rest," he looked SO fucking nervous. So, I said, "aye, go on ahead, I've never had it before. Why not!" (just for the experience) and dropped my pyjama bottoms, giving them a full-frontal nudist view! I turned and bending over I slapped my ass cheek saying, "aye, go ahead stick it in!" This got a few sniggers from the female nurses, which again was what I was after. The Indian Doctor said, "No! Pull up your bottoms, we'll do it in your bedroom". We went into my room and I lay on the bed. I took the injection and the next thing I knew; it was morning. It was not that great an experience but it showed me the power of the drugs they had!

I didn't spend all my time with Harold in the first stage ICU on the 2nd admission. There was an elderly female retired school teacher, Xanadu. Xanadu was 76 years old and had a little shine for me. She was married but fuck was she a rascal. She was highly intelligent and said the same of me. Most of my time in there, was spent with her, and we got touchy-feely. Don't cringe, you would too if you were locked up in there with a woman cracking on to you! Ha! She was good-looking for her age with a naughty glint in her eyes and a saucy sense of humour, very like my own. We were birds of a feather with a generation gap of only 50 years! She was really mischievous and hated all the nurses, with no exceptions. She was in with Bipolar, but once again, she was another patient that seemed fine to me. She just had a problem with authority. A problem that brought her to the attention of the Doctors in the 1970's when things were really grim in a mental asylum. She told me horror stories. She said back in the early 70's she fell out with her husband one time, and he had her sectioned and brought to where we were in St. Pats mental Asylum. They brought her from her home against her will at her husband's discretion (a sectioning fear I was going through with my father) in an ambulance to the hospital. She was very petite, but she told me she fought hard when they brought her in the main doors. She said it was excruciatingly frightening because she trusted her husband so much, the most out of anyone, and then he had done this to her because of an argument. It left her so alone in the world and it was something I would experience myself a few years down the line, as you will read. The male nurses manhandled her in the main doors as she fought them. She wouldn't calm down for them, so they threw her on the ground, smashing all her front teeth. They then just lifted her up and dragged her to her room. They left her until the next day with her teeth smashed. It was a terrible story, and she showed me her false teeth, taking them out for good measure.

She was getting really horny with me every day when we were out of sight of the nurses —looking for kisses and getting frisky. I just thought, what the fuck? Who cares? When in Rome. THEN I woke up one morning after a week in there to the best wake-up call I'd had since my days with Briona when she did it for me. (Fair play to Briona! I told her it was one of my fantasies, and she made my dream come true!) It happened as I was lying asleep in my room, one morning. My bed was in a dorm with two other patients. There was floor to ceiling windows sealing it in from the corridor for high observation. It was bang in front of the nurses' desk, but that didn't stop Xanadu! Thank Christ for curtains, because as I woke, before I even opened my eyes, I could feel something moist yet firm around my cock, massaging it up and down in slow rhythm. My cock was throbbing. It was so hard. I was so turned on. I opened my eyes and looked down the bed, and all I could see was this head-like shape going up and down and a body standing at the side of the bed. I lifted up the covers and had a sudden surge of mixed emotions. My conscience was telling me, "this is wrong!" Xanadu was smiling up at me with my cock in her mouth. She was old enough to be my Grandmother, but fuck did it feel good! She gave it a few more sucks as I watched her, then she kissed the tip and shuffled away, giggling to herself. Not much thought of her husband lol. I lay back down and pulled up the covers. There was only one thing for it! Coinyabeta time! I had a glorious wank releasing all the tension that she had been putting in me for days. It was fabulous! Never be shy about wanking. I know it is a healthy thing for men and women to do, and in my experience, it is great for men to practice their staying power for when they're shagging. It can also help women achieve orgasm's quicker during sex.

When I left the ICU and went to the second stage of the process, they showed me my room. I threw my stuff down and I decided I'd go for a smoke. I went into the smoke room to settle in a bit. I noticed everyone in there when I went in. One of them was a stunning dark-haired beauty called Dawn I found out. I found out later that she was an air-hostess as well. She was wearing a Japanese kimono and who, as soon as I sat down, said in front of everyone "who'd like a blow job?!!" in a soft south Dublin accent. I thought this is directed at me. I looked around at the other options, I knew it had to be me! I put my hand up and said, "I wouldn't mind one!!" She looked over and said "C'mon!" laughing. This place is fantastic, I thought. Flo was bang on. These ladies had no inhibitions, very promiscuous. Great for a licentious guy like me!

She looked to be in her early 30's, I thought. And very attractive. I didn't need to be told twice. I jumped up and went with her to the door, but she said, wait a second as she pulled the door ajar and peaked out. She said the nurses were doing their suicide watch, but she said they'll be done in a few seconds! Very romantic!! And good timing! They did it every 15 minutes, like I said. A second or two later, when the nurses had finished, she grabbed my hand and said, "Let's go!" We ran to her room, then into her bathroom, and she closed the door. She got down on her knees as I pulled my bottoms down and, licking her lips, she looked up at me with her thick dark eye lashes and seductive eyes, she said "Mmmm!!!" I was rock hard. She took my cock in her mouth and sucked it slowly. Jesus, I thought I might be locked up against my will, but this DEFINITELY softens the blow. Pardon the pun! Then after 6 or 7 sucks of sheer ecstasy came the pain! She stopped, kissed the tip just like Xanadu, and said, "right, that's enough for now!" "WHAT?" I whispered loudly. Jesus, I was going weak at the knees! Blue balls again! What is it with these female mental patients? I thought there was a conspiracy or something. I thought, Fuck, do they know how to tease! Thinking of Kena the year before and old Xanadu. I didn't ejaculate in Dawn....YET!!!

Afterwards, we went back into the smoke room, and one of the old ladies in her late 60's asked me, smiling as soon as we walked in, "how was your blowjob?" "Excellent," I said lying. I wanted to cum but it was fun. I was laughing at how open everyone was. The old ladies were just as bad. I knew this from my experience with Xanadu. Time passed quickly during the next week or so. There were a few girls my age in there, so I'd plenty of entertainment. Then a right header arrived on the scene. He was a heroin addict and Bipolar. Bipolar's a myth! I don't believe in Bipolar one bit. I became good friends with him. He told me his story. He said that he had been caught walking down the street by the gardai with a samurai sword going to frighten a guy who'd threatened his girlfriend. That would scare him, I thought, and it gave me ideas for my attack on the Gardai later in life, as you will read.

It wasn't until I got on the open ward after the four weeks in the ICU for my final four weeks that I started to feel a bit of freedom again. I met this girl, Janie, who told me she was in the top 1% of the country for intelligence. I answered her, "fair enough," but I was intrigued and into her straight away. She was the vice-president of the philosophical society in Trinity College, Dublin, at the time. I later told my friend Munhall this, and he said, laughing sardonically, "if she was that smart, what the hell was she doing hanging around with you?!!" I met her as I was leaving the gymnasium after playing snooker with another mate, Gerry, whom I'd made friends with in there. Gerry and I were walking past her, and I noticed her on her own in the big empty gym hitting the punch bag, so I shouted to her to turn her hips. She stopped and said, "what?" so I winked at Gerry and said, "I'll see you later". He just laughed out loud and shook his head, and walked on. I went over to her and showed her how to hit the bag with power. We became good friends and smooched a little but nothing too serious. She had a boyfriend on the outside. She was a really bright girl and a poet from Vanessa ward. I knew she wanted it, though. She was fantasizing all the time when we were kissing. I could see it in her eyes! She rubbed my cock a few times and I knew she wanted to put her lips around it. She was very intellectual but as with all humans, sex is paramount. Vanessa ward is a ward full of women in St. Pats, my dream come true!! Janie was a good yard stick for measuring the quality of poetry that I was writing at the time. We spent most of our time in the next few weeks together. Kissing and fucking driving one another up the wall with no sex! We would have been fucking the life out of one another if things were right in this world! She had the sexiest ass!!! I thought Trinity can make them!!!

However, in the middle of that time, one day as I was sitting on my bed listening to music and writing, Dawn, the Japanese kimono lady came in. I noticed her big sultry eyes and lips first. She shuffled in like a Geisha. She was very sexy. She asked me how I was and sat down on the bed. I said fine. I thought of Janie and a fucking threesome. Janie had told me she had lesbian flings before, even though she was only 19. She said she had a 17-year-old Portuguese girlfriend thing going on. It got me really going. She said we could have a threesome some time!

Dawn asked me if I was up for sex, with a dirty look in her eye, pointing to the bathroom in the bedroom. Again, I said, "YES!!!" without hesitation. We walked over to the bathroom. She bent over the toilet and pulled up her night gown and down her knickers. Her legs were tanned. I knew she came from wealth. As did all these women in St. Pats. I mounted her straight away. She had the sexiest round ass you have ever seen. I felt like cuming straight away. She was bent over the toilet, holding on to the seat, and she said, "Fuck me rotten!!" I fucking stuck my cock in and pumped like fuck. All of a sudden, I became aware of the mirror beside me. I could see the reflection of my cock inside Dawn. It was so erotic. I cheered myself on putting my fists up in the air, laughing to myself. I thought I'll always remember this. She noticed the change in rhythm and looked back and said "what are you doing?" "Nothing!" I said laughing and carried on fucking her. The sweat was pumping off both of us. We were the only two people on the planet at that moment.

She dropped a letter up the following day. I found it on my bed the next afternoon. It read...

"Hey, Juan,

Well, that was a little bit more exciting than that mundane crap in Dean Swift (ICU – 2nd stage). I just lost my partner from drink and ain't over him yet and don't know if I ever will be. This bloody alcoholism rapes you of everything in your life. Even my family doesn't want to know me, but they don't understand that the addiction supersedes all responsibility and reality. That "shag" was great and I say shag that I am so hurt by men that I guess I just use and abuse them the way they did it to me!! That's not to say that I wouldn't like to "shag" you again and maybe have some TLC, even if it's just to pass the time. That isn't meant coldly, you're a great fuck, but we haven't even begun yet. I want to shower with you and drink your juices. That's right, I'm a dirty bitch! I've been called the fuck of the century and I think you fall in to that category as well!

"I did what I knew until I knew better, and when I knew better, I did better.""

Dawn.

My dad and mate, Doyler, came in shortly after that. I showed them the letter, and I told them the story about fucking her and her sucking me off a couple of weeks ago in the ICU. Doyler roared laughing saying, "Jaysus, we put ye in here to get away from all that!!" I laughed at this but I thought you don't lock somebody up for that behaviour. He was severely deluded. My father poisoned everybody. All my friends were alienated by him. I had no-one to believe in me. I let it go and I asked them if they wanted to meet her. They jumped at the chance, but when we were halfway up the stairs to Vanessa ward, my father started laughing and said, he wouldn't be able to keep a straight face. He had a sense of humour on him and he loved women too!!

Janie and I hung out together most days after that. She said I had a real man's edge. It was really nice talking to her at that time, though. She was such an intelligent woman. I had my faith restored that these women existed. I'd always doubted me meeting a partner of equal caliber in intelligence.

I was glad when I got out of the asylum, as far as I was concerned, I was never going back into one as long as I lived. My parents had other ideas and were every bit as bad as the doctors about me taking the medication.

I wanted off the stuff because of the effect it was having on me. I was drooling in the pub after 3 or 4 pints, half asleep and not able to joke and laugh with my mates. I could not keep up with conversations. If there was a lull in conversation, it was impossible for me to think of anything to say to keep it flowing. I was fucking so distraught in those years of taking the poisonous medication. It took up all my brain power to hold a simple conversation. I'm so relieved to be off everything now.

I knew I didn't need it, but I was the only one that seemed to believe in me at that time. My father putting the spin on the story within the community didn't help it. He told everyone that I was off the timing. It hurt me to the core and angered me for years. At least he can't do it now!

I felt undermined when he poisoned the well with my close friends. They all started fucking believing I was Bipolar as well. I'd been away from home for some years, and when I came home, I just didn't fit in with the old troop a bit. I'd changed a little. Got a little more worldly. On top of that, my father had the power to section me by Doctor Lucky, which I knew he would use as a form of control over me. The second admission seemed to convince people I was Bipolar. My Father had lost control of my life when I gained my independence by going away to sea and earning my own money. I wasn't wrong about him coming down on me with his full force when he had the chance. He was such a power freak, something nobody knew about him!

He walked in to my room not long after I got out of St. Pat's for the second time, and said when he saw me sitting on my bed writing "You know that writing craic is the next step back to the mental!!!" Then he walked out of my room. The doctors had told him that the writing was a symptom of my mania. He fucking used this against me. I've been writing since I was 16 years of fucking age. I knew then I was going to write everything I could remember down and finish big pharma off. The aliens have told me that the symptoms of mania are the most all conceivable longing attributes of an extrovert.

25

SHANNON AIRPORT

Prediction: Tuesday 12ᵗʰ of August 2004 (edited in 2021): St. Pats Mental Asylum, Dublin, Ireland

War and Peace

Churchill said,
"War is only just,
when all other means of peace are exhausted."
So, pick your political target,
and shoot it or blast it.
Not like the Americans,
who use collateral damage,
by bombing schools and hospitals,
creating colossal carnage.
What is their agenda?
Is it war and peace?
Or a piece of war?
They enjoy the power rush,
like driving a muscle car,
"overwhelmed and inebriated,
by the exuberance of their own verbosity." (Uncle Jimmy said that)
They plunder and pillage,

all non-American cities,
countries afar from their own lovely land,
and the only disasters they receive,
is by the act of Gods hand,
the weather,
two buildings are flattened,
down to ground zero,
and the stupid yanks,
think George Dubya a hero?!!
His tyranny had to be stopped,
American hearts opened,
I believe in no borders at all,
Pride in a country,
Makes men fall,
Let them see the truth of war for wealth,
Of how their leaders use disguise,
Plausible deniability,
AND lies, lies, lies,
Let's see what the world thinks,
when their true intentions are shown,
When their thoughts of world domination,
are fully grown,
the spoils of war,
and roads of tar,
oil for your car,
and talk about it in a bar,
But the aliens won't let him,
we'll stand tall and be counted,
no prouder an alien now there is on this earth,
we'll smile at the grandiose delusions.
But we'll hide our mirth,
I don't believe in war,
But I do like fighting,
Everybody's a warrior at heart,
It comes natural to us humans,

so, we'll hit the same spot TWICE,
With a single bolt of lightning!
So, come on, Mr. Presidente,
bring it on,
send your best,
I'll take them on!
I'm from Donegal & Derry,
my name is Juan.
—Find this in Anonymous in the town that talks

Protesting at Shannon airport was done on a whim. I thought it would impress Jamima. A couple of days before, I was working in Cork. We were working in a building screwing up Gyproc to beat the band. I was loved up with Jamima, my one-time love from when I was in national school. We had kind of struck up a relationship in the last year. I remember when I was nine years old, she kissed me behind a prefab one evening in our old Drumaweir national school in Greencastle. It was exciting. She was crazy about me. I did not know then what I know now about women. If I had been 20 years older, I would have made her my wife. Now we were older, it was way more exciting. She made me think about everything I had ever dreamed that I could do with a woman in my life. I wanted to spend my life with her. She had a massive impact on me! Even though she thought I was boring because I did not drink when we rekindled our relationship. If only she knew!!

I was 28 years old, just outside the 27 club. I did think about those partiers that died, when I heard about the 27 club from Hollywood – I was no longer in that danger zone!!!

While my mates and I were working, we were listening to the radio and if a song came on, that I liked, I would sing along. I was smiling and singing, but if it was sad, there would be tears in my eyes. I had extreme feelings for Jamima, and I was missing her.

I was working alongside my mate McNulty on the second floor. But on the first day, I couldn't contain my emotions. I was working through the stress of it when I thought, fuck this, I need out of here. I needed something to distract me. I jumped down to the bottom floor (no stairs in yet, just some cement bags stacked up) and I told my old mate, the boss Mac Eas, that I needed to get out of there. I could not focus. He said, "go on to fuck!". "You are no good to me anyway!" He is a hard man to work for, but I thought at the time, he was only joking. My other mate, Tony, who was working for him laughed at it. I threw down my work belt and walked down the road into Cork city centre. I was running; I had that much life in me. Jamima had set my fucking brain on fire. She was causing havoc with my emotions. So far, it was unrequited. We hadn't even had a kiss. We were friends, but outside interference had stopped it from getting hot and heavy. She had come back from London after seven years away, and we had hit it off. She was hot to trot on the Moville scene. I thought she would be the one. It was a weird year. I had stopped drinking before I met her and found it really difficult to get my leg over her without it. I was using marijuana instead of drink. It was crazy what that did to my brain. I was on it 24/7. It was ruining my life.

Anyway, in Cork, I went on the hunt for some weed. I went to a bar down by the docks to play some pool and collect my thoughts. I wanted to see if I could meet a few heads, and it was a bar that was close to my heart with my Merchant Navy background. I was playing pool on my own, when I had a brain wave. I thought I'll just ask the first person I thought smoked it. I left the pub and walked up Barrick Street. I walked into a quaint little book shop. There was a hot young pretty thing on the til. I bought a book on herbal remedies for Bipolar. I was curious. As I was leaving, I took a punt and asked her did she know where I could score some weed. She laughed and said, "You need a hemp shop for that!" and then she flirted. She said, "You can't come straight out and say that to anyone!" I flirted back and said, "If you don't ask, you don't get!" She said there is a hemp shop across the street. I thanked her and left. It was in there that I met an American beauty, a gorgeous woman called Ella. She was beautiful inside and out. It was like we were long-lost buddies. It was so easy to chat with her. There was a little sexual tension going on. She was married, but it did not stop her from flirting with me. I spent an hour, just chatting with her, and I told her I wanted some weed. She said they didn't sell it, but she would see what she could do, wink, wink, nudge, nudge. Her husband came out from the back. He was a long-haired hippy and a cheerful chappy called Paul. He left to run some errands and when he returned an hour later. I was still there chatting. He laughed and said, "are you still here?" I laughed. I felt a bit awkward but carried on chatting to Ella. He went through to the back and left Ella and I to it. She got the wine out and had a little drink. I told her I was off it. I was telling her my life story and how my Bipolar diagnosis came about. I showed her the book I'd bought on herbal remedies for Bipolar and she started to flick through it. She said her mother had the illness. I told her I'd faked it a few years before. Everybody nowadays has fucking bipolar. It's a fucking epidemic. The aliens are stamping it out!!

She flicked through the book for a minute or two then found a paragraph that said people with what I had faked, "are considered a shaman in some civilisations"—more propaganda I reckon. In my discoveries all the propaganda with bipolar was just that. They just wanted people to accept the diagnosis and go on medication. It was to boost the patient's ego. It was a massive pharmaceutical ploy headed by the staff in the hospitals. I told Ella I wasn't on any medication and that I was using weed to keep me calm, but it was not working. I still felt a high from being in love with Jamima. It was an elatory experience!!!

Ella made a phone call and told me to call back in the afternoon the next day, and she would have an ounce for me. 230 euros worth. Worth every penny.

I was sifting through the other stuff that was on offer in the shop. An interesting name on a packet caught my eye. It was called San Pedro. I asked her what it was. She told me it was a cactus extract, very like magic mushrooms. She said the Native Americans used to take it to go on their spiritual journey. I discovered in 2017 from my kiwi cousin Michael McLaughlin, that the main ingredient is a hallucinogenic called mescaline. I looked it up on Wikipedia, and it said that mescaline was the most powerful psychedelic in the world. I thought, "holy shit!" when I found out. I've since read Hunter S.Thompson's FEAR AND LOATHING IN LAS VEGAS and he was taking a ton of it. I thought no fucking way. I bought one of them and I also bought some heroin substitute. It was a brown dust in a little plastic jar. Heroin was always one of those drugs I wanted to try but was always afraid of injecting it. You hear so many stories of people overdosing on it. This was going to have to do. The San Pedro were 30 euros each, and the trip lasted between 18 and 24 hours. I asked her, how do you take it? She said both were to be taken like a tea. She explained that you boil the San Pedro, then let it sit in a pot for 6 hours, then drink it like a tea.

I was walking back through town with my bag of goodies and decided I would take in a show at the theatre. The Chinese circus was on, so in I went. It was a big old theatre. I was up on the balcony and had only a few rows of people in front of me and no-one behind. There was about 5 seconds of darkness between each of the acts and I was itching to get at the drugs! So, I thought I would have a little fun. Surreptitiously, I got out the heroin and placed a magazine I'd bought on my lap. Using my bank card, I cut out a decent line of the brown dust, rolled a 20 and waited until the next dark lull between the acts. As soon as it went dark a few minutes later I snorted the heroin in deep. It nearly blew my eyeballs out!!! Jesus fucking Christ, it stung like as motherfucker! My brain was buzzing. My nostril was on fire but I played through the pain. I was having good craic too so, I cut out another one. The lights went down and BOOM! I had another. I was nicely buzzing for the rest of the show. When the lights went on after the show, I was gathering up my things and waiting for everyone to leave first before I left. As I sat there, I got the funniest look from a woman leaving. She was in her 40's with two kids. She smiled and gave me that look that says "What have you been up to?" Then she looked all about where I was sitting like she was looking for something, then she shook her head smiling and walked on. I had all my stuff lying around me so I thought it was that, that she was laughing at but it was the knowing look that she gave that got me. I gathered up my things and stopped at the toilet on the way out. I went for a pee and I looked in the mirror after I had finished and had an out loud laugh to myself. There were two big brown rings around each nostril. She figured out I was snorting something!

I got a taxi home. Eager to try out my San Pedro. All drug taking was new to me having been in the Merchant Navy since I was a teenager and we were drug tested. So, I never really tried anything. A few puffs of a joint was the height of my drug taking.

I took it back to my digs and waited for the other lads to go to bed. I did not tell them what I had. I put the pot on the stove and poured the San Pedro into it. I put the water in and I went into the sitting room. I put on a DVD based on the music group "The doors" —one of my favourite groups. I love listening to their music. I thought it was very fitting for what I was up to. They were famous drug takers in their day. We already had some hash in the house so I rolled a joint and waited for my tea to be ready. I know this story will probably not go down well with my family and friends who think I went off the rails but it was just experimentation. They would watch a movie about drug taking like this and have no qualms about it. Double standards, I think?! What's wrong with me doing it? I know it's a little dangerous but I'm an adult. I know what I am doing...!

I watched the movie and smoked my head off. When the 6 hours were up, I went into the kitchen and poured the tea from the pot into a mug. "Mugs are for drugs!" As Jamima would say. It was very little tea. I just thought this isn't going to do anything to me. I drank it back then a brain wave came over me. I used a spoon and scraped the residue from the pot into my mug, and to make it more palatable, I put brown sauce in it. I mixed it up and scoped it into me. That should do the trick, I thought! I got ready to go into town to see my new mate Ella.

I still had to wait a while until the rest of the world got up. It was only about 6 am. Mac Eas and the lads got up. I told Mac Eas I wanted the day off. He said, "aye, no problem!" They all went into work, and I made my way back into town. I was walking up Barrick Street when it started to kick in properly. I noticed an orange glow around a passer-by. He was walking past me. I thought wow cool! I went and got my money, then I went to Ella's shop back down the street. The orange glow guy was in the shop. It was a bit surreal. Ella said, "Hi!" "How are you today?" she asked. "Brilliant!" I answered. "A lot calmer!" I said. She asked about the San Pedro and when I was going to try it? I said, "I'm on it right now.". She couldn't believe it and had a big laugh. She said you're supposed to take that in the woods. I told her I remembered her telling me that, but I thought sure, a city is a concrete jungle. That gave her an even bigger laugh. Then, I told her I snorted the heroin substitute too and she burst out laughing again. She told me she would put a short anecdote in Hot Press her favourite famous Irish music magazine of my couple of day's drug adventure. She had a friend who was a reporter there. I read it a few months after. It did not do it justice. I collected the weed and stayed for a good part of the day, meeting her friends and customers. They did not seem to worry about the smell of it. I studied what she had in the glass cabinet counter a bit more intently this day and asked her what each of the things she had under the counter for sale did. I bought three packets of San Pedro and some packets of Lotus leaf. FYI the milder smoke. Ella threw in some paraphernalia, and finally I bought a mini chess board for Doyler for his 30th birthday. He was on the Aran Islands Ferry servicing Inishmore, Inishmaan and Inisheer off Galway. He'd invited me to his party in a couple of days time. She bagged it all up and I walked about the city after that, smoking the weed and not really caring if I was caught, thinking it should be legal anyway. If they ask, I thought jokingly, I'll tell them I'm Bipolar, and it's my medication. I walked about the city smoking joint after joint. I was enjoying myself. I've always loved the atmosphere in Cork City. I thought nothing of it. A guard smelled the weed as I walked past him on Patrick Street and said, "do that at home!" I thought, cool guard. I thought it should be legal anyway. I decided to blow off work with Mac Eas and go to Doyler's party. I had the 90 grands from my car crash settlement I'd got earlier that year, and I thought I would take a bit of time to myself. I spent the night chilling in and around the City and when I was walking along a bridge up to the all-night bowling place, 3 guys smelled the weed. I got talking to them and ended up spending the night paling about with them, then going to Tralee for the night, the next afternoon. One of the guys was from there, so I went for a night out with him. They were a bit of a laugh. One was a rapper, the other a producer and the last one a famous Spanish actor. They were all young, 19 and 20 and 22.

The next afternoon after the night in Tralee, I got the bus for Galway. I couldn't wait to hit the Aran Islands with my weed. I thought I'm going to be very popular! When we got to Limerick, I stepped out of the bus for a cigarette. When I tried to get back on, the driver asked me for my ticket. I'd thrown it away. He said I couldn't get on without a ticket. I said, you seen me get off the bus. He wouldn't let me on the son of a bitch. He was being a real jobsworth! Rot in hell you cocksucker!!! Lucky I had my weed with me!

I knocked about Limerick for a while. I was chilling out, taking in the sites relaxing in a bar with a joint and a cup of coffee by the river. Nobody seemed to care. It was pretty cosmopolitan there. Then it started getting late in the evening, and I really wanted to be in Galway that night. Having the funds, the 90k. I wasn't going to blow it all, but I thought I would have a little fun! I got in a taxi and asked him to take me to Galway. He said he couldn't but that he knew someone who would. The guy he got had long hair and a yin-yang sticker on the dash. I took it immediately that he did martial arts, which made me feel at home.

We set off from Limerick, and we really hit it off. I asked him was it ok to smoke some weed in the car? He said, "Sure! As long as you put the window down!!!"

I smoked non-stop and was relaxed in my skin until it came on the 10 O'clock evening news over the radio that George W. Bush, the president of America at the time, was landing in Shannon airport. I'll call the driver, Yin yang. I asked Yin yang what was the landing about, and he explained that Airforce one was landing in Shannon airport to refuel. He said, there are hundreds of protestors being barricaded about two miles back. He then pointed to a massive cluster of lights on our left and said, "That's it over there!" That's when my head went into overdrive. "Change of plan!" I said.

"What's that?" he asked. And because he'd already allowed me to smoke weed in the car, I knew he would be game for a laugh.

"I've to go to Shannon airport,", I told him. "A friend of mine is coming in on a Ship". "Is he?" he said. "Yeah," I said. "Aviation fuel… I'm going to see him for his birthday". I thought time for a little fun. Do a bit of protesting of my own!!! Jamima would be fucking IMPRESSED when I told her! She always went for the bad boys. I thought I'd be marrying her in no time. This was to be a wedding speech story…

"Righto," he said, getting ready for the turn.

Then he asked me if this was true and I said "no, but you believed it, so will they".

I asked him if he was up for it, and he said he was. I gave him the money for the fare so there'd be no hanging about. I had the bag of grass and other accoutrements in the paper bag at my feet, and I still had a joint on the go. The smell was over-powering (White Widow, Cork's finest). He said, "you'd better put that out," referring to the joint. "Gardai up ahead," he said, pointing to the Gardai roadblock up ahead. It was on the road in front of us as we drove up to the main building. Yin-yang asked me, "What'll I say?" I told him KISS. Keep it simple stupid. Just say "one to drop off." We came to the first barricade. I counted 15 guards. They all looked tense. The taxi driver put the window down as he stopped and said, "Good evening Guard, one to drop off." The Guard looked in and I leaned over and said, "Good evening, Guard". I must have looked a right sight! I had a shaved head with a scar from the top of my head to my left ear, where I'd gotten stabbed. I was wearing a green army jacket with matching combats. They might have thought I was in the army. I had a red T-shirt on that said COMPL3T3 CUN7. The guard just nodded and said, go on ahead. He never smelled the weed. I don't know how he did not smell it. The next blockade was way more relaxed. They were just kicking about. One of them was even smoking. I calmed down a bit when I saw this. I guess they thought if he got through the first one, he must be okay. They just waved us on!

We got to the building entrance. Yin yang was laughing his head off. He said, "I'm sure I'll see you on TV or something!" I laughed and thought maybe! I shook hands with him and said, "Good luck," he said "bye!" with a smile from ear to ear. Yin yang, if you're reading this… well done! You're a man after my own heart lol.

I grabbed the bag and got out of the car. I walked to the main entrance door, and I just thought, show time!

I walked in through the door and thought now to be serious. Everything I do from now on will be watched. I was aware of the security and cameras. As I walked from the door and up to the departure/arrivals board, I gently swung the bag to and fro, getting rid of the smell. I wasn't too afraid. I figured that the security dogs that they might have would be there to smell for bombs, not drugs. The smell of the drug was really overpowering, I don't think swinging it to and fro would have worked BUT remember I was very stoned and still had San Pedro residue in my body!

I read the board as though I was waiting for an arrival and put on a disappointed face as though my plane hadn't come in.

I saw the sign for the bar to my left and walked upstairs. I was off the alcohol for about a year at this stage, so I ordered a coffee and a Lucozade, then sat in the first booth on the left facing the door. I noticed a camera in the corner up and to the right. I thought at the time everything I did was being watched by security, and everything I said and did would be recorded and watched again after I was finished, including lip-reading, or so I thought. I took out the birthday card for Doyler. My original plan of going to meet him on Inis Mór Island, where he was working as an engineer on a ferry, was put on hold.

I began to think to myself.... I'm in a position now to make a stand and make a point. So, if I had control of the world and a president's attention, what should I demand?

First of all, there was peace in Ireland and a united Ireland, so I wrote on the card "30 years have come to pass, now no fences only grass", referring to the duration of the troubles in Northern Ireland and how there should be no border between the North of Ireland and the South of Ireland and the double meaning referring to Doyler's age. With a play on the fact that I believed they should legalise marijuana in Ireland as well. It seemed to calm everyone down. I'd been involved in smoking it for a year at this point and could see the benefits of it. Not to mention the health benefits of helping so many illnesses and the commercial benefits of hemp. Smoking it 24/7 as I was doing, is not the way to use it recreationally. I was still learning. I still love a good toke now and again still. I have an addictive personality and all substances are too much fun for me so I only use narcotics in moderation now!

I sketched a caveman on the card. I was inspired by thinking that the world will go back to being cavemen. I wrote "No.1 Jamima". I was substituting dope for excitement but the urge took over so I started eating the weed out of the bag. It gave me a serious buzz emotionally. I knew it would take a while to kick in. I thought about going to the newspapers with the story. I thought what was going on in the airport needed highlighting. The danger to our national security by letting the American government use Shannon airport for illegal runs with prisoners in airplanes was very real. I thought I would tell them I did it when I was high. Once I got on TV, I would make my point about marijuana. I believed if they made it legal, it would stamp out a lot of crime. I carried on scribbling a few more sentiments on Doyler's card. I was listening to the American accent behind me.

I'd noticed a blonde-haired man and a black man when I walked in. We were divided by a lattice-wooden partition. I could still hear them. The black man looked like the quintessential secret agent. He had the earpiece and spring-like wire attached to his radio. He had a big beige trench coat. I knew he was Secret service. I thought after the whole incident, the FBI were on my case. The paranoia lasted for nearly a decade. I thought they were listening to my phone calls for years. The aliens have told me that they still do that. They said they've been listening to me since that incident. It was exhilarating in there and nerve-wracking after the event with the paranoia! I could hear the agents communicating. It was just short bursts on his radio. I got the chessboard out. The mini travel one I bought from Ella.

I placed the chessboard on the table, in front of me and set the pieces up. I was eating the grass out of the bag to beat the band. I'd the munchies! What better for munchies, than more grass?!!! I pointed my face up towards the camera and mouthed "Up the Ra!" just for the craic. I knew they'd look back on it, if they weren't looking already!! I began playing chess against myself, black against white. I was aware the camera was on me, but no one seemed to care. It was pretty relaxed in there. Not, caught yet! I thought.

I played chess until I checkmated the white king. I picked the black king up and knocked the white king over. I held the black king aloft in front of the security camera. I was wearing the white bracelet for peace on the wrist of the hand that held the black king aloft. It was for the famous Irish charity Concern. The sentiment for holding the black king aloft was to make a point that America, at the time, was ready for a black president. I wanted world peace and an end to poverty. My primary reason for my protest was that I believed Ireland should remain neutral and not be dragged in to a world war which I thought was developing. The aliens have told me that I was bang on. FYI, I stopped world war 3. A little appreciation wouldn't go amiss Letterkenny mental asylum!!!

I thought, at the time, that they were going to use Shannon airport strategically by fuelling planes to bomb the middle east. I decided against going to the papers with my story, in case, the gardai brought a drug charge against me! And I wouldn't be able to travel freely or work without worry. I had so many reasons for protesting, it was funny!

The two agents walked out past me but never batted an eyelid. I put the chessboard away and the girl behind the bar told me the bar was closing. I said, "thank you!" and she said, I could sit out in the foyer, if I liked. It was just outside the bar but it had a lot more open space than the nice cosy bar. It was nerve-wrecking but I braved it anyway, nothing to lose at that stage! I picked a seat to the left as you come out of the bar entrance. Mainly because I'd to go to the toilet and they were the closest seats to it.

I sat down and looked up. I saw another person across from me. He was sitting in the corner on the far left from me. He was casually dressed with a baseball cap on and had long grey hair. I thought he might be a journalist or something. I had thought about being one myself in later years. An undercover one! Anyway, he was typing on a laptop and looked fairly casual. I took out my distraction again, the birthday card and began to doodle but the need for the toilet got the better of me. I'd to pee badly, but I didn't want to pee long! My father's joke!! I didn't want to wrap up everything and take it with me. I wanted everything to look casual. I felt the heat now that I was out in the open. If I was being watched I thought by leaving everything there, I wouldn't look suspicious. I left everything sitting there and went to the toilet. I peed as quickly as I could. It was such a RELIEF!

I came back relieved and sat down. The table was on its own and was about two feet square. It was tiny. I noticed my pen was missing. I had a quick search but I couldn't find it. Paranoia took over. All those drugs were putting me in a heightened state of paranoia. I thought that someone had taken the pen, and they were running it for prints as I sat there worrying. I immediately felt very alone, and all of a sudden, I got a huge rush that the president's security had their focus on me. I wanted to share that heat!!!

I decided to ask the journalist man across the way for a pen. I took Doyler's card and left my paper bag full of drugs on the floor beside the table. I walked over to the guy with the hat and said to him, "excuse me, do you have a pen I could borrow?" He said he did and gave it to me. I sat down at his table and pretended to write something important. I was sitting on the other side of his laptop. He looked confused. The table was tiny. It did look strange! He probably wondered why I sat down. I could see him looking at me using my peripheral vision. He had a look of bewilderment, but I kept my head down and wrote something on the card and coloured in a doodle. I looked like I was concentrating. He shrugged his shoulders and carried on with what he was doing.

He had seemed like an approachable guy, and I was right. Seconds later, the two agents I'd seen before were standing before us. They asked my buddy if he had any ID?

"Sure," he said in an American accent.

"What's your business here, sir?" The African-American agent asked him.

"I'm just waiting on my plane to be refuelled, and then I will be on my way," he said.

They checked his ID, then said, "OK." The black agent handed it back to him and then asked me the same thing. I only had a fake student ID card, so throwing a bit of levity into it. I told him, "There you go!" handing it to him. "Don't use it though," I said, "the travel stamps up." He did not laugh.

He just said, "sure.", and just ignored my quip. It was getting tense!

The next thing, all I heard was, "GOD DAMN!!!" I looked around over at my table, and another guy was taking his head out of my paper shopping bag which he now had on the table.

The other guy shouted over to me, "IS THIS YOURS?"

"GET HIM OVER HERE!" he shouted. "C'mon," the black agent said.

I walked the whole 9 yards over to my table, accompanied by the secret service agent. It was a fucking exhilarating. I was pissing myself laughing on the inside. Inside I was DANCING!!!

"Yeah" I said, "it's mine".

"What is it?" the agent who hollered asked.

At this stage, I thought it's time to play my get out of jail free card. Bipolar mania!!! I speeded up my voice with plenty of pressure (it's a symptom of mania) and said "it's marijuana, gangji, dope.... it's my medication,"

"I know what it is," he said, "But what are you doing with it?"

Another agent came up behind us. The black agent handed my credential to him and said, "Check that out!" I was worried about my UK drunk and disorderly. I had a clean record in Ireland apart from the window break in the hotel at aged 25. The Bipolar story. Little did I know that the Gardai had made up a load of charges. I don't know how to prove that. Maybe someone reading does? The Carndonagh Sergeant Hamish Tigers, a guard from my youth with the eye of a weasel, showed me my record in 2019 in court. I was being done for 11 drunk and disorderlies inside 2 months. Hamish, was being overtly friendly and said, "This is your life!" Laughing! I didn't think it was funny and told him they were false. I read a couple of them quickly and could see they were fake. The ones I spotted were a few years before I was ever even in court. He said I had 56 drunk and disorderlies. That is quite a number. I think it's some kind of record or something! It's a lot of drunk and disorderlies, even over a life time. There was an assault charge from when I was in College in Cork and that never happened. I spotted it immediately when Hamish showed me the charge sheet. It was the first on the list. The Gardai in 2019 were out for my blood. I told Hamish Tigers after he showed me, that I was world famous!!! I was only winding him up! "No, you're not!" he said but I could see the doubt flash in his eyes. I told him you are not going to get away with these false charges. He just laughed. They think they are above the law. Hamish said to me in front of my lawyer in the court room, "take some medication". He said it about 3 or 4 times. He's was trying to force me. I told him "No bloody way!" He said "Why not?" I told him the only thing medication does is change everyone's attitude towards me. If I am taking it, I get all the help in the world and everyone is fucking nice to me. If I don't take it everybody is complete cunts! He left it at that! When the court was being heard, I believe the judge saw through the 11 made up charges and I got off with a 100 euro fine. Fuck did that piss Hamish and the other Guards off. The judge even leaned over to Hamish when Hamish was in the witness box reading out the charges and said in a loud whisper "What are you trying to do here?! I couldn't believe it! I was 30 feet away. The whole court room must have heard it. I felt so much relief that the judge saw through it and was on my side. I think Hamish and the other Letterkenny Gardai wanted me in jail.

When Hamish and the Letterkenny Super-intendant were taking me back out through the court (where nobody could hear them!), Hamish said to me threateningly "Go near young Mac Eas and we'll beat you up!!!" Hamish is an old friend of Willie McCabe, Mac Eas's Garda father. About 3 months before the bullshit drunk and disorderlies, I'd reported Mac Eas for beating up his girlfriend Olive. She'd messaged me for help. I knew she wanted me to beat Mac Eas up but I couldn't put my career on the line for that, as much as I'd love to. He's an evil cunt! So, I reported him to the Gardai in Moville. The fucking attention on me from the Gardai in Letterkenny intensified. Word had obviously spread. I was arrested, it seemed, every time I was in town with a drink in me. I knew after Hamish threatened me why I had gotten the attention and false charges on my charge sheet. Talk about bullying and corruption. Everyone says the Gardai look after their own and I was now on the brunt end of it. Hamish also knew I have been totally discredited by being labelled Bipolar so no-one would believe me if I told about the threat. I told my own father Hamish threatened me and he flat out said "No he didn't." Jesus Christ was I angry at him. (My da was a fucking asshole anyway!!!) I truly believe Olive, Mac Eas's girlfriend now has Stockholm syndrome. He has bullied her so much; she feels even more for him. Only last week she called me a liar and that he did not hit her. She is gold digging. He is loaded. She sent me photographs of the black eye the silly bitch! The Letterkenny Super-intendant was witness to what Hamish said. I ignored Hamish's taunts and never reacted in any way. I wonder how they would fair out in a polygraph test if I examined them? I'll probably do it some day!!

The Sergeant in Moville, who is a close acquaintance of mine, told me in 2017 that if I didn't stop misbehaving with alcohol, there would be no fucking book! I thought it was very fun! It gave me a little anecdote from Malin head. It was food for thought about how much power the gardai think they have in Ireland. They are SO above the law. They fucking do what they want and get away with it! The only record I thought I had at the time was a drunk and disorderly in Campbelltown in Bonnie Scotland. I was in on a ship sailing as Chief mate and got lifted for getting in a bar fight in a hotel there. The fight is a total blank to me. I doubted if the fight even happened. Either way I won! Which I thought was pretty fun!!! They were fucking lying through their teeth. I fell asleep and then woke up. When the cops took me to the hospital for a gash I received on my right shin, they left the cuffs on. I needed to pee really badly. A male nurse had to hold my penis while I went! It was funny as fuck! Really awkward!! I didn't get done in court for the drunk and disorderly in Scotland and have hardly been in court (well relatively speaking) in my life. The life with Fanjita really put a blemish on my career. SO, where did all these charges come from Gardai?!!! Maybe someone reading can help me get them expunged.

Back to the story......Meanwhile, while my I.D was being processed, the black agent, asked me a series of questions. He asked me, "Why do you have it?" referring to the drugs. A symptom of Bipolar mania is rapid speech, so, I began to talk a mile a minute. I spoke rapidly. I said, "it's my medication...... the doctors know I smoke it, my parents know I smoke it, even the gardai at home know I smoke it". Whoa! I thought, can of worms there, I saw the old Commodore garda spark to attention, mentioning the Gardai because as soon as I mentioned it, the old Commodore guard said, "what guards at home know you smoke it?!"

I was going to say, Willie McCabe, Mac Eas's father, whom I have always been good friends with, and who was a very famous guard in Donegal. He died recently. The fucking boyos did not even tell me. I was pissed off at that. I would have went to the funeral. I had so much respect for him. I thought better of saying his name. I thought he would get in trouble. So, I dropped another guard, babyface, in it. He has been the bane of Moville for years. Fuck him! He was giving me a hard time around then! He even made up a drug charge against me but luckily, I got off with a probation. It was all experimentation to me!

"Check that out," the old guard said. He had joined my interrogation. He was a distinguished gentleman of about 65 years old. He had his full regalia on. His medals were gleaming. There were a lot of them. I thought he looks like the boss of Ireland. "Do you know what Bipolar is?" I asked all of them. The two special agents answered no. There were three of us standing there.

"It's manic depression," I said.

The old guard nodded.

"I know what it is," he said

"Anyway," I said to the black Service guy who was in front of me. The English agent was a cockney bloke. I could tell after from his accent, he was standing to my left. The old Commodore guard was standing to attention on my starboard flank.

"Did you ever smoke dope when you were young?" I asked the black agent.

"No," he answered.

"You're a liar," I said.

The MI6 guy smirked at my taking the piss out of the American. I think there was a bit of rivalry. The American wasn't laughing at all. He was under immense pressure. The President was landing.

"What are you laughing at?" I asked, MI6 dude. "Did you ever smoke dope whenever you were young?"

"No mate," he said in his English accent.

"You're a liar too," I said.

He nearly burst out laughing.

"What's this?" the black agent extraordinaire asked impatiently.

I started sifting through my drugs. They'd dumped my bag out on the table, and the little paraphernalia that Ella gave me, as well as the shop's business cards, were everywhere on the table. It was a frenzy of evidence. I hope she wasn't caught.

"That's for taking cocaine," I said, picking up the bullet for snorting coke. I put it to my nostrils one at a time and sniffing rapidly, saying SEE?!! That's lotus leaf for "the milder smoke," I said, half laughing into myself. Then I picked up the green Maglite and pulled a bit of a skit on them. All I was thinking was no sudden movements! There could be a sniper. A reach but you never know! Crazy when I think about it now! I screwed off the top slowly, looking at them all, there was total silence. I was building up the tension, then rapidly at the last turn, BOOM! I pulled it off! They flinched. I was secretly in stitches. I put the top of the light on the bottom of the stock and placed it on the table, and said, "Look, it's like a candle, great for a date, look it doesn't blow out!" jumping side to side as I blew at it.

"Phew, Phew," I said, blowing at it rapidly.

Then they said, "What's that?" pointing at a bag of San Pedro.

"San Pedro," I said.

"Do you know what that is?" I asked them.

"No," they said in unison.

"It's acid!" I told them, "the native Americans used to take it when they wanted to go on their spiritual journey...I'm on it right now!" I wondered if this was my spiritual journey to rid the world of tyranny. The aliens believe that this endeavour ended George W. Bushes world domination attempt. The Amero is the only good thing he brought in. It is going to be the world currency. Everyone will use dollars in a couple of year's time. The new world order that the aliens are bringing in, is going to happen very rapid.

I was fighting for everyone's freedom. The American Indians should never have been abused by the American Government. They deserve lots of money for losing their heritage.

"I know what it is," the American dude says.

"Man, we gotta get this guy outta here...the president's landing in 50 minutes!" he said, addressing the other two.

"What president?" I said, ignoring his panic.

"He's not my president. Anyway, do you not think he's a bit of a dickhead?"

The American guy looked at me, stunned.

I said, "Don't worry, you don't have to answer that...I know you just work for him. I think he's a bit of an asshole myself!"

I thought the MI6 guy was going to have a seizure holding in the laughter!!!

I'd noticed another guy coming back with what I presumed was my ID and a silent gesture behind my back to say that I was cool or something because I noticed all their attitudes change. They relaxed. I don't know what they were told. I'd thought maybe they were told about Campbelltown. That was the only charge in my mind. It had happened very recently. That night in the Scottish cell singing at the top of my voice to the police after being taken in for a bit of R'n'R was fantastic!!! I even got my picture taken. It wasn't what they wanted. I put on a crazy face, and the cop fucking flipped. He said "I'm taking that again!" I said "Do I have to?!!" just chancing my arm! He asked the female cop did I have to take it again and she said "No". So, I said laughing "That's my photo then!" He was so pissed off!!! He left me back to the boat the next morning at 6 am and even stopped so I could get newspapers in a shop to soften the blow with the Captain at me being arrested. It worked. I told that cop I would be famous one day. He said "I believe you". I've always held that belief. It was just a matter of time.

Back to the airport. They were now trying to get rid of me. It felt like the interrogation had heightened. They asked me, "why are you here?" and "what's your purpose?" all simultaneously, so I answered everything at once, in overdrive. Time to get out of here, I thought. I said I was there to see my mate Doyler for his birthday. I said he was coming in on a ship....it was an airport. I knew they would believe it.

"There're no ships coming in. The river's been closed since 6 o'clock yesterday morning", the black American agent said.

"He didn't know that," I said, referring to Doyler.

"He's been at sea for days, and I haven't been talking to him," I said. "Right, well we gotta get you outta here, where are you staying?" he said.

"I'm staying with him!" the black guy threw his eyes up to heaven this time in total exasperation and said loudly, "he ain't COMING in."

"Well, I've nowhere to stay then!" I said.

"Get him a hotel!!" he said to the other guys.

They were about to wrap it up and escort me away until I said "What about my drugs?"

This got another snigger from the MI6 guy. The rest looked exasperated. I was in stitches on the inside. Laughing my little head off. The other men were in disbelief. One of the agent's wrapped it up and pushed it into my chest. I wrapped my arms around it.

As we were walking down the steps, I was accompanied by a tall guard in his late 40's. He was completely silent. It was just the two of us on the long walk towards the front desk by the door. I started singing a song under my breath, the rebel tune 'The Broad Black Brimmer'. *"There's a uniform that's hangin' in what's known as father's room…"* "Shut up ta fuck!" the Guard said. I laughed again into myself. The I.R.A are gonna love me I thought!!

At this stage, I thought I'm on the home straight and allowed myself a grin. I noticed a guy with a skin head out of the corner of my eye. He was about 40 feet away. He was walking past, trying to keep the laughter in. It must have been a riot for the Irish. They were probably all watching it on the security cameras.

When the guard and I got to the reception desk at the front door, the receptionist woman said, "we have a hotel booked for you!". She had a phone to her ear. I decided to stall. PRESSURE, PRESSURE, PRESSURE!!!

"How much is it?" I asked.

"It's 30 euros". She said.

"Not bad!" I said.

"Does that include breakfast?" I asked. She was completely gobsmacked. There was a pause of confusion as she looked at me in disbelief, then she said into the mouthpiece, "He wants to know, does that include breakfast?" I was laughing my head off on the inside. I thought I was going to burst.

I could hear the American voice on the other end of the line say very, very loudly, "YEAH, TELL HIM YEAH!!!"

I looked up at the tall guard, and he said through gritted teeth, "I'd take it!"

I was laughing inwardly as I had been all along as they'd fumbled. "I'll take it," I said.

We walked out the building's main exit towards the road, and an awaiting taxi. The Gardai had formed a line in some sort of salute to me. I had no idea what was going on. There were 5 or 6 guards all lined up. It was a bit surreal. It was a bit of craic though. One of them burst out laughing at me when I caught his eye. He looked like a bit of craic!! If I had gone to the media after, I thought I would have shut down the fact that everyone thought I was Bipolar forever. There's no way I could do all that if I was manic!!! I had my reasons not to. I didn't want a drug charge because I wouldn't be able to go to America. A dream I'd held since I was a child. I've always wanted to be a Hollywood action hero. The aliens have told me this is about to happen for me. I'm getting fit now with no drugs, no alcohol and very little carbs.

I got into the taxi and away to the hotel.

I walked into the hotel and was met by the manager. He was young. He sounded a bit drunk. It did not care. I was buzzing. The other staff were very attentive. They got me a room and I went up to it and sat on the bed. I was in too much of a good mood to go to sleep. It was still early. I thought I'll go down to the bar and have a Lucozade. Things are so boring when you don't drink alcohol. I vowed last year to never give it up again. I have the aliens 100% behind me on that. They told me it's a great drug if you treat it with respect. Probably the best.

I went down to the bar after filling a couple of 50 euro baggies with weed. I planned to find a nightclub. I knew there had to be something on. It was the weekend and Shannon was a big enough town. I went down to the bar leaving all of my weed scattered on the bed. I did not even put it back in the shopping bag. It had been filled to the brim. Much more than an ounce I thought. She gave me a sweet deal!!

When I got down to the bar, the manager told me, no alcohol. I fucking got mad at him and said I don't drink. He looked pissed off. He was a proper idiot. One of the customers said he was the owners son and he was a complete fucking tosspot. I bought a Lucozade and sat at the bar. I thought I would not mind a bit of Donegal. I had spotted a juke box. I got some change and went over. I looked through the songs and found what I was looking for. I put on the song Las Vegas in the Hills of Donegal a tune by the Goats don't shave. One of my favourites. It blasted out. The manager was angry. I could tell he'd been told to keep me under wraps. I decided to leave. I asked my new buddy at the bar if there was a nightclub nearby. He said there was. He said just follow the road up to the left and it was about half a mile up the road. He said you'll see all the cars. I left with a smile on my face. I could not wait to meet someone and tell them the story of the airport. It was busting out of me.

I got to the nightclub. I found it easily. There was very little people in. I went straight out onto the dance floor. I did not even take off my army surplus coat. I was spinning around having a great old time but people were watching me and thought I was a bit weird. I decided to go out for a spliff. I walked to the main door and skinned one up. I was happily toking on it when a car came speeding towards me. A man jumped out and came running up to my face. He roared at me "ARE YOU SELLING THAT SHIT AROUND HERE?!!!" I laughed at him. I did not show any fear. He must have got tipped off. I was easily described. He got fucking angry. He raised his fists and I said quite calmly "I know your game, away and find your own." He started laughing and looked back at the car full of men. He pointed at me and said "GET A LOAD OF THIS GUY!!" "ARE YOU SELLING IT?" he said forcefully. I replied "No it's all for me." He laughed again. He asked me what I was doing here? I said I was protesting at Shannon airport because of George W. Bush landing. He bust out laughing and said "Come on with us!!" "We'll show you a good time!!" I said "Why don't you come in to the nightclub?" He said "I'm barred!" I left the nightclub and went with them. They seemed pretty cool. We went to his house and he got out the hash. He said they were up early in the morning so they weren't drinking. I told him I did not drink. He was impressed. I sat at the table in his kitchen with one of his roommates and told them the story of the nights events at the airport. They fucking bust their holes laughing. They called me a crazy cunt. I told them I mouthed UP THE RA!!! To the camera and sang "The Broad black BRIMMER!!" as the guard was leading me across the way to the front desk. They nearly wet themselves laughing and said "You're one of us!!" We're the young I.R.A. That was it I was in the I.R.A in Shannon. We had a good laugh at the story. They then told me not to worry about the guards and getting caught with weed. The whole of Shannon smokes it he said. And I'm the Daddy. I thought pretty cool. He asked me then did I hear about the riots up in Dublin when the Protestant Orange men were marching down O'Connells street? I said I'd seen something on the news about it. He said that was us. We were throwing bottles of piss at them. There was no petrol in them. It was just a rag soaked in petrol, set on fire with piss in the Lucozade bottle. I laughed at him. He was pretty funny. He said they just threw them at the marching men for a bit of craic!! He said they were at the Opera the night before with their women and they all went on the lash the next day, filling themselves up with beer so they could fill the bottles with piss. He said it was great craic. I took his word for it!! We smoked long into the night. The next day we went to a house to collect some money. He had a laugh when he told me what they were doing. He asked me "Are you not afraid?" I told him "Not one bit!!" He did not give a damn about the guards. He said the young I.R.A around Shannon are a law onto themselves. I thought how cool. The aliens have told me that drugs will all be legal forever in a few years time.

I went back to the hotel and up to my room. When I went in, the first thing I saw was a completely clean bedspread. I'd left it covered in weed. I thought you crazy cunts. Smoking all my weed lol just kidding. I figured something like this would happen. That's why I filled a couple of baggies. Not enough to get a serious drug charge if I was caught. I really did not give a fuck around that time. I thought I'd retired from sea. It was a bit fucking stupid. I went down to the reception and asked for the manager. She said he was away and he wouldn't be back until tomorrow. I said you took my Marijuana. She said it was put away in the safe for safe keeping. I told her I wanted it. I said it was my medication for bipolar. She said there's nothing I can do. The safe is locked until tomorrow when the manager comes back with the key. I said I would wait. I booked for another night.

It was 1 a.m and I was so fucking strung out. The acid was still coursing through my veins. I never thought when I ate all the sediment that it would be in my system for days. I went downstairs for a cigarette and a bit of head space from the room. A taxi pulled up and a woman got out of it. I had a brief moment of clarity. All the drugs were making me fucking dizzy with surreal thoughts. I jumped into the taxi the woman just got out of and asked the driver could he take me to Galway? He said no problem. I got to Galway and booked into a hotel there. I was a day late for Doylers birthday. He did not care. He had a good time anyway. In the morning, I got a bus back to Donegal. I thought to myself. I just lived out a movie…

26

NINJA

··

I got home from Shannon and nothing much was said. No-one knew anything of what had happened. My mate Charlie Barr told me the breach of security in Shannon airport was mentioned on the news in the Dail (The Irish houses of Parliament) and they were all laughing about it. One side of the house was poking fun at the other who were denying the breach. I got a bit of a laugh out of that! Jamima however was not impressed. I was fucking devastated. I thought what the fuck do I have to do to get her to marry me? I told her I thought she would be impressed but she said that's not a mad thing to do, it's fucking MENTAL!!! My plan had failed. Miserably!!!

I told a few of my close friends the story and it became an urban legend. I heard the taxi driver Yin yang did the same in Galway and Limerick…rock on Yin yang!!! But to the rest of the country and the world it did not happen…Mac Eas would not believe me that done it. He said show me some proof!! I thought you are a fucking retard.

I was never questioned by the Gardai about it but the paranoia of it remained with me for years and years after it, until I just thought fucking hell, I have to get over this. I calmed down then. I know they're still watching me but they know I'm ok. They know I'm not a terrorist.

I pursued Jamima over the next few months and I was out all-night smoking copious amounts of hash. I was still off alcohol and it was going well but I was experimenting a lot with narcotics. I felt I'd missed out on all of it growing up. Everyone around me were experienced drug takers – I was playing catch up and starting to fucking out do them!

One night after I got back home, we were out in Buncrana for the night and I was given 4 ecstasy tablets. I'd never tried them before. I was told two would keep me going for the night. I had a great night alcohol free and thought this is much better than stumbling home drunk. I thought I've found my drug. I much preferred it to weed even though I was a little stoned as well. It was a really enjoyable experience. Getting "Loved up!" as they call it. I arrived home and there was no-one in. Both my parents were out. I got into bed and put on some music and lay back enjoying the buzz off the E's.

I lay there thinking about how I'd gotten involved with Jamima on a friend basis but how I wanted more. She said she didn't feel the same way about me. It, wreaked havoc with my emotions. I'd fallen head over heels for her, but she was having none of it. She gave me a few signals here and there over that year of 2006, the year I pursued her and it was all I needed to stay faithful to her. I thought Shannon would be the clincher but obviously not. She just wanted to be friends but I dumped the girlfriend I had in Scotland. Her name was June, an occupational therapist whom I'd met in 2005. I dumped her so I wouldn't be cheating on her if I slept with Jamima. It was disastrous. June was perfect for me and completely believed in me. She had no doubts after six months of going out with me that I was in no way mentally ill. I'd told her my story. She worked in a mental asylum herself, so she should know! It was nice to hear, even though I had no doubts myself.

My Father had gotten me a job working as Chief mate on a log-carrying ship called the Red Baroness through his contacts as a pilot. I was sailing around the west coast of Scotland when I met June at a local nightclub in Troon. She lived in Ayr, Robbie Burns, the poet, country. After we'd been dating a couple of months, she came home to my parent's house where I was still living (I should have moved out years before, I was too old to be living there) to visit me one leave. On our night out, Jamima was there in the pub. Jamima was dancing without a care in the world and really caught my eye. June was gorgeous smart, and funny. However, she didn't like giving blowjobs. It pissed me off a little and ruined sex for me with her. And I thought, we'll probably break up because of this. Her reasons did make me laugh, and the only way she would do it made me gag, she wanted me to swallow my own cum. I wasn't ready for that. If it was now, I would probably have did it. It is such an important thing during love making to give each other oral pleasure. She said in her cute Scottish lilt that she didn't want wee sperm swimming around in her mouth or her belly. It gave her the heebegeebes thinking about it. I should have told her the acid in her stomach would have killed them. I remember one time she came to visit me when I was on the Red Baroness. The Captain had gone to bed. I took her up to have sex with her on the bridge. I was living out a fantasy. I used to imagine having sex doggy style over the chart table. A table used for navigation. It was one of my best fantasies. One I've had since I was about 20 years old. We got busy and June was so bloody up for it. She was a bit of a wild one! All those psychiatric people are fucking crazy about sex with mental patients. She loved that I was a mental patient. She said it turned her on even more. We had sex in the Captains chair. I sat up with my jeans down and she straddled me then we did it doggy style over the chart table until I had cum. It was bloody brilliant. Nothing wrong with June!!

After that, when I was home, I used to leave my parents house in the early evening and not come back until the wee hours of the morning. They were getting worried. They had suspicions I was doing lots of drugs. I was driving my mother's car and hanging out with my mates. I should have been saving and getting out from under my parents law. It was fucking diabolical. No fucking reprieve. I felt trapped living there. I just could not get it together with being on the medication. My father had told me to keep taking the medication even when I got the new job. I thought that that was fucking mental. How bloody dangerous? I don't care what the doctors say. You can not be in a position like that with power and responsibility of peoples lives and take that sedative poison. I fucking thought no way am I taking it and just took it with me to sea to appease them. I never once put any of it in my body. I was way more responsible than any of them. My father probably would have stopped me working if he had of found out. Such was their fucking mentality.

I was living my own life when I was home but I never once thought about getting my own place. There are not that many places to live in Moville. Moville is quite the place to live lol fucking is not. It is boring lol just kidding.

Jamima told me at the time when I confessed my feelings for her that I should have just let it happen. I told her I wanted to break up with June so I could be with her (something not done apparently according to her. It put her off!!!). She said that I should keep seeing June even though there was a spark between us because she wasn't sure yet. I continued seeing June for a short while then dumped her. It hurt a little, I was very confused around that time. There was a lot going on! June was devastated. I could tell!! Another woman caught in the maelstrom.

The Jamima saga dragged out for over a year, driving me demented! Ha! We never even kissed. It was my own fault, but Jamima was not that clear about her intentions. She was giving me the come on too. Then acting the complete bitch. So, it was unrequited. I was trying my best at the time to convince my parents I was better off the medication. The Doctors had me on Epilim. A drug used for epilepsy but one of the side effects was a depressive feature. This stuff was fucking my mind up. I explained to my parents how it was bringing me down, but they didn't care as long as I wasn't elated. Depressed was good! My father said those exact words! My mum would phone me at 10 O'clock every night to see if I'd taken it. It was a nightmare! Eventually, I got off it with my parents' blessing, but they were not that happy about it. I told them it was so fucking dangerous being at sea with all that fucking junk in me. I couldn't function properly on it. Was it any wonder? I didn't need the fucking stuff!!! Being off the alcohol gave me a lot of freedom, but because I got heavily into smoking a lot of cannabis, my mind wasn't what it should be had I been totally sober. The weed was playing havoc with me no matter what way I looked at it. I was getting very paranoid, and I was having delusions. The Shannon airport incident left me believing my phone was tapped and that the NSA, the CIA, MI6 were all after me. I had no proof, and the only thing I could think was that they were all watching me because they were wondering why I had done it. It was ludicrous! I had the peace bracelet on me, the white one for the group Concern at the time of doing the activist shit in Shannon, so I was hoping they would see that it was the main reason for me being there, all other things aside. It so trivial now when I think about it, but the weed exaggerated everything. I was smoking heavily every chance I got.

The job on the Red Baroness didn't last that long —about eight months. I was drinking a lot when I went ashore, then sleeping in. I wasn't surprised when the Captain sacked me. He had already warned me that he would if I slept in again. As Chief mate, you are to be a responsible person. Someone the crew looked up to. I was letting myself down when I look back on it now. A lesson for all you young sailors, take it easy on the booze. You can read the common theme throughout this book concerning alcohol, and it's not good. I would have had a dream life without it. I wasn't taking the log boat job seriously enough to take it easy on the drink. I got off the boat in Scotland after being sacked and stayed with June for a couple of weeks which drove everyone at home crazy because when they found out I'd been sacked, they thought I had gone off the rails again. I was actually grand enjoying my time in Ayr with June. She can vouch for that.

When I eventually went home, June said as I was leaving...."you aren't coming back, are you?" I said I was, but in hindsight, deep down, I knew I wasn't. I went home to regain control of myself and pursue Jamima, much to the annoyance of some of my other friends at home. One of them said "she's a mate. That's a no-go area when you're in that zone!" That was according to Farren. What a dickhead?!!! He told Jamima that I fancied her before I let her know, and fucked up my chances. What a cock block cunt?!!!

The tension in my parent's house was palpable when I got back. I had fucked up the job my father got me, but because of the apparent illness, he wasn't too annoyed. He got the shock of his life a month before that. He was piloting the Red Baroness up the River Foyle and talking casually with the Captain. They were good friends. They'd been coming for years to Derry with logs. My father was getting ready to put the vessel alongside when he noticed a new Chief mate on the deck. He asked the Captain where is Juan? The Captain couldn't believe it. He said to my father "Didn't he tell you? I had to sack him. He was drinking and sleeping in!!" My father lost the plot. He told the Captain that I hadn't said a word. He asked the Captain where the fuck I was? Lol. I had jumped ship. Not really done these days. I'd stayed in Scotland buried up to the nuts in guts. Every day I woke up I was lying lee of bum island. Having a whale of a time shagging June every morning and every evening. She told me that I was like one of my favourite performers… Robbie Williams. She said I reminded her so much of him. She fucking idolised him and in turn idolised me as well. She told me a terrible story though of a past boyfriend. He fucking raped her 5 times in the one 24 hours. He locked the doors and the windows and held her down and continuously raped her. I was going to kill him. She said to leave it. I was so fucking angry. I eventually came home and I gave up the drink, which pleased everyone. What did annoy my Dad was the time I was spending out of the house away with the mates from years before that I had reacquainted myself with and who all did drugs. This came to a head for me one day when we were sitting watching TV together, and I started laughing at something on it. Immediately I could feel my father's attention on me. He'd stopped laughing and was studying me out of the corner of his eye. He had read half a book on Bipolar (I was taking note of his progress, he never finished it!) that was written by the head of St. Pats Mental Asylum. The same Doctor I had quizzed about the Unipolar up. I now felt that my Dad saw himself as some sort of expert on bipolar. He had the power to section me so, I said to him, "look, daddy, I can't go on like this," wanting to get everything out in the open. I just wanted things between us to go back the way they used to be a few years before. He was a fountain of wisdom, and I enjoyed being around him. He was respected by everyone in the community. Something I aspired to and was proud of, but this felt like I was in a pressure cooker. I couldn't show my emotions. It also led me to have a serious neurosis where if I began feeling happy, I would think of something bad to stop me from feeling happy to counteract the feeling, so I wouldn't appear elated! This habit stayed with me for a couple of years and drove me fucking de-mented!!! I got over it after 2 years of driving myself nuts. It took some logical thinking to break the habit but I was ok in the end.

I also felt my independence had been stripped off me. I said to him, "you think I'm showing signs of mania if I am laughing, and if I'm quiet, you think I'm depressed, it's driving me insane...I feel like you are just going to lock me up". The sectioning card that had been put in place had not only stripped me of my independence, it had swallowed my confidence too. I couldn't settle in his company. He started laughing when I asked this, and as was his humor, he said, "what? you think we're going to run after you with the big net and catch you and put you inside again?"

"Joking aside", I said, "yes, that's what it feels like." I was glad I broached the subject, but it didn't ease the feeling much. I went to my local GP a few days later. He had been my Doctor most of my life, and I told him about my worries. I said that the pressure was getting too much in the house between my father and I, and I felt he was about to section me. The Doctor told me not to worry because it wasn't that easy to section someone. It's not just my father's word. I told him "you don't know how manipulative he can be!!!" "You have to be a risk to yourself or others" he said, so as long as I didn't do anything like that, I would be grand. It is way fucking easier than that to section. They gang up on you and you are fucked. You have to do what they say! The system is so fucking militant. I was really angry at my father for being put in this position. I told the Doctor in anger that if he put me in the asylum, I would have people break me out and burn the place down! I was really pissed off. It probably didn't help my case, but I didn't mean it, nor could I have done it, but that was the level of anger I was feeling. All that was going through my head as I lay there buzzing off the ecstasies after coming home from Buncrana. There was a knock at the door. It was my mum. I said come in. As soon as she came in, I could tell she was drunk. It was about 3 weeks after I'd gone to the doctor about my worries about my father sectioning me. She denies being drunk now when I recount the tale. Selective bloody memory. My father was the same as her when I recounted these stories over the years, selective memory! They fucking deny everything. She came into my room, and I asked her where she had been? She told me she was over at the Drunken Duck, the bar that was formerly ours and that my father was still there.

Then she asked me, "what is wrong with you?" and how come I never talked to them anymore? I said, "I was fine" and that I was just keeping myself to myself with my writing and seeing friends. There was nothing to worry about. She said she did worry, so I pulled back the covers and told her to get into the bed beside me, and we could talk. She got in and we talked about how I was spending all my nights with my friends. I said that the narcotics I was experimenting with weren't affecting me badly. This was not true. The weed was leaving me very paranoid. I thought I'd set her up. So, I said to her that because she was a nurse, she would know if I was on anything! This set up was to my detriment, as I found out by both my parent's reaction. Then I said, look, and I took out the silver paper with two ecstasy tablets on it. I said, "look there are two E's there, there used to be 4. I have two in me right now!" It wasn't a nice thing to do, especially to your mother, but I was buzzing, and I felt in control of it. She had never seen an E before. When I put them away, I told her that the effect that she had been told was that I would be up jumping around the room going mad, yet here I was sitting back listening to music, chilling out. Next, I said, "mammy would you mind if I had a joint?" and she replied, "well, I wish you wouldn't! "Good enough for me!" I said, and I skinned up and had a smoke. We talked for a while and settled some of the problems, then she left and went to bed. I was so fucking horny for Jamima that I slipped off my boxers and had a glorious wank. It had been nearly a year since I ejaculated. I had been holding back waiting for her to sleep with. Have you ever had a masturbatory experience on ecstasy? It is fucking mental. All those feelings!! Wow!! The next morning, I opened my eyes and I woke up to see my local GP that I had confided in the three weeks previous, at the end of my bed saying, "Juan just remain calm!"

"WHAT??!!! I said "WHAT THE FUCK IS GOING ON?!!" My parents were standing beside the bed saying the same thing. "Please be cool, Juan". I knew immediately what was happening.... they were about to section me. I said, "Nope, this isn't happening", lying back down in the bed, I said, "anyway, who's going to make me?!! I'm not going anywhere!" At that, two gardai stepped into the bedroom saying loudly, "YOU'LL BE COMING WITH US!" I sat bolt upright in the bed and said loudly back, "WHAT? YOU AND YOUR BIG LOUD VOICES?!!" Then I verbally attacked the Doctor first, saying, "I told you he would do this!!" referring to my father. "What about your Hippocratic Oath?!!" I shouted at him. "I told you in confidence that this would happen!" My feelings were that they had all gone behind my back. I was so fucking angry!! I remembered the stories the likes of Xanadu had told me about losing the trust in the closest to you because of it. My world had come crashing down!!! I couldn't believe my Dad had called the law. I was so fucking disappointed in him.

We talked about it ten years later when I was trying to get him to watch a documentary called 'Marketing madness – Are we all insane? (You'll find it on YouTube) It shows the awful treatment of psychiatric patients – misdiagnosis, sectioning, and the terrible effects of the medication that they give you. It's a Scientology movie, even though they are bananas they do good work in that field. Everything else about it is fucking nuts. I studied it and thought what a bunch of lunatics? A science fiction writer creating a religion and all the well to do people spending their money having an audit, that is where they tell all their thoughts and feelings and pay Scientology thousands of pounds. It is fucking mental. They were forcing me to sign up with them. I thought no fucking way. It is just an outlet for pent up aggression. The documentary was exactly what I went through. It brought a tear to my eye when I watched it, I thought I'm not the only one who sees the truth. I tried civilly to get my point across to my Dad that he was wrong to do it. He fell asleep during it; such was his interest. When I woke him up and put it to him that he was wrong to section me. He said irately, "it was for your bad behavior!" I was so fucking angry. I've lost fucking years of my life inside because of this shit. I said, "You lock people up for illness, not bad behavior!" We left it at that. Never to be resolved.

My worries about being sectioned in 2006 were not unfounded after all. The faking of the Bipolar down in Dublin 3 years previous had snowballed out of control! I jumped up from underneath the covers, naked as the day I was born. All I was wearing was the white bracelet for Concern on my wrist. I really believed in it!

I stood up on the bed, putting my hands behind my head and swirled my cock around doing the chopper. The two Gardai jumped back. I screamed at them "DOES MY NAKEDNESS SCARE YOU??!!!" Then I roared at my father, "YOU FUCKING TOERAG!!! CALLING THE GUARDS ON ME!!! FUCK YOU!!! I'M NOT GOING ANYWHERE!!!" My father lost the plot. He made moves to strike me. The two Gardai held him back then ushered both my parents and the Doctor out of the room. The two guards steeled up then the minute everyone was gone. One guard was in his late 40's the other in his mid-50. They said in big deep voices again, trying to be authoritative, "right that's it, c'mon, you're coming with us. Get dressed!" SO, while still standing up on my bed, naked and with the skin-head, I had at the time, so looking quite scary already, I said, "just one second..." to them and walked to the end of the bed and picked up the two samurai swords I had left there for such an occasion. I knew the sectioning was coming, and I had bought the two swords in a shop in Malin Head called the Curiosity shop with my mates, thinking this'll make for a good story when I put it up to whoever comes to section me! I knew as I was going through all this, I would write about it someday. Makes for good reading. Doesn't it?!! Ha! I picked up the swords with the sheaths on them, and while facing both of the Gardai, I walked halfway up my bed, then standing looking down at them both, I screamed, throwing the sheaths off either side, "C'MON THEN!!!" They fucking ran out of that room, quick smart. The one behind was climbing over the one in front trying to get out of there!!! I PISSED myself laughing!!! I closed the door, then I went over to my TV/DVD combi and played the Godzilla theme tune of Jamiroquai's "I'm Going Deeper Underground"!! Up to full blast.... very apt for what I was feeling, I thought. I lay back down with the samurai swords across my chest. I had only been joking with the guards. I wasn't about to attack. I was only scaring them enough to get them out of the room. They didn't know that, though!

After a couple of minutes, there was a knock at the door. "Yes?" I said. Another guard, Hamish Tigers, the plebe, whom I've talked about, faking all those charges, opened the door and put his head around it, and asked how I was? I said, "Look, Hamish, I've known you a long time, but I just want to be left alone. There are two people I will talk to, one is Jamima (because she knew the whole story and that this was bullshit), the other is Willie McCabe." Wille believed I faked the Bipolar. Willie was the retired Guard I spoke about and was the father of twin brother friends of mine, Mac Sea and Mac Eas. He was a good Garda in my eyes when he had been one, and I trusted him. Hamish said "dead on" he would see what he could do. They were friends. I was close to tears at this stage, thinking about what my father had done sectioning me. Jesus, did I feel alone in the world. Nobody believed in me! My mother was involved in the sectioning too. After all, I thought after, I had told her about the drugs the night before. The E's were the icing on the cake. I gave them the excuse they needed. That was the fire I was playing with back then!!!

My Dad was getting all the blame in my eyes. At that time, I thought in my heart my mum would never call the Gardai on me. I know now that is not the case because she did it in later years. She called the guards when I was one day out of a 3-week stint in the asylum because I put a joke up on Facebook. I put a picture of myself with a belt around my neck, pretending to be hanging. I was drunk and thought it was funny. I went to Willie McCabe's house the next day after putting the post up to see Mac Sea. He was home from Holland with his girlfriend, Babette. Hamish was the guard on duty. Hamish said it looked real to him when he came to section me. I said it was just a joke then I said "yeah! I'm thinking of taking up acting!" Babette smiled at me when I said this but she was worried. "That's not funny!" said Hamish. He really was being a proper wanker. It was obvious there was nothing wrong with me. They fucking arrested me anyway and took me in again. I was fucking SO pissed off at my mother. The staff laughed, when I went back in, at what I had done and they let me out 2 days later. The whole thing surrounding mental illness is a complete fucking sham!!!

My mother always plays the innocent when talking about anything to do with how I was treated comes up. She says she can't talk about it because of her blood pressure. More excuses! My mum always said through the years that she wasn't sure whether I was Bipolar or not. It was my Dad who had been with me in Dublin in 2003 in the beginning, but she did go along with his decision to break my balls about taking the medication. I believed completely when this sectioning in 2006 happened that she had Munchausen syndrome, by proxy (MSBP). Munchausen syndrome, by proxy, is a mental health problem in which a caregiver makes up or causes an illness or injury in a person under their care! She was fanatic about me taking the medication. I felt it was the nurse in her. She even got me the silly fucking box where I could put my tablets in for each day for the week in advance, she was so excited giving it to me. She loved having a patient to look after. Some of my parent's close friends I talked to in the months running up to the sectioning, said when I complained "ah, they're your parents, they mean well!" I couldn't win with my parents, but the majority of the public were on my side. It did not matter, it wasn't a popularity contest. My parents had the power over me, and they used it with all their force. I learned very quickly that because of the Bipolar label, all your rights in the real world as a human being are walked upon. I feel sorry for anyone who has been through the system. It is hell.

Well, I can say now, with all honesty, I'm not mentally ill, nor have I ever been. The sectioning was very wrong! I hope to Jesus this book is a testament to that!!! Every problem I've had socially has been caused by alcohol and cured by abstaining. Don't ever come at me with that medication again, any of you, you assholes!

As I lay there, waiting on Willie and Jamima, my anger at the sectioning was overcome by the sheer frustration at the situation. I had my mobile phone, so I phoned my friend, TC's father. He was a Doctor. I had his number on my phone as another contact for TC. He answered, and I told him the situation. I told him I was dead on, to which he said sorry, but it was out of his jurisdiction. He couldn't help me. He asked me how I was feeling. I said, "metaphysically wrinkle-free!" I told him there was nothing wrong with me. He laughed and said, "play it cool," "go to the mental asylum, they'll see nothing is wrong with you, and you'll be out in no time." It wasn't what I wanted to hear. I wanted him to fight for me, but it wasn't going to happen. I felt so alone. I thought it was good advice. I just didn't want to hear it. Willie arrived after 15 minutes. He came into my room and sat down beside me on the bed. He said, "do you want a cigarette?" and took one out for himself. He was a cool cat. I said, "yes". Then he said, "Give me those swords!" in his low Cavan drawl sounding like a movie star. It made me laugh at how cool he was about the whole thing. I gave him the swords and told him, "they're fake! They're only toys," I said. "I don't care. Give them to me anyway!" he said. He took them and put them at the bottom of the bed." You's whore's!" (referring to his son's Mac Sea and Mac Eas, the terrible twins and our loveable capers growing up) " how we going to get out of this one?!" he said puzzled. He smoked his cigarette, and I broke down a bit, getting tearful. There was a lot of pressure on me, and his comfort made me feel a little safer. He said, "C'mon, you're alright!" making sure I didn't let myself down by sobbing like a baby! I stopped myself from showing weakness, and I agreed with him that the best solution was to go to the asylum and show them I was ok and get it over and done with. I thought I would be out in no time when they saw I was not fucking elated. I told him I would go but not in the Garda car. Willie said he would take me in his own car. Jamima arrived five minutes after Willie. I had already decided the course of action. She came into the room and, taking the dominant role like she always did, said, "first things first, get dressed!" I dressed all in black and packed a bag, but I didn't tell her that I packed my Leatherman tool and planned to escape as soon as I got in there. I needed to breathe, but I wasn't being given a chance. I was very angry, and the colour black-suited my mood. I wanted everyone to feel it. I was being locked up against my will. I wanted Jamima to be there so she could hear the stupid questions that I was asked when I went into the Doctors and see that I wasn't being listened to by the people who counted. Doctor's, parents etc...

I arrived in Letterkenny mental asylum and did the interview with what I took to be a Nigerian Doctor by her colour and accent. I was angry at this, too, because she wouldn't understand my sense of humour or attitude. She asked me a series of questions, one of which was, "how did I see the future?" To which I replied "the futures bright the futures orange"...it was an advert on TV for a phone network at the time.... she didn't get it, but Jamima did, she had a laugh, Jamima was in the interview room at my request so she could see how ridiculous the whole system was. I was admitted anyway.

That night I was in my room with the door closed and I was waiting in anticipation. It came to about 11 pm after the medication had been given out so, I put my plan in action. I had hit it off with one of the other patients, a settled Irish traveller from Letterkenny, whom I'd asked to keep a watch for me at 11 pm. I'd explained to him that I was going to make a run for it. He was to let me know when the nurse minding the smoking area, which had a view of the garden and where I'd be running past, wasn't watching. It was to the right of the window I was getting out of. It meant whoever was minding the smoking area could see me as I ran past the smoking area to get out, if they were looking in that direction. I got dressed and ready to escape playing Beethoven on my stereo and recording it on the camera on my phone, which I thought I could later put on YouTube. Unfortunately, I lost the chip from my phone not long after I got out. I then phoned a taxi for 11.30 to meet me outside the A&E of the general hospital. I had screwed off the screws, using my Leatherman, on either side of the wooden bits of wood that only allowed the window to be open only about 12". I left the wood in place in case the nurses came in. I was looking out the window over to the right where the smoking area was. As soon as the traveller friend of mine, Jimmy, gave me the thumbs up, I pulled the bits of wood out of the way, pulled the window down, and jumped out, and ran across the garden. I jumped with one foot onto the window sill that was beside the 7-foot wall that closed the garden in, between the buildings. I was free-running. I scaled it easily and jumped down the other side. I ran a little in the darkness keeping close to the building, then walked when I hit the light. The taxi was there waiting. I jumped into the taxi and told him I was going to Greencastle. He just asked me if I was coming from A&E, which I wanted it to look like, and I said "yes." I then tried to knock the price down a bit. He'd said 60 euro, so I asked him, could he do it for 50, and he agreed... We talked a little, but obviously, I never mentioned what I was up to. He dropped me off at my local bar, the Sean ti, where I thought I could wait and see my next move. I could not believe it when I walked in and saw Jamima was with another man, not that I had dibs on her or anything. She was her own woman but it hurt...she knew how I felt about her. I got over that quickly as we were friends first, and I needed help badly. I was all over the place emotionally but very determined there was nothing wrong with me mentally. I just needed to be believed by my parents. I thought by escaping, I could prove the point that they couldn't hold me and that I didn't need to be locked up. It obviously worked the reverse in hindsight. A couple of the asylum staff nurses believed me, a couple of wholesome nurses listened to my plight and believed I was telling the truth. Jamima couldn't believe her eyes when I walked in. She said quietly as I walked in, "come out here..." signalling to the smoking area outside on the veranda, then said, " what are you doing out?" I told her I didn't need to be in there, in the first place, and I didn't know what I wanted to do but that I was proving a point that I was sound of mind. How else could I have orchestrated that escape? The main reason I had done it was in protest.

We tried figuring out my next move. I called Charlie Barr, my mate who lived about 20 minutes away by car, deciding I could hide out in his house. He came in and collected me, and I stayed up all night listening to music. I was up dancing with it up to full blast, I was so in love with Jamima. Just seeing her earlier on in the night set my mind on fire. I was ready for marriage. I wanted her. I couldn't sleep with what was going on. Charlie went to his bed early, leaving me to chill. The next morning when he got up, I contacted Jamima again, and she said she was in Ballybofey, which is not far from Letterkenny, where the asylum was. We agreed to meet her and her friend there.

When we all met up, my thought was that because Jamima at that point believed me, she could plead my case. It was a lot to put on her shoulders, but she did believe me at that time that I didn't have Bipolar. She also believed my explanation that I reacted with the swords and escaping because of the position I was put in and the pressure everyone put me under. I was on a happy high after making the escape, but I also thought with my friend's belief behind me that I had a good case. It wasn't to be. When I met with Jamima and her friend, the first thing Jamima said was that my father had been in contact with her and that he was nearly in tears. I told her it didn't sound like him but I said ok, I'd give him a call. He answered the phone, and the first thing he said was, "what are you doing out of that asylum?!! Get back in..." Tears my ass, I thought, laughing inwardly bittersweetly to myself. That sounded more like him! I loved my father and his attitude to life, but not when all his force was directed at me. I believed fully he was wrong in this case. It was like he'd become my nemesis. That CUNT of a Doctor all the way down in Dublin, Dr. Lucky, had driven a wedge between us that was Bipolar, convincing my father and not believing me, and I have had to live with the consequences ever since. I told my parents the story of how I met Flo and what she had told me about the place. I said it was the only reason I went in! That and not to disappoint my Dad. They put what I said to Doctor Lucky about Flo, and he said it was just one of life's coincidences that I'd met her and that he was full sure I was Bipolar! What a dick! Jesus, have I proved him wrong!!

As I stood in Ballybofey talking to my Dad on the phone, we agreed against my will that I would go back into the asylum. It was tearing at every fibre of my being to agree, but I just thought, "let's get this over with!" I said I wanted to get something to eat in Letterkenny, have a few games of pool, then go in. I wanted to feel the normality I was getting with my friends who were there. The whole thing was a joke as far as I was concerned, just not a very funny one.

I went back to the asylum and I remember my eyes welling up in the backseat of Charlies car on the journey there because not them in the front, nor my other friends, or any of my immediate family who thought they were trying to help, knew what I was going through in the asylum. I was being treated like an animal and talked to like I was a kid. It seemed to me like the cunt's of nurses were enjoying the patronizing! And I knew now that I had upped the stakes by escaping it was going to be even worse. They would be even stricter with me, and hell-bent on making my time there harder. There were nurses and Doctors in there with a sadistic streak in them. I wasn't wrong!

I was told recently when writing this that they have all retired since, but there are new ones there from my recent experience. The nurse who is hellbent on fitness said to me in 2018. "You're GOD!" He was looking for a fight. I was just walking out of my room. He was definitely trying to antagonize me. Berndan the nurse was standing at his side as nurse fitness freak sat in the chair. The nurse is a fitness freak for a nurse with not a lot of cop on and his son, the little work dodger, same as his Da, looking for a handy number of a job, said to me "BELVEDER!" as he was walking out of my room. He said it in a really loud posh, take the piss accent. The admission happened when I had come back from the yachts. They were trying to wind me up. I didn't react to either. Much to nurse fitness freaks non-amusement, he wanted a punch up! It's all because I am going against the mental health system and saying there is no mental illness. They are trying to fuck my life up. The little cunt that said "BELVEDER!" had his back turned to me when he said it. I stopped him and asked him what he meant? And he denied saying it. There was no-one else around to hear it. Gas-fucking-lighting!!!

The treatment I have received in Letterkenny and Sligo at the hands of these animals, and mental bullies of nurses young and old have left me with tremendous mental scars and anger. I'm sure I'm not the only one. What is hard is when people doubt your mind, it's near impossible for them to ever forget it and totally trust what you have to say ever again. It was the bullying and the lying that was getting to me. They are always saying derogatory things, then deny saying them. Then they would ask me, "Do you think you might have Schizophrenia because you're hearing things?" FUCKING sadistic cunts!!! They are SO cruel. It is really, really heavy to work in those conditions for any good nurses. They have to keep in with the bad nurses and play along. I have witnessed some serious malpractice in Letterkenny asylum. I would NEVER recommend a young person to go into psychiatric nursing. One nurse said, without looking at me, as he walked out of the canteen "It's never going to stop Juan!!!" referring to the abuse.

Back to 2006, they treated me like a child when I was an officer in the Merchant Navy. They were loving having the authority over me. A lot of the nurses loved me back then and I had a bit of banter with them but most of them turned against me. I was persona non grata because I wouldn't lie down and agree to being mentally ill. I was an authority figure in my line of work and usually in charge of giving orders yet here I was being told when to go to sleep and having to ask and then be accompanied when I wanted to go for a cigarette. It was demoralizing.

After they had taken me after escaping, I was trying to sleep with the radio gently playing. The doctor came in and said turn that down. I said it was down. Any lower and I would not be able to hear it. She said I don't care, turn it down and she turned the knob down. I argued with her and she said if you don't behave, I'll get the injection. I said trust me I don't give a fuck, eyeballs are very soft I said. What do you mean by that she said? I said what do you make of it? She said it's a threat. I left it at that. She fucking annoyed the hell out of me. The next day I rebelled, playing my music up full blast after they had taken me in after escaping. I was giving the nurse that had the duty of sitting outside my room on watch, a hard time slagging him off. I had a lot of anger in me at being locked up and he was getting the full brunt of it. My door was to remain open at all times so they could watch me, and that included my toilet door.... I couldn't even go for a shit in peace. He looked in one time when I was having a crap, and I stood up, turned around, grabbed my ass cheeks with both hands, and spread them shouting, "SEE ENOUGH?!!!"

When I was slagging the nurse off and playing the music, they decided I was becoming overly elated. It was just the pressure I was being put under, and I had decided to give some of it back. They organized all the male staff, about 6 of them, to come into my room to subdue me as they put it. What was frightening was I knew I couldn't fight back because I felt I could end up in there forever. Also, my family believed I should be in there, and I was literally at the nurses and Doctors mercy. This was nothing like the fun times I had in St. Pats Mental Asylum with my many women. This was gritty torture. I haven't written about my many incarcerations in Letterkenny over the years because it was boredom personified! I've had 30 admissions in total. 25 of them were in Letterkenny for fucking nothing. I just wanted to get them over and done with and move on with my life. That all didn't come about until this year 2023, as you will read.

I would wish this feeling of helplessness that I felt at the time on nobody, and I feel for anyone incarcerated against their will and having to put up with the ignorant brutality that goes on.

The male nurses came into the room, and I jumped back up onto the bed. The highest point possible. One of them dived on the bed and grabbed my ankle, tumbling me flat on my back on the bed. They all jumped on me, holding me down. I didn't fight, but one cock of a man reached over after I had been pinned to the bed and squeezed my throat. I tensed the muscles in my neck and said, "I'll get you, you cunt!" Nasty bastard. I never did get him back. I've carried no vendettas. As much as I thought about it when the nastiness was happening throughout my times locked up. It's not worth it. Let it go and move on is my advice.

They injected me with the sedative, and I was out cold until the next morning. They did it to put manners on me. Another time around 2017 they knocked me out for 2 whole days and fiddled with my chart to say I was awake. It was fucking scary!

In 2006 the nurses on the night shift whom I had warmed to and who believed me after one on one talks with them said they felt sorry for me.

They said they knew I was sane and didn't believe I should be in there. They gave me the Irish Mental Health Act 1945 to read one evening. I found a section that said it must be a Doctor external to you, not your own GP, that decided on whether you were deemed unfit and in need of sectioning. The sectioning party did not do this, as they had my local Doctor do it. That has all changed now. The mental health act now does not give mental patients any leniency. The next day, I asked to use the computer, wrote this law out in word, and printed off about 10 copies. There were other patients in there who'd had similar experiences. I showed it to my Doctor, who just laughed. He said it means nothing. "You need to be here," he said. I had no rights. I decided after this and what had happened with the injection that I needed out of there and planned to escape again. They had the window fixed in such a way that it could not be opened again, so I needed another way. I waited two weeks before I decided to escape again. I needed the heat to calm down. They were watching me like a hawk. I had 24-hour surveillance. I had a new nurse every night. The nurse that had been allocated to me the night I decided to escape this time was from another asylum. He was in his late 50's and didn't really say much. I told him I wanted to go for a shower, and as was the case, he had to accompany me to the communal showers. He stood outside the curtain as I was showering. Then thinking of a joke while I was showering, I put my head around the curtain and asked him to wash my back? He looked really uncomfortable at the request and said, "No!"...obviously and I said, "well, the other male nurse, Tall Gerard, did it for me!" The joke I thought of was about a guy who got stiffed in a taxi ride in New York then spotted the taxi man who done it a few weeks later in the front of a line of taxis. As part of a plan, he went to three taxis before him, asking each of them for a lift, saying he had no money, but he'd give a blowjob for the fare. As he expected, they all told him to eff off but as he got to the corrupt one, he just told him where to take him as he had the cash leaving the man's colleagues believing he'd accepted the blowjob!! By that reckoning, I thought I'd give the last nurse whom I didn't like either a slagging too. He still didn't do it!! LOL.

When I got back to the room, I got my casual clothes on, but I dressed in such a manner that I could withstand the cold. I had on a Liverpool football jersey, an Ireland rugby shirt, a fleece - a pair of shorts and my sandals. It was about nine at night, and I asked the nurse could I go for a smoke. He said yes so, I put my army surplus coat on. I went to the smoking area, which was outside but blanked off to the garden by a 7-foot-high wooden sheet of ply wood.

I crouched on the bench with my feet up on it, sitting, smoking, looking at him and talking about my Merchant Navy days, waiting my chance. I had everything I needed on me. My Bank card being number one. He began asking me questions then about my time at sea. We were the only two there. He asked me if I had ever abandoned ship. I replied, "We did safety drills for it, but I never had to do it in reality." I thought to myself as he asked me this, "did he know what I was thinking?!!" That I was about to abandon ship! Stupid, now thinking back but not hard to make the connection at the time. I was nearly finished the cigarette when I thought this is it...he had a momentary lapse in concentration as he relaxed into the conversation and was standing 20 feet or so away. I leaped with one foot up on the window sill inside the smoking area and jumped up to the top of the wooden partition. As I scrambled over it, I could feel him reaching for my ankle but I got over the partition and fell flat on my face. Smacking my hands and knees on the concrete on the other side of the ply. I squashed the cigarette that was still in my mouth to a right angle when I hit my face off the deck. I spat it out. I didn't have time to feel pain! I got up and, slightly half-dazed, ran at top speed towards the window sill and wall that I had jumped before. I got over it again in a flash, same as before. This time I ran like my life depended on it.... zigzagging in case of snipers. Paranoid city! I was so paranoid about what had happened in Shannon airport a couple of months before. I pictured snipers on the roof!!! Lol. When I got to the housing estate on the other side of the road, I began walking. As I walked down through it, I met this guy walking up with a can of beer in his hand. I asked him the way down to the town. I told him I had just escaped from the mental asylum. He laughed and said, "I done the same thing myself ten years ago!" I hoped at the time I didn't end up on the booze like him. He pointed me in the right direction. I thanked him and walked in the direction he had given me. I did it at that time of the night because of the darkness, and my thinking was because it was a Friday night, there would be a lot of people on the streets mulling about going from pub to pub. I was right. I didn't stand out in the crowd at all, even though I was in shorts and sandals. I made my way down to the Port Road at the bottom of the town where I knew of a friend of a friend's house was. As I was walking along the road, I spotted the Gardai in their Paddy wagon coming slowly towards me. I had my hood up and only glanced in their direction as they slowly passed me. They didn't look at me either, and they looked straight ahead so as not to startle me, I presumed. I knew they were looking for me. The asylum would have alerted them immediately. They would have my description, I thought. They didn't look my way at all, but I figured they were using their peripherals. As soon as they passed me, I bolted, running at ninety degrees to the road straight across it and over a fence into a garden, then ran to the back of the house and lay in a ditch at the side of their garden. I heard the police van roaring to life. Tires were squealing, turning and pulling up and stopping quickly. What a rush! I was enjoying it! They pulled into a wasteland right beside the fence I was hiding behind. I could see their shining torches, and I heard the shouts of the guards to each other, asking one another could they see me? I could see them in the lights of the van looking for me. When they couldn't find me, they got in their van and left. I was laughing to myself. I'd gotten away with it. Now for Belfast! I took out the two Valium I had kept under my tongue during the medication dispensing and that I spat out afterwards, keeping them for this occasion so I could sleep wherever I was. I wrapped up then in my coat and went to sleep in the grassy ditch. When I woke in the morning, I realized I'd had a great night's sleep and that I was free, but I needed to be on my way out of Letterkenny quickly because they'd still be looking for me. I walked quickly to the main roundabout to grab a taxi into Derry. My plan was to go to Belfast, where I knew Jamima was. I thought once again that from there, if I crossed the border, the Guards wouldn't be able to touch me (Which I found out later was true) and that I could argue my case from there. I really felt I had no one to help me or listen to what I had to say about what was happening. I quickly walked to the main roundabout that lead out of town and got a taxi at the rank there. He gave me a lift to Derry. I paid him with what I had then, and I was just in time for the bus, as it turned out. I was a few pence short for the bus, but the lady at the desk said, "On ye go," winking, which I thought was very nice of her. The next thing I know, I'm in Belfast, and all I felt was freedom! I felt like I could breathe again. I was listening to my tunes on my headphones oblivious to the traffic noise. Still, I focused on having my say against my treatment and catching up with Jamima. I booked into a hotel into the Europa hotel. It was always on my bucket list. The most bombed hotel in the world. It was in the city centre and I then phoned Jamima. She told me another friend of ours McCourt was in Belfast too, so we should call him too. He was like a brother to me. I loved his banter. I did this, and he brought me some normal clothes to wear but they were way too big. He was a bit outward lol. He said I had to change my clothes because they said I looked like an escaped mental patient the way I was dressed!

I bought a new set of clothes that day and relaxed into the city. I went looking for a new hotel after buying the clothes. I walked into one and as soon as I opened my mouth, they were immediately wary. It was at the top of the Falls road. A predominantly Protestant area. They are so fucking obscene with religion up there. They figured right away I was Catholic. They treated me like a terrorist lol if only they knew. I spent the week exploring Belfast, chilling out, and really enjoying the place. I was walking along one of the side streets one day and I felt like I was under surveillance. The heat could be felt. I knew the security forces would have all been alerted of my presence. I was an escaped mental patient after all!! As I was walking passed two fucking assholes in trench coats, they definitely looked like undercover cops, they said, while not looking at me "She's nothing but a slut!!" I knew immediately they were talking about Jamima. I always have an alert buzzing inside me. I have read all of Andy McNabbs books. The SAS guy. He has helped me become a secret agent. I have lived my life undercover for all these years. I got over that little fracas and got Jamima to liaise with my parents and pass on a message saying that I did not want to go to the bloody asylum. I was in such a dire position. I thought Jamima could help. But she just bowed to my parent's pressure and said she thought I was Bipolar as well. It was the end of my life, I thought.

Jamima spoke to them, but they would not budge. They believed me about my bad treatment in Letterkenny asylum, but I still had to do my fucking time. This is bullshit! I thought! So, to take the heat off myself because of what happened in Shannon just before all of this went down, I went to the mental asylum. I thought it would get the security forces off my back as well. My father came with my mother to Belfast and we had the weirdest drive to Sligo, the new asylum. Jamima came for the run, but she wasn't much bloody use to me.

THEY FEED YOU UNDER THE DOOR

When we got to Sligo, I decided I was going to give the entire staff the silent treatment. I was told I would be there for 3 whole weeks. I thought, fuck them, easy peasy. I'll stay silent for the whole time!!

We had come to an agreement in Belfast over the phone that I would go to the new asylum. The dreaded SLIGO INSANE ASYLUM. I'd heard stories from other patients who were threatened with being sent to Sligo for not conforming in Letterkenny mental asylum and that it was a fucking torture chamber there. Very bad conditions, so bad in fact, that if you misbehaved there, they would lock you in your room and feed you under the door. I laughed at the time when I heard this story. It couldn't be that bad, I'd said. I was about to find out.

The first night was eerie, there were high ceilings, and an old-world adornment on the walls that looked drab and worn out. There were only a few other patients and one around my age who I got on well with, but he was only there for a few days. There was another guy too, but he was only in the high observation unit when he misbehaved in the general population on the other ward.

There wasn't much going on in there apart from a lot of conforming to what the nurses said and being made aware that the cameras were watching you all the time. Without putting a feather in their cap, the paranoia of cameras stayed with me for a good two years after the admission. The feeling of always being watched is not a good feeling. You can never relax. It was terrible.

A lot of my time was spent sitting listening to the radio that I'd brought with me and looking out the window of the smoke room. The silent treatment was really pissing them off. I only spoke when spoken to. I decided to stay on my own in the smoking-room and get my time in. It was a terrible place to be. The three rooms that we co-habited – the smoke room, the TV room, and the games room were large. I just sat in the smoke room, looking out the window listening to the radio and smoking cigarette after cigarette. I was allowed outside in the sunshine only twice in the 3 bastarding weeks for fresh air, walking back from Mass, and kicking a ball about one sunny day. The rest of the time there, I sat on my own, recounting my memories in my mind. I wouldn't watch TV with the nurses because I felt like it was giving in and they were the enemy. I spoke to them as little as possible.

I got up every morning, and made time for myself. I started shaving my head with a razor so that it took longer to get ready, and then I had sort of time slots, and I worked it. I got up in the morning, got dressed, had a shower, got shaved, and then by that time, it was breakfast time. I spent a bit of time smoking in the smoke room. Maybe a few games of pool if they let me play. Then I would have lunch and then spend more time just looking out the window listening to music. There was only a couple of times I had people to talk to in there, the other times, I just sat listening to the radio, and that was it.

All in all, now, when I think back, I got the time in pretty easy. I stayed out of the way, but there were a few assholes for nurses in there. There was one nurse, Norman, whom every time I asked him to go to the toilet, he would say, "just a minute", "in a minute," then he would finish watching whatever he was watching on TV, or he would finish reading the newspaper. He wouldn't just get up off his fat ass and let you into the fucking toilet. It's not like you were asking every five minutes, but he would just do it to play with your head, and because it was locked, it had to be opened with a key. Norm was a lazy fat prick! He would stand outside the toilet, then I would go to the toilet, and he would wait for me to come out, and when I would come back out, he would lock the door. Simply said, waiting for him was a form of control that he exercised every chance he could. I was locked up in a place for the criminally insane as well. They told me "we lock the criminally insane up here too." How did it come to this, I thought?! Flo was right. The whole thing had escalated exponentially on me after the first admission.

It was fucking SO bad. When I was asking for cigarettes (I had to ask for cigarettes), another nurse Alex who was in his late 50's, would only give me a couple at a time. He wouldn't give me a full box. That was their rule, and he wouldn't give leniency. The other nurses did give leniency to it but he was a prick! The other nurses used to give me the whole box. They did this because they were a little bit more normal. Not like the sadistic fucking cunts with nothing going on in their lives outside the asylum. I have found out from other nurses that many of the nurse's steal medication and get high on it. They have alcohol and drug addictions and fuck with the patients for pleasure. They are always SO full of themselves that they bully the good people working there into doing what they do to patients. It is about to stop!!!

Alex enjoyed the power trip. They were my cigarettes, so I wanted them all. This one time whenever I was down the hall at the locker where they kept our belongings, I sort of sneaked up behind Alex. He didn't know I was there. The other nurse Mike, with him knew, he had let me in. They had stopped at the cupboard that housed all the patient's cigarettes and started talking. I was standing a distance away, but I went up closer to see what they were saying whenever they started talking. They had their backs to me. The younger nurse Mike, who wasn't as bad as Alex said, "will I give him the box?" Alex, the head nurse, turned around to him and said, "Ah, sure, just give him a couple of cigarettes. You don't have to give him the whole box". So, I said startling him, "No you have to give me the whole lot because they are mine. I bought them. So, I own them". He was just making life difficult for me, and then when I went to reach for them, I cut my finger on the metal door of the cabinet. I flicked the blood at Alex, saying, "look, they are my fucking cigarettes!" It hit him on the face!! Lol. This freaked him out, so he said quickly, "we will give you the cigarettes, we will give you the cigarettes. It's ok…it's ok". And then that was it. He fucking shit himself!!!

At this stage, these places were wearing thin on me. It was my fourth admission, and the games the bullies played were growing tiresome.

Then another night, one of the women in there had her birthday. There was only three other people in the ICU constantly when I was there. All of them were in there long-term, one was in 16 years, and another one was in 12 years and another in 14 – long-term patients, years living there! Freaky and scary.

I wasn't in the general population due to the fact that I was a high-risk patient for escaping, so solitary and a rubber room it was for me. After over two weeks in there, it was my birthday, and my mother and her twin sister Aine came to see me. They brought with them a cake with Spiderman on it because I kept escaping. I had escaped twice from Letterkenny, and I escaped once from St. Pats mental asylum. I even broke back into the Dublin one! One day in St. Pats I went on the piss, drinking. It was easy to break security there. Another night in St. Pats I got some leave, and I could go freely into the city. I went out with a couple of other patients who were allowed to stay out for the night. I wasn't allowed, and had to be back by 12 midnight. I told the other patients I felt like Cinderella! We went to a nightclub. I even scored in the nightclub. I got a girl, Susie Farrell, and her number! She left quite an impression on me. I wrote this poem (also in 'Anonymous in the town that talks') the day after I met her and sent it to her through a text message but I never got a reply. I think the fact that I was in the asylum, freaked her out ha ha! I dunno why? We mental patients are great shags. VERY very naughty, so we are lol. I told her in the message, to come and visit!

UP

Susie

When I saw the tassles shake,
My brain applied lusts brake,
But the more I watched,
the more I admired,
lust took over,
as my brain was inspired,
a kiss on the lips,
from those tassled hips,
cigarettes tossed aside,
passion surpassing,
the will to hide,
the dance floor we'll clear,
as we seek, hide, and glide.

But I had to leave her because it was half eleven. I had to be back before the gates closed. Whenever I got back, the gate was closed. I walked back down the road outside the asylum, looking up at the perimeter wall. I wondered if I could climb it. It was too high at the gate, but I noticed the wall got lower the further up the road you went. I nearly walked to the end of the road where it was about 5-foot-high, then I climbed up on it and walked back up the length of the road on top of the wall to the main gate of the asylum. When I reached the gate, I was inside the grounds, so I jumped down. When I walked to the door, a young Scottish guy appeared out of the shadows and said, "ah, are you Juan?" I said, "yeah," and he said, "We were expecting you," and that was it. He just opened the door and let me in. I thought it was a bit weird. The managerial staff laughed about it, and the nurses thought it was hilarious as well – breaking back into the asylum. But that was alright. Those were better times. I didn't know the gravity of my decision to go into the place at the time or the impact it would have on my life. Hindsight?!! Eh?!!

I asked the woman whose birthday it was, did she want pizza? I had my Visa gold card with me. She said "yeah. I wouldn't mind some!" She was the victim of bullying as well. She asked one of the female nurses for water one day. The nurse came back in to the smoke room with the water in a plastic cup and showed it to her then walked over to the plant and poured it in to the plant, laughing and said "There's your water!" That nurse was such a sadistic bitch. She squashed the cup in her fist in front of the patient then left the room laughing to herself. She looked at me expecting me to laugh. I thought, if I'd a gun I'd shoot you!

The visa card wouldn't work over the phone when I tried ordering the pizza, so I said to Norm, the lazy cunt for a nurse, "look, I want to order pizza," and he said, "Well, you have no money". I said, "I have a Visa card, and I can use it," but he said, "Your Visa card doesn't work". I said I could use another visa card, so I phoned my Dad, and I asked him could I borrow some money. I had money in my bank account, but I just couldn't get access to it. I used his visa card to phone the pizza shop in Sligo town and ordered up 3 big pizzas, and we all sat, myself and the other patients and ate out faces full. The three of us sat there in the smoke room and ate the 3 big pizzas. It was a little victory. We didn't give the nurses any of it but we left all the boxes open to let the smell fill the place. I let the nurses eat their sandwiches. It was a bit of craic with the other patients. We were watching the nurses have their evening meal, looking in at us jealous. They were expecting some. It was a small victory, but an enjoyable one.

Another night wasn't so funny. Big bad John came in, a new guy on the scene. He came in to the games room while I was playing pool. He was a tall cunt about 6"4' and in his 50's. I knew he had a mean streak in him, the way he spoke to me. He said threateningly without even introducing himself, "You're going to bed at 12 O'clock, SHARP!" It was on my final week. The other nurses had become lenient with me, but he was asserting his authority on me. I hate cunts like that. I just shrugged and said "whatever!" It pissed him off. He stormed out of the room. I had my little routine, and I was used to it. I got a late-night cup of coffee, and I sat and smoked until it was time to go to bed and got the call to go. It was sometimes later than 12.

I carried on playing pool after the interruption. Then, after, I went back into the smoke room, where I spent the majority of my time away from the nurses and had peace to smoke. Five minutes to 12 midnight came, and Big bad John shouted into the smoke room "time for bed...." I shouted back, it's only 5 to 12. So, in they came in. Big bad John with his young lackey, Damien. Another male nurse in his mid-twenties, well-built with his arms swinging by his side like he was carrying two TV's, spoiling for trouble. They had it in their heads they were going to put manners on me, I could tell. They walked up to my side where I was sitting with my feet up at the window ledge listening to my radio. John spoke. He said loudly and more authoritatively this time "I said, it's time for bed!!" I said to him, staying seated and repeating the words he'd said to me earlier, "you told me..." "You'll be going to bed at 12 O'clock sharp!" "It's not 12 O'clock yet!" I said. This annoyed him even more and he said angrily, "I don't care what I said you're going to bed NOW!" half shouting and grabbing at my arm. I stood up with the cigarette hanging from my lips, turned, and faced them. I took the cigarette back into my mouth, lit and chewed it for a second, then blew, spitting it all over their faces. I was out to annoy them. They'd annoyed me! 5 to, is 5 to. Not 12!!! I wasn't going to be pushed around. At that, they both grabbed my arms and tried manhandling me out of the room, but I had other ideas...I made myself limp, so they had to drag me across the floor. I put my feet out in front of me so it was like I was skiing across the wooden floor as they dragged me. I looked across through the windows into the TV room as they were dragging, huffing and puffing, to where the pretty young female nurse was stood shocked at what was happening. I could see by her face she was distraught. I gave her a cheeky little wink. It was funny as FUCK!!! She kind of laughed. Good enough for me, I thought. The two male nurses were struggling with me but I thought "Fuck them!". "Let them sweat! They can drag me the whole way to the room, I thought. Which is what they did, with a lot of anger, I have to say. Every time we got to a locked door of which there were two before my cell door, I would fall on the ground because John had to let me go to open the door. This was purely to annoy them and show them that I couldn't be intimidated. I went completely limp. He'd pick me up then continue to drag me through each door to the cell door. By the time we got there, there were two other male nurses in the room. The rubber room was a fucking jail cell. So, there were 4 nurses in total. Two holding me by either arm, and the other two in the cell. I'd stopped the limp act when we got to the door. I had bigger fish to fry with the behaviour of the young nurses in his mid-thirties. The adrenaline had got the better of him. He flipped my bed which consisted of a sturdy mattress on the rubber floor, while the other two restrained me. He was laughing manically when he done it! Then he kicked over all my books and picked up the rubber duck I'd brought as a memento from the Europa hotel, in Belfast. It was yellow, and he was saying, "AW look Juan," "Look Juan!" squeezing it, teasing me with it. Fucking idiot! It was rubber. He was doing no harm. I thought, this guy's a retard!! I said in a cool but authoritative voice, "Put the duck down!" Quoting from the movie ConAir where Nicolas Cage said, "Put the bunny down!" I was laughing inwardly at him. These piss ants had no life except bullying people like me. They squeezed me through the door into the room with one nurse on either side. I rolled out of their grip onto the flipped mattress, as an example of what I could do. They had no chance against me, if I decided that, that was their fate. I decided to go easy on them. I was having fun! They lifted me back up and pinned me against the wall. I wasn't going to strike out at any one of them even if they struck me because I wanted out of that asylum. And I knew the extreme disadvantage and inferior position I was in. They could lie about anything that happened, and there was fuck all I could do about it!! Sure, I was mad, according to them.... the evil cunts. And I was right! They did lie but not before Big bad John threatened me. He grabbed me and held me by the throat, after I rolled out of their grip then pinned me against the wall as the other nurses had an arm each. He raised his fist to my face drawing it back like he was going to hit me and he shouted, "YOU'LL DO AS WE SAY!!!" I remember the gleam of his wedding ring and thought I'm sure his wife has seen that before. He seemed to like that kind of guy. So, I shouted back at him, "GO ON, HIT ME, SEE WHAT HAPPENS!!!" I meant that I had the law on my side, not that I would attack back, but that is not what they thought, and they accepted the challenge. He said calming down, "Why, what are you going to do?" "Nothing", I said, with the feeling of amusement in me, "but there's a camera up there and a camera up there!" I said, directing him with my eyes (there were two cameras in the rubber room) and that was it. They backed down and stormed out of the room. They walked out pumped up but not happy. The only points they scored were for the bed toss, but I also didn't give a toss. I was about to take those points away from them. I was fucking enjoying fucking with them. Dangerous and all as it was. I just shrugged as they banged the cell door. They then pulled back the spy latch, which was about 3" inches high and 12" inches long and goaded me through it, saying sarcastically, "Goodnight Juan!! Niiiight!! "Have a good sleep!", another wanker was saying. They all laughed insanely. They took a lot of pleasure out of roughing me up, again, I had no rights. I just ignored the dickheads and proceeded to make my bed. I turned over the mattress and methodically put on the sheets. They continued to taunt me until I replied, "Goodniiight!!" in a sing song voice, smiling at them like I was happy. When I did, they shut up and closed the hatch angrily. It ended a little too abruptly for my liking. I knew it wasn't over. They were vindictive pieces of shit!! I lay down under my freshly made covers and called out for them to turn the light off...just to really piss them off! Ha-ha!! I knew this would annoy them because they couldn't leave them on. They turned them off, and I rolled over to go to sleep. About 10 minutes later, the lights went on again, and I could hear the keys rattling to open the door. The door opened, and as I expected, the on-call doctor walked in. He had an injection with him, and his first question was, is everything ok?! He looked like he had just woken up, and he was surprised to see that I looked half asleep. I was putting on an act to get one over on the nurse pricks. "Huh?"...I said, rubbing my eyes. As if I'd been sleeping. Which obviously, I wouldn't have been able to if I was very manic. "Yeah," I said, "everything is fine." He told me that the nurses had called him in saying that I was in a manic state and needed to be controlled. Lying bastards, I thought. I knew as soon as I saw the Doctor what they were at. I was waiting for it. I was angry, but I didn't show it to the nurses or the Doctor. The nurses were all standing at the door, watching, excited at getting one over on me. The Doctor turned to them with a confused look on his face and said that I was fine and that there was nothing wrong with me. Which was true. The nurses were trying to get me knocked out for the night to teach me a lesson. The injection was something the nurses threatened you with regularly if you didn't agree with them at night or misbehaved during the day. They left you to believe they could do anything to you when you were unconscious. They do this in every mental asylum I've been in. They probably do it in every psychiatric asylum the world over for all I know. I was relieved the Doctor had some cop on. He went against them. He got up to leave, and as he turned to go out the door facing them, I winked and smiled at the nurses pissed-off faces. It felt good to get one over on them.... if not a little scary at what could happen in these places if they took spite at you.

The rest of my time went smoothly enough until they were putting pressure on me to mix with the nurses in the TV room. It was in my final days. I'd been told by a criminal from Dublin, that I wouldn't get out unless I sat in the TV room and was nice to the nurses. I couldn't bring myself to do it. The nurses put pressure on me to sit with them. So, to show I couldn't be pushed around again, I sang 'Flower of Scotland' at the top of my voice, pretending to be crazy in the smoke room, looking in through the windows at the nurses in the TV room, then started running up onto the window sills and jumping up and off and around with a spinning high kick showing them what I could do if I wanted to. It was designed to intimidate them like they were trying to do to me. It worked but not like I expected, as I found out the next day. I was called to an interview room around lunchtime and had a sit down with the on-call Doctor. The nurses had ganged up on me and told the on-call Doctor that I had a short manic episode. The bullshit that surrounds Bipolar! It was complete horse shit. I was putting on an act and they fucking knew it. Lying fucking pricks!!! They told the doctor that he needed to increase my medication. I told him I was fine, and I asked who reported me? He said that all the nurses had got together and said I was manic. I asked him if I looked manic to him, and he said no, but they had gone together and that was it. He had to respond. I said, this is bullshit and not fair, but I had no rights. The doctor upped my medication so much so that it left me drooling looking out the window in the smoke room the next day. I could barely move. I was scared shitless of what it was doing to my brain. I was still compos mentis but my body wouldn't function. This is kind of thing they did to me in St. Pats as well. It was not all fun and games in there, just in case you think I had a brilliant time! I think there has to be some brain damage because of the shit they put into me. Some of this medication causes people to be suicidal. I repeat - check out the documentary on YouTube 'Marketing madness – Are we all insane?' I was forced to take the extra medication and if I hadn't of fought against it, I would have been on it for life. I stopped it soon after getting out. It was a lonely fucking place to be mentally and physically. Just before I left, a male nurse, whom I'd been told, just to scare me was a brown belt in Karate, came in to the smoke room and apologized for any wrong doing of the nurses. He said "I hope you have no grievances with us?" He thought I had plans to get revenge on them. He looked really fucking worried. I told him "No axe to grind" but I was angry in my eyes. I could tell he wasn't sure. Fuck them, I thought. Let them worry! I finished my time out and went home.

When I got out of there, I didn't move into the newly renovated house of my Grandmothers like my Father had told me I would. The dreams of my new life in it had kept me alive in Sligo. I sat everyday planning how to best spend my 90-grand settlement on it. My father had promised me my Grandmother's house when he asked for the 20 grands, if you remember, from my car crash settlement to finish the renovations saying, "sure it'll be yours someday". I gave him the money.

When I got out of Sligo, he said I was to live in our home house alone. The whole family had moved into my Grandmothers and were on cloud nine because of it. They had given me the broken house. My Father, my mum, and James had moved into one side of the semi-detached, and my sister and Kestas had moved into the other. My Dad knew I had the money because of my car crash settlement and charged me 160 euros a week to live there. I told him it was fucking extortionate, but he said it's a four-bedroom house – take it or leave it. I told him I would pay the mortgage and own it but he said no. He was bleeding me dry. It took me years to get over not moving into that new house of my Grandmothers. It was such a kick in the teeth. The old house was picked dry by them. They furnished the new house with pickings of the old house. Even leaving me without a bastarding couch. I was being treated like dogshit. My mother was walking all over me. When I pointed out that I was a fucking Officer and how dare she look down on me. She replied sarcastically "well you're not now!" and walked away happy with her little fucking put down! It was one of the worst periods of my life in Shrove. Nobody came to visit me. I've been blackballed by the entire community because of my families well poisoning.

I was so used to the old house; it gave me no inspiration at all for my writing. I was looking forward to the new house and a new lease of life. I think that's what pissed me off the most. The TV was broke in the old house and there was stuff missing that they had taken for their new house.

I hadn't the energy to put the house back together because of the heavy medication I was on. They had put me on a ton of Seroquel. It was so fucking strong. I just lay in bed all day wishing I was off them. I felt suicidal at the time. The medication had zapped me of everything. I thought about slashing my wrists but I thought NO! I am not fucking letting anybody do that to me. I knew I had too much to live for but the thoughts were coming because of the medication. As I was lying in bed, I felt a pull on my forehead. It was the aliens. They were disconnecting me from the psychic connection I had with all my family. The O'Donnell's are a psychic family. They are the most evolved family in Ireland. The pull on my forehead lifted me off the bed. I had to sit up because of it, then I felt it release and fell back down. It was the weirdest feeling. All the emotions that were bubbling up inside me disappeared.

I asked my Dad for my 20-grand back, and he just laughed at me. "What 20 grands?" he said. I said, "you think you're some sort of Soprano (referring to his favourite TV show)" he laughed even more at this. Sadistic fuck! He had the law on his side too. I asked a lawyer in 2019 when I was on the bones of my ass without a penny, could I sue him for that money? She told me that if it was a gift, then no. I wonder if he knew this, or was he just being an arrogant prick like he could be?

I never got it back, and no one listened to me complain about it because of the Bipolar diagnosis. My father played games like that until the day he died. So, do not ever tell me "He was a good man." He was a house devil and street angel. I had no one to turn to for help. I was completely drained of my get-up and go. I have this in abundance. Any yachtie that knows me will vouch for this. I dockwalked and dayworked with the best of them. I hustled and was proactive every day in Antibes to get a job. It is SO difficult to get a job on those yachts and I got a ton of them. So, you cunts of nurses and doctors, do not tell me I am mentally ill. It does NOT exist!!!

The heavy medication took away my get up and go. I was completely out of my head on it. The worst part was, that I knew I did not need it. It was the most torturous feeling I could ever imagine. My entire family was happy as long as I was in my box, causing no hassle. I thought fuck this after a couple of months and got off all the medication. My Dad spent the entire 300 grand he got for selling the pub in 2004 on stables, horses, and the renovations. He hardly left fucking anything in his will for us. Jesus Christ, all those hours, days and weeks, and years we spent working in the godforsaken bar of ours. James lucked out, he got left everything. The horses and stables were such a dream of my father's, and he calls me mental!!! It was a real waste of money! I couldn't wait to get out from under my Father's regime when I came out of Sligo. I should have moved to my nearest town of Moville and got my life back together, but like I said, my head was fucked from the medication. The Seroquel is a fuck-ing evil drug. I was taking it every day. After I took it, I would lie on my bed and try to recall my memories. It was like the memories were being zapped out of my brain. One second, I could picture them, then suddenly it was like the connection had broken. I knew I wasn't going to be on that medication long.

It felt at the time like I was under house arrest. I felt like I was under constant scrutiny about my mood from my family. Even after I gave up the medication, my brain was fried from all the months on it. But I managed to hatch a plan on how to escape my father's clutches. I headed for Superyachts in the South of France. This was 2007. I was more than qualified to work on them with all my certificates. I was in the mood to emigrate and never come back, such was my frustration with life in our household at the time. Some mental patient to be able to do that?!! My life was a farce in Ireland because of the blackened name I had gotten of being Bipolar. My Father didn't want me to go to France, but he couldn't stop me. The minute he saw me getting excited about going into yachting, he flipped. I was at his computer in their nice new house because I didn't have the internet at home, reading emails from my friend about life there in France, and my Dad said attacking me, "You just want to go over there and live the high life again!" I said "no" "I just want a job." He couldn't argue with that.

I went to France, stayed away from the booze, and after two weeks of going to all the agencies in Antibes, I landed a job as 3rd Officer on a very high-profile yacht called 'M/Y Kingdom 5KR'. It was once owned by ex-president of the United States of America – Donald Trump. It is now owned by a prince of Saudi Arabia.

This job had wider implications because I was still worried about being watched by the American security forces after the Shannon stunt in 2006. I was paranoid as fuck about background checks even though I had no record apart from the many drunk and disorderlies that I didn't know about. It worked out well for me because of U.S – Saudi relations, I thought what better place to hide out from the Americans than on a Saudi yacht! Things went smooth on there. It was like living in a high-class espionage movie for a while with the glitz and glamour of the South of France and then the edginess of the worry of security forces being on my ass. It took a while for my brain to come back to normal after all those heavy medications. I also felt socially awkward because my brain wouldn't function properly. It took years to come back normal. I am only feeling 100% now in 2023. The carrying of the big bad secret that I'd been in a mental asylum was bringing me down as well. I was being, in my words, accused of being Bipolar. A nurse said when she heard me saying "accused" in the asylum "you're not guilty of anything!" "Just accept it," referring to the Bipolar. Fucking Jesus, did it rub me the wrong way!

I was the object of affection from a young Spanish stewardess but she liked another guy better lol.

I travelled from Antibes, taking the yacht down through the Suez Canal to Sharm El Sheikh in Egypt. The owner of the yacht owned the four season's hotel there as well. I did my watches, glad to be back in a state of normality for me after being treated like a fucking no-hoper. A strange coincidence occurred on the journey. About 30 miles from the entrance to the Suez Canal on the Mediterranean side, I noticed a ship's name on the ECDIS, one of the computer navigational screens, "Maersk Barry" I couldn't believe it. It was the ship my brother James was working on. He was 2nd mate on it. I was so proud of him. He really is a good brother.

I got on the radio immediately and called the ship up. It was about 2 miles from us, and as it was an early evening, so I could see it clearly. I called them up, "Maersk Barry, Maersk Barry, this is the Motor Yacht Kingdom," "Do you copy?" I said calling them. My brother answered right away! He was on watch. It was another coincidence. "Motor yacht Kingdom this is Maersk Barry... JUAN, is that you?!!" I could hear the laughter in his voice. "Yeah, James it's me!" I said. "How you doing?" "Doing good!" he said. I said the same, then I said I would phone him when I got in to port. I was aware everyone was listening in, so there wasn't much we could talk about. It was just good to hear his voice. We had a great relationship. We never had an argument until I took the piss out of his now wife. He went fucking bananas at it lol.

Both of us were at sea at the same time BUT in the size of the whole world, what are the chances of that happening?!! I thought after that there were higher powers at work setting it up. It's a crazy thought, but not when you are dealing with the uber rich.

The crew who were on watch with me told our Captain about it when he came up for his watch. One of them said "it was like radio Ireland up here, a while ago!" and then let me tell the Captain the story. He was amazed at the coincidence. My only problem with the coincidence occurring was that when my mum found out, she told the local newspaper, the Derry journal and they wrote a full-page article on it, pictures included. So much for me keeping a low profile, I thought!!!

When we got to Sharm el sheikh and tied up, the harbor we were docked in had a wonderful view of Mount Sinai, the place where according to the bible Moses received the 10 commandments. The Captain organized a snorkelling trip for the whole crew, they were 40 of us, and I went snorkelling on the reefs there before the owner arrived. I got on great with the crew. I am friends with some of them to this day. The Captain's son and I really hit it off. He was a really nice lad and made me feel really at home on there. It was a great introduction, and welcome to yachting. I found everyone in yachting to be the salt of the earth. They really look out for one another! His Father, the Captain, was a really nice man too. It was a new life for me! I couldn't get enough of it. The job was only temporary, but I relished it. It was a start and my first reference. I did let my hair down a bit in Malta, when we stopped for fuel on the way there. I went drinking with half the crew. There were about 15 of us in a bar doing shots, and I got up on the bar counter and danced with one of the scantily clad dancers. It was my first drink in over a year. This went down a storm! The crew talked about it for the rest of the trip, laughing their heads off! It was great having the guests onboard. I was used to entertaining from my time on the Jeanie Johnston and all the bar work I had done in our family bar. I left after this trip and went home. The aliens told me at that time unbeknownst to me, that I must go home. They said I had big things to tie up. They were talking about bringing down the mental health services. They were bringing me home to finish them off. It was going to take years but that was my mission. I did not know any of the aliens plans at that time. I just heard an authoritative voice in my head giving me a command. It sounded important. I'd had this lots of times. I did not know it was aliens. They talk to me in a normal chatty way now but they still command me to do things. It is up to me whether I do them or not so don't be thinking I am under any bad influence. They never ever tell me to do anything against the law.

I crab fished for a little while during the 4 years at home between the time of my first yachting experience and the next yachting experience. I said on my CV that I fished continuously. Everybody lies on their CV!! I always wanted to go back to yachting, the trip on Kingdom had whet my appetite. I found yachties to be fantastic go-getters and great to be around. Full of energy and life. I knew I wanted to finish my career there. Hopefully I'll be an owner soon and employ the best crew ever! I plan to give them rotation, 2 months on, 2 months off and full pay for the year. I'm going to boost the wages as well – treble what we're on! I hope to create a revolution in yachting too. The yachts have been stagnant for too long. They need a shake-up! I'm going to give it to them!!!

The next four years before my return to yachting were fucking mental. I had a fucking diabolical relationship with the craziest little fucking slut you have ever heard of in your life, Fanjita as you've read already! That was 2008 to 2010. I had some good times as well, these are the good times!!

CRÈME DE JUAN

Being off the drink was boring me to tears when I came back in 2007. I'd come back from France and stayed bloody sober. It was such a mistake but I am aware I was only having delusions that I can not be without alcohol lol just kidding. I was getting my life back. The only fun people had around where I lived was drinking alcohol. I'd been threatening to give up alcohol since I was 19 years of age, and even though I broke loose in Malta when I was on the yacht, it was the only time I did in a year and a half. I got a great reference from Kingdom, which means a lot in yachting. Alcohol has destroyed my life, but I have some great memories on it too. Go figure! I had been off it for all that time before this night. I wasn't going out much hence the boredom. I'd bought a car with the crash settlement, and I was back living on my own in the house I grew up in. I didn't blow the settlement money because of good advice from my elders. I was looking for alternative things to do that didn't involve drinking. I went to the cinema on my own this evening in Derry, but on the way back, I stopped in Moville, parked up, and went into the late-night bar/night club there. I forced myself to go in even though I felt awkward, sober. I knew it would be tough going into the battle-field in my sobriety, but what awaited me arose my wealth and health.

It was around 1 am, so the party in there was well on the way. Everyone was a little tipsy when I went in. Jacinthia, a lady whom I had fancied the hell out of as a teenager, spoke to me as I came in the door. She was the older sister of the friend of mine, Olive, Mac Eas's girlfriend. Olive is a little vixen and she fancied me too. Jacinthia was about 35 at the time. I was 29. I knew by looking in her eye even when I was young that she was a dirty bitch! Ha! She was too old for me to even think about back then, but I always thought she was cool. I used to think her boyfriend was a lucky man. They used to cut some swathe in the pub. I always had eyes for her. So had a lot of other men. I hadn't seen her in years, but suddenly we seemed closer in age. There was a definite attraction between us. She introduced me to the guy she was with, Kav was his name. She then introduced me to her friend. Her name was Ava. Ava had the same look in her eye as Jacinthia. It got my engine purring. I seduced Ava. We hit it off right away, but I had to drag her away from three hornball of young guys before I did. She seemed a little flighty, and the boys had raging hormones. I spoke with Jacinthia, comparing her with Ava in my mind, trying to figure out which one I thought was sexier. Kav was a bit of craic too. When Jacinthia heard I was driving, she offered all 4 of us to go down to her house. I was more than happy to oblige. The club was ending, so we threw some shapes to leave. She gathered up Ava, who was a little more than tipsy and behaving a little slutty much to my liking. We all got in my car, and I drove us down to Jacinthia's house. Ava was the same age as Jacinthia. When we arrived at the house, we sat in her sitting-room talking for a few minutes. Then the two girls excused themselves and went into the bedroom for something. I'd guessed it was the same discussion Kav and I was about to have. He could see I was into Jacinthia as well. Kav said to me as soon as they left, "which one do you want?" he said. "I'm easy, it's up to you," he said. He then produced some Cocaine, smiling, and said, "have you ever taken this?" "No," I said smiling, but I told him I was willing. "Wait until you see them after they get this into them. It drives women wild!" he said. I picked Ava because she was on holiday here, so I thought I could have her that night then I could have Jacinthia another night, when Ava was gone. Sound reasoning, I thought!

The two women came back to the sitting room, and we had a few lines of cocaine. Then Ava and I went into the bedroom, and Kav and Jacinthia stayed in the sitting room. Ava got undressed, and so did I, then to stop the noise, we had sex on the bedroom floor. She didn't want Jacinthia and Kav to know we were fucking because she was still married. I doubt if they'd have believed her! She didn't mind them thinking we only kissed a little, which she was going to say if she was asked. She told me she was in the middle of separating from her husband, it was happening in a couple of weeks. She said that when she was back in a few weeks, we'd be free to fuck as much as we wanted, if I wanted to, that is, of course. She was really fit and had a great body, 6 pack to boot. I was ready to eat her alive! I told her I'd love to fuck her more. She told me she played rugby and that she had loads of lesbian flings with her teammates. They were at it all the time. It sent my mind in overdrive. She knew it would, she was smiling telling me. She was really turning me on. A cat couldn't have scratched my cock, it was that hard. She wanked me, massaging my cock before entry, warming me up, then she straddled me as I lay on the floor. She had petite breasts, but like they say, anything more than a handful is a waste! I pulled at her nipples with my teeth, driving her wild and kissing her passionately. The cocaine was doing its job. She was horny as fuck, and her pussy was dripping wet. I was in pretty good shape too physically at that time, so we fucked like wild cats in total silence but for the heavy breathing. Our sweaty bodies were writhing on the floor.

After we rode, we cooled off for a minute or two then went back out into the kitchen to Jacinthia and Kav. They all had some more to drink, and then I left and drove home. Ava had given me her number. She told me that even though she and her husband had split up, they were still living in the same house for their kid. I started texting her over the next couple of weeks. She was really horny, to say the least!!! I loved getting her messages. It was really good banter. She was telling me all the things she wanted to do to me and all the things she wanted me to do back to her, when she came back there on holidays in a few weeks. She said in her texts, this time, she wanted a threesome with her, Jacinthia and I, or Cin as Jacinthia liked to be known, whom she told me she had been sleeping with too at the time. That set my mind on fire too. I could imagine them naked fucking! It was great wank bank material.

A few weeks later, Ava arrived back in town, and I met up with both her and Cin in the Sean ti bar in Greencastle. It was the weekend, so there was a good few people in. We talked for a short while, then with seductive smiles on each of them, they finished their drinks, looking at me with a horn on them. We were all thinking the same thing. Of what was to come.

We left and drove to Cin's house in Moville, chatting sex all the way. We settled into the sitting room for a while. They were both having a drink, and they were telling me to relax and have one too! This happened to me with women all the time when I was off the beer. They all wanted to see how I behaved when I was drunk. They thought it was funny, they knew I wasn't a real hard fucking drinker. I just messed up sometimes. They all thought the drunk me would be fun! The three of us were getting cozy swapping sex stories. It wouldn't be the only thing we'd be swapping; Ava had been explicit in her texts. She wanted me to urinate on her, and make her kneel before me and order her, saying "suck my cock, slave!" She said she would say "yes master..." then I was to spank her ass! I couldn't wait! I thought, gas craic!!

The stories were good fun, and I bowed to the pressure and had one can of beer. It was fabulous foreplay. These girls really knew how to get your motor running. Ava was pretty drunk.

After a while, the conversation turned to bedtime. Cin said she would go up and get the bed warmed up, with a cheeky smile and a naughty glint in her eye. Ava said as soon as Cin left, that she wanted to fuck me on the couch first before Cin got her hands on me. She had the naughty glint as well. I was loving it! She got undressed and so did I. She lay across my lap naked and asked me to spank her bottom. I'd never had this happen to me before. I'd had women ask me for a little slap on the ass during sex but not this domineering malarkey. It was kind of erotic. She had this little girlie look on her face. I kind of laughed into myself. I didn't want to spoil the mood by laughing in her face. She was horned to the last! "I've been a naughty girl master!" she purred. Lying her full weight on my knees with her ass skyward and looking back up at me with an innocent schoolgirl look on her face. "Spank me, master!" she said. I didn't know how hard to hit her, so I slapped her a little spank with my right palm. "Oooohhh!!" she said. "Mmmmm....!!! Harder master!" she pleaded. I slapped her again. "Harder master! HARDER!!!" So, for the craic, I hit her on the ass cheeks with all the force I could muster! The crack echoed around the room! She squealed, "Aghhhh!!" she said. "Not so hard!" "Oh!" I said. "Sorry, it's my first time!" She sat up. "That hurt!" she said. "You said harder!" I said, laughing. I couldn't keep the laughter in.

She lay back on the couch, a little pissed off. I kissed her to soften her up. She started moaning. I lay on top of her between her legs and guided my cock into her wet pussy with my hand. She forgot about the slap as we locked lips kissing. She wrapped her legs tightly around my mid-section, drawing my cock deeper inside her. She was whispering, "fuck me, master!" "FUCK ME!!!" I didn't want to cum and ruin the threesome that was about to happen, so I thought of my training with all my wanking and paced myself, gently pulling back my balls when I felt like cuming to keep the love juice inside! I kept it going and I was giving both of us lots of pleasure. I had my head buried in the cushion above her shoulder. I was waiting for her to orgasm. I was slowly, rhythmically making love to her when I heard a little snore. I pushed myself back up to see her face, and to my shock and horror, she'd fallen asleep!!! I had never had this happen to me! What a blow to the ego that would have been if I had been any way sensitive! Luckily, I didn't give a fuck! I couldn't believe it, but she was so drunk, I wasn't surprised! I laughed to myself again and gave her a little smack across the face with the back of my hand, James Bond style! She woke up startled, and I laughed again at the shock on her face. "Do you really want to do this??" I asked. "Yeah!" she mumbled, half closing her eyes again. "Are you sure?" I said. "You look like you're about to fall asleep again!!" "No!" she said, "Fuck me!!" So, I carried on fucking her. I knew from her noises she was still awake. A few seconds passed, and as I had my head down going for it, I heard a soft snore from her again. That's it, I thought. I'm going up to see Cin...BUT before I do, I thought to myself (my mischievous side running wild because of her snoring!) I'm gonna have some more fun. Fall asleep on me?!! How dare you?!!! I thought. I stood up naked facing her as she lay on the couch passed out. I shook her shoulder, waking her up a little. As she came to, I asked her, "did she want to do some of those things she text me about, like peeing on her?!!" And without even opening her eyes, she groaned "yeah, do it, do it!" So, as my cock softened up a little, I stood back and peed all over her. I stopped mid flow so as not to soak the couch, a bit of respect, I thought, but it was enough! Ava amused me as she writhed with pleasure. She lay there on the couch with her eyes closed, moaning and rubbing my piss all over her tits and pussy. I was laughing quietly. I thought for the craic, then that I would stick my pissy cock in her mouth. She sucked it dry. I had to stifle my laugh. She really enjoyed it. I thought there was a bit of subliminal intuition going on. I'd got her back for falling asleep on me. "Fall asleep on me, BITCH!!!" I thought!!! Maybe I should have defecated on her?! I thought, laughing.

Although it was kind of cute. I liked the woman. I left her lying on the couch sleeping and climbed the stairs, still with the sexual juices raging through my veins. I went to the toilet to finish off my pee. As I was just finishing peeing, I felt two hands slipping around my waist and grabbing my cock. I didn't know who it was. I thought it was Cin. I looked around and was surprised when I saw Ava again. It was dark, but she was smaller and I could make her out from the light in the hall. She'd woken up and followed me upstairs. "Fuck me up the ass..." she whispered. As I turned around, still very surprised to see her awake again, I said, "what?" kissing her and going rock hard again. "I want you to fuck me up the ass before we get into bed" Dirty bitch I thought, but fuck it! I also thought. She hunkered down and sucked my cock deep in her mouth then spitting on the tip of it, she bent over the bath, spreading her ass cheeks. She said, "Fuck me hard!" I stuck my cock up her ass and fucked her hard for 5 or 6 seconds. She was gasping. She whispered breathlessly, "Ok" "Ok!" "That's enough!" I pulled out, and then she stood upright. As she did, a big blob of shit, fell from her ass and hit the tiles! It was my first real experience of anal sex. Nothing like Riverdance's lap shit!!! I cringed, but Ava was totally unperturbed. She reached over, pulled some toilet tissue off the roll, and in one swipe, wiped the shit off the floor and flushed it down the toilet. That's happened to her before! I thought. I was getting life lessons from these ladies and enjoying every minute of it! Anything goes! "Go you on into the room." She said, "I'll be in, in a minute" she said as she sat on the toilet seat for a poop. A wise decision, I thought!

I went into Cin's bedroom. The light was on. She sat up, looking at me seductively, as I walked in. The feeling of being around these two ladies was surreal. I didn't speak. I growled as I crawled forward on my hands and knees towards her on the bed. "Oooohh," she said. She laughed her dirty devilish laugh that I remembered hearing in the bar as a teenager, another one of my fantasies was about to come true, I thought to myself. "You're a bad boy!" she said, putting her hands around my neck, drawing me towards her, kissing me on the lips, then forcing her tongue in my mouth. I returned the favour. The juices flowed in our mouths. I pulled back the bed covers, and she spread her legs. I lay between her legs, pulling the cover over us. I was aware after fucking Ava up the ass that I wasn't clean. I had seen a documentary on sex hygiene. They said always wash after anal before vaginal sex.... all of a sudden, that didn't seem to matter. I wondered did Ava take some sort of pleasure out of that. It was a private joke for her knowing that Cin would more than likely have my cock in her mouth at some stage through the night. It made me laugh, too, I have to say. I reached down to her pussy and put three of my fingers inside her. She gasped then said, "Mmmmm..." I slid my cock deep inside her, drawing back my face from her to see her expression. It was an ultimate fantasy fulfilled! One I'd harboured since I was a teenager. She smiled and moaned. Her expression was divine. She never took her eyes off mine. A real turn-on in my book. Her vagina felt silken after Ava's tight arse! We kissed more. I knew I was going to do nasty things to her, and it must have showed. Her dark eyes came alive with pleasure. They showed depths of degradation that gets me every time. She practically purred at me. Only a few deep strokes later, as Cin and I were just getting comfortable, the door flung open. I looked around as I was lying on top of Ava's fuck buddy, and there stood Ava, fists clenched and ready to riot. She hollered, "SO, YOU'VE STARTED WITHOUT ME?!!!" indignant and jealous as hell. Fuck was she drunk! I laughed and said, we're just getting warmed up, rolling off her mate. "C'MON!!!" I said to her and threw back the covers so she could get in. She got over the indignation quickly. There was sex to be had! She climbed in between Cin's knees and seductively caressed her pussy with her tongue, licking everything from Cin's knee to her soaking pussy. I watched as she slowly licked Cin's pussy, thinking, so this is how women do it to each other in real life. It was my first threesome. FUCK ME, I WAS HORNY!!! Cin was arching her neck in pleasure while playing with my cock, slowly rolling her fingers over the tip, searching for spikes of arousal in my eyes. She slowly masturbated the mainframe of my soul as I lay back and watched them both with pleasure as they pleasured one another. Ava was going at it, like an expert! She was caressing and kissing with her tongue deep inside Cin's pussy. She was holding Cin's ass with one hand and had her other hand on Cin's tummy, holding her down to stop her from rising off the bed. Cin was writhing with ecstasy. I could feel the sexual energy pass through my body to the tip of my cock. It was orgasmic. We all kissed, and we fondled until Ava wanted to try something else. It was the height of eroticism.

Ava showed me where to stand at the side of the bed on the bedroom floor, and then she stood facing away from me, bending seductively over in front of me. I slipped my cock up her cunt without a second's notice. She was bent over in front of me. I kissed her back and rubbed her tits, licking the curvature of her spine. I ran my fingers down her back giving her shivers. She loved it!

Cin lay back on the bed in front of us. Ava spread Cin's thighs and started sucking on her clitoris. She spread her vaginal lips entering her pussy deep with her tongue and fingers. She licked Cin's thighs, as Cin moaned with pleasure and looked at me, smiling, straight in my eyes. It was the most erotically charged I had ever been. I did not want to orgasm. I wanted to make it last forever. I could feel the psychic connection. The aliens have told me those ladies opened up my destiny. I will become the world's greatest lover!!! Don Juan!! My Superyacht will be called M/Y Licentious guy.

Cin was smiling at me, knowing I was enjoying it. Ava ran her tongue slowly towards Cin's pussy, left leg, right leg, and then licking her pussy lips again. Ava was dripping wet. I could feel the moisture from her pussy running down my legs. Cin was holding Ava's head with both hands, pulling her tongue deeper. Cin never took her eyes off me except when she closed them in absolute orgasmic pleasure. I held Ava's ass as I came like the thundering wreck of an absolute God. Cin was squealing. She was cuming too!!! I was like Billy the Kid on speed! Her doggy style was barking hyena! Cin came as Ava wrapped her arms around her thighs, gripping ferociously, to get more purchase, sucking her deep. Cin exploded with wealth. The greens were flying out of her. Who said money doesn't grow on tease? Ava was like her gardener, tending her every need. I watered Ava with my wealth. I came at the same time. I thought I was going to faint. My knowledge spilled forth. I'd fucked her like a demon. We three curled up together and sped at breakneck speed through the night. I took turns fucking them while the other watched, kissing and caressing, then I fell asleep between them. I felt like a King. We'd driven until the gas was empty and slept until it was full again. I awoke in the morning with alarm bells ringing. I thought I had died and gone to heaven. I smiled to myself when I opened my eyes fully. A naked lady on either side of me. Which one first, I thought?

STAG DO IN GALWAY

In late 2007 I decided I could have a few social beers. I started to drink again, and it was my downfall. I was still 29. We had my friends stag do in Galway. We left early in the morning to get down there and give it a good lash. We had good craic on the bus on the way down. We met loads of people in the different pubs we went into when we got to Galway. There's was 11 of us in total, so we were kind of separating into groups, talking and having the craic but trying to stay as a unit.

It was about 11.30 pm, and I was a little distant from everyone, which the mood can take me sometimes when I'm drinking, so I wandered off for a bit of a breather, thinking I'll probably try another pub then go back to the hotel. I told Sean ti man, the stag, I was leaving and went for a walk. So, knowing Galway city centre a little I tried one of the night clubs I remembered. I asked one of the bouncers if it was ok to go in and have a look to see if I liked it first? He said no problem. I went in, but there were very few people there, so I left, thanking him. Then I tried another doing the same thing. It was very early for there to be anyone in any of them, so I decided to go back to the hotel. I thought to myself I wouldn't mind something to eat before I go back, so I made my way up to the chip shop on Eyre Square.

I went in, ordered, got my meal, and sat down. The place was packed. I ate my meal, but I thought I would have a bit of craic and banter with the staff behind the counter as I was leaving. I tried old faithful, the one I'd used in Dublin that got me in the fight, I hadn't learned my lesson! I asked one of the Indian-looking men serving, "how come the price of chips down here is so expensive?" He looked at me quizzically and said, "what?" frantically because they were busy as hell! Which is what I was expecting him to say, so I said, "How come the chips here in Galway are more expensive than the chips in Donegal?!!" "Are your potatoes more expensive?" He didn't look too happy this time...even a little perplexed, but I was only joking and about to leave when I heard a voice of authority behind me saying, "Excuse me are you causing trouble?!!" It was the Garda Siochana...3 of them...the one who was speaking looked like he was fresh out of Garda school, so I said, "no, I was only having a bit of craic!"

These young Guards tended to be the worst I have found because they are looking to make arrests and make a name for themselves, so I was on my best behavior, not just because it's the kinda guy I am but also because he needed no encouragement to do his worst.

Unfortunately, as I was talking to them and explaining my case, I spied my, when drunk, cantankerous friend Mac Sea through the windows and thought, "aw shit, he's spotted me!" This is going to be fuel on the fire, knowing he'd come in and try and plead my case too, which fair play to him he did, but in his state, I was better off doing it on my own. I was cooling it. I was saying to the guards, "I'm no trouble." Then Mac Sea comes in and says, "Juan, what the fuck??" and pulls the guards arm saying, "leave him alone he's not well!!" Referring to my apparent bipolarism! I told Mac Sea to be quiet and that I'd appease the situation telling him, "Mac Sea, shut the fuck up, I'll handle it!!" To which the guard said to me, "less of your bad language!" Then turning to Mac Sea, he said take your hand off me... "that's assault grabbing a guard's arm like that". I knew what Mac Sea was doing was a bad idea! I said calmly, "Mac sea, fuck off!" To which the guard said to me, "one more swear word out of you, and I'll arrest you!!" I couldn't help it... "What the fuck did I say?!!" was my reply! I was kinda drunk, and it felt, in that state, that I couldn't miss the opportunity of the quip, especially as the guard was being obnoxious. The guard said to me, "right, that's it. You're coming with us!" I put my hands out in front of me as the whole chipper watched on. He put the cuffs on me, cuffing me in front instead of the back as he is supposed to. He must have been really annoyed not to remember that one. He led me out to the car with the other two guards in tow to the Garda car. I couldn't figure out how they got there so quickly! I was told the guy behind the counter has an emergency button that he can press when he needs help. A bit far-fetched, I thought. I imagined one of the other staff called it the minute it started. I was only messing, but they were taking it very seriously. We got to the car, and he put me in the back seat, and all the while, I could hear Mac Sea arguing with them, saying for them to release me into his custody and he'd make sure I got home safely. I was laughing at him. I was waiting for the end result. I knew it was coming! Their answer was…. "if you don't leave it alone and go home right now, we'll arrest you too!"

As I was sitting in the car listening to Mac Sea's heated conversation with them behind the car, I looked around just in time to see Mac Sea's face going up against the back window and them cuffing him, telling him he was coming too! I started laughing! He was way more drunk than I was and a lot more vociferous. They put him in beside me, and he started on me then!! Saying I was an asshole getting us both arrested, and he began trying to head butt me with his cuffs on behind his back. Pretty funny, I thought, smirking, head butting him back but only messing. He meant it for real!! I said, "You're the reason for us being in this mess because you upset the situation so much!!" He was saying loudly to" fuck up!" Then one of the guards got in and told us both to calm down. We went to the Garda station and got checked in to what I have to say was one of the nicest cells I have ever been. Decoration and art on the walls…I sang my heart out for about an hour at the top of my voice just to annoy the guards, then fell asleep. They let us out separately around six, and we made our way back to the hotel independently.

It was a couple of months before the hearing for the incident. We were being charged with drunk and disorderly. I wasn't too worried because I had an idea of what I was going to say. I was only joking at the time, and I was hoping the judge would see the light-hearted side of it.

Before the case started, I was advised by my appointed solicitor on the day to apologize for my actions to the Garda for what I said on the night in question. I really didn't want to do it because I thought the Guard was wrong to take the action he did, and I really thought the young fucking arsehole had overreacted to the situation. So, against my better judgment, I went over to where all the guards were sitting in the court room, and just before I got to the point where I was face to face with him and apologize, I decided not to do it. I thought fuck him, he's an arsehole and carried on out of the court room and went for a cigarette. As I was standing at the top of the steps on my own smoking, I noticed a rather fetching blonde lady of stature coming up the court house steps with a spring in her step. I immediately guessed her to be the judge. I flirted with her right away! "Hi there!" I said smiling naughtily. "Hello!" she said returning my flirt with a mischievous smile. I finished my cigarette and went back inside. I told my solicitor I would represent myself. I felt the story could only come from me.

We were all told to rise as the judge entered and I felt my heart lift! It was the judge that I had the moment with before on the steps. I thought she might go easy on us.

It came time for the judge to see our case. She asked me to stand up. Then she addressed the court and said that there was a Mac Sea involved in this case too and asked him to stand also. The judge then asked me what happened? Mac Sea's solicitor had told him not to mention that he was down from Donegal on a stag do. He'd said the judge would look unfairly on it because they detested the stag do mentality that Galway attracts a lot of. I thought I'll go with the truth. When it came to my turn to speak, I explained in my own words exactly what happened, outlining that I was only trying to have a bit of banter with the staff in the chip shop and get a bit of a laugh going, but it had been taken the wrong way. I explained that we were on a stag do, and I got separated from the company and I was on my way home to the hotel when it happened. I also said I worked in the Merchant Navy, and a charge would limit my chances of getting work again and affect my travelling to countries like the United States. She listened to my story and looked fairly on me. Mac Sea had told me to play the Bipolar card, but I said

I saved that for special occasions! He thought it would be a good idea for himself to get a letter from his Psychiatrist to say he was suffering from the after-effects of a car crash. A car crash we were in together the previous year, but she tossed the letter aside, saying, "it has all become very Americanized!!" I laughed inwardly. I'd told him she would think it was bullshit! The fine was a bit steep; it was 500 euro and we were bound over to the peace for six months but no serious record. A good result, I thought.

After the 6 months were up, we were called to the court in Galway again. I was with Fanjita. I'd taken her along to pay my fine. My father had so graciously given me the 500 euro. I was penniless. The bitch fanjita could not wait to get her grubby little hands on it. I told her no bloody way. That's for the court room.

30

SLEDGEHAMMER!!!

It was shortly after the Galway stag do incident and I was in a local bar in Moville. Now, this incident may leave you feeling I am a bit crazy, but I prefer to think of myself as inventive when drunk! It is my creative side!!!

I was smoking a cigarette out the back of the bar in the smoke room when this tall guy started throwing his weight around for no apparent reason. He was spoiling for a fight! He was starting to annoy and antagonize everyone standing there, and then he started to challenge the friend I was standing talking to. I didn't know the angry guy personally, but I had seen him around and I knew that he was an asshole. My friend told him to get fucked, so he changed his attention to me. I said to him, "Don't even think about it. What, you can't get a reaction out of them, so you're going to try me?" I said.

I was really pissed off watching him ruining the ambience of the night. I hate dickheads like that. So, I asked him, "what? Do you want a fight?" I knew by putting it up to him, he couldn't back down in front of everyone after acting the hard man. He couldn't lose face. He said, "yeah, I want to fight.". My mate laughed because he knew I was about to kick this guy's ass. So, I said, "let's go outside then.... follow me". He reluctantly followed but he tried to maintain his dignity too. I knew that it wasn't going to work. He'd already lost. I walked through the crowd with him trailing to the front door. I looked back every so often to make sure he was following. I didn't really want to fight, but I wanted to teach this guy a lesson. I got to the front door and opened it. I walked out to the street. It was after closing hours, so it was a lock-in. The place was very busy.

When I went outside, I left the door open for him. I was ready to kick his scrawny ass. He was part of a gang in town. They were all a bit younger than me and they caused fucking mayhem. I heard the door banging after me. I looked around and figured out someone else had closed the door after me, and the other guy had chickened out. I thought, you fucking cunt!!! I didn't give a shit about the ass-kicking. What I did give a shit about was him ruining my night and getting me locked out for no fucking reason. I knocked on the door to see if I could get back in, but no-one answered it. So, standing there pissed off about 15 feet from the door, I shouted, "THAT FUCKING ASSHOLE!!!" I was angry at myself, too, for letting him get to me, leaving me in this predicament. All of a sudden, a car, a boy racer type, that I was standing in front of started revving up his engine as though he was going to knock me over.... that was all I needed!! I ran up his bonnet onto the top of his roof, but as I did, he took off and I fell from the roof. I fell right on my face on the tarmac. I wasn't in the mood to be pushed around by anyone this night. I stood up again, and I thought, what now? Where do I go? I looked up the street square, and I could see a crowd outside the late-night bar night club. I had been barred from it a month or so before for something I thought innocuous, but the bouncers obviously hadn't thought the same! It was a stupid argument. The barring was only for two weeks, so I thought, yeah, I should be fine. I walked up and joined the queue. When it came to my turn to get in, the bouncer put his hand up in front of me and said, "you're not getting in!" "Why not?" I said. He said, "because you're barred" "I said "that was only for two weeks and it was a month ago now, so it should be ok now" "I have been going everywhere else but here in that two weeks" I said. He said, "I don't care you're not getting in!" he was holding up the queue at this stage, so I told him I wanted to see the manager, and he said, "right, I'll be back in a minute." He went inside, and the other bouncer was letting people past to get in. The main bouncer came out again and said the manager of the club at the time, whom I knew and had gone to school with, said I was too drunk. I said, "I couldn't be. I was only out and I'd only had a few drinks in the pub down the street". I said, "anyway, how does she know when she hasn't even seen me?" He said, "look, that's the way it is." I was really pissed off at this stage. I wondered how she could see me? Then I spotted the security camera above his head at the door. I said to him "I'll be back in a minute".

I went down back to the square where there was a taxi waiting and asked the taxi driver Terry who was an ex-fisherman in his late 50's to run me back down home to Shrove. He did this, and when we got to my house, I told him to wait on the street for a few seconds. I jumped out and went into the garage, picked up a sledge-hammer, and got back into the front seat of the taxi. Terry asked me where I was going with that? I said, smiling to him, "I'm going to pale some posts." He half laughed and said, "fair enough". I paid him before we got there, as I had done in Shannon, so there would be no waiting around. I was on a mission!!

When we got back to Moville, Terry pulled up in front of the nightclub. I got out of the taxi and I concealed the sledge down by my leg. The queue was all the way from the top of the ramp of about 20 feet and longer, maybe a 30 feet queue waiting in line down to road level. I put my right hand close to the head of the sledge for control and my left hand at the top of the shaft so as to get a good swing. That camera was coming off the wall, I thought in my pissed off drink induced wild state. I ran up past the queue of people, and just as I was about to swing the sledge at the camera, while passing the bouncers, one of the bouncers was quick off the mark and jumped out and grabbed the shaft of the sledge and held me with my back to his chest and the sledge shaft up to my neck. Everybody went crazy. I was pretending to get choked by it. My cousin Red started shouting at the bouncer to let me go!!! And that the bouncer was choking me.... I was making all the noises of it! Not to make a fool out of Red but to get the crowd going. The bouncer wouldn't let me go. He waited until the guards got there. As it turned out, it was the bouncer's first night on the job, so he didn't know anyone or who to listen to. The crowd was telling him to let me go and that there was nothing wrong with me, the anger had long left me after he grabbed the sledge hammer, and when the guards got there, I knew one of them. The guard I knew Paul took the sledge from the bouncer and told me to go home. He said if he saw me in the town that night again, he would arrest me. That was it. I got a taxi down-home and went in for a quiet beer in Michael John's pub beside where I live, then went home to bed. In hind sight, it was a bit of an overreaction to not being let in, especially as I was bound over to the peace still for the incident on the stag do in Galway at the time!

I met the owner a few days later in another pub. He was laughing about it. He said it was like something out of Scarface the movie lol.

I went in to my local in Moville a little while after that and sat down at the bar. As soon as I got a drink, the song 'Sledghammer' came blaring out of the juke box. Everybody cheered looking at me!!! It was a bit of craic…

31

M/Y OBERON

2011 started with me wanting to go back to sea on the yachts in Antibes, South of France. So being on the dole, I had to save up my money using the credit union to get a loan with the ballpark figure of 1000 euro in my head to sustain me in France. I gave myself 3 weeks there. I'd gotten rid of fanjita and was so relieved. I had PTSD from the trauma of going out with her and that was the most fucking terrible, atrocious time of my life put to an end. I just thought, time for a bit of a good time. I got to Antibes and felt the heat of the sun and was so relaxed. I knew it was gonna be potluck if I got a job but I was loving it. The rent in Debbie's crew house was 200 euro per week. Well worth it for the amenities you get. I used the 1000euros to keep myself in Antibes with the rent and food. The plan worked. I was reading the book 127 hours by Aaron Ralston too and it gave me real good inspiration to persevere. The yachting is gruelling when you are looking for a job. I did the agencies first and the girls second!

The first couple of days passed uneventfully. Then after one interview in a certain agency, the woman who was interviewing me, who was really nice, said that she had two yachts for me and it was up to me to choose which one. There was a 50m that needed someone right away or a 60m that was on its way across the Atlantic from America and would be needing someone in a week or so. I chose the 50m and told her I thought it might be a better idea to go for the smaller one because I would learn more because I would be working on deck with the deckies. I remembered from Kingdom that if you worked on deck, you got way more experience. There wasn't much difference between a 50m and a 60m but I thought the smaller one would be more hands on.

The 50m, as it turned out, was more of a party boat because it was a shadow boat in a fleet of 3 with a sister ship the same size and an 80 metre mother ship. I thought I could practice on the 50m range then move to the 60m but the partying onboard was fucking crazy.

There is a general hierarchy on board all boats, and it's the same on every ship worldwide from the Captain down. You have to learn to be in the management side of things but know the deck and do both.

I took the Oberon job anyway and did the interview with Gillet, the Captain, who was really sound and someone I thought I could get along with. I did the interview along with another guy, Joe, that I had just made friends with in the crew house. It was a bit of a coincidence. He was really sound as well, and when we did the interview, Gillet said that both of us had jobs as long as our references checked out. Unfortunately for Joe, one of his references was a bit of a dickhead and wouldn't give him the reference, so he didn't get the job. I got the job as a Second mate, and they got me my 10-year B1/ B2 visa for the United States. Getting the visa was a bit hair-raising to say the least.

Putting my hand on the laser scanner in the US embassy in Rome had me sweating bucket loads. I wasn't sure what would show up on their records after the Shannon incident.

Captain Gillet had told me in Monaco, where I met him and his missus for drinks before I joined, that the crew would probably offer me to come out for drinks with them when I arrived. He said to go and to get to know them. It was so laid back. I was a bit shocked. I thought I'm going to enjoy this. I was so fucking stressed from all the mental health trauma that I could not feel any joy. I love yachting and I will tell my children to go into it.

I flew to Miami and joined the yacht in Fort Lauderdale. When I got to the boat on the first night, I was collected by the then Chief mate whom I was replacing for a month until the new Chief mate, Rab, arrived, then I was going Second mate. That night, I arrived, I drove the old Chief mate to the airport. It was my first time driving in the States, so I got a good buzz out of it and a feeling that I had landed... it felt exhilarating.

I went and met the crew. They were a great bunch and I clicked with them all straight away. They were in Las Olas in downtown Fort Lauderdale. It was my first time meeting them. I got introduced to one of the young deckies, Punchy as I nicked named him later because he told me he was always getting in fights in Antibes, France, where he grew up. He seemed like a bit of a lad!

The first question Punchy asked me when I met him on that first night in Fort Lauderdale or Fort Liquordale as it's known was, "do you do drugs mate?!" He said it, laughing, putting me on the spot in front of everyone there! I could see the pensive looks on everybody's moniker. "No," I said. I was not wanting to give anything incriminating away. I was his superior Officer, and I had left all my drug-taking behind me in another life. This was a fresh start. He just laughed and said, "You'll not get along well here then!!" That being said, I didn't want this job to go pear-shaped from drinking and partying because I had all that done in the lead up to getting this job and didn't want it to end like that. This was a time for work, and I didn't want to go down that slippery slope again...like at home where I was drinking a lot and simply idling away waiting until I had the money saved...it was no life. I'd spent 4 years doing fucking drugs before that and this was such an opportunity. I did not want to fuck it up!!

Unfortunately, I didn't stick to my guns! Punchy and Aztec, another deckhand, got some acid pills one night. I dropped two of them that night when we were all out in Fort Lauderdale. A couple of days later, the worst thing that could have happened, happened. The Captain got an email from a crew agency to say we were all on drugs. A deckie from the crew agency who was new to the crew dropped everybody in the shit. He left a couple of days after joining and told the crew agency that had got him the job that everyone was on drugs and an alcoholic. The Captain asked the Chief Stewardess "if I tested the crew, who would pass?" She said "no-one!" The Captain went fucking mental. He waited a week so we'd all be clear, then he tested us. It came up negative for everyone. Thank fuck it did. I thought my career was over. I've often thought afterwards that drugs and alcohol are omnipresent in yachting. Yachts should really set the precedent for the rest of the world to legalize all drugs. I had never been so stupid in my life concerning drugs as that time. The Captain was a bit of a playboy himself. He did not take to kindly to being dropped in the shit. I always admired him for the way that he handled the situation.

After about a month of being on board getting the yacht ready for the Boss trip to Alaska, Rab joined. It was not the best introduction. I was fucking pissed out of my head. I had just come back from a night out with the crew. He did not like me immediately. He said to the Captain. "Sack him!!" The Captain said "No bloody way. He got us through an audit. He's our main guy. I love him. My missus loves him too!! Rab was so fucked off. That was it. Rab was on my case. It had to end in tears. What a piece of shit?

We left Fort Lauderdale and we sailed from Florida down to the Panama Canal. We spent two nights in Cristobal in Panama before going through the Panama Canal. It was great craic!!

A gang of us went ashore this night, Captain included, and ended up in an all-night brothel bar. I broke the ice! The other guys were not used to being in a brothel. The Stewardesses were cheering me on! I picked a black-haired Mexican beauty and went upstairs with her. I was excited to experience a Mexican woman. Jaap the Chief Engineer said "There's a Mexican mistress in every sailors heart!!" I laughed when I heard it. He was full of fun!! I got the woman to get the craic going for the Stewardesses. They were loving the brothel. I finished up and went back down stairs. The Captain said to me the minute I came back down "That was quick!!". I said "yeah I'm a fast worker!" He said "You didn't shag her! You had a fanny wank!!" It made me laugh. I then tried to convince Aztec to burst his cherry and get a hooker. He said he'd never paid before. I told him it was tradition in the Merchant Navy in this situation for the Captain to pay for the cherry boy, if you remember, the cherry boy is a sailor who has never been with a hooker? He laughed at this. I said "I'll pay!" So, he went for it. He went with her upstairs and burst his cherry. I meanwhile started table surfing and nearly got us kicked out! It was a bit of a laugh.

Then I saw this hot skinny black babe hanging out of our Captains ass. I knew he didn't want to do anything but I had no money left. I really wanted to fuck her too so I got a sub of the Captain and took her upstairs. I spent a bit more time with her and had a nice little relaxing exotic shag!

The next day we travelled through the Panama Canal and sailed up the west coast. Just as we were passing Costa Rica, we stopped the boat and went swimming in 2 kilometres of deep blue Pacific Ocean water. There were thousands of turtles migrating. Swimming along minding their own business! It was really cool.

We sailed on up the west coast and stopped Cabo St. Lucas, Mexico for fuel. Jaap and I went on the screaming piss along with Ivan, Aztec and Punchy. It was fucking mental. I went to climb aboard the yacht just as we were leaving but they had taken the stanchions down, so I had no railing on the gangway to stop me falling in. I was so unsteady on my feet, that I had to get down on my hands and knees and crawl up the gangway on to the boat. It was the worst I'd ever been coming back to a boat. I always have been quite ok.

We left there and went to San Diego, California. The Captain wanted to go to Las Vegas for the weekend. He asked the crew who wanted to go? I jumped at the chance. I'd never been. 3 of us took him up on the offer. Pez the Chef, Rab the Chief mate and I. We hired a Mercedes Benz and filled an ice box full of beer and drove through the desert to Las Vegas.

We arrived on the Friday night and checked in to our hotel then went out for the night. We went to a club called Espionage and shit was it expensive. We paid $400 for a 70cl bottle of vodka and 4 red bull!! It went off pretty quietly that first night but we had planned to go to the Cirque du Soleil on the Saturday night. We drank a shit load of alcohol all day the next day and were fairly drunk going in to the Cirque du Soleil in the Bellagio hotel. Just as we were about to go in the door to the theatre my legs collapsed! I didn't feel too drunk and I remember the sensation of complete lack of power from the waist down but I fell to the ground anyway. I thought I'd been poisoned. I thought someone had spiked my drink. Rab was the culprit in my head. I fucking hate that cunt. He was an asshole. I was always watching my ass when he was onboard. The door staff were staring at me. The Captain yelled to get up! I was slapping my legs for some feeling, it was really scary, but they wouldn't respond! The lady working there called on her radio for a wheelchair. The wheelchair arrived and Pez said he would wheel me back to the hotel. He wheeled me out through the foyer where all the gambling took place. The carpet on the floor of the foyer was about an inch or two thick. Pez was sweating buckets pushing me. He said it was like pushing me through sand! We got to the entrance and my legs got some feeling back.

I stood up and on shaky legs and I told Pez I was ok. We walked outside and as we passed the famed Bellagio fountain, I thought in my drunken mischievous state it would be fun to have a piddle in it. There were tons of tourists taking pictures of it. I jumped up on the perimeter wall and started to urinate into it. All the tourist cameras in the vicinity turned on me and the flashes were going off. I waved laughing at them. Then when I finished peeing, I jumped down. It was just as the fountains were going off. We walked on back to our hotel. When we got to the door of our room, Pez asked me was I ok to stand straight without him holding me? I said I was. He let go of my arm to open the door and as he did, I slid sideways down the wall beside the door with a big sweep of my right arm and smashed one of the walls lights off the wall. There was glass everywhere and I got a gash on my arm. Pez took me in to the room unperturbed and left me there. I woke in the morning on the tiles in the bathroom with blood all around me. It was a bit of a wild night. I was so fucking lucky I didn't hit an artery.

The next day we were due to go home but because of my legs collapsing we missed the Cirque du Soleil show so the Captain decided to stay another night and get the Sunday night show. He made me pay for the extra night in the hotel for everyone. Fairs fair he said!

Rab, Pez and I arrived back at one of our rooms after the Sunday show. There was no sign of the Captain. He'd gone off on his own. After about half and hour, there was a knock at the door. Pez opened it and there was the Captain with two gorgeous looking hookers.

They came in to the room and the Captain said to me and Rab, "One each!" "On me!" he said. Rab was on one bed and I was on the other. I got my cock out straight away. The horny hooker put the condom on my cock with her mouth, then started sucking. I smiled over at Rab. Brother's in arms! But he was such a dickhead. He really felt threatened by me. I had higher ships certification than him. He looked so pissed off when I smiled at him. He was getting the same treatment but he couldn't concentrate with me laughing over at him. He stood up and took her in to the bathroom. I thought what a fucking pussy! I lay back and enjoyed being pleasured. A few seconds past and out came the other lady. It hadn't taken long with Rab! She slid on top of my bed beside her mate with a seductive smile and a real dirty look in her eye. She had finished with Rab in seconds. Not much of a man, I thought! LOL. Rab and I were having friction all the time. Rab was a complete fucking arsehole. The horny bitch started sucking my cock as well. The two hookers were giving me the star treatment. One was wanking me as the other one was sucking me off. Then as the original one started sucking me again, the seductive one stared in to my eyes smiling until I exploded!!! The Captain and Pez had women at home so they didn't get involved.

We travelled on up to Alaska after that. Punchy earned the nick name I gave him well when we got to there. We were alongside in the harbor in Ketchikan for the duration of those 2 weeks before the owner arrived. We were in a bit of a party mode. This night Jaap, Punchy, and I were in a bar. The boat had been in town for about a week. The bar was called The Asylum. We were doing shots and having a great time. There was hardly anybody in, but we were having fun on our own. I danced on the bar counter and got my picture taken by the beautiful Filipina barmaid called Elvimarie. I believe the story of my dancing spread throughout the town! I figured it put a lot of noses out of joint because three guys came up to Punchy and I at the side of the street when we had left the Asylum to go home to our yacht. Jaap had gone to another bar and got a taxi home later with Elvimarie so he missed it. I hadn't laid eyes on these assholes before they started the hassle. We were the blow-ins, and they were obviously out to teach us a lesson. It didn't work! We gave as good as we got. The asshole that started it was obviously a few synapses short of a thought. He came up to my face with his two mates on either side and demanded angrily, pointing his finger at me "who do you think you are?!" he shouted. I laughed to diffuse the situation. I'd had this a few times in my life before, but Punchy had no time for it. "BOOM!" He hit him on the jaw with a right hook full of venom. He knocked the guy flat on his ass and then took on the guy beside him. I laughed again with pride because he didn't put up with their shit! I got in a tussle with the other lad. A load of locals got involved helping us because the assholes had other men waiting in the wings to fight as well! A full-scale riot broke out. There were about 20 people fighting. It was closing time, and half the town were drunk on their way home.

A taxi driver who saw the fight start jumped out and hit one of the instigators over the head with a wheel brace. Three more guys tried squeezing Punchy between a building and the wharf into the water, but they didn't succeed. He's a tough little cunt, he's a funny one too!!! We had a post mortem after on the boat when we got back, and he told me about it. There were skirmishes everywhere. When it had cooled off, we walked back home to our yacht unscathed. I think we gave a good account of ourselves! We were laughing our asses off! It was a crazy night.

The next day the rest of the crew were all up in arms when we told them about the night's events. Jaap was so pissed off he missed it. All the crew were worried about going back into town but I said we had to! We had to show those assholes that we weren't afraid of them. They all agreed, and we all went on the screaming piss again! We painted the town red all over again! The two engineers, Jaap and Ivan went with Punchy and I on a pub crawl. We had no trouble, but we were hyper vigilant all day. It was really only enjoyable when we met with the Captain and the stewardesses later in the day. We all walked into this popular bar. The place was packed. Everybody looked at us. The head barman shouted to us "WELCOME!!! with big open arms and a big laugh! He shouted over the noise "HOW Y'ALL TODAY?!!!" "We haven't had a fight like that in Ketchikan in years!!!" he said. We were guests of honour!!!

The partying was so much fun on Oberon but the problem I was having with it was, I wasn't saving a lot of money which is what I wanted to do. I had my eyes and mind focused on getting enough money together to do my Chief Mate/Master Mariner (Captains ticket) certificate. It had been my ambition since I started going to sea.

The Boss arrived and the trip went off without a hitch. After the boss trip, which lasted a week, was over, we journeyed down from Alaska down and stopped in Vancouver, Canada. We had a couple of nights out there when we arrived, and found it to be a really nice and friendly place. One night we were all out in a pub by the docks. This girl, Marilyn, came over to our table and started hitting on me. She was really drunk. I decided I would take her home, back to her boat. She was a stewardess from one of the other boats. One of our stewardesses said she would walk her back, that I could stay where I was, but I said it was no problem. I would walk her back. It was lucky it was me that walked her back because as we entered the secure marina, after walking through the gate back to the boat, she took a big stumble to the right on the floating dock and nearly fell in! If it had of been one of the stews holding her, I don't think she would have been strong enough to stop her from going in the drink! I got her back to her boat. I hit on her right away. She said flirtingly to me before I bade her good night and went back to the bar, "What do you see when you look at me?" "A drunken mess!" I said, Negging her. PUA's (pick-up artists) will understand what I mean. She stormed off. I went back to the bar laughing. I thought I'd gotten to her!

It was a couple of days before I talked to her again. We had a soiree on board for Canada Day a few days after that, and as happens on some of these occasions, the crew from other boats in the marina are invited, so she was there too. We were in a prime location for the fireworks over the water, and there was a great atmosphere when the fire-works were going off. The other crew and I were doubling up as bar staff to the guests on board, maybe 30 people. Marilyn was really laying it on thick for me. She was making eyes for me every chance she got, but I was ignoring her. I didn't want to get involved with her because of her alcoholic ways. I didn't want anything to do with her because I found from experience that if a girl is worse than you on the partying scene i.e. drinking front, it ends in oblivion...for me anyway! I learned this with Fanjita and Marilyn reminded me of her. Sex crazy BUT fucking mental!!! The ignoring made Marilyn worse... now she really wanted me!

I tried to stay clear of her, but she wanted to hook up. As the guests petered out, everybody started egging me on saying, "go on, go on!! Go for it!!"...quietly then eventually in front of her! She didn't seem to mind and was actually laughing about it. It became an out in the open joke by the end of the night! She wasn't that drunk either so the negging I gave her must have worked! There were only few guests left and it was near the end of the night, so, it was mostly the crew, and they were saying, "why not?" "Why don't you go for her?" and I said, "she only wants to get pregnant!" This got a laugh. I went for it anyway. We were standing between her boat and our boat on the floating dock, my whole crew were leaning over the railings above us cheering us on! Marilyn said "right, c'mon on to my boat"....

I was about to go on board when I had a crisis of conscience and asked, "do you not have guests onboard?".... it was a big no-no on all yachts to have someone on when there were guests on board. She said, "yeah. Right let's go somewhere else," so I said, "let's get a hotel." We went up to a hotel that I knew and as we were going in, she said, "let's have a game with the desk clerk and make him feel uncomfortable!!" "I'll come on to you big time and you play it cool!" When I went to pay, she started rubbing her hands all over me. She was grabbing my balls and I was saying, "stop...hang on, contain yourself, woman!!" Brushing her hands off me totally nonchalant to what she was at...telling her to stop it and saying "get off".... it was funny. The clerk was definitely trying not to watch what she was at. He was keeping his eyes on the job. Then came the problem...I was trying to pay with my American Visa card, but it wouldn't work. I asked the clerk could he try it again, but he said no, it's not working (it turned out as I found out later that my mother, whom I'd left in charge of transferring money across from my

Irish account to my American one, had forgotten or not got around to doing it.... thanks mammy!!!!) I asked Marilyn could she pay and said I'd give her the money the next day, but she said "no! I've never paid for sex before, and I'm not about to start now!" She was a little bit older than me so, I took this to be over a long period of time, but it did make me laugh.... I felt like a bit of a Gigolo. We walked down through the park back to the yachts, and I was saying things like, "what about that park bench?!" "AL FRESCO?!!!" "What about that nice secluded grassy area?!" Telling her, it was late at night and no one would see us!! She was saying, "No..No...No!!!!!"

We got down to the dock, entered the marina again, and there we were, standing between our two yachts, and she said, "well, I have got guests on my boat! You don't!!" "Shit!!!" I thought.... I really want to get it on with this woman!! I hadn't had sex in a couple of weeks. I was horn fucking crazy living on a boat with all those gorgeous stewardesses. I said I was horny, and I said, "if I take you on board, I could get fired!!" Very naive of me, of course I could. She replied, "well, only if you're caught!!" I said, "right, let's go, but you have to be quiet!!" We walked onto the boat and inside. Then as we walked past the guest cabin she said, "what's in here?" and opened the guest cabin door saying, "let's do it in here!" I said, "no way!" get out of there. She said, "it'll give the stews something to do!" I said, "get out of there!" grabbing her hand. The last thing I wanted was the stews angry at me! They were so good to me on board. I told her to be quiet. I took her into my cabin, which I shared with the Second Engineer, Ivan, but he wasn't there. He must have gone to another cabin, so Marilyn and I fell to it.... we had the sex! It was pretty damn good too. I fucked her like a wild thing. I was living out my fantasy of sleeping with a stewardess on a yacht. I woke up the next morning with her arm around the back of my neck, and I thought, "Aw naw, what the fuck?!!" It felt like a man's arm! I fucking shat myself. I didn't remember the night before for a split second! Then I looked over at her face and thought, "oh yeah that's right, I remember now!" I woke her and we had sex again. It was very sensual. I told her then, looking at the time, that she had to go, so get up and go out quietly please because the Pez the Chef, Rab the Chief mate and I were going to watch a rugby match in a sports bar that morning at 07.30 am. She started joking around, obviously still a bit tipsy, but I was telling her to be quiet that we were going to get caught, which wouldn't go down well! What with me being the Security officer on board too! I got her out with a quick kiss goodbye, and off she got with no-one seeing her. I went back in to the cabin and got into the bed quickly with my clothes on waiting on the shout from Pez. And in what seemed like only a few minutes later, Pez gave me a call. He put his head around the door and asked was up? I shouted, "yes!" "See ye on the dock in 5!" he replied. "Righto," I shouted back. I got up, splashed some water on my face, and went out onto the quay.

As we walked up the quay Pez turned around to me and said, "you had sex last night, didn't you??" I said, "no" not wanting to be caught by Rab. I didn't want him to hear that I'd had sex on the boat. But Pez persisted in front of Rab whom he knew for a long time. I naively then thought it would be ok for Rab to know, so I said, "yes...how did you know?" "Because I could smell it!! He replied. I laughed at him. He was on about the cabin. He was a bit of a character. I always like a character. They make the world go around!!

I was used to other boats like in the Merchant Navy, where it is a lot more relaxed about that sort of thing. I didn't think it would be that big a deal!

Pez, Rab and I had a great morning getting drunk. Then we met up with the Stewardesses later on, and went for something to eat. Then on the next day, Sunday, I went for a few pints on my own around the bars but came back early. I was just in time when I got back to go for another few drinks with the Engineers, so it was a very heavy weekend. The next morning, I woke and went out on the deck for work. I was probably still a little bit tipsy from the night before and definitely hung-over. I was feeling like shit. Rab was handing out the jobs. He asked me to de-rust the 16-ton crane on the aft deck. This meant climbing up on it without any safety harness. My fault for not wearing it or asking for it, but I did it out of guilt for going heavy on the beer all weekend. He was a fucking sadist. He knew I was fucking hungover. I also thought he wanted me to fall and injure myself such was the malice I felt out of the guy. After

I had finished doing the job, he called me on the radio, asking me to come to the bridge. So, with the impending sense of doom coming over me, one I knew from years of getting in trouble, I went to the bridge, and when I got there, he slid a piece of A4 paper across the chart table. "Read that" he said arrogantly. The Captain was off on leave. I don't think this would have happened had he been on board. I read it, and it said that due to me breaking the security rules by bringing a woman on board and being regularly intoxicated the following morning while working, I was being fired. I was about to knock him out. He had such a fucking glow about him. He was getting what he wanted. I knew he'd wanted me off and now the Captain was behind him. He'd got his way, the little fucking weasel. After all that went on, on that boat! I was so angry at the time, but it passed. I enjoyed my time there though; it was 4 months of complete hedonism! Punchy knocked his CUNT out for hitting on his girlfriend, who was one of the stewardesses, shortly after I left. I heard it through the grapevine. Fair play to Punchy! I thought. I think there was a little anger in there for my dismissal too. It made me laugh when I heard!

So, that was it I got off in Vancouver. That sacking sent me on the wildest rollercoaster ride imaginable.

32

LOST IN FRANCE

They flew me back to Nice from the Oberon fiasco. I arrived back and went to stay in Debbie's crew house, again, in Biot, which is the next town over from Antibes. I wasn't sure how to approach the fact that I had gotten sacked with the crew agencies. It was all new to me. So, I thought I would go to one of the smaller crew agencies and practice for the others. I wasn't sure how to broach the subject. I thought I would keep it quiet. I wanted to tell the truth because I would be starting on a clean sheet again, but I decided to keep it quiet. When I sat down to talk to the woman behind the desk, she looked at my CV and the first thing she said was, "oh, you were on, Oberon!" "My best friend's son aka Punchy is on that boat!" Ahhhh, I thought...shit there goes that game plan! I said, "yeah, I know him. He's a friend of mine." She said, "tell me what happened? Why are you not on the boat anymore?" I said, "it's kind of a long story. I'm not really sure if I can tell it or not." She said, "yeah, tell me the truth. It's the best way because this is a very small industry, and it could come back and bite you on the ass if you lie." So, I said, "right ok." I told her what happened. That I brought a woman back to the boat, and I was drinking too much. She said, "right...ok..." She said, "the best thing to do is tell the other agencies the same thing because the truth will come out, and you are better telling the truth in the long run." I did as she said and told the truth, some of the reaction's I got were kind of funny.

I went into the agency that got me the job on Oberon and the crew agent was delighted to see me. She "Hi Juan, great to see you again. Come.." she said "Come into my office." It was the first time I had spoken to her since the sacking. As soon as she closed the door to the office and no-one could hear her she said "Ok tell me exactly what happened? It was a real party boat, wasn't it?" I did not want to drop the crew in the shit as well so I told her it wasn't. She was really pissed off. I said "I don't think it was that much of a party boat!" She said "Well that's not what I heard!!" I was so fucked off at being put in that position. Especially after having been sacked. I did however feel loyalty to the crew. We had some great times together and I did not want them all to get a bad reputation. She said that I was going to have difficulty ever getting a job again. I thought you fucking bitch. She cut me off from the crew agency. I made it one of my stops when I was touring the crew agencies every week but she was so cold with me. It was demoralising. I fucking stopped in the end. It was bringing me down too much. I cursed Rab, the cocksucking cunt.

After a couple of weeks of staying in Debbie's I went out for the night into Antibes to blow of a bit of steam. I had an epiphany. I thought I could make some contacts in the party world of yachts. Always a good idea if you are a bit fucking wild. Get on a boat that doesn't have that much rules as the normal boats. I went into town and got absolutely hammered on alcohol. I did not do any drugs but there was plenty around. I was wearing the t-shirt the stewardesses had given me on Oberon. They had bought it for the Captain but he did not want to wear it so they gave it to me. It said on the t-shirt "PARTY LIKE THE IRISH". They thought I would like it but I was extremely uncomfortable wearing it. I wanted to make a good impression on people and not be throwing it in people's faces that the Irish tend to drink a lot. I wore it anyway thinking I would draw some attention. I did draw attention but I did not have a clue who they were. I woke up the next morning in a barn 5 miles out of town. I was lying on my back in the clay of the barn. I woke in a panic. I did not know how I got there. I was so drunk the night before. I was so confused. I immediately thought I'd been kidnapped and brought there. That is definitely what happened. I could not fucking believe it. I reached around and felt my asshole. I was checking to see if I had been raped. I was so relieved that there was no signs of it. It did not mean that it did not happen. I could have been raped with a condom and some lube. I would have been none the wiser. My father always said when I was growing up "You better watch your drinking, you were so drunk last night there could have been a marching band of queers up your ass, and you wouldn't have known." He said it a few times. I never listened. These words were ringing out in my ears at that very moment. I was fucking going mental. I thought the Oberon fraternity had kidnapped me to teach me a lesson about getting too drunk. They were Russian Mafia and I thought that that was the sort of thing they would do for a laugh. I pictured them chloroforming me and putting me in the trunk of a car and taking me miles out of town. I was justifying my actions in my head. I thought it was just another hiccup and proceeded home. I got home after asking for directions. I went straight to the Supermarket and bought a load of wine. I chilled out in the summer sunshine and put it down to experience.

After a few more weeks of Debbie's, I got kicked out! I was having a great time there before that. One of the male deckies there nicknamed me "Hasselhoff" from Baywatch because there were so many women hanging around me. It got a laugh! They didn't mind. But a twat called Rob stole a wallet, and I apparently became his partner in crime because I'd spent the night drinking with him. Debbie was apologetic to me but she said she had to do it. Well, it had nowt to do with me.

Anyway, I moved to an even wilder place in Bel Air, Antibes. I waited the whole summer there for a job. It was called Caroline's. It was way more relaxed than Debbie's. Debbie's was very like living on a yacht. It was very professional and I loved living there. I highly recommend it. Debbie is like a mother figure to you. So much like the Chief Stewardesses I have come to know and come to love. These guys were smoking inside the villa in Caroline's. It was a bit of a culture shock. I made great friends with them right away. I had a great time living there. I got lucky with a hot American Chef one night we were out in Juan le Pins as well, the next town over from Antibes, the other way from Biot. I took her back to the crew house and no exaggeration, I made love to her 5 times! She was so fucking horny. I EJACULATED EVERY TIME!!! I hadn't had sex in months and I was surrounded by gorgeous scantily clad women every single day. I was more than ready for her! Wraggamuffin aka Gypsy told everybody about me shagging her. He had video footage. He quietly recorded me in the morning as I was getting my morning glory from her. I asked her in the middle of shagging her was she educated and he burst out laughing. That's when I noticed the camera on me. He been videoing for a few seconds. He got a great laugh out of it. He was a bit of a wild man. I really liked him. He was salt of the earth.

I was looking for work periodically but not getting any and running out of money fast, but luckily enough, I got a job at the end of the summer. It was on a 50m yacht called 'M/Y My Trust Fund', which I got when I was in Amma's crewhouse after being kicked out of Caroline's. Wraggamuffin and I got kicked out of Caroline's because her patience with all our shenanigans wore thin. We were drinking all the time. The final straw was one night when Caroline wanted us to go to sleep, Wraggamuffin wouldn't turn off the light in our villa and go to sleep like she asked so she said "Right! That's it! You're out of here!" and kicked the two of us out the next day. I did have a romantic interlude with her 19-year-old daughter while I was staying there. Much to the enjoyment of her mother's erotically charged eyes. Her daughter was a bit of a looker.

My Trust Fund was a deckhand position. I was sailing below my rank but I took it because money was running tight and I thought, take it because you don't know what opportunities will open to you when you do. It had taken over three nearly four months in different crew houses in Antibes, but I finally landed a gig. This was still 2011. I joined the boat as deckhand in Toulon. We sailed from there to La Ciotat, further down the coast, to go into a dry dock, where they took the boat out of the water for repairs and maintenance. "Up on the hard" is the term they use. Once we were there, one day when I was up on the bridge, the Captain said while doing his paperwork "well, the boat has been sold, and it looks like we'll be going to America..." This was great for getting a B1/B2 visa for the States, but I already had mine from being on Oberon...he said, "I need a new Chief mate, a new Second mate, a Chief Engineer and a Chef!" I told him immediately that I had my Chief mates ticket, and if he was willing to put me forward for it. I was willing to do the job. At the time, we had a skeleton crew (as little people as it took to keep the boat running) because the boat was being sold, so we were between owners and waiting to go into action again. He said to me, "right then, I will put you forward for it, and we will see what the office has to say." He was a really sound Captain. He did this, and they accepted it. I was promoted from deckhand to Chief mate inside a week.

So, to celebrate a little, I went to the Irish bar there in La Ciotat. Such a fucking idiot thing to do! I went ashore, and I met other crew from the other boats. It was fun. I did a bit of arm wrestling, and I showed this big muscly guy, who couldn't believe I beat him twice, the trick of arm wrestling and how to put your whole body into it. It spread like wildfire throughout the Saffa's (South African people) ...Everyone knows it now, so it's made arm wrestling a lot tougher. I had some drinks, a few shots, and it was good. On the way back about 2 o'clock in the morning, I made to go into the secure area of the harbour where the Superyachts are, but I found that the main gate was locked, well I thought it was locked. I looked at the fence to see how to get over it. I thought shit, I better climb it because I had no other way of getting in. I started climbing the fence, but it was very narrow wire, and it made it difficult to climb, definitely the point of it. I climbed up to the top of it, and someone said I should have thrown a jacket over it, but I never thought of that, I got to the top and threw my left leg over it, but I didn't have the strength to pull myself up and over it because I was too drunk —all a bad idea when I look back on it now. As I was leaning on the wire with my left leg, trying to pull myself up and put the right leg over, I felt the wire piercing my left leg behind the knee. It left me stuck at the top of the fence, and I thought, shit, what do I do now? I can't let go. The pain was serious. I knew my leg would be ripped apart by the wire, and I couldn't pull myself up because I was too drunk. It took all my strength, so what I did was hold on to the wire with my right hand and put my left-hand underneath where the wire had pierced my knee, then pushing down with my left hand under the left knee and pushed down on the wire so as to lift the left knee from where the wire had pierced it. As soon as I did this, I fell on the same side of the fence again, still outside, onto my face and smacked my mouth off the tarmac. I looked up and seen a bit of grass, then crawled to the grassy bit and passed out. I was so drunk that I fell straight asleep. I slept until the wee hours of the morning. About 6.30 am that morning, I woke up. I didn't know exactly what time it was, but I could see the daylight. I thought, shit, where am I?? I realized that I had been sleeping at the fence for a couple of hours. I got up and looked at the fence again. Then I looked and saw a door size gate in the fence. I hadn't realized it was there, so I checked it, and it was open, and I thought you fucking dickhead... thinking it about myself, half laughing too. I walked in and started running back to the boat because it was getting daylight. I didn't want to be seen coming back in that state as I had some blood on the front of my shirt. I got back to the boat, got on board and cleaned myself up, and got into bed. Then at 7.30 am I got up again for work and I was fine, but my teeth were a bit sore where I'd smacked the tarmac, and the back of my leg was cut and needed tending to but I was in pretty good shape. I got out the medical kit and put a patch on my leg with some disinfectant, and it was fine. I worked for two days, then cleaning the boat and doing general duties, dressing my leg every night when I finished work. The thing was I knew it was going to get infected if I didn't get it treated. It was behind the knee on the joint, so every time I stretched my leg, the wound would open. I'd had the foot ulcer before from the foot balling injury, so I knew the signs of festering if they were to come. I told the Captain that I had caught myself coming over a wall when I was coming back to the boat, and he said, "Right, ok. Go get it sorted out".

I contacted the manager of the shipyard, and he gave me a lift to the hospital to get the leg seen too. I got the wound treated, and they bandaged it up and said I had to get it treated every day for a few days, then it was every three days for about two weeks. One of the nurses flirted with me. After she patched me up, she rubbed my crotch and gave me a wink. It was so fucking funny. She was gorgeous!! If only I had the time!!

After that, we left the shipyard on the boat and went to Monaco. The boat was going to be there in Monaco for about a month before we sailed to America. We were going to do a charter with the new owners to Villefranche. This day a couple of days before the owners joined, I got in some dayworkers who were friends of mine and we worked till late. Ditsy and his mate Al. Then afterward, we all went to the Rascaz bar in Monaco. It was a local yachtie haunt. As we were sitting outside having our drinks, this group of ladies were walking past and obviously heard us talking because one of them asked over the small hedge, "are you guys from Ireland?" Ditsy, my mate, shouted he is pointing to me. I said "Yeah, I am why?" "Because so are we," she said. We asked them in for a drink, and they joined our company. We were all sitting there talking, and one of them, Alice, who was paying me a lot of attention, she was really attractive and a great fucking body on her. She asked me what our boat's name was and laughed when I told her "My Trust Fund!" We carried on talking, and she said to me, "You are so nice. How come you don't have a girlfriend?" and I said with the type of work I do; I have just not settled down properly yet. My French friend on the boat, Flossy, told me earlier on that day that a lot of people have sex on the shore front in Monaco in the open where the dock runs along and where all the boats are. I started laughing when he told me this and said I thought that's cool, but I gave it a bit more consideration now confronted with this opportunity. Alice was an occupational therapist too so brains and body, ticked all my boxes. My second occupational therapist to have as a partner. It's the mental illness card. They can smell it off you!! We laughed and joked. Then I asked her did she want to go for a walk with a knowing wink, and she whispered to me, "Why? Do you know somewhere? "Yes," I said... She made her excuses, and we left. We walked along the dock that is the seafront in Monaco. There was a load of playground rides all set up but they were closed down for the night, so halfway across, I grabbed her arm quickly and said, follow me through the fence that was there around the playground rides.

She followed, and we got inside where the rides were and she giggled a bit and said, "what do we do now?" I patted one of the rides there and said, "what about this one?" "Want to go for a ride?!!" I asked. "How?" she said. I said, "we can do it doggy style over it." "Ok" she said, "Just gimme a second to get myself ready," and she went behind the ride saying, "Us girls need our privacy!!" I wasn't sure what she was doing. I think she was taking off tummy flattening panties! It made me laugh. She came back and said, "Right, ok, I'm done!" We started kissing then she lay over the ride. I fucked her like a mental patient. I was going at it like a jack hammer. She was moaning so loud. It was so sexually charged. It was about 1 am so not too many people about. They were all in the pub. I was about to climax, and I said "I'll cum on your ass. I don't want to get you pregnant!" She replied much to my shock, "well, it isn't the worst thing in the world that could happen!" It made me laugh. I thought these fucking mental health service people are the crazy ones.

We got tidied up and she was gasping for more. She was hanging out of me. Rubbing my cock all the way back across the sea front. I did not stop her. I thought she would marry me. We went back to the pub then and back to the rest of them sitting there. It was like we were never gone. Good, I thought I didn't want them to start talking about it. There were more girls to be had. Ditsy Gilbert, the womanizing sod from London town, was talking to Alice's friend Jennie. I call him Ditsy because he's blonde. He was getting on rather well, but she was paying me a lot of attention too. So, although Alice looked a little miffed, I talked to Jennie as well but more to annoy Ditsy than anything!! Jennie was sitting between myself and him, and Alice was sitting beside me. Ditsy was getting really annoyed and telling me in whispered tone to fuck off from behind her back.... then, as she turned around to take a drink, he jabbed me square on the mouth with his fist, right on the sore teeth. The little CUNT "Aghh...." I said, and Jennie looked at me, but kept it quiet in an unwritten rule. Thinking honour amongst players and laughed it off. She didn't know what was going on, and no more was said. It was a little funny, but it hurt, I thought right on my sore teeth. They offered us back to their hotel, but I said I had to get back to my yacht.... Chief mate... responsibilities and all that, so I left.

I kissed Alice goodbye and thought I've joined the ranks of all those Al fresco Monacans.

The next day my teeth started playing up big time, and because I knew we were going to the States. I knew I had to get them checked out. It was a couple of weeks crossing, I didn't want to be half way across the Atlantic with a toothache. They felt a little loose and very sore. I decided to go to the dentist. I told the Captain I had a toothache asking him was it alright to go to the dentist. He said, "Does this go back to the incident where you were out drinking??" He got annoyed, and I said, "yeah, I banged them when I fell." He said, "Right, ok, you can go." "Get them checked out." He was really pissed off!! I could understand why. I was the Second in Command.

I went to the dentist in Monaco, and he took an X-ray of my teeth and said, "they are broke." "Both your front tooth and left incisor are broken at the root and have to be taken out." I wasn't happy, but there was not a lot I could do or say. He said if they stayed in, they would rot. I went back there the next day and got them taken out, and went back to the boat with no front teeth. It was pretty full on. I thought I was going to get sacked. A couple of days later, I got a plate with two false teeth on it.

It was a temporary fix and I thought when I'm wealthy I will get screw in teeth. And that is the first thing I will do with the royalties of this book.

I was so fucking broke for money after that. I came up with a dastardly plan. I emailed the owner and told him I had an accident on the boat. He went mental and called the Captain from Canada at 2 O'Clock in the morning. Waking him up out of his bed. What the fuck happened my front teeth, he wanted to know? I told the owner in the email that it would cost him 9 thousand euro to get them fixed. It was a ludicrous thing to do but I was fucking desperate. I told the Captain when he asked me what the hell I did that for that I would sort it out with the owner. He was so cool with it. I think he thought it was funny. He called me a dreamer after I asked him for a lend of his phone to take a picture of the moon lol. I emailed the owner again and told him that I would incur all costs and not to worry about it. I apologised for bothering him with it. It was all forgotten about.

We left Monaco and went to the States. Halfway across the Atlantic we had a bit of a party. It was Rob, my best mate ever's birthday. He was such good craic. He was another head the ball. I let him go party in Monaco with Ditsy whom he had never met until that night. They really hit it off. He said he would be back to the boat before work in the morning. I let him go. He did not get back to 5pm the next bloody day. And when he got back, he didn't give a fuck. I'd been keeping the Captain updated with his arrival but he'd gone on the piss again with Ditsy. Anyway, it was his birthday onboard and we had to test the Jacuzzi. So, I organized with the Captain that we could coincide the two. He said we could have two beers each but we had a little more than that! We had a great laugh. We took pictures of us in the Jacuzzi, and a couple of the crew put the pictures up on Facebook, which we found out later was definitely not allowed. We had to take them down. The now deceased Chief Engineer told us "You fucking idiots. You tried out the jacuzzi before the owner even did." We had a laugh at the that.

Whenever we got to America, the new owners decided to sack the whole crew and get an American crew. They were going to keep me but my drinking changed their mind. It would have been a great time. The Americans are fantastic to work with. So, bubbly!!!

The owners said my drinking had to be kept under control, and I kept going out of control with it, so that was it. They had enough of the party like the Irish lol.

Now that I was sacked, I had three choices for my next move, work wise. I could stay in Florida and look for work there. And because it was Christmas, it was a good time of the year to be there. The season was hotting up there. I had good qualifications and I had experience. It gives me the shivers now at how out on a limb that yachting takes you. The second option was to go home because I had been away for nearly a year and felt I needed a bit of a break. I'd lost my fucking mind on that boat. I could not concentrate on anything. My mind was all over the place. It was the alcohol. I had drank a substantial amount of the owners vodka and the Captain was not impressed. The other option, which was suggested by a friend of mine, Will, from Dublin, was that I could go to Sint Maarten in the Caribbean and look for work there. The aliens have told me that Sint Maarten is paradise on earth for a party animal like me. They have told me to go there to live when I make my first million from this book. I am going to do that. They are adamant that I will be a Billionaire from the sales of this book. Anyway, I'd been sacked but it wasn't a bad sacking. I still got a reference from the Captain but it was useless. He did not put anything about my ability or personality. I was excellent with the crew. I kept everything ticking over. Will my mate said Sint Maarten was a busy place with lots of jobs going and probably better than Fort Lauderdale in Florida. So, Sint Maarten sounded good to me. It's a small place too, so I thought it would be more concentrated for work, and less people were likely to have my certification.

I got there in a fucking shambles. My mind had left me. I ended up in the most expensive hotel there. I was fucking winging it. I hadn't a clue where the crew house was that Rob had told me about. I was so fucking demented from alcohol. I was in the expensive hotel thinking 250 dolllars a night is not that bad. I was so fucking out of it and only by chance I saw this taxi driver sitting in the foyer looking like a gangster in his big fucking shades lol. I thought he would know the island. He looked local. He was a black man. I went over and asked him did he know here the crew house for Superyachts was. He said no but he had contacts and he could find out for me. I was so relieved. I had no internet and I definitely knew that there would not be an internet café on the island. I put my bag into the back of his car and sat in the front. He started making his way out of the airport when he got a message on his phone. He changed his attitude and got fucking weird. I was so fucking scared. I'd stories about yachties getting killed on that island. It was legendary. He asked me if I wanted another hotel? I said no take me back. He turned the car and drove about 100 yards. I had no possible way of finding the crew house. I decided to trust him. I told him to take me to the hotel he was talking about. I figured that I could find my bearings. He told me it was cheap. He said it was only 60 dollars a night. I thought not bad. I had about 7 thousand euro saved up. I was pretty content. Fucking mental when I think about it now, so risky. I was so determined to find a job on a Superyacht and become a Captain. We arrived at the hotel and got checked in. The taxi driver told me his son was the manager and anything I needed he would get it for me. I knew right away he was on a about drugs. I went to my room and had lie down for a minute. Then with a raging horn on me, I got up and went down stairs to see if he was still there. I asked at reception when he wasn't could they call the number he had given me. He came back and I asked him could he take me to a brothel. I knew there were tons of them on the island. It was legal there and the drugs were more or less legal too. I was so excited. I felt like a real adventurer.

I went to the brothel and got my leg over. I felt better after it. My mind was clearer and I thought to myself I'll give the alcohol a wide berth for a while. That's what I did. I went back to the hotel and holed up in the room ordering room service and lying low for a week. My mind came back. I was so fucking happy. I knew I'd be fine.

At the end of the week I got a call at the reception from the taxi driver to say he had a contact of the best people on the island to do with Superyachting. I was overjoyed. I felt so relieved. I got a taxi with him to the crew house and Riselle said the minute I got there "So, you're the famous Juan?" I laughed and asked her what did she mean? She said "We have Rob here and he's been asking everybody all the time he has been here has anybody heard of you?" I thought fucking hell. So much for a new beginning. Everybody would know my bastarding name now. I went in to the crew house with Riselle and Rob was lying on the couch fucking passed out drunk. I woke him up and he nearly kissed me. I was not very happy. He had invited himself along to my new beginning. I was so fucking pissed off. I got over it and we went for a drink. I was in the mood for a little partying before I went near the yacht agencies to look for work. I wanted to get a bit of the island atmosphere before starting work. I needed to relax after being sacked. I had a little steam to blow off. Rob was the ideal man for that!! We went to a local bar and as we were sitting there the radio was playing. I started laughing. The song on the radio was a local station. It was playing Reggae. I was listening to the words. They were singing about going down on your woman before washing your teeth in the morning. I thought it was hilarious.

The next day, Rob and I went to the Soggy dollar. It was a local yachtie bar. We were so fucking drunk. It was the end of the new beginning. We were in the party zone. It lasted 4 months. I never got a job. I only dayworked on a couple of yachts. I was so fucking annoyed that I did not listen to my instincts and keep my new beginning quiet on the yacht My Trust Fund. Rob latched on to it and thought Sint Maarten would be fucking mental to party in. We had different goals. The crew house was right beside the airport. There was a ton of yachties staying there. There was a bar in the grounds of the compound. It was called Shadows. He was a character. I liked him a lot. I ate his food prepared in the grottiest fucking kitchen you ever seen in your life lol. I didn't give a fuck!! When in Rome!!

I told Riselle that I was looking for work right away. She said "You need to stop partying!!" I was alarmed at the idea. I did not want to stop. I had a serious Cocaine addiction within a week. I was spending hundreds on it every bloody day. My money was disappearing rapidly. I needed a job right away. I stopped partying and left that crew house with Rob and moved to a big Resort with other yachties who were looking for work too. We got a cheap deal. 100 dollars a week. I thought it would be a better environment. I was so fucking wrong. It was worse. They were fucking mental. Partying non stop. I never had a chance. Riselle told me as well when I told her my plan about moving in with the other guys into the Resort "That's a lot of balls in one place!!" I did not know what she meant. It became evident when there was friction. Boys were throwing their weight about but I could handle it. I was in the Resort and thought to myself I need work. I went to the agencies and they said "We've heard about you. You've got a bad reputation. We don't think you'll find work here." I was fucking heart broken. I had no idea how I was going to find work. I did not even think about what I would do when my money ran out. I was so wired in to getting a job. I always had my brother and my parents to rely on. I was lucky like that. It relieved the pressure.

I got kicked out of the Resort for drinking. Rob and I went back to the airport crew house and had whale of a time. We partied like there was no tomorrow. It was crazy. We were doing Cocaine with breakfast.

There was lots of women but I never got near one of them. I was always drunk. It was like the time in Antibes, I was with a girl from the crew house I was staying in. She said "Come on into town. You will not get a job drinking like that". She was absolutely into me. I thought fuck it and went with her. I was out of my head staggering. She thought I was so much fun that people would love me and I would get a job immediately. She was so fucking stupid lol but her looks were out of this world.

We went down town Antibes and were outside the Hopstore. She introduced me to a yachtie stewardess she knew. She said to me this could be a job for you. I asked her what kind of yacht it was? She said charter. I thought fucking hell. The holy grail. Her friend was just coming out of the bar. I could tell she wasn't that drunk. She looked quite proper. My buddy introduced us and the stewardess said "Not another drunk Irishman!!" I was so fucking pissed off at myself. I got the kick up the ass I needed from her. I was really letting the side down. She brushed passed me. My buddy said "Don't mind her!!" "Come on let's get a drink." I could not believe the mentality of the fucking whole lot of them. They just party like there is never going to be an end.

The yachting fraternity is the best fraternity in the world to be looking for work. They look out for one another. I have always, always had a brilliant time with the new crew in the crew houses. They are so full of life. They bring joy every morning and after the shit life I've had at home for a century, that's what it felt like, I was so happy, happy, happy to be alive.

When Rob and I were in the Resort with the gang of guys looking for work instead of the airport crew house I was asked by some of the crew from a yacht to a barbeque at the airport crew house. I went with Rob. We were drunk before we got there. Rob suggested we get a beer in the Supermarket for the journey to the crew house. I was fucking so dismayed at how much I had fallen from grace. I was drinking in the street in front of perspective employers. Rob didn't give a fuck. We got the beer. And I bought some corn on the cob. It reminded me of Briona, my ex fiancée. Her name was COB. We went to the barbeque and they put my corn on the grill. It was ready in a minute or two. I never thought that it would totally destroy my life. I bit into it and all I felt was my two front teeth give way. They popped in my mouth. I went mental. I spat them out and in front of the yacht crew I told them "Fuck that anyway." And was about to throw them away in anger. The yacht crew jumped at me. They were not drunk at all. A few social drinks is what they had in mind. Rob and I was were fucking out of it. The yacht crew said all at the one time "Keep them, they can stick them back in again." They were so cool. We drank on. I put them in the pocket of my board shorts. I went to bed. And woke in the morning with hangover from hell. I rubbed my teeth with my tongue and had forgotten about breaking them the night before. "Fuck!!!" I thought. I'd forgotten about that. I remembered putting them in my pocket. I checked the pocket and they weren't there. I went fucking nuts. We went back to the Resort and got some booze and I slowly lost interest in finding a job. I got down on myself. I was suicidal. I got up one night and walked to the water. I went into the water and thought to myself in the darkness, all I have to do is swallow the water. I was out of my depth in the water. I was the pivotal point for me. I stopped drinking. It only lasted a couple of days but it was enough to cure me.

We went to La Bamba beach bar this night. Everybody was there. It was two for one at the bar. You could get double fisted on 5 dollars. That meant two beers in your hand. It's a yachtie phrase. One I'd learned. They have lots of them. The other one that sticks out in my mind is a Saffa one "First world problems!!" Those were what I was having. Yachting is so elite.

Rob and I were standing on the beach outside La Bambas with beer in each hand. There were women everywhere! Rob was eyeing them up and so was I. I decided to show them a little Jiu Jitsu. I said to Rob, hold my beer. He said why? I told him "I'm gonna jump through that fire." He said "Don't be fucking daft!!" I said watch me and gave him my beer. He played the cool cunt and took them from me. It was in front of about a hundred people. All the yachties from the Superyachts were there. I ran at the fire and dived over it. It was ablaze. There was 5 pallets stacked up on fire. It was 10 foot in the air with flames. I break falled on the other side. I'd put my hands in front of me pushing the flames out of my way. I don't know why I done it. It was moment of madness. I have a lot of them.

I walked back and the flashes were going off on a ton of phones. All I heard from the women was "Who is he?" I was so delighted. I'd had an impact. I said to Rob "Lets pick up some women now…" He laughed at me and gave me my beer back. It was so fucking cool in my hand. My hands were on fire and I was in pain. I ignored the pain and went with Rob to some gorgeous women sitting down beside the fire. They were the ones who said "Who is he?" I was looking my greatest that I have ever looked. Thin and tanned. We sat down and started chatting to them. One of them was from New Zealand. She had such an exotic feel to her. I can feel people's presences. It was surreal but she got up and left as soon as we sat down. She went to the bar. I started talking to the next best looking chick. Rob got angry. He started butting in. There was not much other women to choose from. I had the best looking one. He fucking cock blocked me. We went home empty handed.

I went to bed and fell asleep. The next morning a guy who I'd helped the night before with somewhere to stay said "Holy fucking shit, look at your hands!!!" I opened my eyes and took a look at them. They were ballooned right out. He took me down to reception. He was another gangster from the island. Rob went nuts at me taking him back. I thought he was dead on. We got the manager and he took one look and said "I'll take you straight to the doctor". He brought me there and the doctor said there is nothing I can do. It will subside. You have 3rd degree burns. I thought fuck that and when I got home I burst the blisters and pealed off the skin. I knew from having burns before that that was the best thing to do. The pain left immediately. We went drinking again. My new partner in crime was a local named Shaun. He told me that he was not liked by everybody. He said that his mother was high up in Google. She had a really well paid job but that he never got a penny from her. He was broke as fuck. I took him on the piss. We went to a casino with my last 80 dollars. I had more money in a bank account in Ireland so I did not mind.

We were loving the casino. He had Cocaine on him and was sniffing it in the toilets. I declined. I'd had enough of it. We drank for free in the casino. He told me they all do it on the island. They go in with a couple of bucks and get fucking hammered. I thought it was brilliant.

We went to the Soggy dollar and bought some Vodka. He said "I'll have the good stuff." And I knew then he was fucking playing me. Fucking swindelling the tourists. They all do it. He said his cousin Big Mike was the man around there. He owned the Jet Skis outside La Bamba that were rented out to tourists. He was so proud of him. He told me that he sold Cocaine as well. He said that he could get it for 10 dollars a gram. He said it was Columbian Cocaine. The best stuff on the planet. I did not take him up on his offer. I was not in the mood. We parted company and I went back to my Resort. Rob was furious. He said that was fucking dangerous. He could have killed you. I told him that it was dead on. I was in safe hands. He's cousins with everybody. I said that is was good to get to know the locals. He did not agree.

We moved back to the crew house shortly after that. Then one night in Shadow's bar there. I got in an argument. It was very unlike me. The guy I argued with was a bit of a plonker. I was a little too drunk and I punched a hole in the sign for the crew house. I was walking out of Shadow's bar to get away from the dickhead from Scotland. I was very surprised at him being such an asshole. I always got along well with the Scottish. It was either him or the sign. I think I made the right decision. I apologized to Riselle and paid for the sign but because there was a complaint also about me cracking on to one of the girls too, who didn't like my banter, Riselle said I had to leave. She said she was sorry but I had to go.

Finally, after I moved from the airport crew house to another one, I got some day work through a friend I had made there called Ghost. I got two weeks working on a yacht called "M/Y Starfire." Ghost and I became pretty close. He nicknamed me Guinness after his favourite drink so that was my Caribbean nickname!! He wanted me to sell Cocaine to the yachting fraternity. He knew I was running low on money. He offered me a line of Cocaine the length of a magazine and gave me a book called "How to think yourself rich!" I laughed at his idea but I took the Cocaine. It was the best on the Island, according to him. The book wasn't bad either. The one anecdote I remember from it was about a gold prospector during the big gold rush in the 1800's, in California who stopped two feet short of hitting pay dirt on the land he was searching for gold on after months and months of digging. Another man bought the land from him after he gave up in desperation and carried on digging form where the man had left off and hit gold the following day. The moral of the story is to never stop 2 feet short! Persevere. It always stuck with me. The other one in his book was to keep your how to get rich idea in your mind every day. Always be working on it in your mind. Think about it 24/7 until it happens. Mines has been this book and a variety of other things as you will see over the coming years. It works. You are constantly honing and new ideas arise all the time of how to make your dream come true. You have to be 110% focused. In saying that, there wasn't a chance in hell I would jeopardize my career to sell a bit of Cocaine. I would have gone home before doing that.

Then, the same night after I finished the two weeks of daily work. After we'd got paid. I went out for the night. Out to Philipsburg. I took a few hundred dollars, enough for the night, and left the rest of the 1,200 dollars in the crew house. The next morning when I got back, I checked in my bag where I had left the money, and the money was gone! I could not fucking believe it. It was the only money I had in the world. I felt devastated. It was the most money that had ever been stolen off me. I literally had nothing else, and I wasn't sure how I was going to survive there without any money. I was stranded!!! I knew I could ask my younger brother for a few quid but not for the amount I needed to stay until I got a job. My parents were my only way of getting home if I did not find a job. That was a lot of pressure on me! I blamed Ghost for taking it because he was the only one that knew I had it but he denied it very convincingly. I do not believe he took it. He was a good guy. There was one other little toe rag there and I think it was him. I raised a bit of a stink with the land lady about how this could happen, but she and the other few people staying there said I had been told to lock my door, so no sympathy. It was not what I was looking for. I was looking for a refund, but it wasn't happening. She had told me to watch my stuff and that all sorts of people walked through there, that it was a bit of a thoroughfare. Luckily enough, it was April time, and most of the yachts were going back across the Atlantic to the Mediterranean. So, a couple of days after, I got a call from the Chief mate of another yacht called 'Solemar' that I had been day working on too. He asked me did I want to do a crossing with them from Sint Maarten back to France? It was only to make up crew numbers for insurance purposes, but it served me and suited them too. He said it wasn't an Officer's position, but it would get me across the pond. He said I would be on watch with the Captain and do deckhand duties. It suited me down to the ground. I would get deckhand wages and have enough money to survive until I got a job when I was in France again. He also said it was a two-month gig, and if I wanted, I could stay for their shipyard period and do night watchman, which I agreed to. It all meant it would leave me in good stead for looking for another job when I got there. So, I took it. Before I left my mate Ronno from Dublin came to Sint Maarten. He was the one nicknamed me Juantheman and it never stuck. I went on the screaming piss with him. He knew I'd no money so he paid for everything. We got Cocaine and went on morning booze cruise in a taxi owned by Big Pappy. He had become a friend of mine. Ronno got angry when it came time to pay. Big Pappy charged him 400 dollars. It was extortionate but I would have paid it. Ronno only gave him 200 dollars and told him fuck right off. I had to laugh. I would not have the balls to do that in Sint Maarten. Ronno was more or less a local. He'd been coming there for years. We had a good time. I joined the next day and the Chief mate said to me when I was passing my luggage up to the yacht. "This is very light!!" I said "It's the way I travel!!!" He laughed and said "Welcome aboard!" He was so bloody cool. I had great craic with him. Probably the best Chief mate I'd met in yachting.

It was a 2-week crossing and in just over a week the Captain said to me that we would stop in the Azores for fuel, and because there was 3 birthdays onboard, he said he knew of a great restaurant there, where we would get our food served on hot volcanic rocks. When we arrived, we went to the Captains favourite restaurant and had a fantastic evening. Then the next day we did the volcano tour. On the second night, the second mate and I went out for a few beers and had a good time. We got split up because I met some of our other crew and stayed out for another few beers. He went home. I was walking back to our yacht shortly after that with a young guy I had met in the pub. His small 10m yacht was tied up behind ours in the marina. Ours was the 60m in front of it and as we were walking back to our respective yachts, he said "Wow that's some yacht!!" He said, "what's it like inside? It must be cool as fuck?!!" "C'mon!" I said. "Take a look!" We got on the passerelle and walked up and went inside. We were sitting there in the crew mess, and I asked if he was hungry, and he said, "yeah!!" So, I got him some food from the fridge in the galley. At this point I have to say it's not as strict in the commercial world of shipping that I grew up in to do something like this, but in yachting terms, it was a *definite* no, no! Then the stewardess came in, and she said, "JUAN!! What the fuck?!!" I said, "What???" She said, "come here a minute!" and I went out of the crew mess with her and she said, "You can't have anyone on the yacht that is not part of the crew unless security is passed on them first!" I said, "shit, I never thought about it!" I went back in and said, "Look, you're going to have to go!!". He said, "don't worry, I'm gone, I'm gone!" I showed him out, and he left. The next morning, I got up, and we'd sailed. I went up to the bridge a bit apprehensive. I did not get a good feeling about not being called for letting go the ropes for sailing. I have been at sea for years and I automatically knew I was in trouble. I met the Second mate on the bridge, and he said, "what happened last night...?" laughing. He said, he saw the Captain down picking peas up off the deck in the crew mess. I said, I didn't think it was that bad. He said, "I think you should be ok. It's your first offense ". But later I met with the Chief mate and he told me that if it was up to him, it would be fine. He said because I hadn't been told the rule about bringing people aboard, but he had to ring the regular Captain who was off on leave. He explained to me that this sort of thing had happened before where he had let people away with things, and it had come back to bite him on the ass, so he had to tell. I told him not to worry. I knew it was cutting him up. I had done wrong. He talked to the permanent Captain, and he just said, "He gets off in Gibraltar" where we had to stop for more fuel. So, I did.

Whenever we got to Gibraltar, they had to let me go. I got on a plane and went straight back to Nice and Antibes. I rocked up to Caroline's crew house again a little on the tipsy side. I was drinking the whole way there. I knew I had been kicked out before but I was going to apologize to her again and see if I could stay? But when I got there her husband arrived shortly after me and said in a raised voice "what are you doing here?! He angrily blamed me for causing trouble last time I was there but I said "no I didn't, but I'm getting the blame for it!" so I left. I've seen Caroline since, and we get on well.

I then went to Amma's crew house that I had stayed in before as well and asked Carol could I stay? She said no problem. I stayed there for a few weeks. Things were fun, and I was meeting new people. I didn't really go out much. I was drinking, but I was staying in, knowing I had to save my money until I got a job. There was another thing where I had met this girl the last summer I was there in Caroline's. I had spent a lot of my time talking to her on Facebook when I was in Sint Maarten. So, when I got to France, I had a thing all built up in my head that I was going to meet her, and it was going to be all love, fine and dandy. It wasn't to be. My imagination had run away with itself. I had bought her a painting in the Azores, and I was going to give that to her. The plan fell on its face. She was an air stewardess and she was working on a private plane in the Philippines when I arrived in Antibes. She said on Facebook that she was going to be there for a couple of weeks, so I had to fill my time while waiting until she got back.

I was into my fitness before I got back. Training in the gym on the sundeck on the boat during the crossing, but when I arrived, that fell by the way side, and I got more into the party scene again. I wasn't eating very well either, but I was trying to lose weight, so I wasn't too worried. Although I did know it was better to do it through fitness. Anyway, things fell apart at the seams job wise. I met loads of cool people who I am still friends with, but the jobs were hard to come by, and it was June...a bad time of year to be looking for one. It was halfway through the season, so unless someone left, got injured, or sacked or it was a new build or something, it was going to be difficult to get a job.

My money began running low, and I got kicked out of Amma's. Again, for my drinking! My brother had helped out a couple of times with a couple of hundred euros when I was in Sint Maarten. The money in my account kept getting sent to me by my mum when I was on the island because my bank card wasn't working, and I had to get money transferred to me through the western union. I thought at the time because of my paranoia with the alcohol, that they thought, the customers and bank staff, from their expressions that I was getting money from home and that my parents were keeping me, I so was paranoid every time I went in. It made me mad because it hurt the independent in me and it made me feel bad. I was self-sustaining apart from the couple of hundred that my brother had given me while I was there and the couple of hundred in Antibes, but I didn't like asking him. So, I was down to my last 100 euro and Carol in Amma's crew house asked me to leave. She said, "Juan, you have partied too much...I have to ask you to leave". I said, "I'm sorry about that.... I'll go....no problem". I left that night and went to find another crew house, but all the crew houses were full, so I went down to the beach. I had heard stories of people sleeping on the beach until they got a job, so I thought I'll do that. I decided I would have a good meal to myself before going there and stopped at a little restaurant on the Prince Albert Boulevard on the way down to the Royal beach. I had lasagna and a nice bottle of wine. Then I bought another bottle of wine before leaving to go down to the beach. The weather was fine, so I knew I'd be warm. It was summertime after all.

As I walked down, I began thinking that I'd had enough of these Superyachts and wanted to be a writer, and I was thinking fuck it all. I was in a rebellious fucking mood. In the dusk of the evening, I remember looking out at the water, grabbing my luggage drunk as hell, and throwing it towards the water. I thought fuck this shit, then lay down and fell asleep. When I woke up in the morning, it was shit!!! Because as I looked around, I could not see my luggage anywhere!! It was all gone! Including my laptop, all my documents for work, my passport, everything. The only thing that I had left was a phone and a bank card that were in my pocket. I thought fuck! I'm going to have to report this. I went up to the police station in the centre of town.

When I went in and spoke to them, the first thing the cop said was, "Have you been drinking, sir?!" I said, "yeah but it was last night!" He said, "no, I think you are too drunk". I said "look, I just want to report my stolen luggage ". He said, "yes sir...come back in the afternoon. You are still too drunk". I was like, right, ok, fuck it! I left there and thought I need some help, so I went back up to Amma's crew house. This was early morning, about 8.30am. I went in and sat down around the back where the crew quarters are and waited for everyone to get up. One of my friends whom I'd made there, John McGrath (who has written 3 books called Chef for sail 1,2 & 3 – out on online bookstore everywhere) said as soon as he saw me "what the hell happened?!!" I told them all about the events of the night before and that morning. They were all saying, "You need to get down to the police station and report it! You're not that drunk!!" I said, "I know, I thought the same, but the police told me to wait until lunchtime and come back sober!" They all said, "no man, the sooner you get it done the better because the thieves will be getting further away." I never thought about it but that was a ridiculous thing to think. They would never find them. At the time, it was what I was thinking as well. "You need to get on the case right away" one of them said. I left there and went back down to the police station. Whenever I went in, it was the same police man I had been dealing with and he said: "ok, come with me." I was so happy. I walked behind the counter and walked through the backdoor, as he led.

We got to their office at the back and I went to sit down but he said, "no, come, come," gesturing with his index finger. We went through another door, then he walked me down the corridor a bit. He opened the cell door and motioned for me to go in. And I said, "what the fuck?!" He said, "you cannot go. You are too drunk," and I said, "no, I am fine!!" He said, "no, you are too drunk. You must stay here until you are sober." I was like, "ah fuck sake!!" But I didn't protest, I just went in. He locked the door and left me there. Banged up abroad!!! I sat down on the bed (wooden bed, no mattress or anything), and then I lay down and went to sleep. I was so fucking hammered. Wine really gets you drunk. I'd been drinking it for weeks by then.

After a couple of hours, they took me out and breathalyzed me. I walked out of the cell and into the interview room, where they had a breathalyzer and sat down. One of the cops said, blow into this. I took a big breath and blew into it. I remembered what it registered it said 1.0. Afterwards he said, "What have you been drinking?? Whiskey??" I said, "No, why is that a good score?" Trying to make light of it. He said, "No.....you have been drinking whiskey" He thought it was a massive score!! I said, "no... wine, some beer, no whiskey". He said, "no! whiskey!" Then they were speaking French, and I understood one saying to the other "repatriation", and I thought no fucking way. They are going to send me home. I thought I don't want that. I felt I could pull it back. All I needed was a job. Not the clearest of thoughts at the time, but I didn't want to go home in that mess. I stayed quiet, then I said, "when do I get out?" He answered, "when this reads zero," pointing to the machine. "That could take a while!" I said. They put me back in the cell.

They took me out another time after that, then the third time, it read clear. I was in there about 30 hours or so. I'm sure they have a record of it, but it was over 24 hours anyway. When they let me go, they said they would look into the stolen luggage, but I wasn't holding any hopes for it. I walked outside, and as I was standing there, I thought to myself, where do I go now? I had 50 euros still in my pocket, and I had made a friend in the crew house called Jake from South Africa. He had said he was going to La Ciotat, to the shipyard there to look for work. He said a friend of his could help us get work. I said no at the time because I wanted to stay in Antibes because I was looking for an Officer's position, but I thought now it might be a good idea. La Ciotat was where I had been the year before. I decided to get in contact with him and go to La Ciotat and see if I could get some work too. First of all, I wanted to get in contact with my mate Ditsy. I knew he would help me out with some money. I had given him 300 euro for his birthday, but I needed the money back now! I went to the stoney beach on the outskirts of Antibes on the other side of the fort. As I was sitting there on the beach, I was staring out at a yacht just outside the harbour. It was waiting to come in, and as I did, I heard a voice in my head saying, "how fucking dare you? How dare you?!" It seemed to be coming from the yacht. It was the spirit of an old salty seadog from Antibes. The aliens have told me that the spirit was so pissed off that I was becoming a local in Antibes. He was jealous of me. Then the yacht started making its way in towards the port. All I was doing was lying on the beach resting. I didn't know what I had done, but I did think it was the aftermath of having drank too much. I did not know then that I could talk to the dead. I heard them chatting to me all the time but I just thought it would go away. The aliens told me they were not one bit worried about me. They have always been talking to me as well. They were guiding me with every thought and inspiration. They knew what was coming. The adventure of a lifetime!!

I walked on around the front of the fort facing the water. I sat opposite M/Y Kingdom 5 KR. It was slightly dusk, and I was sitting on a rock between the path and the water's edge, texting Ditsy and trying to explain in not so many words what had happened. As I was sitting there, the yacht, Beretta went in past with a small zodiac boat trailing behind it. I was looking at my phone texting when I saw this flash hitting the wall of the path beside me. I thought it was a bullet at first because I was so on the edge from all the drinking shenanigans that had gone on the days leading up to that. I was feeling guilty too from what had happened over the last few months, but I realized when it happened that it wasn't a bullet, it looked like the flash of a laser. I looked out at the zodiac, and I could clearly see one guy driving and another guy standing up facing me, it looked like he was holding something on his shoulder. It looked like a bazooka. My mind went into overdrive! I thought that it was some special technology that wasn't heard of yet, and they were firing it at me! I was so paranoid at this point it is hard to explain. I thought because of my time in Sint Maarten where drugs and drink go hand in hand and flow pretty freely, that in some way, I had pissed off drug dealers there, and it had followed me across the Atlantic, and now the gangsters on this side were after me too! I didn't know whether I had let people down, and they were annoyed, but I wasn't a bum. I was just trying to get some rest.

As I looked up, there was a guy sitting there on the bench with a 2 litre bottle of water, and I thought right.... they are going to shoot me. Then the guy on the bench is carrying acid in that bottle, and they are going to pour that over my face when I'm lying there dead so that I'm unrecognizable. I thought I had become a victim. That they had taken all my luggage, and now they were trying to kill me. I had made a joke on Facebook saying I had been erased, and now it was happening!! Some of the stories I had heard of deaths at the hands of some of these gangsters in Sint Maarten had tweaked the morbid side of my imagination. It felt very real. One of the stories I heard before I got on a plane to go there was of a stewardess who ran out of money and couldn't get home so she prostituted herself. The story went that she was addicted to Cocaine and owed dealers thousands of dollars. She tried to pay them off but it was impossible. They kidnapped her and took her to a secluded beach and killed her. They gouged out her eyeballs and set her on fire. Everybody said that the gangsters probably gouged out her eyeballs when she was still alive. There was lots of jokes about it. Totally fucking bonkers but that's yachting for you!! The local police found her dead body naked burned to a crisp. I sat there for a couple of seconds, not moving after seeing the flash. I continued looking at my phone, thinking about what to do next. I stood up slowly, not wanting to run because I would look guilty, and he would maybe take another shot at me.

The guy with the bottle sitting back on the bench from where the flash had hit, got up and moved off to the right a bit standing facing the water too about 15 feet away. I climbed back up and sat down on the bench, trying not to show any alarm. As I sat there, I looked over at the guy with the bottle of liquid. He was in his 50's, and he just smiled at me, then turned and walked away towards the town. I stood up and walked in the same direction. Not running and thinking as hard as I could about what I had done wrong. I had a lot of paranoia from coming off the drink. I had done so much drugs in Sint Maarten that my mind was a fucking minefield of paranoia. I hardly touched any weed the whole time I was there because of the testing onboard. Cocaine is out of your system in a couple of days. Weed stays in it for up to a month depending on how much of it you smoke. The alcohol was my biggest downfall in the Caribbean. I had the shakes and paranoia while I was sitting there, but I had had all that before, so I knew what it was. This all felt very real and made sense in my head. I had the feeling that people were trying to kill me before. I had annoyed people in Sint Maarten, or so I had been told by Ghost, and it was all coming back to me tenfold. He told me he saved my life. He said that they were so pissed off at my behaviour that they were going to kill me. I believe him!!

I spent all night walking around Antibes, trying not to settle in one place because I felt the spirit of the ninja was after me too, training me in a way. It had happened at home when I was in Donegal, where I was on a higher state of alert.

As I was driving one evening to Letterkenny. I saw a vision of a ninja in front of me. I stopped at a petrol station, and as I turned my back on the guy who was putting in the petrol, I felt a knife going into the back of my neck (not in reality). I heard the words in my head saying "you're got!" So, it felt like I was fighting with the spirit world as well. In a surreal kind of way, it was as though it was keeping me alert, but it left me really on edge, not knowing who to trust and that an attack could come out of anywhere.

It was all supernatural before I even got there. I was lying in my bed at home shortly before I left for France, and I felt like I was in a harem and could feel three women around me and see their purple images naked toying with my cock and playing with me as I lay there naked, masturbating with them. You could say I was fantasizing but to see them in front of me, it felt like there was something greater coming when I got out there.

So, I was outside Amma's crew house, and it was about 3 or 4 in the morning, and I had nowhere to stay, so I thought, ah, I'll just sleep outside the crew house. There was a grassy part beside the road shielded with bushes, so, I sat down and put my back to this reed-type tree with reeds so tight that whoever I thought was after me couldn't stick a spike through it and into me, so I didn't have to watch my back. I did think they could stick a needle through it, but I figured I was more or less safe. I didn't sleep, and then in the morning, I was walking down to the port again to look for day work. I thought this has got to work! I have got to get something. As long as I kept my chin up, it will happen. There is a lesson in there to all you dockwalkers. Keep the chin up!

I was crossing the road, and a guy in a lorry flashed the lights at me. I was so paranoid I thought he knew me, and everyone was in on it. I decided then to go to the train station and skip looking for day work there and go straight to La Ciotat to Jake and look for work there.

I got on the train and sat down. When I did, three young Arab guys in their 20's got on and sat in the seat on the opposite side of the aisle from me. I think they were Arab. There's a big Arab population in Antibes and the area. I thought afterwards they were there to be friends with me, not to harm me. My friend, Punchy, in Antibes, has a lot of Arab friends. I thought they might be friends of his. My head was in a spin. I felt under immense pressure and because I thought that everyone was trying to kill me, so why not them too. I was sitting there as we moved off, and I had had a Chinese takeaway the night before, and I had taken the chopsticks and put them up the sleeve of my coat and I was thinking, one of them is going to get stabbed if they come at me. I half slept on the journey, but I was aware they were there. I did wake up startled and made a stabbing motion with a chopstick at them as if one of them had come at me. It shook them a bit, I could see the surprise on their faces, but they stayed standing where they were. When we got to the station where I was to change for La Ciotat, I stood to leave, and as I was walking down the aisle, one of them said in English, "Non...non-go back to Antibes!!!" He looked kind of worried and I didn't ask why he had said it but I said "No. I'm going to La Ciotat." He looked more disappointed than anything and let me go. I would have listened to him because of the fear in his voice, but I had nothing to go back there for. I also thought I would be alright when I got to my mate's place and had some rest and out of public view for a while. Lots of weird things were happening to me. It had been like that since the moment I stepped of the plane in France in 2007 for the first time. I was in a nightclub in Antibes in 2007 and when I was dancing with a hot bloody chick my name JUAN came over the speakers, booming out. I hadn't a clue what was going on and carried on dancing. It was surreal!!

I remember at the time on the train that I was listening to a voice in my head that was guiding me. It was the aliens. They have told me now in 2023 that they were instrumental on this journey. They wanted me to have a Billion dollar adventure and win the Palm d'Or. It was telling me everything. It spoke when I went to decide something. It would say yes, no, when I was trying to decide something, then it would direct me. The aliens hear every thought and they respond with their voice to them while I am thinking. They spoke about everything, right down to where I walked. It would say left.... right. The aliens have now spoken to me in full narrative form. It only occurred as a full narrative in the last couple of years. They are telling me all about this adventure right this minute. I am editing the book for the final time. They are reminding me of the whole adventure. It is wild!! I didn't know what the voice was at the time. It wasn't my own inner voice, so I didn't know who it was. Whether it was god...some spiritual guide, or who? God does not exist. The aliens have told me that. I know now! It is not scary one iota. I do not listen to radio. I do not watch TV. I sit or lie in total silence and have conversations with the alien race Pachsion. They are going to guide me to lead the world in to the 23rd century. They are going to use my writing as a guide to the human race.

I was also having visions at the time of this woman I had met in Letterkenny mental asylum when I was in for drinking again! She told me that she was a Billionairess and she asked me to go to her house in Scotland and stay with her when I got out. It didn't work out. I did not want to be with her. She was extremely needy. The other woman I was having visions of was a Kiwi girl I had been partially seeing the summer before in Caroline's crew house. It had ended kind of badly too. She had gotten in to bed with me and to give things a bit of excitement I ripped her knickers off quick. She was getting ready to make love spooning. When I ripped her knickers down, she leaped out of the bed and said "What are you doing?!" I laughed and said I was just having a bit of fun! She was not happy and we never had sex.

These two women were appearing in visions and they were telling me they were going to kill me and that I was a coward. I could see a meat cleaver coming at me at one stage. I firmly believe these hallucinations are down to the San Pedro I took about 10 years before and that they were flashbacks due to alcohol withdrawals. The alcohol withdrawals seemed to exaggerate them. All I knew is that as I was going through it, it all felt very real...

My reason for not going home was that I thought if I toughed it out and showed the underworld, I meant no harm or didn't mean whatever they thought I had done, then they would leave me alone. I liked this part of the world and didn't want to be chased away from it and never be allowed to come back.

As soon as I arrived in La Ciotat, I knew I had to make contact with Jake. I hadn't much battery on my phone. I had kept it off as long as I could because I had no charger. I got in touch with him and told him there were no buses working because it was Sunday. He said it's a long walk from the station to town. I set out on foot. I walked from the station into town. It was the longest walk I've ever done. My feet were aching. I met up with him. We went shopping to get some stores then to his apartment where his friend was. He knew I hadn't been eating and that I had no clothes because I'd got robbed. He gave me new clothes, and I got washed up. It had been a good few days since I'd had a warm shower. So, it felt good!

We ate, then chilled out as I caught him up on the story so far. He and his friend listened. When we finished eating, he cracked open a beer and asked me did I want one? I said I better not. Then I thought it might be good to help me relax, and after all, I was coming off a major bender the last few weeks, so it might be good medicine. We had a beer, then they were having a joint, and he asked if I wanted some? I said again, "well, I shouldn't really.... but what the hey, I'll take a blast. It might calm me down as well".

It affected me big time, whatever it was that was in it. I thought it was Sulphur. I thought they were trying to poison me! I WAS sooo paranoid!!! It was maybe my weakened state...but my whole vision left me, and all I saw was a wall of fire, and all I could hear was my father's voice saying "Juan let go...they're making fun of ye.... let go..." I could feel a pull in my chest like all I had to do was give in. It felt like I was going to die. I stood up, slapping my face trying to get my adrenaline going. All I could see was the fire in front of me, and it did feel right to let go. It felt like I was dying, but because I didn't trust my father at the time, I wouldn't listen to his advice. I felt if I had listened to his voice, I would have died. It looked like the gates of hell or heaven in front of me. I wasn't sure which. I wasn't afraid of what was in front of me, but I didn't want to die. I felt it wasn't my time and whatever or whoever was in control was wrong. I was trying everything I could to stay alive, trying to pull back from the fire and slapping myself in the face as hard as I could. I ran for the bathroom right beside me and looked in the mirror just to see if I was still alive. It was a stronger drug than anything I had ever smoked before, or again, maybe it was my weakened state. I came around, and I could see my face in the mirror. This all happened in an instant. I said to Jake when I came around, "right, I'm not having any more of that!" I told them what I had seen, and they were like "yeah, I don't think you should, you better rest."

They were both going out for the night, so they left, and I sat down on the bed a little stoned and a little warm from the drink. It was the first time it had happened but as I was looking at the wall of the apartment, I could see channels of thin vine-like streams of energy coming from the top corner of the room down to the middle of the wall 5 feet in front of me in a diagonal translucent "S" type shape on the wall. It was a visual from the aliens. They told me this in 2021. They are eternal beings. They have 3 suns on their planet. The serotonin generated in their bodies keeps them young. The suns are so strong. Their planet is 100 times the size of earth. The equator is 1 million miles around. They are coming to earth on the 11th of April 2026. They are going to evolve earth. And they have put me Juan in charge of the planet. I am the King of Pachsion. They are calling me the King of the Cosmos. I am King of earth as well.

Then as I looked at the visual's I heard the words and the music of my life. It was telling my story. The aliens were singing to me. They still do that. They communicate by singing to me sometimes. It is really easy to listen too. It does not distract me one tiny little bit. I can live my life as normal. I don't remember the words now from back then but it was about the previous months. At the time, it was being played to me in a singer's voice I didn't recognize. I didn't know if it was coming from me or where but it was playing on and on. I now know it was from another planet. 100 Billion light years away!!! I sat and listened. I was intrigued. I watched this for a good 15 minutes and listened to the aliens. It was so bloody cool!! The vines of energy seemed to have an energy stream moving through them. It was out of this world. I listened to it until it stopped. Then I lay back in the little camp bed and waited for the guys to come home. I could not sleep after that.

My South African buddies came back later that night. I told them when they came in that I had been prepared for someone to break in and try and kill me. I had a razor ready to slash because I thought my life was under threat. I had not told them about getting shot at yet. I figured they would ask me to leave. I was right! I told Jake when they came back that I had been shot at in Antibes. It freaked him out and he said if that's what's going on you better leave. He said "If you got shot at, that makes us a target as well." I said "I know!" "That's why I am telling you now! So, you can make up your own mind." I left in the morning but I went back for a razor. I wanted to maintain a suave look for dockwalking!

Jake also gave me a pair of sunglasses and said, look here, you can pawn them off if you need some money. I'm sure you'll get 50 euro for them anyway. Sound man. I took them and thanked him for having me. Apologizing for bringing it to their door, but he was fine, and so was his mate. I didn't do that with the sunglasses. I kept them. They were a good pair. I decided then, as I knew the lay of the land and it was early morning that I would go to the shipyard where all the yachts were and chance my arm dockwalking. I thought if I hit lucky, I could pull everything back again!

After going around all the yachts and getting nothing, I walked back out through the yard. But before I got to the main entrance to leave, I spotted a rusty fallen down hanger behind the security fence. It is massive. I'm sure all yachties who have been there will remember it.

And having nowhere to stay, I darted through a fence that had the old broken-down hanger cordoned off. I went inside looking for somewhere dry to settle down for the night. As I went into it, I noticed a small prefabricated building in the corner on the right and steps leading up to its roof. I walked up the steps thinking it'll be safer up there because I'm out of view from anyone who can see me and rats. Only one entrance point as well. Good for security.

I hunkered down and got comfortable, thinking this is going to be a long night. I was sitting on one of the steel girders frames with another girder above my head. As it got dark, I was thinking safety, but I had a plain view of anyone coming up the steps, and I could hear anyone clambering around trying to get in through the fence, so I figured I was safe.

To make sure I was, there was a piece of wood like a small staff about 3 feet long lying beside me, so I broke it in two. It was like two stakes, and I had them in my hands and thought I would use that to defend myself if anyone tried to attack me. I was still having withdrawals from all the drinking I had been doing, too, so I was having nightmares, and visions like hallucinations, and my body and hands were shaking too. Some time passed into the night, just as I was settling in when all of a sudden, I could hear voices from outside saying, "let's get him, let's get him." I thought with the two stakes in my hands that if anyone breaks in, they're going to get STABBED. I just thought, I'll stab them if they come near me. Somebody will have to die to kill me. I was going to put up a fight whatever happened.

As the night wore on, it started to rain, and then a full-on thunderstorm started. I had no shelter above me for the rain coming down, so I used a piece of slate that was lying there from the roof years before and put it on the girder above my head. It wasn't much use, but it kept the rain from falling directly on me. While I was sitting there, I had a vision looking down on the half-lit derelict floor of the building, and I thought I'm giving up drink if I have to go through this afterwards. As I said it to myself, I saw an image coming towards me and then enter me. I felt a sense of serenity and wellbeing that I had never felt before. It felt good, but then I rebelled, thinking boldly, ah,

I'll just have one or two, and the image and the feeling left. I've been told it was the aliens putting the spirit of Pachsion into me. It was my feeling on Pachsion when I was living there. Absolute power. I then saw another vision of translucent Wario from the Nintendo game Mario Carts. He was sitting in giant size on the ground in front of me, about ten foot-high like a big fat cat. It was like being on acid, but I hadn't taken anything in years. I'd had the joint, but that was the day before. I could see the vision down in front of me as I was sitting huddled upstairs on the prefab roof inside the hanger. The hanger was very run down with massive holes in the roof, and the wind was blowing through it. I kind of liked it too, being there it was a bit rustic, exciting. At the same time, too, I had all this stuff that was going on to contend with, so it wasn't that exciting. The feeling would come and go.

I woke up in the morning, and as I woke up, I took a big breath of air, stood up and shouted out "England, Scotland, Wales, France." I don't know what it meant or why I didn't shout Ireland! It was probably what I was dreaming about, but in my head, at the time, I thought these are the people who are looking out for me. Crazy as it sounds! I also felt a pain in my heart and down my left arm. I thought I was having a heart attack and that it was plausible because of the drinking withdrawals. So, to get my heart pumping, thinking this would be the best course of action, I started doing press-ups to push the embolism out. I did ten quickly, then stood up, and the pain left. I thought, right I cannot stay here. It's too open. I need shelter. I moved from there further into the town. I found an old abandoned warehouse. I was walking past, and I saw the entrance to it barricaded by a 5-foot high gate. I jumped that and walked halfway up to the left, and picked a steel stanchion that I could sit behind, shielding me from the road. My plan was to stay there and dockwalk along the shipyard every single day. I was dry shaving and not looking too bad. I thought, get a job, get some money, find a place to stay with the money, and get back on my feet. Simple! It nearly worked as well!! I docked walked and got some work (There's another lesson to all you dockwalkers. Persevere! Something will happen for you!!!) BUT unfortunately, I didn't have a passport. The Captain said he would have given me the gig no bother but the office said no, not without a passport. It was a two-week gig on a Shadow boat. That was a real kick in the bollocks. The Captain said I would have got a 1400 euro for it. "It would have kept the wolves from the door!" he said. He was pretty dead on. He looked ex-military.

I contacted Ditsy by phone and arranged to meet him in Toulon, where he was on a yacht as deckhand. We met up, and he gave me 300 Euros. He said he was going away for the weekend with a stewardess who was on the yacht with him and to get myself together. He said get some new clothes, a hotel, showered and some food and I would feel better. I stayed for two nights in a cheap hotel, then I went back to La Ciotat with a bag on my back and some money in my pocket. I thought I would just dockwalk again and get some day work. Unfortunately, it did not happen for me. I went down and out again. I stayed in a small motel there for two nights but decided not to stay any longer because my money was running out and I always had the big warehouse. I told the Italian motel owner, who looked like a bit of a gangster, about my plight and about being shot at in Antibes. He just started laughing, which cheered me up a little, making light of it. The only actual problem I encountered whenever I was in La Ciotat was one afternoon, when I was dockwalking and I'd walked across the towns seafront there a little too often because I had no money and nowhere to go, and a guy who was standing there with two other guys pointed his finger at me like a pistol and pulled the trigger. I thought the Italian guy had talked. I was about 30 feet away from the guy. I put my hands out to the side and made the universal signal for what? What did I do?!! He didn't do anything and just stared at me angrily with the two other guys, then I shook my head and walked the other way. I was laying the crazy lost boy look on a bit, but I felt I was getting closer to the people who were after me. I wanted to meet them to find out what I had done and explain I was innocent. Another guy shouted at me after this as I was standing outside the Italian motel during the day. He was walking by the laneway I was in, and he roared in English…"What no bullet holes?!!" looking at my legs. I didn't know what was going on. I saw a fishing line hanging outside on a tree and thought I was going to be garroted. I felt like I had been set up. It could've been because I was walking about so much and had become suspicious.

Either way, it didn't help my sleep pattern when I went back to the warehouse that evening. After this happened, I decided to go into the shed and chill. I was walking past a pizza van and with some euros I had left, I bought a pizza then went back to the building. I ate the pizza crouching down in the spot I had picked out, then put the box on the ground underneath me, and used that as my seat. While I had been walking around earlier, I had been feeling the deaths of people like a hanging with a rope around my throat, bullets and knives going into me, and I kept feeling a knife going across my throat. I know it was because of the aliens. They were training me to be alert so I could not be killed. I stayed in the big warehouse for a couple of days.

The first night there, I sat down on my pizza box and stared in the darkness at the wall opposite me. As I sat there, a vision appeared saying, "this is the HUB!! the hub, the hub, the HUB! You are listening to the HUB!" It seemed to be coming from a ball of energy fiery gold and red in colour, with energy streams coming horizontally out of it against the back wall. Then the music started playing, and again, the story of my life in the song was being played to me. I sat there and listened. It was like country rock. I looked away to see what would happen, but I was really interested in what it was saying. It stopped when I looked away, but when I looked back, and I relaxed, kind of meditating, it reappeared again. I listened for a long time. I have been told since writing this original text that the alien race was watching out for me. It was them who were singing to me. They are going to make a movie out of my life when I'm on Pachsion again in 50 years time. All these adventures are well documented on Pachsion.

As I listened, I felt the darkness engulf me. It was very dark, and I still thought I was a target. As I sat there, I looked around to see where a sniper could shoot me from. Up and to the left, there was a block of apartments with a light on in the top one, the one that had a direct line of sight to me. Someone came out onto the balcony with a shaved head, and at that time, I thought it was Big Andy. He was the gangster who I thought was after me. Him and his gang. I thought even some special agents were after me. Although nothing happened to me at the time of Shannon airport, I still felt a deep paranoia because of it and it made me conjure up all sorts of scenarios in my head. I heard someone landing on the roof. I immediately thought, they are parachuting in. It was fucking frightening. I heard the two feet landing on around the middle of the roof of the building and running as soon as he hit. I thought, right, this is it. They're coming down, and they are going to shoot me. The roof was about 50 feet high and about 100 feet long. The place had been gutted, and it was just a shell. I stayed in the shadows, hunkered down, waiting for the fight of my life!

Nothing happened, and I stayed all night in the same position. I stayed there a couple of nights. Then having had enough of the fear of having a death threat over me. I decided to make my way to the train station, and get out of there. I knew Antibes better and thought I would be safer there. I thought the local people in La Ciotat thought I was dealing drugs or something or they just didn't like dossers, and at that point, that was the way I was living. Not all of them were like this. As I was walking around the town a day or two before this before, a group kids, in their early teens came over to me in a park. A girl and two boys, and the young girl offered me a puppy to take care of. It was a really nice gesture, and I appreciated it big-time, but I thought to myself deep down, I can just about look after myself at the minute, never mind a dog. I knew I wouldn't be able to feed it because I had no money so I thanked them but declined the offer.

I left the building and struck out for the train station. I put the deck shoes that I was wearing into the bin as they were smelling and put on the flip-flops I had bought in Toulon. As I walked out of La Ciotat towards the train station, I got the feeling something terrible was going to happen to me. That I was about to be killed or kidnapped and tortured. Severe paranoia, but the drink can have that effect, so I was trying to calm myself and not become overwhelmed. I felt like I was a target. I walked out of town as calmly as I could, but I couldn't help it and began to panic, so I started to run. I saw a cafe beside the road and went in and tried to tell the waiter in English that I needed help. He looked at me blankly. I said I needed the police, but then I thought that is the worst thing I could do because then I'm a snitch, so I apologized and left thinking I just had to tough this out and get home on my own. I was getting closer to the train station, but my mind was in overdrive, and I thought as a show of good faith, from me, that I am not a drug dealer or anything and I mean no harm, also, so they would think that I was a little crazy! I put the "sandals in the bin", a bit like the song Elton John wrote about Mother Teresa, very like princess Di's song, and continued on, on my bare feet. The flip-flops had the Jamaican flag colours on them, so Rastafarian in my eyes. I was sending them a message that I had nothing to do with drugs. Looking back now, it was like being in the movie, by Jean-Claude van damme were rich people bet on the lives of criminals giving them a chance to run then hunt them down with a killing squad while watching them on a bank of TV's. I continued walking, feeling vulnerable because I thought I was being followed when I spied abandoned train tracks perpendicular to the road. I immediately thought, well a car can't follow me up there, so I walked up the tracks. While I was walking up them, I was thinking I feel safer now, for a while at least. Getting out of the town was a big relief, even if I did think I was being followed. When I was walking up the tracks, I heard a voice in my head saying, plant that there, referring to the backpack I was carrying. It was the spirit world. I know that now. The aliens have told me. I had my suspicions then and did not follow their orders. It was an entrance to a small housing estate. I did not know why the voice was telling me to do this, but I felt it was an evil spirit within me and the bag was supposed to be a bomb. I didn't do it. I ignored the spirit and carried on, but it made me wonder what the spirits around me wanted from me? I wasn't playing games with anybody. I wanted to find my way home and get out of this debacle. It was as if I had broken down and I had to get out of it on my own but they told me to leave the bag there, and I didn't know why? Maybe the spirits thought the people in the houses were drug dealers. I thought of the French Resistance and paramilitary groups from home were chasing me home, and all the paramilitary groups of the world were connected up. Then all the drug dealers had connected up, and all the business people had connected up.

I thought the whole world was trying to get me! Or they were playing a game with me, and I didn't know why or what for?

As I was walking up the train track, I got to a country lane. I wasn't sure which way to go, so I turned right, just hoping I would find the right path back to the main road leading to the train station. It reminded me of home, where I lived in the country. I continued walking down the road feeling safer already because of the narrow roads and high ditches. It was about 2 in the afternoon at this stage, so it was warm. I was wearing two t-shirts, a pair of levis jeans and walking on my bare feet. I thought after a short while that I needed to sit down for some rest. I had been walking for what seemed like an eternity. It felt like it was a bad idea and I should have kept going. I would have got a train and got out of there.

Instead, I saw a gate leading into a field on the right. It was between two very high ditches about 20 feet high. I jumped the gate onto the short grass and walked over to the left so I couldn't be seen from the road. The field where I was sitting was facing the town and this voice said (not my inner voice but voices of other people all the time (not audio hallucinations either!)) "this is not a good idea. Keep moving!!!" The aliens have told me since, it was them. And that I was in mortal danger. I did not take the advice! I was very wary though. I thought then that even at that distance, I was still a target for a sniper. I thought the blue polo neck shirt I had on me would stand out a mile in the green field. I sat and rested anyway, not dozing but resting my eyes all the time, still aware or feeling aware that there were people after me. Next thing I heard, someone. This guy leaned over the fence to me. I looked up at him, and he said in English accent, "I would stay there if I was you." I thought fuck! I knew there was people after me! It was the first confirmation I'd had. Jesus, was it high octane! I sat there anyway, thinking they were on the other side of the fence in the gate house I had noticed on the other side of the road. There was a big manor house further in off the road with land that had stretched all the way up to a forest on a steep hill.

It started to get dark. I hadn't moved an inch! I was getting very edgy, the darker it got. I thought to myself I am going to make a run for it. I noticed a hole beside the gate that I could fit through. I was in fear and ready for a fight, but I thought, how do I get out of this? I thought I was going to be shot or tortured. I was thinking the worst. I crawled towards the hole in the darkness, leaving my bag to the side, and as I did, the heads of three Rastafarian black spirits, complete with dreadlocks appeared in front of me as I hunkered down, the visions are always translucent. And because I was just back from the Caribbean, I thought Voodoo.

I'd expressed my interest to the local guy, Shaun, I met when I was there, and he said, "no man, you don't mess with that. It's real." I kind of made a joke of it, but I believed him and know it for a fact now because the spirits are with me and still appear. They are appearing as I write this, and I'm in a quandary to reveal what actually appeared in front of me and what they said. They are guiding my eyes now to different words on the screen, making up a message and telling me not to write it! Aghhh, so annoying! Here goes anyway, they told me to stay where I was and that I was going to die and that I was going to be skinned alive and set on fire! They were talking in a Caribbean accent. I don't know if it was because of my circumstances that the visions appeared because of my fear, but they made it worse. They also gave me the energy and urge to take flight. I thought fuck this, I'm not hanging about.

I remembered the green hedge on the other side of the road about chest height, and I planned in my head what I was going to do. I thought, right! If they have a gun trained on the fence waiting for me to move, then I'm dead. If they don't, I can catapult over the fence and get away, making for the forest at the end of the long field on the hill. I was hoping there wasn't a house foundation or some sort of blockwork on the other side of the fence, which there can be, thinking of home where it happens that I could land in. Fight or flight, and in this case...flight was better. Ignoring the three spirits in front of me, I crawled through them and out the hole, steadied myself ready to run to the other side, and then ran like fuck! I ran across the road and put my two hands on the wooden fence, and somersaulted over the fence, landing in the field. I took stock quickly then ran like hell for the woods. I could see a tree halfway up on the left and aimed for that. I ran with all my might. I got to the shadow of the tree and lay down, catching my breath. I thought this is a nice place to lie down. It was a moonlit night. I looked up the field to where I had just come from and saw that no one was following me. I felt relieved but I was still out in the open. As I lay there, the visions started again. This time as I looked up at the sky, it came down from a star. Two people. One was of a gorgeous young blonde South African girl whom I had proposed to in Antibes a couple of weeks before. She was saying to get up and run!!! I did not listen. I was still on edge but I felt pretty safe there. I had said in Antibes, if it doesn't work out with your boyfriend, marry me, and she emphatically said yes! She was really pretty, and I got on well with her, but it fell apart when I couldn't stop myself from drinking. We had gone for a walk up over the hill from the crew house and were looking down over the harbour, it was very romantic!

Then the other apparition was Meredith, the Scottish Billionairess I had met in the asylum in Letterkenny. They were a few feet away from me. Then as I looked back down the field towards where I had come from, the guy Big Andy who I thought was chasing me was standing with his arms out holding what looked like a silver or white gun. In my head, I thought he's holding a Glock, but from that distance in the moonlight, I didn't know if he was a vision or real. It looked like Andy with his big bald head. I had got in a fight with him in Antibes. I was drinking all day with him and ditsy. Ditsy was a friend of his. Big Andy was a Cocaine dealer and an ex-British army soldier. He'd said to me "I know why the I.R.A don't like the British army, the army used to come into their houses and steal their TV's." He had a laugh at that. He was a UVF man. Ulster volunteer force, a paramilitary group from my country. They were protestant and the I.R.A were Catholic. It was so stupid to be in a country like France and be talking about that stupid war. I got annoyed and took the piss out of him. He was huge. Definitely the biggest body builder I'd ever met. He was about 6' 3" and had bulging muscles. He looked like he could crush you. He never said a word at my piss taking. Then later that day, I went for a piss and woke up on the toilet floor. I was so drunk that I never thought about what happened. I just got up and had a piss then went back out and sat beside them all again. The big man who was with him and who was about 6' 7" had told me earlier in the day that the pub I was drinking in was a UVF pub. I couldn't believe it, in the middle of Antibes. Then I thought about it. Old town in Antibes was nicknamed Little Britain. I looked up at him and said "I thought all that shit was over with…" He just looked at me in bewilderment. I'd faced him down and he didn't know what to do. He was trying to intimidate me. It did not work. The next morning, I woke up. I sat up in my bed and ran my tongue over my front teeth. They were very sore. I told Gypsy who was lying on a mattress on my bedroom floor that my teeth were fucking killing me. He laughed at me and said "Ha ha ha…Big Andy hit you last night!!" I asked him why? And he said "because you were taking the piss out of him all day." I thought fucking hell, I never really get in fights. It was just before myself and Wraggamuffin moved to Ammas crew house and I got the job on My Trust Fund. That was the first of 3 slaps I got on my teeth in 2 weeks.

No wonder they were broke. One punch from Big Andy. One slap from falling off the fence drunk in La Ciotat and Ditsy the little tyke!!

The spirit of Meredith said to me, "you're going to get it now!" I took flight again!!! I thought "I better not lie here or I'm caught!!!" I got up, and when I looked around, I could see defense forces standing up, translucent figures. About six of them with camouflage over them and guns sticking out. They looked real in the moonlight. They looked like snipers. I thought it was the army ranger wing of the Irish defense forces, whom I had some contact with in Antibes that summer. They tried to sign me up to do their close body protection program. They said I'd be a real heavy hitter.

They were facing the forest. It was as if I was watching a mission in progress. They were hunkered up for a few seconds, then they lay down again undercover and disappeared. It was so surreal. I was having lots of visions. It was kind of fun! I looked back up the field, and I could see Big Andy getting ready to chase me. I thought he was about to start running at me and shooting.

I didn't think twice! I took off and started running towards the forest on the hill further up the field. I zigzagged over and back the field, in quick darting movements, hoping to hell there was nothing that could cut my bare feet in the grass. I zigzagged over and back in case Big Andy would start shooting at me, but nothing happened. I got to the first of the trees, and it was all brambles. I climbed through them, ignoring the pain and all the time in my bare feet. As I climbed up and through at a 45-degree angle, I felt a grip going around my ankle. I looked down, and there was a translucent apparition of Big Andy holding my ankle with one hand. But as I looked at him and pulled my foot away, the image disappeared. It was just tangled in a briar. I got free of that, and as I climbed further up through the undergrowth, I looked up, and there were four ninjas with their costumes on, in midget size, and they were sticking me with needles. Jabbing me over and over! In my head, they were injecting me with AIDS. It was the worst thing I could think of. It was only fleeting. I realized they were just images, and it was just the thorns, so I burst through them and kept on going. They disappeared as I climbed through them. I got halfway up the hill and decided to rest. I could see the top of the hill where the trees stopped, but I didn't know what was beyond it. Then I heard a deep voice in my head saying, rest here, rest here but stay standing. It was the alien race!!!!! They kept ME alive. I kept standing, and a black guy appeared, then another one appeared. It was bright in the moonlight, and I could see their apparitions. Then the whole crew appeared, black and white, and they were all around me. They were saying just rest. Then they were giving me heroin. They were hooking me up, and the heroin was going to cure the AIDs that I had just been given. They had me on a drip, and if I stayed standing on that one spot all night, I would be cured. It was fucking mental. They chatted to me all night. They kept me going. I stood and listened to them even though it was getting cold. I hardly moved an inch. If I moved at all the voices and surrounding spirits would disappear. They would only reappear when I was still for a few seconds again. I don't remember now what they were talking about. They were just talking, and they were all around me. It was really comforting. The bushes and trees were forming their shapes. It was really painful to stand in my bare feet in the sharp undergrowth without moving a millimetre BUT I did it!!

Then in the morning, about 6 O' Clock, when it got daylight, I saw out through the trees, a guy at the bottom of the field feeding animals. He disappeared from view then a military aircraft flew low overhead. I was in a kind of valley. It looked like an F14, but I couldn't be sure of the make. I thought I was getting a salute from the military. I thought they were watching me on satellites. It was a weird bloody time. It flew past as I was about to make my way down through all the trees and brush again to get my bag. Then I thought, fuck my bag, I'll make my way up over the hill, find a road, and head for the train station. I climbed up the steep hill.... still in my bare feet! Climbing through all the bushes and trees, up to a clearing near the top. I kept on walking and I got to a fence. As I was about to climb over it, there was guy standing in front of me about 100 yards away. He had a shotgun in his hands. I could see the side by side barrels. Suddenly he fired a shot literally across my bow and shouted in English...."Go back the way you came!!!" I was like, what the fuck have I done!! What did I do?? Jesus Christ, why was everybody after me for?! I turned around and started walking back down again. I didn't get upset because I had been through so much. The fact that he was giving me a warning shot was good enough for me. He wasn't firing it at me! I didn't know where I was to go or what I was to do. I walked back down through the forest, and it was pretty painful. I was climbing through briars and bushes to get to the bottom. I got to the field again after a lot of torture, and what a relief it was when I got to the grass. It was so soft and free. I could feel it between my toes. It was lovely, wet, and cool. I walked until I got to the end of the field. When I got to the end, I thought, well I'm out in the open now. They can see me, but I thought they are not going to do anything to me, like shoot me in broad daylight. At least that was my thinking. I climbed over the fence and got back out on to the road. There didn't seem to be anybody. I looked over at the house and saw no one, so I walked over to the hole in the ditch where I'd left my bag, and to my relief, it was still there. I thought maybe they would have taken it because they knew where I'd been lying. I put the bag on my back and struck out for the town again.

I thought, right, that's it. I'm being threatened, and I didn't know who by. I'm going to town to find out by whom. I'd heard horror stories over the last few months of horrific things that had happened to people in drug-related crimes like people being tortured by having their fingers cut off with tin snips, and all these stories were running riot through my head and I thought they were going to do the same to me. It was very real to me. I walked back into town, and as I was walking along the road, this guy stopped in a car about 20 yards in front of me. He got out and was eyeballing me in an intimidating way, but I faced him down and kept walking towards him because I had done nothing wrong in my eyes. He got back into his car, pissed off, and drove off. I was going into town to meet the main drug dealers and resolve it. Whoever or wherever in La Ciotat they were. Whenever I got to the outskirts of town, I changed my mind and thought I just wanted to get out of there, so I turned and started walking towards the train station again.

When I got to the train station, I went inside, and with the last of my money, I tried to buy a ticket. I was at the computerized ticket dispenser. As I was choosing, I got a sudden rush! I could feel someone coming at me fast and close. As I looked around, I heard a loud bang like a crack of a gun. This guy ran out past me through the doors that lead out on to the track. He had long black hair tied back in a ponytail and a hooded army jacket on. He was in his late twenties. I think the gun was blank. There is no way he could have missed from that range! They had finally got me. It was as if I had been a target for days and nights, and they had finally got to me. I looked at the teller to see if he saw anything but he kept his head bloody down. He was letting on he didn't see anything. It scared the living fuck out of me!!! I was the only one in the small train station building. I thought, holy Christ, I have got to get out of here. I turned back to the ticket dispenser, and as I was choosing my destination, a voice in my head kept saying go to Marseille. It was the spirit world, I now know! The aliens have told me that the spirit world wanted me to die there and then. I'd been listening to this voice and the alien voice for years. Someone told me it sounds like your conscience! But the aliens have told me it is them. They have a running narrative from their alien planet and it is wonderful. They talk to me psychically. I thought at the time my inner voice had gone to someone else. Like a transfer of consciousness. I thought, maybe it's still in there. I just have to find it. I thought it had maybe gone to my brother or my dad because of the way they were behaving. It was not like them and it was so like me. I wasn't sure but I thought it had gone somewhere else. I now know that it was the aliens and the spirit world all along. The aliens do not suggest anything bad. The spirit world is evil when they want to be. You just have to know what to listen too. They give some good advice as well.

I thought, why go to Marseille? It would have been the end of my dreams. I didn't know why or who it was telling me, but the voice was telling me Marseille. I thought of reasons for it, but I wanted to make my way home, so I ignored it. I also thought about the Bourne identity movie, how he turned up in Marseille, and thought maybe that was my inspiration. I couldn't choose the ticket. I had pressed too many destinations then cancelled them because I kept doubting myself, a quality I never had before being brow beaten by that little bitch of a Fanjita, that little twisted FUCK-ING cunt!!! The machine froze. I couldn't buy one! So, I could only go one place now, and it was wherever the train stopped, leaving me that I had to change for Antibes, which was my destination, meaning I had to get off in Avignon.

Before the train arrived, I was standing on the platform and I had a vision of Meredith again. While I was standing there on the platform, I saw a vision of a guy holding a meat cleaver. As he came at me, I froze, and he struck me on the chest with the cleaver and said, "That's what I thought.... you wouldn't defend yourself! Chicken!!" I was scared, I have to admit, but I felt prepared after it. If it happened to me in real life, I would react. The train came, and I got on as if nothing had happened. I'd been doing that all along, as soon as something happened out of the ordinary, I'd wait until it had passed, then carry on. It was the only way I had of dealing with it.

Whenever I was in La Ciotat, I felt like I had been shot at a couple of times, but I kept on walking — ignoring all the bullets. There were no bullets on the ground when I would look, but I heard things hitting the ground and walls beside me, and I would just carry on and letting on I didn't notice them, hoping whoever was shooting at me would just think I have done nothing wrong. It was as if they were trying to scare me by missing. I don't know. I'm sure they could have hit me if they wanted. I was feeling the deaths of people too. As I was walking around, I was soaking up the spirits that had left their energy traces in whatever space I walked into. I would walk into a certain spot and receive a message. I could feel that someone had been killed on a certain spot and felt how they died. I was told by a really well-known Psychic that it was the world war residue. It was really interesting. It only happened in France.

I got on the train and winged my way to Avignon. When I got to Avignon, I had another spiritual vision. It wasn't until later that evening after it got dark. I looked it up on the internet when I got home. I put into the search engine what I felt at the time, and the result said I'd achieved a State of Grace. What I was experiencing was religious ecstasy. Often experienced after long periods of fasting. I'd gotten off the train in Avignon early that day and chilled out at a picnic area within the station's ground. I was sitting on the step outside the train station that night about 10 O'clock, the birthplace of the Foreign Legion my Father had later told me. As I sat there a laser came forth out of my eyes. It projected images up on the gable end of the houses there. It was really well projected. I cannot remember now what it was but I felt it was a very holy experience. I had just decided to give up alcohol for good and I had stopped smoking and I was never ever going to touch drugs again! I stood up with the glowing feeling of serenity in me and I walked into the square around the corner in the centre of town. As I sat there, the small bush in front of me, circular in shape, roughly the size of a human head, sparked into life. It took on the shape of a face and started talking to me. I felt like Moses and the burning bush! It was really giving me a load of information. It spoke to me for about 15 minutes, and I talked back to it, but I mostly listened. Then two people, a man, and a woman came to get in their car that was parked beside me. The woman said to the man in plain English with an English accent. "If he wants a drink, the bars over there." They were trying to upset things. I was suspicious of them right away. I thought they were the secret service agents. I looked back at the bush but it became normal again.

They left, and I looked over to the bar on the corner that they had pointed out. I hadn't noticed it before. I thought I wouldn't mind a glass of water. I was resolute I would never drink again. I felt out of this world. I have never experienced that feeling since but I hope to one day soon. I walked over to the bar, still in my bare feet, and went in. I asked at the bar for "d'leau", "water"? There was a man there in his 20's and who looked like he would be pretty handy in a fight. He had a skin head and was behaving pretty boisterously. We were the only two there. He was really loud. He was talking in French. I did not understand what he was saying. He looked like he wanted to be in charge of the bar. He looked at me and spoke aggressively to me in French. I said, "Je ne parle Francais. Je suis Irlandais!" "I don't speak French, I am Irish!" "Ahh!!!" He bellowed. "Irlandais!!!" Then he took a big swing and punched me right in the gut. I took the punch! I have a very boisterous friend at home in Moville. He behaves the exact same way as my foreign legion friend as I later thought him to be. He was the quintessential soldier. So, I reacted the same way as I did with McCole and punched him back. I put my arm around his shoulder laughing with him, then surprised him with a punch in the gut too. He went, "Oh oh OOooh!!!" Bending over and putting his hand on my shoulder, laughing jovially, then he said to the bar man, "BEER! BEER!" I said, "no, I don't drink!" "Non?!! He said. "Irlandais!! Beer! Beer!" I thought of what I had just decided about an hour before, the euphoria I was feeling, and then I thought just to be sociable, one can't hurt. I said to the barman, "demi", a "half." I saluted the man santé, and as I took a sip, while looking at the bar, the feeling of euphoria left me, and I saw the translucent golden fiery aura of the saint that I thought that I had become leave me and disappear. It folded into itself behind the bar. It was accompanied by a voice saying…"St. Brendan, it is then!" I felt like I had achieved Sainthood and took it that the voice said I was now like Saint Brendan because he drank alcohol. I had real thoughts of making a pilgrimage to Rome for some direction. I was pretty holy at that time. I know now that God does not exist. The aliens rule my world.

I left after this, really disappointed and went back to the train station where I was staying in the picnic area to ride the night out. The next day I walked around for a while exploring, and looking for somewhere better than the train station to chill out and get my head down because I was wrecked tired at this stage. I couldn't find anywhere, but I found the police station. It was close to the train station, and I thought that's good to know.

I went back to the picnic area where I had set up camp. It was enclosed from the road by hedges, so I felt safe. People couldn't see I was there. So, I thought if I lay down, the only people who could see me were the ones that walked over to the area. I lay down and rested but I could not sleep. The next morning, I was hungry and thirsty. I noticed a half-full bottle of diet coke that I hadn't noticed before. Someone must have thrown it away. I never thought I would ever have to be in the situation of nourishing myself with other people's garbage, but I'd read enough survival stories to never look a gift horse in the mouth, so I lifted it and drank. It was like nectar. If only there wasn't more of it! I thought someone could have put poison in it but thought fuck it, I'll take my chances! I was glad of the sugar rush.

Then unable to sleep, I sat up in the warm sunshine. I was looking out over the tracks when the sunflowers that were in my field of vision turned into people's heads. There was Big Andy and two others, an older man and an older woman. They started talking to me. They began threatening me, asking me why I was here? It was as if I was in a room sitting on a chair, and I was being interrogated. Then Big Andy said, "where's your gun?" and I looked down as though I was sitting on a chair looking for a gun, but there was none there, and he said, "that's what I thought.". The old guy said then in a cockney accent "you can travel the world, but we'll get you." "You'll be lying in some resort somewhere, but we will find you." Then, my great aunt, Lilian's voice came into my head and said, "Run, Juan, RUN!!!" and I thought then I was seeing the future of what was going to happen. I jumped up, terrified. I ran onto the platform, out through the station, and ran for the police station. When I got to it, a car pulled up fast and stopped outside the police station. There was one guy driving and one in the back. The one in the back had opened the door and said, "get in." He wasn't threatening, but I was afraid of what was going to happen if I did. I declined the offer, thinking no way! Then he said, "go! Check-in then" referring to the cop station, in an English accent. I have to say I nearly did get in because it seemed like they wanted to help me, but after the vision I just had, I thought it was a premonition. I turned and went into the station. Before that happened, I was walking around town. The voice in my head was saying "You are dead. There is going to be a sniper that will shoot you. You have no chance." The aliens have told me it was a dead soldier a bit like the old salty seadog in Antibes, if you remember? He told me that the Antibes people were trying to kill me. This spirit was telling me the exact same thing. I fucking went nuts. I walked around town trying to avoid everybody. It was impossible. It was so bloody hot. I was sweating like a pig. I got to a shop and thought, as a distraction I'll go in and try on a pair of trousers. I went in and tried them on. The voice started laughing and said "Try on the bra as well…" It was so vile of an accent. It was creepy as hell. I did not do what it said and put my Levis on again. They were so comfortable. Definitely the best jeans on the planet. The aliens are all going to wear them when they get here. I went outside and the voice said "If you do not do what I tell you, you will be killed.." I listened this time. It said "lick that dogshit!!" I looked down and there was an old pile of dogshit on the pavement. I didn't want to do it but I was so fucking frightened. The voice was so confident. I got down on my hands and knees and licked the dogshit. I nearly made me vomit. I stood back up and the voice was laughing it's head off. It said "You are fucking mental…" I walked back over to a bus shelter and had a seat. A young guy sat beside me. He took out of his pocket and a little vile with liquid in it. He looked at me, then put the vile to his mouth and drank it. He was trying to tell me to take medication. That's what the voice said. The aliens were laughing their heads off. They said it was the bloody stupidest thing I've ever done, licking dogshit and do not listen to the spirit. I was standing there when the spirit said "Take a look up to your right." I looked up and looked at a window. The voice came on in my head again. It said "That's where the sniper is…you just avoided being shot!!" I could feel an energy coming from the window. One I felt when I had my life threatened in Ireland years ago by the I.R.A. They were out to scare the life out of me. I was told by another guy who was in them not to worry. They were only carrying on.

While I waited in the police station, I could smell marijuana which I could not explain, but there was a girl there about 20 years old sitting in the waiting room crying. I asked her what was wrong, and she said she'd had her laptop stolen by a guy that day. The police took me in and asked me what was up, and I explained that I had been robbed of all my possessions, including my passport, and I had no way of getting home. No money, nothing. They phoned the consulate in Paris, and a really helpful Irish girl there told me they had a representative in Cannes so to make my way there if I could, and they would issue me with a temporary passport. I thanked the police and made my way out, and started walking around again. I was really hungry. I was walking past a butcher and thought I would go in with my bank card as ID and in some way tell them if they let me have some food, I would send them the money. I hadn't eaten in days. He shook his head and said no need and reached over and gave me a full chicken in a bag. I couldn't believe it. I'll never forget it. They were really nice people there. So helpful!

After I ate it, I thought I would find somewhere to relax. The voices in my head were telling me not to eat. They were telling me to lose the weight, make my way to the countryside, and if I lost enough weight, I would feel weightless and be able to fly. It was the aliens. They do not believe in eating food all the time. They are so aware that earth is a planet of excess. They are going to change all that. The voice was saying that I was the matrix. Earth dwellers are so fucking over weight it's ridiculous. They carry around all this excess flab and wonder why they need pharmaceuticals to keep them alive. All they need is a balanced diet. They will have a much longer existence on the planet earth if they do not over-do eating and drinking alcohol and smoking cigarettes and doing narcotics. The aliens kept telling me that I was the one and it's very true. I would see energy streams coming out of people like vines, and I saw them running parallel to the street. Really thick ones, as if they were everywhere, and we plugged into them as we moved around. It is different universes Juan was seeing. It is down to the San Pedro. I'd had enough, though, and just wanted to get home even if I had to go to the asylum and agree to being bipolar even though I knew that I definitely wasn't. The pressure that I felt from home was making me rebel, and also the circumstances of how it all came about. I thought I saw the ether where thoughts and inspiration came from. I continued walking around, and as I was looking up at the hills admiring the view, a voice of an elderly gentleman said in my head in a wistful way, "you'll be old and grey before you come back this way." It was an old spirit of the town and I was communicating with him. I walked into the centre of town and spotted a big hotel there. I walked past it and saw a charcuterie. I went in and thought it's time to phone home. I felt like I was admitting defeat, but I knew it had to be done. I asked one of the guys behind the counter to use his phone, and he said yes, no problem. I explained that I had lost all my luggage and I needed to phone home. I did this, and my mum called back, I answered and then my dad was speaking. I explained what was going on. I told him the gist of the situation, and he said that he would send money to a Western Union office and I could collect it there. He also asked me was there a hotel that I could stay in? I told him the name of the one I'd just saw. He said he would book me a room and to go find where the Western Union was. Then in the morning, I could make my way to Cannes, and we would sort out the passport situation. He said not to worry. I was grateful. He was such a good man to have in a crunch situation. Cool as fuck. No fucking drama. Straight to the point. A great man to help you when you're high and dry!!

After I finished on the phone, the other guy behind the counter came out with a pair of crocs in my size and gave them to me. I said, "really??" And he said, "oui! Yes, for you!". It was like walking on air. I thanked them profusely and left to find the post office. As I was walking up one of the streets, I saw a tourist office and went in and asked for directions to the post office. A really pretty young French girl behind the counter gave me a map and a flirt of the eyes and showed me where to find it. I thanked her, and went on my way, and found it. I had a little trouble getting the money because I had no passport but after going back to the police station and explaining the situation they let me pull up my email, print out a copy of my passport, then I had the cop signed it to show I was who I said I was. The Western Union accepted it, and I got the money. I went to the hotel, got a shower, and a bath, and got cleaned up. The next morning, I got a train to Cannes. It was a Friday. I was booked into a hotel there and waited it out until the Monday. I got the emergency passport and flew home.

33

LETTERKENNY

W hen I arrived home, the rain was torrential. I was still feeling very summery. As I disembarked the plane the rain hit me in the face. It was nice to be home in Belfast, I thought. I was wearing my T-shirt, shorts and the crocs the butcher had given me. I'd travelled the world in the last year and a half. It was time for a bit of chilling. I couldn't wait to get home. The T-shirt I was wearing had an American flag on it. I'd bought it in a market during the weekend I was waiting in Cannes because the clothes I had been wearing had been on me for weeks. As I looked at the T-shirt in Cannes at the time of buying it, the voice in my head said to me not to buy it. It was the spirit world. I thought of the ramifications of buying it. Maybe the voice suggested not buying it because I was in France and they didn't like each other. Or because American agents were chasing me, although I didn't think that really. The spirit didn't give an explanation. I just felt on edge for years because of what happened in Shannon. I wondered why they had let me away with it? I bought the T-shirt and wore it with pride. I wasn't angry with anyone and really just wanted everyone to get along.

My father was waiting for me outside the airport building. He wasn't happy. I could tell by his manner. I walked over to the jeep and threw my bag in the back. We chatted about my trip but I was very reticent. We stopped for something to eat in KFC, and I never thought too much about anything. I was happy to be home after a year and a half away. It was the longest I'd ever been away. And what an adventure I'd had!!!

After an hour of driving along. I was engrossed in a story I was telling him and I didn't pay too much attention to the direction we were travelling. It wasn't until we got to a place called Bridgend on the border, and we took the road for Letterkenny, that I asked him where he was going? He said I'm taking you to the asylum. I said "what the fuck for?!" He said "we better get things sorted out". I asked what he meant? I said I was dead on. He said he felt that I needed help again. It was the biggest kick in the fucking head I'd ever heard of in my life. I'd been away for a year and a half without any fucking medication. He wanted no part in helping me get my shit together. He was a fucking waste of space when it boiled down to it. He spread rumours that I was emaciated when I came back. The lying fucking cunt. I joined a gym to lose more fucking weight after that. He was such a lousy father to me in those years. I knew I could get back on my feet easily and very quickly if I had the security of my family around me.

Not a fucking asylum and more fucking medication. I feel like I should have jumped out of the car now when I am writing this, but I had no other choice. I was angry, but I let it go. The fucking pain of these bloody admissions were driving me round the fucking twist.

I went into the asylum and got medicated again for no reason. It was just to keep my father happy. I was a bit paranoid about my safety for a couple of weeks after I came home. But it is really understandable how that could occur when you have just been chased around the South of France in a death-defying manner.

I wrote down what was bothering me while I was in asylum. The paranoia passed because of this. I knew it would take it out of my head. It was the reason I started writing in the first place when I was 16 years old. I was so angry with my father at that age when I was working in our bar, that I came home from work and began writing in a fury. I'd heard about writing therapy and I gave it a try. I wrote down about how much of a cunt he was for putting me under the pressure he was putting me under in the bar. It was the relief that it gave me that made me continue to write.

A few days into the admission, my parents came in to see me. We went into the visitor's room, and I sat down opposite them. I asked my father could I come home. I hadn't lived at home with them for years so I thought it would be ok under the circumstances. I had nowhere else to go. I told them that "that was it for me with the drink and drugs," I said. "No more partying." And my Dad was like, "yeah, right, Juan!" and smiled with his arms folded. Then he said, "no" that I couldn't come home and that he thought I would be better of living in Letterkenny. That I would be closer to the services i.e. the asylum. I didn't agree with him and told him I would be better living at home. I could get back on my feet then head off again. I knew it would be less of a struggle and easier on me, which is what I needed. He said on a personal level, it would be better for my own independence to live in Letterkenny. He was such a cunt to me and all the while trying to be the cool cat. Always talking about the yachts when he was out in public. I heard him quote me while I was sitting at the same table. He was so fucking into my life on those yachts. I knew he was really jealous.

To be honest I wasn't too worried about the pride of the independence angle. I was more interested in getting my life back together the quickest way possible, but I acquiesced. I had no money and nowhere to stay. Loving parents who wouldn't let me stay and made it as difficult as possible for me to get back on my feet and I felt fear, unfounded or not of people trying to kill me. I just thought, fuck it, and got on with it. I'd been on my own long enough and thought I don't need them. I knew if I had moved home, I would have got into my fitness, and I knew it would have cured me because I had done it before. It was a short-term plan in my head, but they didn't go for it. I thought to myself then, well, at least when I do make my millions, I could say I literally started from nothing!

I began to get my shit together then with the social welfare. The nurses and services in the asylum were very helpful and helped me out getting the forms and somewhere to stay. They got me a place to stay, albeit, a homeless shelter. I would never have done this shit to anyone. I was thinking about my parents and how I had helped them out with money to fucking build the cunting house they were living in. It made me SO fucking angry!!! I would and have always helped people out. It doesn't make you stronger it just pisses you off forever and ever. My brother James, did not fucking help me out one bit when I was out of money, that time. He was on really good money around that time. I thought nothing of it at the time because I am really independent but in later years when I looked back, I thought if it had of been the other way around where he was out of money, I would have offered to help him. I would have supplemented his weekly welfare payments with a good balance of money to make his life easier. Instead, he was off buying himself a fucking Porche. He hardly phoned to find out how I was. He only called to see me once. All I want from him is contact. He is my younger brother. I love him to pieces. His wife Catherine is a beautiful, intelligent woman. He done really well for himself. The writing of this has left me so angry that I find it difficult to even write about it. I felt such a sense of abandonment. I felt that quite a bit for years. Everyone else had a great family connection apart from me because of the Bipolar diagnosis and being shipped off to the mental every whack about. It is soul destroying. It took a lot of resilience to keep my spirit alive. I knew my family were there if I needed them but I wanted the family security of close proximity such was my vulnerability at the time.

Ah well, I guess you could say it toughened me up. When I had come back from Africa after the best Merchant trip I'd ever had, if you recall earlier in the book, I had come into my own. My confidence had come back to me after being destroyed by Briona's criticism's and the car crash. My confidence coming back put everyone's noses out of joint. Mainly my fathers. He wanted to be the fucking boss! He was so fucking hard on me. I was trying my best to overcome the fucking stupid mental illness stigma. I am not mentally ill no matter what your opinion is after reading this book is. I will prove it in the coming year. The aliens are visiting me in one year from the 11th of April 2023. They will be coming to my house in Rathmullan and staying with me for a week. We will drink and have a good time. They will tell me how they want to be received by the earth. I will organise everything to do with their arrival en masse in 3 years time. They will tell the earth when they arrive that I am not mentally ill. They will tell them that I am an alien.

I moved into the Homeless shelter after leaving Letterkenny mental asylum. I met the owner of the hostel, a really nice woman there called Cynthia and her husband Joe. They ran the place together. They gave me my own unit, which consisted of a bedroom come kitchen, and a bathroom. It was the end apartment, and I enjoyed my time on my own when I settled in. I went up to the main house the day I moved in and signed the terms of agreement.

The next day was a beautiful sunny day when I woke up, and I felt in the mood for a cold beer. I had bought a couple of books the day before and I thought I wouldn't mind a few cans and chill. I went to the local off-license and bought 12 cans of beer, and went back to the apartment. I sat and drank them with the door open in the sunshine, reading my book and enjoying the day. Later that evening Joe walked past the door when I went to put some empty cans in the bin outside. I asked him which bin I should put the beer cans in. He looked at me bemused and said I could put them in that one over there and pointed. I put the cans in the bin, then went back into my apartment and chilled out for the night.

The next morning, I woke up about 11 o clock. I got dressed and thought to myself, I'm a bit hung over. I'll have a can of beer to take the edge of it. I had just finished the beer when the phone in the apartment went. It was Cynthia asking me could I come up to the main house. I went up to the main house and into her office. She said to me to take a seat. I sat down, and she said, "Juan, have you been drinking?" I waved my hand in front of my mouth and said, "Why can you smell it?" She said, "No I meant yesterday, why have you been drinking today?" "Noooo!" I said. "Ok". She said believing me. Then she said, "Joe said you asked him where you could put the empty beer tins." I said, "Ah right!" She said, "That's the number one rule on the agreement!!" "No drinking!!!". I said, "I never thought about it. It was such a nice day I thought I would have a couple of beers and chill out". She asked me, "Do you have a problem?" to which I replied, "No, I have no problem. I don't need to drink. I just never thought about it. I'm fine without it." She said, "that's ok then, I'll give you a chance." I thanked her and went back down to my apartment. I thought it was kind of funny!

I was taking medication every day after I came out of the asylum. They really had me convinced it would help. I was SO fucking distraught I thought, I'll give it a go. I know it goes against everything I have been talking about but I nearly believed them that I had Bipolar. I knew it wasn't true, though. They were so fucking powerful in my head. They manipulate you so bloody well. Every sodding time I reached up to the cupboard to take the medication, it brought me down. It had the Nocebo effect on me. It had the opposite effect of placebo. It brought me down and made me feel like I was under the careful, watchful eye of the mental asylum every time I took it. I hated being reminded of it. I knew I didn't need them. The doctors said the medication would help with my paranoia, but locking my door had a more positive effect on me.

I met a guy from Shrove shortly after that on Letterkenny main street, and he told me about a really good gym called the Warehouse, which was only 20 euro a month. I went along one day. The man that ran it was a body builder, and I told him I wanted to join. I told him I had never done the gym properly before, so he asked me, "how many days a week I could come?" I told him, "all of them" so he said, "right, you will come Monday to Friday and rest at the weekend." I agreed, and he said, "First we will strengthen your heart and lungs, and then you will do the weights." "I will make you number 1," he said. I laughed, but he said, "no seriously." He made me walk on the treadmill for the first three weeks, increasing the speed over the 3 weeks then when I finally asked when I was doing the weights, a question I had been holding back for a few days(I felt like the karate kid with Mr. Miyagi -wax on, wax off) he said, "We will start tomorrow." I trained like this for two months and really enjoyed it. I could see the results, which made me proud of all the training I was doing. I went to my friend Farren's wedding at the end of the summer and did quite a bit of drinking! The drinking threw me off my training for a couple of days, but I went back to it after that. My trainer asked me, "did I enjoy my few days off?" He knew I had gone on a bit of a bender. I continued training every day. I met some really nice people in that gym, and everyone was super friendly.

I moved out of that homeless shelter and in to a flat as soon as I had enough money saved and all my paperwork sorted out for the rent allowance. The apartment was just up behind where I had been staying. It was there that I began writing this book. I sat down and thought about it, and after a few days, I thought. I have waited long enough to write my story down. The story was exploding inside of me, waiting to get out. I got a pen and a writing pad and wrote constantly for 5 hours long hand and got the book started with 'Shannon airport' and a couple of other chapters. It felt really good. That was 2012. I have been working on this project on and off for 11 glorious years. It has been so much fun writing it. It has been part of my life every day.

I was feeling good about myself after moving in to my new apartment and decided to visit a friend of mine in the Letterkenny mental asylum. I had made friends with him through AA a few years back and I had met him again when I was in the asylum and I knew he was still in. I thought it would be nice to visit him. When I went to visit him, he told me he wanted out of there and asked me could he stay with me? I thought fuck it anyway! I knew that it was going to be terrible experience. He was a gambler, a drug addict and a fucking raging, raging alcoholic. I said no problem but I was worried. I wanted to help him get bloody out of there. It was driving him demented. I said he could stay for a couple of days until he got his own place or went home to his parents. He stayed for a couple of days. It was not that much fun. He moved out and in with friends that he'd made. He invited me up one evening but there was an altercation with some travellers. He had accused one of their women of neglecting a child and they said that he had reported her to the welfare. They wanted to kill him. They fucking wrecked his house. Smashing everything, they could find. I was caught up in the middle of it. Letterkenny is full of settled travellers. I've always got on with them but these dudes were fucking nuts. I knew they probably had weapons on them. They were going to leave him dead. I left my mate to it but I was really worried they would come after me too. The next day I talked to Mac Sea on the phone and told him what happened. He did not put my mind at ease. He said I'd get out of town if I were you. So, that's what I did. I put an add up on Facebook that I wanted to move back to Moville and a good-hearted mate answered me.

A couple of days later, I moved back to the flat that I had been living in before in 2010, after I had broken up with Fanjita. It was above my mates restaurant.

I decided I would go back to the Superyachts. I should have gone back to the Merchant Navy. I would have had a stable life and become a Master Mariner. I was not thinking straight. I just wanted away from the mental health services. They were destroying my life. I came up with a dastardly plan. I planned to save 50 euros every week from my social welfare money with a ball park figure of 500 euro. I was going to get a loan for a 1000 euro and do as I had done in 2011.

I was still on medication such was the brain washing they had done on me. I was drinking every single day. The drinking was totally out of boredom. I never really got that drunk. It was really only beer, wine and cider that I was drinking. I was just trying to get the time in so I could go to France. I was trying not to get too pensive about having to wait for the season in the yachts to come around that March. I tried to relax and hoped the jobs would happen for me when I got there. It was a big bloody risk as usual. I did what I planned to do and achieved my goal. My father left me to the airport, and I said to him that I would stop drinking when I got to France to give myself a good chance this time.

ANTIBES

23/10/18

Antibes

Love in the sun,
Summer has begun,
Fun, frolics,
and a tight little bum,
muscles galore,
head straight and square,
now for a job,
and so long despair!

W hen I arrived in France, I got settled in to Debbie's again. It was like home from home! I was there a couple of days when a good mate of mine, Magic from Poland, contacted me on Facebook. "I knew you wouldn't come!!" Was the first thing he said. I told him I was already there. He said, "cool, I have some daywork for you on my yacht 'M/Y Stormbringer'." He was Chief Mate on there. "He said its three weeks work, and you'll need someone else, someone with engineering skills" he said. So, I hung up and went up to Debbie's sitting room and asked if anyone had engineering skills. Louis answered, putting up his hand, and that was it, we went to work the next day. It was good craic with Louis and Magic and the other guys there. Not long after we finished, my money ran low for the projected time I wanted to stay there. Big Dan, who was a fucking loud mouth cunt lol such a fucking boy. I had no qualms about pulling the piss out of him all the time. Debbie said "there is no chance in hell that Dan would get a job on a yacht!!" She was right but he really wanted one. He tried so hard. He was also living in the crew house and was working as a taxi man for a yacht transport service that had started up in Antibes predominantly for yacht crew and yacht guests. Big Dan asked me did I want to work for them. I really thought about it. I thought about the pro's and con's, then decided it would be really good for making contacts so I took the job.

I really had some fun driving everyone about. It was a joy every bloody day. I wasn't drinking in the beginning so it all went really smooth for me. Unfortunately, when I did get a job offer on a yacht, the boss of the taxi service would not even speak up for me. I needed his reference and he would not give it. I was really fucking pissed off about that. The taxi service folded at the end of the summer, as you will read, but luckily enough I got a job on a very famous English yacht called M/Y La Masquerade.

There was a few Dan's living in Debbie's around that time. There was Big Dan as I said, then there was Beer Dan who drank every single day but his golden rule is he wouldn't start drinking before 12 midday. Good-looking Dan was a bit of a smoothie with the Stewardesses.

Around this time, I told Louis about the medication I was taking and how I knew I wasn't bipolar. We were sharing a room. I told him as well the story about licking the dogshit. He said that it was the funniest thing that he had ever heard. I told him some other stories as well, and he had a good laugh. I knew by his reaction, that people would enjoy reading this book. I stopped the tablets and immediately started losing the weight that had blighted me for over a year because of the reaction in your body. The fat cells are created by the carbs being turned into fat cells because of the substances in the psychotropic drug. It is fucking nuts!! It was bloating me out and making me look terrible. I've always been pretty well kept with my weight. The weight I am now, is the same weight I was 3 years ago. I do not put on anymore weight. I only eat when hungry. I do not over eat. I only over drink. That is a joke!! I stayed off drink all that summer and even though I wasn't going out partying with the crew house gang every night I did score with one lucky stew.

She was a 23-year-old South African staying in the crew house. I was 33 so I wasn't doing too bad, I thought! She had a degree in psychology and talked about doing her master's in Cambridge, England. She was very street wise as well. I offered her to go to a work mixer I had been invited to in Monaco by one of my cab fares. The fare was a crew agent. Sara the South African stew jumped at the chance but I had ulterior motives. She was really giving me the come on in the crew house so I saw my chance to get her on her own. She had the sexiest ass in a pair of jeans. I'm a real ass and eyes man. I love erotic eyes and anus's that you just want to fucking eat!! I didn't have enough money to stay in a hotel in Monaco so I thought we could wing it, hang about all night then get the early train back in the morning. She was happy enough with that. We did the mixer and it went really well. There was an arrogant Chief mate there who was running down my certification. Sara stood up for me. I really liked her for it. She said Juan's a Captain. Do not speak to him like that. The guy was shocked. I just laughed. We left the mixer and I took her to another bar where she couldn't get enough Tequila into her! She said she loved Tequila. She was firing one shot after another into her! After shot number four she asked me how I would make the move on a woman? I thought this is it. She is coming around to my way of thinking! I said "I usually let the woman make the first move". There was silence for a second, then she slid across the sofa we were sitting on and kissed me full on the lips. We snogged for a few seconds then she pulled back. She then started serenading me with psychology compliments. She said I was the Captain of the crew house and everyone looked up to me. She said I was "the Alpha and the Omega!" She said I was so knowledgeable. "You're like the Dalai lama!" she said. Then she asked "why did you pick me?" "You could have had any woman in the crew house". I said "because I was attracted to you". "What attracted you to me the most?" she asked. I was about to tell her a joke of mine when I get asked that question. I've had it loads of times. I normally tell the woman who asks me that it was their mind that attracted me the most. They fucking love that. They always go all mushy. Then I say yeah, I wanted to fuck your brains out!! I thought about it this time but she was too intelligent and probably would have taken offence so I told her it was her personality, hands down. That was the truth. She was really wild. She was desperately trying to get me to drink. I wouldn't. I was happy being sober. We left there and I took her to the swimming area near the harbor. It was really secluded from town and I reckoned it would be quiet at that time of night. She stripped off naked the minute we got there. I was horn fucking crazy the minute she done it. She dived in and swam out about 20 or 30 yards. I thought it was a bit dangerous with all the drink she had taken. I told her this. She was laughing at my concern. Then she started playing games with me. She shouted "I don't think I want to sleep with you now!" I was so pissed off. "Why not?" I shouted. I was sitting on the steps watching her swim. "I don't want to get a bad name!" she shouted. "I won't tell anyone!" I shouted back. There was silence and I was thinking fuck this anyway after all that effort! Then she swam back in towards me. I was sitting on the steps. I didn't say anything to her. She pulled her naked body up onto the steps and crawled towards me. I was sitting back on my elbows with my legs outstretched. She crawled up my legs, looking erotically into my eyes and reached for my trouser belt. It was dark but I could still see her erotically charged eyes in the street lights. She pulled down my boxers and took my hard cock in her mouth. She sucked it in deep. Licking the tip and spitting on it. Then she gorged on it more. I was so aroused. She rolled over on to her back and said "Fuck me". I rolled over between her thighs and entered her vagina with my throbbing cock. We made love passionately. She was so beautiful and had a great body. I was so fucking relieved that she fucked me. She was so divine. I could not believe that a girl that young would be into a man in his 30's. She did not care. We fucked some more and I came like a monster. I roared like King Kong when I came!!

We got dressed and made our way to the train station. We got the train home in the early morning. It was a really good night.

There was another beautiful Canadian girl in the crew house that I had very big attraction to as well. However, she was with another crewman. It went ok with her but I felt if I had of been in the loop with partying, i.e. drinking, I would have landed her. We all went out one night to Nice to let off some steam. The Canadian girl was so into the drink scene I thought fuck this. I'm getting drunk! We all got drunk and she had an argument with her boyfriend. They both went home. I stayed on that night in the hotel with Cyan, another guy that had come with us. We went to the beach the next day and continued drinking. I'd had my wallet stolen the night before. I was looking for some cocaine after the nightclub and the guy who said he could get it for me ran off with my wallet! I tried giving chase but I was too fucked from the drink to catch the little cocksucker. Cyan and I made our way back home to Debbie's a little worse for the wear. The Canadian girl cancelled my bank cards. She was really sound and switched on.

My money was running low so I moved out of Debbie's and into The Crewhouse in town. It was cheaper. I made very good friends there too, but the transport service folded due to bullying from the local Police and taxi men. I started to drink and party again with everyone. Unfortunately for me, I partied too much for the owner of The Crewhouse and got thrown out. Not very becoming of a Chief mate. I am really sorry for it. I let myself down. I moved from there into my friend Ace's apartment across the street. He let me stay with him, which was really kind of him. He's a good mate and he had a lovely fiancée Alice at the time. Ace and I drove his illegal taxi to make ends meet.

Around this time, I met an elderly artist, Karen Le Fleur. One evening I was picking her up to take her home to Juan le pins from Cannes. As we were driving down the Croisette in Cannes, I thought to myself because of her paintings that she would be a spiritual person. I'd had a little spiritual trouble so I took a chance. I told her of my trouble hearing voices in the crew house I was staying in. It was just before I got kicked out. I told her that the voices were not around me, they were in my head, and they were of the other people in the crew house. I could hear them talking in my head when I was lying in my bed. I told her I even spoke in tongues one night. The South African deckhand in the next bed was really freaked out by it. I'd woken him up. He said I sounded like the Devil. I had a real sense of being inhabited. I explained how I felt things touching me and entering and leaving my body when there was obviously nothing there. The visions were translucent. She smiled and said I was talking to the right person. She told me she had written 6000 papers on the subject. She said that I was seeing and feeling all these things because I was a very powerful psychic. She signed me up to the Royal College of Psychics in London, and said to visit when I could. She said that they would show me how to communicate with the spirit world. I never went and figured it out on my own. Her help though, at the time, really set my mind at ease.

Ace and I drove his taxi for a week or so. I was doing the night shift with him on days. I was drinking regularly and hadn't really stopped since the end of the summer. It was taking its toll. I did the phone interview for La Masquerade while I was in the crew house, shortly before I was kicked out and had been narrowed down to 3 candidates. It was a total fucking coup. Nobody could believe it. I was picked out of thousands!!

A week after I moved into Ace's, I got an email to say that I had the job. Another mate picked me up two days later, early in the morning, but I was still a bit drunk when I got up. I had a bit of a party in the days leading up to going away. I flew to St Lucia in the Caribbean and joined the boat with the mother fucker of all hangovers.

SHARKS IN THE WATER - M/Y LA MASQUERADE

I didn't drink all the way over on the plane to the Caribbean but jeez was I humming of alcohol! It was coming out my pours the minute I landed. The heat was melting me. I only had a hoody and t-shirt on but I couldn't take the hoody off because of body odour. The hoody was one my mum had got me of the Fleadh Ceol in Derry. I wondered how that would go down joining an English boat? My head was so fucking fried from the beer that when I was asked to sign my own passport at customs, I thought I had to give him my autograph. I thought well this boat is famous!! I didn't think well of course you have to have your passport signed! They could tell I was hungover. There was smiles of sympathy.

When I got to the boat, the effects of all the alcohol were taken their toll on me. The crew were all really lovely for the first few days. But I couldn't wait for the days to end and the next one to start so that one would be over as well. I was so fucked from drinking!! The effects left, but there I was on the new boat, and things weren't going too well. I was having what I can only describe as total and utter inhabitation. Every spirit that wanted to talk to me was obliterating my concentration. I was losing weight and not able to concentrate on anything. I'd gone from having drank every single day for a month to cold turkey. And that was very heavy drinking. I was drunk every day. I never once thought of what it was doing to my brain. My body recovers very rapidly, leaving me ready for more. I'm told the recovery is a Family O'Donnell trait. My Grandfather O'Donnell was the same. Whiskey was his poison.

The effect the drink had on me was diabolical. I thought the whole job, the whole work...the actual idea of me working on that English yacht was some sort of espionage plot to jail me and that the crew had been told in secret that they were my jailers. I felt like I was a target when I was on deck too. I thought someone was going to take a pot shot and shoot at me because of my time in Sint Maarten. If you remember Ronno and I stiffed the taxi driver there and he was asking every yachtie that came to Sint Marten did they know me? My mate Clyde from Malta told him he knew me. And the taxi driver said "That madman owes me $200. Give it to me!!!" Clyde said "Fuck off!!" and that was it. He fucked him off. Clyde messaged me. It worried me about going back there.

Anyway, while I was on deck, I felt like I was under scrutiny and being bullied by Jonoz. He was a jumped up deckie from Oz. He was cool when I started but he turned nasty on me. The Greek deckie was my favourite on board. He'd a good sense of humour and he was Greek special forces to boot. I had never had any trouble with crew on a yacht before this. I later found out that Jonoz was after my position. He had already gotten rid of the last guy. The last guy was Merchant Navy as well. Jonoz hated them. As do a lot of yachties. It is so stupid.

I put myself under a lot of pressure in the first few months trying to work as perfect as possible.

The previous year, the guy that I told you who had the argument with the travellers in Letter-fucking-kenny and I had to move back to Moville because of it, died just before I left home to go away this time. He had a lot of connections within the drug world, and in a way, he had warped my mind. I tried laughing it off to myself, but I felt that his spirit had stayed with me when he died. I could see his head entering and leaving me as I wrote this in 2016. I was hearing messages from him. They were a bit of a head wrecking experience. They still come when I think about him but I know how to tell him to go away now.

Even thinking the thoughts about him at the time of writing this, it conjures up translucent visual images of him in front of me, and I can see them moving through the air. The idea of him still being in my life was there for that whole trip. I did not have any closure on it but the aliens have closed all that down for me. No spirits annoy me anymore. It is such a fucking relief!!! The aliens have told me how to deal with them. They talk to them too. It's a pretty weird world we live in – extraterrestrials, the spirit world and me a fucking half human, half alien. Fun times ahead!

One night, as we were anchored off the Island of Mustique, a beautiful island but very quiet. Not much going on there. It was about 2 months into the trip. I was lying in bed sleeping, and I woke up with a voice speaking to me in my head. It sounded really erotic. It was a woman's voice. I checked the time. It was 2 a.m. The voice was telling me that I had to kill the owner. He was an old English Gentleman that owned the boat. I realized at that moment I was an I.R.A sleeper agent. I never knew I was IN!!! I couldn't take the kill. I did not follow my instincts. I stood up in the cabin and thought fuck-ing hell. I don't want to do that!!! I thought about it for a split second. It felt to me like I was about to throw a punch but I did not want to do it. I knew it was a spirit from the Underworld and it was not to be listened to. But it was so seductive. I knew it was a calling from my homeland. I'd had them before but never acted on them. The swell of pride when they occur is overwhelming. Sometimes I cry with passion and pride and downright fucking anger at the injustices the English have put us Irish through. The spirit voice then told me to go and kill myself when I refused to kill the owner. I thought yeah fuck it. I have nothing to live for anyway. My life at home was in ruin with Bipolar allegations and I was so fed up with being locked in the mental asylums. Then I thought on the plus side my death might lead to a rebellion. The spirit was telling me to commit Hari Kari. I am a Samurai and that is the way I should die. I did not complete my mission. I thought so be it. I got dressed in a t-shirt and shorts and walked to the swim platform at the back of the boat. The voice told me to jump in the water and take a breath when I was underneath. I slid into the water and sank down a few feet. I always open my eyes underwater. My father taught me that at a very young age. That and how to float on your back forever. I thought of both my parents in that instant. They were getting a divorce at the time. I thought my death might bring them back together. My dad was a bit of a playboy when he was young. I know this for a fact. He told me one night that he cheated on my mother when he was away at sea before we were born but would not go into the details. I was 17 and didn't give a rat's ass, monkeys fuck about it. I was actually proud of him and thought I'll probably be like that some day!!! I love having lots of women.

I opened my eyes underneath the water and the first thing I saw was a tropical, multi-coloured fish about 2 foot from my nose. It was breathtaking for someone from Donegal. I thought this is beautiful. I don't want to fucking die. Then the voice reiterated it. "Take a breath!! Take one for the team!" I figured who the team were right away. The I.R.A. I didn't know they had sleepers up until that moment. But it did not surprise me. My up-bringing made total sense in that moment in time. All the books that my father had fed me. There were loads of books in our house growing up about the troubles in the North of Ireland. I did not know my father was in the I.R.A. He never told me. I did not find out until he died.

I came back up to the surface. I thought I need some headspace from this boat and my first thought was swim to the Island. We were anchored off quite a bit, about 500 yards but it was dark, shark infested water so I was a bit uneasy. I thought I'll take my chances!!

I struck out for the beach on the dark side of the Island. It was a tough bloody swim. My clothes were weighing me down but I needed something to wear. I couldn't ditch them. All was going fine until I hit the coral reefs about 50 yards from the shore. I climbed over them. It stung like fuck and it brought me back to my childhood of climbing over rocks bare footed at the Shrove beaches. I was lost in thought as I cleared my head. I know it was crazy but I'm a crazy guy. I got over the coral and swam ashore. My feet were stinging a little, I have to say!

I lay down between two rocks for shelter. My right leg went dead as a doornail. I didn't know what was wrong. I thought something had stopped the blood supply to it. I never thought about poisonous coral. I stood up and started Karate kicking with it. Doing sweep kicks from back to front as high as I could get them. The blood came back to my leg. The whole thing lasted 10 seconds but I reckoned I could have fucking died. It spread up my leg so quick. I was lying there thinking about my trip on the yacht when all of a sudden I saw an image of the owner in gold fluorescent light flying about the boat. I watched it in the harbour. I knew it was the owner. It looked like him. It was massive. He was telling me "Juan get back to the boat!!" I decided to go back to the boat. I thought fucking hell, that was weird. I thought I am knackered from the swim in. I could picture myself standing on the quay in the morning waiting for the crew to come and collect me. I thought that would not go down well. I went to the water and on the way there, I noticed a green boogie board jammed into the rocks. I got it out and as I did, I heard a voice say "He's bloody found it..." I did not know who it was talking. I heard it in my head. It was the American defence forces. They had a satellite on me. The aliens have told me this. The aliens were enjoying the adventure. They always knew I'd be ok. They would have stepped in otherwise and told me it was too dangerous. I took the boogie board and went down to the water. I pushed myself out and floated over the coral. It was pretty cool. The sky looked awesome. I was paddling away with my feet and looking up at the stars. They were so bright. I felt so alive...I thought at the time, you lucky cunt, finding the boogie board. I was curious what it was doing there. I never thought about it but it was probably some kids. I felt a little guilty afterwards but needs must.

It was good to get the adrenaline pumping and some head space too. It got my head back on straight. I paddled on back and as I was nearing our yacht, which was all lit up with lights, I thought, do not tell anybody onboard this adventure. The boat looked so cool all lit up! There was another boat anchored beside us so I paddled out around that and I got back near our yacht I decided to let go the boogie board and swim the rest of the way. I thought that if I ditched the boogie board beside the boat it would stick to the side of it and raise questions in the morning. Good thinking, I thought. As I was swimming back to my yacht there was a sudden surge against me. The yacht started swinging on the anchor. I could feel the engines pushing the water against me. I heard the owners voice saying "You've made your escape..." I wondered if he was in control from his cabin and that he knew I'd swum ashore. It frightened me. Fucking crazy cunt, I thought. I climbed aboard, dried off and went up to the bridge to talk to the night watchman. I had already thought about this as I was paddling back to the boat. I just thought that I would tell him I went for a swim and leave it at that. I went up the bridge and the Greek guy was sitting on his computer. I had to laugh at that. Anybody with a gun could have done what I had just did and killed everybody onboard and got away. I told him that I had just been swimming. He said "bloody hell, you're soaking wet.." I said I know I was in swimming I said. He said "You crazy bastard, do not do that again, you'll get into trouble..." I laughed inwardly. I knew he'd be cool about it. I went to bed and forgot all about it. I got up for work the next day a new man. I started enjoying the work then.

A couple of weeks later we arrived in Barbados. I thought, nice one. I've never been here before. I went out for the night much to the Captains disappointment. He did not want us drinking when the owner was onboard. I did not know that those are the normal rules when the owners are aboard. I went out with two of the stewardesses and the cook. They were all women and just me. I was having a ball. The regular chef said to me "I'm the Daddy in Bangkok where I come from..." He was driving the little boat to take us ashore. We were anchored off. I said to him "I'm a Daddy too.." He said "I'm serious.." I knew he wasn't lying. He was a total gangster. I wondered how he got the job on such a high profile boat. I never asked him. We got ashore and the chef who was the crew chef started hitting on me. She was hot. I loved it. I went to the nightclub and bought a load of rum. I got drunk and decided to dance. The Chief stewardess was already on the dance floor. I walked up to her and started dancing with her. She turned away. She was not on any wavelength that I was interested in but I was having fun. She was Jonoz's girlfriend. She was hot as well, as all the stewardesses I met in my travels were. I never once met one I wouldn't have liked to have shagged. She turned towards me. We were the only two on the dance floor. She'd had a few drinks as well. She was enjoying herself. She started flirting with me. I laughed my head off. I thought fuck Jonoz. I'll shag her for the craic. She was flirting like crazy. I thought, you fucking bitch, you're power hungry, just after the stripes. A lot of stewardesses are like that in yachting. I've heard of 60 year old Captains wiping deckhands eyes with women. They love the status onboard if they are fucking an Officer. It's the same on cruise ships as well in the Merchant Navy. It did not go down well with Jonoz when he heard off the crew chef. She told him that I was cracking on to his girlfriend. I wasn't one bit. She was cracking onto me!! The next day I got up late for work. There was hell to pay. I took it on the chin. I got a warning from the Captain and it was the end of a nightmare. I knew I was going to get sacked. It was a matter of when.

A few days later, when the dust had settled from the night with the stewardesses, I went ashore with the chefs. I was a fucking maniac for alcohol. I went with them and had a delicious night romancing the local girls. I scored with a Bajan beauty! She was fucking up for it but I had nowhere to take her. The boat was in port but I couldn't take her back. It was a definite no no in Superyachting! I got a hand job and left it that.

The next day I slept in again and the Captain said I was sacked. It was music to my ears. I could not leave if I wanted paid, so I did what I had to do to get my marching orders. I was playing a game with them. It was a bit high end. All the posh kids that ever want to go on Superyachts should take note, you are only a piece of meat to them. It is not as glamourous as you think. I lost my memory with the stress. I tried writing a sorry note to the owner but I couldn't even write my name. I thought I had been poisoned by the regular chef. The Bangkok Dad!! He was on my hitlist for years afterwards. I was sure it was him. I was definitely poisoned. It was not that stressful.

I flew home to France and booked into Debbie's crew house again. She was such a help to me. She got me a doctor. And told me that he was military. She said he didn't speak English. I thought that was a bit weird. I saw him and told him that the doctors at home said I was bipolar. He said no. You are definitely not bipolar. It is only stress. I wasn't so sure. I was positive I had been poisoned. I lost all my memory of everything I had ever done. It scared the fuck out of me. The Doctor told me it was just the pressure, that I was under that caused it. He said it would come back and it did. He was a good GP.

36

ANOTHER EXPERIENCE OF A MENTAL INSTITUTION

When I arrived home in 2014 from La Masquerade, my brother, James picked me up from the airport in Belfast. My head was pretty fried from the pressure. I was still worried about us being followed because of what I had just been through. I didn't feel safe. I told my brother my worry even though I didn't want to worry him. He was pretty cool about it, but everyone thought I should go back in to the goddam asylum again. It was so cliché at this point. I didn't want to go in yet again.

I was worried about my memory and my safety but I knew the worry of the threat would calm down. It had before. It was because my life had been under threat. We went to the mental asylum and they put me on that fucking poison Olanzapine once again. The one medication that had me piling on the weight every sodding time. My life has been blighted for 20 years by it.

My parents had split up over this time which did not really affect me. I was old enough to let them do their own thing. I was homeless again when I came back and ended up staying in the homeless shelter again. I stayed there for a while then in 2015 I moved back in with my mum. It was a great feeling and what I needed all along. A bit of family support. They did not give one fuck about my feelings since the age of 25 years old. It has been the loneliest life that anyone can imagine. I got used to it!

I started writing my book properly that summer of 2015. I sat down and wrote most days. I'd bought myself a laptop. I went back to France in July to look for work, and finally, just as my money was running out, my mate Aztec, from Oberon, called me and offered me work on his yacht, the charter yacht Passion, he was Chief mate. I jumped at the chance and spent three incredible months there. They were lovely people. I was on depot injections for the fucking bipolar, which I had agreed to take because I was just trying to get out from under their grasp. It was fucking MENTAL!!! The power the mental health services had over my life. I had to lie, cheat, steal and borrow just to get where I was going. That is the reason the aliens have decided that I was the one. They have watched every little shenanigan that I have been party too. They have said I will be the best world leader the universe has ever witnessed. We did a crossing on Passion that year from Palma, Mallorca to Florida.

Before the crossing I gave myself one of the depot injections on the boat. I fucking hated doing it. It left me sluggish, distant, and a second behind everyone else. I only had the one injection with me. It was a real-life scam. I pulled the wool over the systems eyes just to get away. Every time I left for France, I had emigration on my mind! The bad memories of my years gone by kept coming back to me on that yacht. The memories left me tortured and I found it hard to concentrate.

I came home after that crossing and had a lovely Christmas with my mother, my sister, her partner Kestas, and their children. Ditsy then asked me to come over to London and change my allegiance from being a Liverpool fan to West Ham United. I supported them too for a match against Southampton, which they won. He then got me a temporary gig on his boat M/Y Emotion, which lasted from January until April of 2016. Too much partying affected me a lot, and the death of my friend all had me at an ebb. The Captain fired me for causing an electrical fault on a light switch which I thought was a bit harsh, but I didn't go home straight away. They said I could stay on the boat for a couple of weeks day work. It was a bit fucking weird doing that. I felt I should go home straight away. The spirit world was wreaking fucking havoc with my emotions. My mate who had just died would NOT leave me the hell alone. He loved being dead. He kept saying "Join me!!!" I was also getting very paranoid because of the Cocaine Ditsy and I took. I became very wary again. I left the yacht and went home after a week. I'd gotten sacked on my birthday. They put me in the fucking asylum again. It was SUCH a God-awful routine!

I was lucky enough to meet another author on Emotion. His name is Dean de Servienti. He gave me a copy of his book about aliens. It was so intriguing. It's called Quantum. He's Italian and a genius. I said to him after reading it "If only it was true…" I love the idea of aliens coming to earth and now it's happening. The book is still a great read.

I met the doctor a few days after I was in the asylum, and we discussed what had happened. I said, "right, that's it I'm bipolar. I'm fed up with all of the medicating and my fight with the system. I feel I have proved I am not. "No-one believes I am Bipolar where I work and they should know!" "They spend 24/7 living with me!!!" I told her. I said "I have had the same mind my whole life! I remember everything and I've had the feeling of living in a movie since I was a kid". I said to her "How can you tell me that is an illness?" I said "the reactions and blow-ups I have had are due to the positions of great pressure I have been put under with the mental health system!!" The stress caused was abominable. She agreed with me that I wasn't Bipolar but she was just bullshitting me. She said because of the things I was seeing. The spirits entering and leaving my body like forces of energy and hearing voices from the other side that she thought I had schizo-effective disorder. I thought, not another stupid diagnosis. I'd told her about the San Pedro psychedelics, and that it had opened up the spirit world to me. I told her that was it! Enough! No more labels. I told her that psychiatry was the biggest sham in the world!!! She said "ok!" trying to cool me down. Then she asked, "what about your drinking and any drugs?" I told her I had stopped all drugs and didn't smoke weed anymore because of the paranoia. I was paranoid enough! She said, "what about your drinking?"

I told her that I had gone off drink 7 years before that for a year, and it had been the most boring year of my life to which all the doctors present started laughing. I told her I had cut down on it, and when I moved home with my mum, I would abstain. That was 2016.

I crab fished in Donegal then for a while after that while I was living with my mum. It definitely increased my endurance. It is such a physical job. I nearly died on that boat. Crab fishing is the most dangerous job on the fucking planet. I got a message while I was on the crab boat from Aztec to work on Passion again. I asked the Skipper of the crab boat would he hold the job open for me while I did the Atlantic crossing? He said he would BUT didn't. ASSHOLE-AMIO!!!

I went to Nice and did the crossing to Florida. I gave up smoking and drinking before the crossing. It was only when I got to the States that I went drinking again. I lost the run of myself a lot but really learned my lesson to take it easy on it. It was even more difficult than I thought to spend 1000 euros in one week. I went bloody crazy! They only took dollars. I spent it though... every single penny!

I came back and moved back in with my mother. Then in 2017 I moved out of my mothers and into an apartment in Moville. I was on Facebook all the time in my new apartment. I was romancing up to 15 women. It was a real turn on. I was honing my chatting up skills. Then one afternoon I got in contact with a woman called Hanne from Dublin. She seemed very well to do. I told her the domestic abuse that she told me her husband was putting her through had to stop. She acted on what I told her straight away. I made a joke, telling her she should drop everything and come up to Donegal and see me! She did exactly that! She told me she hadn't made love to her husband since she had her daughter 9 years previous. I thought it would be like fucking a nun! LOL. She was a bit of a fantasist. She was constantly telling me lies. I let them go. I was more interested in getting laid and getting out of my head on alcohol. The little white lies she was always telling eventually ended in her gaslighting me and ultimately got me to dump her sorry fat fucking ass. She was so fucking into me. She was a very pretty woman but she was very overweight. We were staying at her family getaway in Mayo and I asked her could I fuck her up the ass? She rolled over in the bed immediately and spread her butt cheeks. I put the pillow under her chin for her to bite down on. I wasn't using any lube. I knew it was going to sting a little. I pumped her 5 or 6 times. She was biting into the pillow and yelling out in pain but mostly pleasure! She was enjoying it. I wanted to see how much she really wanted me. She was really getting on my nerves. It was SO fucking overboard the way she was behaving. It was fucking over bearing. I think she thought once she got rid of her husband (whom she got done for gaslighting. The first divorce on those grounds ever in the country of Ireland!) that she would marry me! So, I pulled my cock out of her ass and asked her to suck me off!!! I laughed to myself. I thought "No way!" "She is not going to put it in her mouth after it being up her ass!!!" I couldn't believe when she gobbled it up! She was SO fucking greedy in everything she put in her mouth. She told me my cum tasted of apples. It did not surprise me the amount of strong cider I was drinking! She even yelled out "Gethsemane!!!" as she was giving me the blowjob. She thought it was a religious experience! She was sucking my cock SO hard!!! She was a Jewish princess and my first Jew!!

I thought she was an undercover cop and got great enjoyment of sticking my cock up her ass then in her mouth! She really behaved like one! I got fucking rid of her anyway.

After I got rid of Hanne, I had trouble all the time with the recurring trauma of being locked up in the mental asylum in Letterkenny. It happened SO many bastarding times!!! The recurring trauma no longer happened to me for a while when I spoke with my father. I spoke with him just before I did another Atlantic crossing on Seven sins in 2017. We sailed that boat across the Atlantic on the tail end of a hurricane. We had stormy seas for about 6 days. There was a big window near the water line on the bow and one rogue wave smashing through that and we were at the bottom of the ocean. Hair raising stuff! I did learn one thing from the Captain that I did the crossing with that still makes me laugh when woman say they are married and you're trying to chat them up. I use it on them all the time – the licentious guy that I am! I don't believe in marriage or monogamy anyway. He said his female kiwi mate gave him advice when he got married and he told her "That's it!

I'll never sleep with another woman again!" and her answer was "A ring doesn't cover a hole!!!" I sat down the day before I left for the crossing and had an adult discussion with my father. I had a little closure about the beginning of the whole asylum admissions, it was such a fucking bane in my side! I finally got to sit down with him and tell my side of the story without him blowing up saying, "that's not how it happened!!" We fought about it again after that.

BUT I have turned the whole thing on its head now because I am telling the truth. I FUCKING FAKED IT!!!!!

Unfortunately, like I said, my Father is now dead! I would love to see him say he is FUCKING wrong.

I had a MENTAL time in Palma after the Atlantic crossing on Seven sins. I went there to see if I could get a permanent job. It was my 40th birthday. I'd joined Seven sins in the Caribbean on my birthday. I was still celebrating by the time I got to Mallorca. Palma is not a good as the Cote D'Azur for looking for work on yachts. There was very little harbours to dockwalk on. I went drinking instead. I was with my mate Ronno from Dublin. He took me into this little bar that sold Cocaine under the counter. I thought this is great to know. I availed of it quite a bit. I was staying in a hostel that Ronno found me. I was walking along the street this day and spotted a book in the window of a quaint old book shop. It was on the paranormal. I bought it and took it back. I opened it up and started reading it. I'd bought 3 grams of Cocaine. I was sitting on my bed in the hostel this afternoon reading the book and snorting the Cocaine. The book was brilliant. It told me that mescaline was the only drug that left you permanently able to talk to the spirit world. The drug that was in San Pedro. It explained everything. Mescaline was underlined in biro in the book. I thought, this is meant to be. It stopped me worrying about what I was experiencing. Another day, I was walking along a street in the city when I caught the eye of a highly provocative temptress. She was so fucking charged up when I looked into her eyes. She had the coolest haircut you ever seen. It was shaved at the sides and long at the back, mullet style. She was skinny with blonde hair and beautiful blue eyes. She was sitting at a small street café having a bottle of Heineken. I stopped immediately and said hello.

She smiled at me with sex on her brain and without any introductions got up from her seat and grabbed my hand! I knew right away what she wanted! I was looking everywhere around the street to see if there was something, we could go behind to have an almighty FUCK! There was an instant sexual connection between us. It was all in the eyes. It's always been like that with me. I can tell when women want to have my cock between their legs. She tried speaking Spanish to me but I told her in English that I was Irish. She said she was German but she only spoke German and Spanish. I was trying to get her to fuck behind a parked car in the street. It was only the afternoon. I would have fucked her in the street with people watching no problem. I couldn't have given one little fuck. She refused it but she was as determined as me to get her rocks off. She thought hard about going behind the car but grabbed my hand again and took me along the street a bit. I recognized the brothel right away. I'd been there a few days before. We went in and she signalled "you pay!" The woman only charged me 15 euros for the room. I figured out she must have worked there. She knew the lady at the counter. We went in and stripped off like lightening. We were all over each other. I licked her pussy, she sucked my cock, it was fabulous sex. I was on top of her, going like a freight train. She had her head buried in my shoulder moaning but I could not cum. The fucking alcohol! I rolled over on my back and started to wank off as she looked down at me. She was rubbing her pussy and her tits as I did this. I felt the surge of orgasm and pointed to my cock, giving her a universal language signal for cuming. I showed her I was about cum everywhere. She put her mouth over the tip and wanked me off into her mouth until I came. She sucked every last drop out of my cock and swallowed. I felt so good about myself. I felt that glorious shiver down my spine. I love that feeling! We got dressed. Then, as quick as it started. It was over. We walked out of the brothel and went our separate ways. She had a real grin of satisfaction on her face. It was like a short movie! Palma was great but I nearly died from alcohol poisoning. I spent 7 thousand euro in 7 weeks on alcohol and Cocaine. It nearly fucking killed me.

When I arrived home after a fruitless time looking for work in Palma, I was homeless again. My sisters partner came up with the idea that I go into the mental asylum in Letterkenny just so I would have somewhere to stay. He thought they may be able to get me a place to stay. It worked. I left the asylum after 3 weeks and moved into a drug den for a hostel. It is closed now. It was a flea-bitten torture chamber but it was a roof over my head. I stayed there for nearly a year. I met Riverdance after leaving that place. I got a job inbetween leaving there and ending up in Riverdances hostel. It was with a Saffa Captain who used to be the Captain on Passion. The yachts name was Elysium. It was a large 70 metre. The Captain told me I was only there to do a watch. It was a strange atmosphere onboard. All Saffas. They were a bit weird. I was up on the sundeck as we were crossing from Antibes to Gibraltar. The stewardesses were sunning themselves as I weight trained. I finished my training and had a bit of craic with them. I told them about the book iCon. They were intrigued and asked me about it. I told them I was going to go to Hollywood when we got to Florida. They were so impressed. They asked me to tell them a story from the book. I told them I would do my stand up routine for my comedy act for them. They sat up excited. It makes me laugh now at the reaction I had to their fun loving yachtie nature. It went down like a ton of bricks. They went fucking crazy. They went and told the Captain. The one stewardess said "What kind of fucking lunatic have you got driving us across the Atlantic? I do not feel safe." The Captain, instead of backing me up and telling them I was medically fit to be doing the job, said to me "I have to let you go, you must keep the Juan stories in, that is what Aztec called them on Passion." He told me what the girls said. It was another little adventure. I got off in Gibraltar with 1,700 euro. I'd only been on the yacht 9 whole days. It was the shortest trip I ever had. I thought fuck this, I'm going on the screaming piss. I was so pissed off at losing the job. I drank for a week, spending the full weeks wage. I had no money to get home. I phoned my mother. She said she couldn't help me. I was fucking frightened. I phoned my brother and he said "Juan this getting fucking ridiculous..you have to stop doing this shit." He got me home. I went back to Letterkenny and had nowhere to live. I was homeless for a couple of days before moving into Riverdances hostel.

Letterkenny was such a pain in the ass to live in from 2017 to 2020. I was constantly abused by the local people. I found people in general in Letterfanny to be quite decent BUT I drank myself to death there. I ended up homeless at the beginning of 2020 after a stupid argument in Ariadne's hostel. You read about some of my experiences in my few years of living in Letterkenny in the first chapter. The mental asylum in LK(Letterkenny), LK as the cool folk call it, was the only place I could go after getting kicked out. They took me in for one night after I bullshitted them saying I was suicidal. I told them I imagined standing out on the road in front of a truck, a bit like a superhero, and the truck would drive in to my outstretched arm and catapult over my head. The admissions doctor believed it! LOL. The doctor said ok we'll keep you for a night but you will have to leave in the morning after seeing your doctor. Doctor fucking Noir kept me for 4 long fucking months. I got a home out of it with Housing first, a homeless help group, but that was the only good thing that came out of that 4-month admission. It scared the hell out of me. I thought I could be in there forever. I knew deep down I couldn't but it would fucking scare anyone into thinking that. It was blessing in disguise because I had nowhere else to go.

ONWARDS AND UPWARDS!

It is now May 2023. As I said I am living in Rathmullan, County Donegal. It is such a small town. They have no consideration for my feelings either. There is so much gossip here. They got me locked up in Letterkenny mental asylum for a week about 3 months ago. About 2 years ago, I was lying in bed and I heard people talking outside my window. It was early morning. They were keeping me awake. I've been told since by the aliens that it was the spirit world. They were trying to scare me. I'm the leader of the spirit world as well.

I've had some time of it in Rathmullan. I've been drinking like a fish lol. It passes the time. Some people don't like me for it. I couldn't give a damn!! Like I said, I was told in Letterkenny mental asylum that IT was the Republican party, Sinn Fein that were abusing me. The party followers tried to make a joke out what they were doing by saying to me "What's it like? The whole Island giving you stick?!" IT is not stick!!! IT IS FUCKING ABUSE YOU SICK FUCKING WASTER CUNTS!!! Imagine the whole of Sinn Fein abusing one man? It is fucking weird as fuck having everybody talking about you when you're within earshot. I was in Letterkenny last week and this little sadist of a coffee boy in the café I was in said to a customer after I ordered and sat down, "We're not lighting him(he meant gaslighting) but it doesn't stop us talking about him…" Then he proceeded to talk about my drinking. I couldn't give a damn. I'm over all alcohol. I'm on the dry for 6 months now. The aliens have told me to give it up along with the cigarettes. They are going to make me thin again. They are going to regulate my diet with light walking. 5 kilometres a day. 5 days a week. I am 16 stone now. I'm getting down to 12. The medication bloated me out and I've been fat for 3 years. I put on 3 fucking stone in those 4 months incarcerated. The aliens are so delectable in their interest of my vanity lol it's my health they're doing it for. The women will be fucking very impressed around Rathmullan when they see how good looking Juan actually is. He will have muscles as well. They were fucking disintegrated by all the medication and his lack of motivation to do anything exercise related because of the sedative effects on him. That is the new Juan coming to rule the earth..JUANSTANTINE!! LOL.

Like I said the services got me a house and it is the one which I now live in. Although I only write about being homeless a few times, I have ended up homeless 4 times because of my drinking. It has not been drinking alone that has done this, I have been forced into a the mental asylum so many fucking times over the years, that I could not get back to work properly. I've been on the poverty line for 12 years because of this as well. I've been doing really well since I finished this book. The aliens are helping me every day with the recovery of the mental health trauma that I've endured. My life is getting normality back. My emotions are coming back to normal. I cannot wait to get to the Caribbean and sit on a beach with a big fat spliff and smoke my head off!! I will do Cocaine as well. I will have 3 women to suck my dick. They can fight over it!! The aliens are coming with me. They are in my head. They can travel anywhere in this planet.

This book has been a joy to write, very therapeutic. I will write many more. I feel such a sense of freedom when I type! I'm looking forward to my blog!!!

I hope ultimately this book helps people. I've met a lot of people in these institutions over the years with the diagnosis of Bipolar and other illnesses and I am aware that the diagnoses are bullshit. Mental illness does not exist. The Doctors are brain washing you. They think by telling you that your kids are really intelligent, but they need a certain medication to stabilize them, that you will believe them. Do not fall for their manipulative doctor ways. It has become so common place that the general public do not care BUT I care and I will rid the world of mental illness forever. That has been my mission. The aliens orchestrated it.

I noticed in all my years at the front line that so-called patients had something in common. They were all a bit on the wild side. They all had that glint in their eyes, joie de vivre. Some of them were worn down with the stress of the medication and life as a mental patient but they always had a good sense of humor when I got them talking. The patients help one another more than any Doctor or nurse ever could. I figured out that the patient's, in every circumstance, did not fit in with their family. There was always friction. It was a common theme. It did not matter whether they were male or female, young or old, they were always the black sheep of their family. This has to end. They were always the dominant kids and the less dominant siblings would fucking gang up on them. Their parents were proper cunts to them. It happened me. I tell you this from 100% experience. I am about to change the world forever. The Alien race who have made contact with me ARE going to fight the pharmaceutical companies using my gnarly personality. They are closing them down. There is not going to be any psychotropic drugs anymore.

The aliens are going to help me become a Zillionaire. They are so fucking determined. They also know the future. They are telling me some of it. They keep most of it hidden. They do not want to spoil the surprise for me. I am so delighted to have them in my life. It is not a joke. They really do talk to me. They are writing these final words. They are speaking and I am typing what they say. I do it all the time. I have got to be the luckiest alien alive. I am King of earth now. They have told me this. This book will be read by Hollywood executives and be immediately made into 10 movies. They will make me millions of dollars!!

The end is nearly here for mental illness. There will be no mental illness anymore on planet earth. I have completed my mission. That is all folks. Watch this space. There are more books to come.